MERMAIDS IN THE PACIFIC

PEYTON BROOKS, FBI

Volume 2

ML Hamilton

www.authormlhamilton.net

Cover Art by Karri Klawiter

www.artbykarri.com

Photography by Jared Lugo

MERMAIDS IN THE PACIFIC

© 2014 ML Hamilton, Sacramento, CA

First print

After writing a fairly decent number of books, I still marvel at the good will, the dedication, and the loyalty of my readers. You keep me writing and inspire more adventures for Peyton. Thank you so very much.

And to my family, as cheesy as it sounds, you are my backbone, my foundation. I love you.

O' train me not, sweet mermaid, with thy note,
To drown me in thy sister's flood of tears!

-- William Shakespeare, *The Comedy of Errors*

CHAPTER 1

Friday

Marco stared at the television, vaguely aware people were running around, chasing a baseball. He'd been sitting here for a while. In fact, except for ordering a pizza and going out for booze, he hadn't left this spot.

Someone banged on the door. He glanced over at it, but he didn't bother getting off the bed. This motel saw a lot of traffic – some of it illegal, *the cop in him whispered*, but he didn't give a rat's ass right now. Based on the whiffs he got when he did venture out, he guessed the guy next to him burned bricks of marijuana on a hibachi 24 hours a day.

The banging started again.

"Open the damn door, D'Angelo, or I'll kick this bitch in!" came an angry voice.

Cho.

Nathan Cho would be as good as his word. Cho was five feet six inches of badass cop, who wouldn't hesitate doing whatever he felt needed to be done. He was also a good friend.

Grabbing his cane, Marco levered himself to his feet. His vision swam and he closed his eyes until the dizziness passed. Hm, when had he ordered the pizza? He wasn't exactly sure any more.

Limping to the door, he turned the lock and yanked it open. A tall black man with wild dreadlocks pushed his way into the room.

"Abe?"

Abe wandered around the perimeter, looking into the garbage can and then heading for the bathroom.

Marco shifted and gave Cho a glare. "What the hell's going on?"

1

"You tell me," said Cho antagonistically. "You've called in sick to work the last three days, and no one knows where the hell you are. You missed your appointment with Ferguson on Wednesday and he reported it to Defino. She and a woman from Internal Affairs are going to be at the precinct Monday morning."

Well, shit. That wasn't good. Marco scratched the back of his neck. "I just wanted a few days off."

Abe came out of the bathroom. "Get your stuff. We're going."

"*We're* not going anywhere. How the hell did you find me?"

"Good thing I know detectives," said Abe. "Get your stuff or we leave it behind."

"Look, Abe, I'm not a child. I don't need you riding in here to the rescue."

Abe gave him a cool glare. Marco realized he looked like shit. He hadn't shaved in three days and he wore a pair of athletic shorts and a ratty t-shirt. "There are three bottles of Jack Daniels in the bathroom trash. The guy next door is having a pot barbecue, but you don't seem to care, and there's a pimp doing double duty in the lobby who had no problem telling us your room number. You're coming home with me."

Marco glanced at Cho. He crossed his arms over his chest. "He's right."

Releasing a weary sigh, Marco knew it wouldn't do any good to argue with them. He didn't have the energy. "I'll go somewhere else."

"Where? Your parents?"

Oh, hell no. That would never work.

"Your brothers?"

Shit, that was worse.

"What about Peyton's house?"

Before Marco could answer, Abe shook his head. "Nope. For whatever dumb assed reason, you broke off your engagement with her and left her wondering if you're alive or dead. Guess that ship has sailed."

"Look, Abe…" He didn't want to talk about Peyton. It hurt him just to think about her, but he knew they expected some sort of explanation. "What happened between Peyton and me is our business. I'm not discussing it."

"Did I tell you to discuss it, Angel? No, I didn't. I said get your shit, we're leaving." He snagged the Charger's keys off the dresser. "I'll be waiting in the car." Then he moved determinedly toward the door, pushing past Marco and heading for the stairs.

"Peyton called me," said Cho.

He figured as much.

"She was scared to death."

Marco didn't know how to answer that. He thought he was doing the right thing walking away from their engagement, from her. He was trying to protect her.

"She was crying."

Marco's eyes whipped to Cho's face. The thought of Peyton crying made him feel sick inside.

Cho took a step closer to him, a muscle in his jaw bulging. "I've never heard Peyton cry before and let me tell you something, D'Angelo, I don't like it."

Marco forced himself to hold Cho's gaze, but it was hard. He ached thinking of Peyton, especially hurt and upset. He hated thinking he'd caused it, but he knew he had.

"Now, get your damn stuff…*Captain*!" said Cho.

*   *   *

Marco watched Abe toss booze into a garbage can. He'd disappear behind the bar in a corner of the living room, re-emerge with bottles, and dump them into the can. Sitting on Abe's modern, minimalist red couch, he wondered what the hell he was doing here.

He knew he couldn't stay in the motel for the rest of his life, but he was hoping something would come to him.

Except he couldn't summon any energy to do anything but sit and watch television. And he wasn't really even watching television. He'd been so sure he was doing the right thing, breaking it off with Peyton, but the moment he'd left her house, he didn't know what to do, how to live without her. He loved her more than he loved anything, but right now he was poison and he was so afraid he'd do irreparable harm to their relationship if he stayed.

"You don't have to do that, Abe. I'm not going to drink."

The precinct's medical examiner paused in the midst of chucking a bottle of Courvoisier. "No use keeping temptation around."

"I'm not an alcoholic."

"Are you certain of that?"

Marco didn't answer.

Dropping the bottle into the trashcan, Abe came to the low-slung white coffee table and took a seat on it, facing Marco. "You broke off your engagement. You love Peyton. How could you do that to her?"

"I did it *for* her."

"How do you figure that, Angel? She's devastated."

"I know, but…"

"But what?"

"I got scared."

"Scared? Of marriage? That's normal. Most people get cold feet."

"No, that's not it. I want to marry Peyton. I want to marry Peyton more than I want my next breath, but I got scared of what was happening to me where she's concerned."

"What do you mean?"

"I mean I was getting possessive and jealous. Not just a little, either. Whenever she was out of my sight, I got anxious, afraid." Marco leaned forward, bracing his arms on his thighs. "She's gone beyond me, Abe. So far beyond me. She has her job and her new colleagues. She doesn't need me."

"She loves you."

"No, she loved who I was. I'm not that man anymore."

"That's ridiculous. You aren't a leg, Angel. It was your leg that was damaged, not you."

Marco looked down. "I wish that was true. I wish I was still the same person I used to be, but that confidence, that security is gone. I got knocked on my ass in my own precinct. I can't protect anyone. I can't go on the street anymore. And I'm a lousy captain. I hate telling people what to do. Then the one case that gave me a sense of purpose got thrown out of court."

"The Carissa Phelps' case? The revenge porn case?"

"Yeah."

Abe reached over and curled his long fingers around Marco's clasped hands. "I know it's been hard. I know you've had a lot of adjusting to do, but this thing with Peyton is just stupid. You adore her, she adores you. I don't say this lightly, Angel, but you two are meant to be together. I believe that."

"Even if it was wrong for her, Abe?"

"How?"

"I didn't want her out of my sight. I couldn't stand the thought of another man touching her, even looking at her. Every time she went to work, I wanted to drink because I felt so damn insecure. I almost ordered her to quit. I almost gave her an ultimatum."

Abe sighed and leaned back, his hand sliding away. "That's not good."

"No. I could see it wasn't good. I could see it wasn't right and I knew I had to leave. I had to get out of there. If I demanded she quit, I knew she would because she loves me that much, but in the end, that love would turn to hate."

"So what now?"

"I don't know. I thought it would be clear what I had to do when I left, but all I've done is drink and think about her. I miss her so badly. I feel empty. I can't imagine a life without her in it. For so long, she's been my everything."

Abe didn't answer for a moment, then he reached for the cell phone Marco had placed on the coffee table, hoping for Peyton to call. "Call Dr. Ferguson. Get an appointment for tomorrow."

"Isn't tomorrow Saturday?" He scratched the side of his neck. "I can't even remember what frickin' day it is."

"Yeah, tomorrow's Saturday, but I think he'll see you. He's been waiting for your call. That's the first step, Marco. That's the first thing you've got to do to get well. You've got to call Dr. Ferguson. And me, I'll go back to throwing away booze."

They both looked at the filled garbage can.

Abe made a snorting sound. "Clearly this is a two can job. Maybe I need to reevaluate my own alcohol consumption."

* * *

Marco sat across from the psychiatrist. Dr. Ferguson gave him a level look, tapping his pen against his lower lip. He wore a polo shirt and wrinkled khaki pants with sneakers today. Marco had forced himself to shower, but he hadn't felt strong enough to use a razor. He feared he might slit his own damn throat by accident, since his hand wasn't steady enough to shave.

"You look like hell."

Marco rolled his eyes. He was only here to protect his job, a job he didn't know if he wanted or not. And also because maybe Ferguson had some insight into how he could make things right with Peyton.

"You've been drinking, haven't you?"

"Some."

"And not eating?"

"Some."

"Sleep pretty non-existent?"

Marco shrugged. Sleep was pretty non-existent because he kept dreaming about Peyton. Every time he dreamed about her, he was trying to find her, searching through the back of cargo vans.

"Do I need to have you committed?"

"No."

"No? You broke off your engagement, you were staying in a sleazy hotel, and refused to go to work for three days. You're drinking and shutting out everyone in your life, including your family. I think we've gone beyond a minor counseling need here. I think we're dealing with full blown depression now."

"I'm not depressed. I'm…"

"You're what, Captain D'Angelo?"

"I'm pissed. I'm lost. I'm frustrated." He gave Ferguson a snarky smile. "And seeing you isn't helping."

"I gave you a tool to help, but you wouldn't take it."

"You wanted me to go to a group meeting where people sit around and moan and whine about their lives together. Yeah, that's gonna help. Here's the thing. I don't spill my guts to people. I don't share all of my hurts and pains and sadness with the world. I don't make myself a fool for other people's amusement."

"No, you sit in a sleazy motel and drink."

Fair enough. Marco looked at the table and ran his finger across a scratch on its artificial surface.

"I'm increasing our meetings from once to three times a week – Monday, Wednesday and Friday."

Marco's eyes snapped to his face, but Ferguson held up a single finger to stop him.

"Group meeting is Thursday night. I'm adding that to your schedule."

Marco started to protest, but he wagged a finger at him.

"Nope. You just listen."

Marco clamped his mouth shut. He'd never seen Ferguson so forceful before.

"You go or I report to Chief Defino that you disobeyed a direct command. As I'm sure you've been told, she and an officer from Internal Affairs will be at the precinct Monday morning to interview your officers. I'm not certain I can save your badge now, but I can promise you that if you fail to attend any of the sessions I've laid out, I will personally recommend you surrender it." He leaned forward, clasping his hands on the table. "Are we clear with one another, Captain D'Angelo?"

Marco nodded. He really didn't think he wanted the job, but if he lost this too, he'd have nothing, and in the absence of everything, he wouldn't be able to stand losing Peyton.

* * *

Ruth poked her head inside the study and gave him a sympathetic smile. "You okay?"

Jeff glanced up. "Yeah." Laying the picture on the desk blotter, he forced a smile. "It's just so hard. All this stuff. I see her in all of it."

Ruth moved into the doorway, leaning on the filing cabinet. "I know."

He laid his hand on the pile of papers he'd taken out of his mother's desk. "Did you know my mom went to D.C.? I found a photo of her."

Ruth came to his side, laying a hand on his shoulder.

He held up the photo for her to see. "See, that's the Washington Monument."

Ruth smiled, taking the grainy black and white photo. "No, I didn't know that. She had a whole secret life before you were born, huh? How old is she here?"

"Um, she had to be in her late twenties, early thirties. That was before she met my dad."

He picked up a stack of envelopes tied with a pale blue ribbon. In the center of the envelope, in the most beautiful handwriting he'd ever seen, were the words: **Mrs. Aster King**. Someone had written letters to his mother. Not just a few. There was an entire stack, all neatly gathered, the top slit precisely with a letter opener. He gave a snort of laughter. Leave it to his mother to have a pen pal. She'd never trusted computers.

When he'd bought her one for her birthday about five years ago, she'd given it to the neighbor kid, said he needed it for his schoolwork, that there wasn't anything she needed doing that couldn't be done with paper and pen.

Ruth rubbed his shoulders. "I'll make some lunch. You gonna stay in here?"

He picked up her hand and kissed the back of it. "For a while. I just want to spend a little time with her."

"I understand." She walked to the door, but paused on the threshold, looking back. "Simon and Josephine will be here tonight."

"Good. The viewing starts at 5:00."

"They said they'd meet us at the funeral home."

He nodded, distracted by the photo of his mother – a handsome Caucasian woman in a dress with a hat positioned at a jaunty angle on her head. She stood with a number of other women, the tall obelisk of the monument rising behind them. Why the hell hadn't he known she took a trip to D.C.? Why hadn't she ever talked about it?

Turning to the letters, he untied the blue ribbon and picked up the first one, pulling out the yellowed piece of binder paper. The same beautiful script leapt out at him as he opened it and began reading.

* * *

Dear Aster,

My name is Finn. I was named after my mother's favorite literary character Huck Finn. She said she always liked the idea of floating down a river, having an adventure. She used to tell me the greatest adventure was in books. I like to read too. I spend all of my free time at the library.

We don't have a very big library, but the librarian is nice and she orders me any books she thinks I might like. Her name is Mrs. Elder. I think that's funny. She must be about 95 and her name is Elder. I wonder what her name was when she was young.

I just finished reading <u>The Guernsey Literary and Potato Peel Pie Society</u>. What a long name for a book, but in it, these people in World War 2 become pen pals with this author. That put me in mind that I'd like to have a pen pal, but you know, everything's computers nowadays and we're not allowed to have a computer.

Anyway, I went to Mrs. Elder and I mentioned that I'd like to have a pen pal. She told me of this site where people write in asking for a pen pal, then the librarians all make a list and match people up. That's how I found out about you.

So, Aster is the name of a flower? That's nice. I wonder how old you are, but from what I read, you really aren't supposed to ask a lady how old she is. I'm fifteen. I don't mind telling that, since no one much cares about being fifteen. It's not one of those fun ages, you know, like ten – a decade, sixteen – driver's license, eighteen – adult. I don't much care about turning twenty-one. Most people get to drink then, but we don't drink in my family. At twenty-one we leave.

Let's not talk about that. It makes me sad. See, I live in this incredibly beautiful place. Big redwood trees, a lot of ferns. We have a creek that runs along the back of the property and sometimes the deer come down to drink. Usually that's in the morning or just before dusk. I like to see the deer. They're so peaceful, so quiet. They make me happy.

Once in a while we go to the beach. I see you live in Reno, Nevada. That is definitely not near a beach. Do you ever wish you could see the ocean? I would be sad if I couldn't see the ocean, but let me tell you, the Pacific is cold, really cold. It's impossible to get into it all the way, but some people do. I like to watch the surfers. I can't believe the way they ride the waves. I'd really like to try surfing, but that's not allowed.

Wow! I just read back what I wrote and I talk a lot about what's not allowed. There's a lot of good stuff allowed too. I get to walk the trails in the hills for as long as I want and once I found a baby rabbit. His mother had been killed, so I got to keep him for a while. My chore is to work the garden. I like that. I like planting things and waiting for them to become food.

It's better than chopping the wood. A lot of the boys have to chop wood or do other hard stuff, but not me. I get to dig in the dirt and pick vegetables.

I know why I want a pen pal. I want to hear about places far away from here, but why do you? Don't you have a computer to talk to people? Sometimes when I'm in the library Mrs. Elder lets me get on the computer. That's pretty neat. I see some of the kids at the library with their phones. Their phones are like a mini-computer. Isn't that funny? People carry computers around with them now.

Anyway, that's a little about me. Here's what I want to know about you. Are you married? Do you have kids? What's it like living in Reno? Don't they do a lot of gambling in Reno? Do you not have a computer because it's not allowed where you are?

Your new friend and pen pal,
Finn Getter

P.S. I guess my last name is weird too. Hee! Hee! What do you think?

CHAPTER 2

Saturday/Sunday

Peyton sat on the couch, her knees bent, her arms hugged around her legs, watching the display on the phone. She wore Marco's jersey, it still smelled like him, and a pair of raggedy sweats. Pickles lay beside her, pressing his back against her hip as if to keep reminding her he was there for her.

The crying was spent. She was sick of it and sick of herself. She'd been crying off and on for days now and she wasn't going to do it anymore. Come Monday, she was putting on a boyish black suit, pulling her wild curls into a ponytail, and going back to work. She was done wallowing.

Still, when the phone rang, she snatched it up, thumbing it on. "Hello?"

"Hey, little soul sista," came Abe's voice. "How you holding up?"

"I'm fine."

"You're definitely not fine, but I get you. I'm sorry I'm not there."

"It's okay. How's Marco?"

Abe went silent. Peyton realized she gripped the phone so tight, the edges pressed into her flesh.

"Abe?"

"He's a mess, sweets. He's been on a binge for days and he doesn't seem to want to get out of bed. I finally forced him to go see the shrink. He won't talk to me. I've tried and tried, but he just keeps saying the same thing."

"What?"

"That he left because he had to. He left because you deserved a whole man and he's not that anymore."

She closed her eyes and drew a deep, calming breath. No more crying. No more wallowing. No more sorrow. "Couples are supposed to work through these things together. He didn't give me a chance."

"He was scaring himself with his possessiveness over you, darlin'. He was afraid he'd demand you quit your job and you would because you love him, but then you'd grow to hate him. That's why he left. He almost asked you to quit."

"I wouldn't have quit!" she said angrily, but she knew she was lying. She would have done anything to prevent this from happening. God, she missed him. Even when he was breaking her heart, he was doing it for her. Shit! She hated that. "Honorable bastard!" she hissed into the phone.

Abe gave a laugh. "He is that. He's also pretty as hell. Have I told you that?"

"A million times."

"What are you going to do, honey?"

"Go to work. Give him space. What else can I do, Abe?"

"Nothing."

"What about the drinking?"

"I threw out all the booze, every last drop. Do you know how long that took? Do you know how badly that hurt?"

"I'm sure it was crippling."

"I had some damn fine stuff here, Peyton. I had a 21 year old bottle of Macallan Scotch. Into the recycle bin it went."

"I thought you didn't like Scotch."

"Everyone likes 21 year old Scotch, but it was worth it. He's scaring me with this drinking. I swear, he's damn near pickled."

"Do you think you should call Dr. Ferguson and tell him?"

"I don't want to lose his trust, but if I catch him with anything, I will."

A knock sounded at the door. Peyton glanced over her shoulder. "Someone's knocking."

"I know."

"You know?"

"Yeah, I know."

"How?"

"I sent them."

Peyton went still. "You sent who, Abe?"

"Open up or Nathan says he's gonna kick this bitch in!" came a loud voice.

"Have fun," answered Abe and hung up.

Peyton scrambled off the couch, racing Pickles to the door, and yanked it open before Cho could *kick this bitch in*. Maria pushed her way into the house, carrying bags and other paraphernalia, and bussed a kiss across Peyton's cheek. Cho followed her, his arms filled with stuff as well.

Peyton turned and watched as Maria dumped her stuff in the kitchen, motioning Cho to deposit his on the coffee table.

"What's going on?" she asked, trying to sound as normal as she could.

Maria gave her a severe once-over. "It's worse than I thought."

Peyton pushed some loose curls behind her ears and tried to smooth out the wrinkled jersey. Cho looked down, avoiding eye contact.

"Maria, why are you here?"

"We're having a slumber party," she said as she began unpacking her bags.

"*You're* having a slumber party," said Cho, motioning between Peyton and Maria. "Me, I'm going home."

Peyton shut the door and moved to the barstools, watching as Maria pulled out ice cream and donuts and chocolate syrup. "A slumber party?"

"Yep. You know, I'll do your hair and nails, and…" She sucked in air and let it out slowly. "Make-up."

"I've never been to a slumber party before."

15

"Never?"

"No, and I think I might be too old for one now."

"Nonsense. It's Saturday night. We'll stay up and talk, watch movies, eat popcorn." She pulled out a stack of DVD's. "I brought *Grease, Pretty in Pink, Dirty Dancing*...all the big ones."

"If you were born in the 1980's."

Maria stopped rummaging and came around the counter, taking Peyton's hands. She was distracted for a moment, looking at Peyton's left hand where she still wore her engagement ring. "I'm here for you. This is what a best friend does. Come on. You'll see. We'll have fun." She held up Peyton's hand and studied her nails. "Besides, girlfriend, you desperately need a manicure."

Peyton's mouth opened, but nothing came out.

Cho tucked his hands in his pockets and moved toward the door. "That's my cue."

He stopped and gave Maria a quick kiss.

It wasn't any romantic kind of kiss – just a quick touch of their lips to each other, but the intimacy of it was like a blow to Peyton. She sucked in air, but it was too late. Tears filled her eyes and she made a strange hitching sound, trying to stop the tears from falling.

Cho looked like he wanted to bolt, but Maria gave Peyton a sad smile and held open her arms.

That did it. Peyton collapsed against Maria and the sobs came wrenching out of her.

* * *

A knock sounded at the door. Peyton put down the dish towel and went to it, scooping up Pickles as he danced around her feet. Jake stood on the other side, offering her an uncomfortable grin.

"Jake?"

"Hey, Mighty Mouse, I'm here to take you to lunch."

Peyton gave him a stern look. "Abe sent you, didn't he?"

"What?"

"Maria just left and now you're here to take me to lunch?"

"Can't a friend take another friend to lunch on a Sunday without it being some national event?"

"Not when it's you and Abe. Look, Jake, I'm fine."

"Then come to lunch with me."

She let out a sigh, then handed him Pickles. "Let me change my clothes."

A few minutes later, they were in Jake's purple car with the yellow daisies painted on the doors. He had enough money to get a paint job now. Hell, he had enough money to get a new car, but he was attached to the Daisy and wouldn't part with her.

Peyton grimaced as she got inside. He'd duct taped the seat to stop the stuffing from coming out and the dashboard sported a hula girl covering a cigarette burn-mark. Peyton flicked the hula girl.

"This is sexist and you need to get rid of it."

"It's a classic. I'm thinking of getting those mud-flaps with the woman's silhouette next."

"You do and I'll slash your tires."

He started the Daisy and she choked to life. "That's a fine thing for an FBI agent to say."

"We could have taken the Prius."

"Naw. I feel guilty when we ride in the Prius, like I should stop and recycle some cans or something."

"Heaven forbid," said Peyton, smiling at him. Actually she was glad to see him. He could take her mind off Marco if only for a few moments. "Where are you taking me to lunch?"

"The Cliff House."

As he drove toward the coast, he kept up a steady stream of conversation. Most of it was silly, but Peyton didn't complain. It gave her time to not dwell on her loss or the emptiness she felt inside.

The Cliff House sat on a rocky cliff, jutting out over the ocean. No matter how often Peyton had been here, she'd never seen it when the sun was shining. Fog caressed the sleek white buildings, slithering among the rocks like a snake. Jake got them a window seat and they looked out over the ocean, watching the waves crash against the boulders.

The waitress took their drink order. Peyton just wanted water, but Jake ordered a draft beer. Then she handed them menus and left.

Jake reached over and took her hand. "Look, Mighty Mouse, we don't have to talk about anything, but I want you to know that I'm here for you."

She squeezed his fingers. "I know, Jake, and I appreciate it. I'm just so raw right now I'm afraid I'll burst into tears if I talk about it."

He nodded, then turned back to the window, releasing her. "This was one of Zoë's favorite spots. We'd come out here on a Sunday morning and get an omelet."

Peyton smiled at him.

"They used to have this mechanical museum below this building, you know, with model trains and those old motion picture viewers. You could put pennies in the machines and watch things happen."

"I remember that. My dad used to bring me here. I liked to see the seals on Seal Rock. He'd give me a couple of quarters and boost me up so I could look through the binoculars."

"I think they moved the museum to Pier 45. We could go there after this."

"Maybe."

The waitress returned with their drinks. "Are you ready to order?"

Peyton opened her menu. "I'll have the crab sandwich."

"Excellent choice. And for you, sir?"

"I'll have the same."

She smiled and gathered the menus, then left again.

Peyton looked out at the ocean and ran her finger through the condensation on her glass. "Do you think you'll ever date again, Jake?"

He lowered his beer and considered her a moment. "Why do you ask that?"

"It's been almost two years since Zoë died. Do you ever want to try again?"

He studied her face for a moment. "I don't know. It's hard, Peyton. Zoë meant the world to me."

"I know she did."

"Whenever I think of having that sort of relationship with another person, I get scared."

Peyton nodded.

He leaned forward on the table. "It's going to be all right, Mighty Mouse. Adonis loves you. He's gonna wake up and realize that."

She gave him a sad smile. "Sometimes love isn't enough, Jake. Sometimes it doesn't fix everything."

"What are you saying?"

"This is something we should have worked out together, but he left. He didn't give me a chance. How do I forgive him for that? How do I ever trust him again? And if I can't trust Marco, how can I ever trust another man?"

"It's too soon to be thinking about that."

"I know, it's just…"

"Just what?"

"I hate being alone. I hate feeling like there's this hole inside of me. What if Marco was the only one who could fill it? What if he was my only chance at happiness?"

"Do you really believe that?"

"I don't know. For so long, no one measured up to him. I love him so much, Jake. I can't imagine life without him. That must be how you feel about Zoë because you've never moved on. You've never considered anyone else."

He gave a laugh and looked into his beer. "That's not exactly true. I've considered moving on, Peyton. I've considered someone else."

"Who?"

He lifted his eyes and met hers. "It doesn't matter."

"How can it not matter? Tell me, Jake. Give me some hope."

Jake reached over and took her hand again. "I don't think you have to move on yet, Peyton. I don't think you have to give up on Marco just yet, but I promise you, eventually, you'll be ready. You'll meet someone that's different than he is, but you'll realize that you could have something really great with that person if you just take a chance." He looked directly in her eyes. "You aren't meant to be alone forever. Trust me on that."

* * *

"Hey, Dad, Mom wants to know if you want a sandwich?"

Jeff looked up from the letter and blinked at his son. For a moment, his mind was slow to process what he said. "Sorry?"

Simon stepped into the library, tilting his head to see what his father held. "Mom wants to know if you want a sandwich."

"Uh, no, no, I'm not hungry."

Simon nodded his chin at the letter. Jeff couldn't believe how much he resembled himself when he was a young man – tall, thin, gangly. Simon had his mother's brown eyes, but *his* freckles. "What's that?"

Jeff glanced down at the letter, giving a fond chuckle. "Your grandmother had a pen pal, it appears. They wrote to each other for years. The boy was just fifteen when they started. I'm up to sixteen now."

"A pen pal?" Simon held out his hand for the letter. "You mean real letters? Stamps and all?"

"Yeah, go figure. It was a viable mode of communication for a long time."

Simon glanced over the elegant script. "Texting's better. You don't have to wait long for an answer."

Jeff took the letter back from him. "I don't know. There's something nice about a handwritten note. It's more personal."

Simon gave him a bewildered look. "Okay, Dad. Look." He sank down into the chair across the desk from him. "I miss Grandma too, but you gotta eat. You can't spend all your time in here. People are waiting in the other room for you. You gotta come out."

Jeff glanced at the door. He really didn't want to make small talk with people. "I hate wakes."

"Well, take your own advice."

"What advice?"

"Come out and talk to people. It's more personal."

Jeff chuckled. "Using my words against me."

"Whatever works."

Jeff settled the letter on the desk, resisting the impulse to smooth it, then he rose, crossing around the desk, and draped an arm around his son's shoulders, directing him toward the door. "You're getting pretty smart there, boy."

"Well, college'll do that to a guy."

*   *   *

Dear Aster,

It was nice to read about your son, Jeff. He sounds like a good man. It must be hard to work in business, but then again, I don't know. We mostly stay here on the farm, but sometimes we go to town.

Mostly I go to town because I have asthma and I need to see the doctor. We save up for a long time to go to the doctor. We have to take turns. Mostly we take care of ourselves.

You asked if I like living in Santa Cruz. Well, I don't actually live in the city, but whenever we go, I like it a lot. Except there are a lot of people. That makes us all nervous. So many people. And they look at us strange. I think it's because we wear clothes that aren't bright colors. I told Thatcher that we might blend in better if we went to the thrift store, you know, where you can buy used clothes, but he said that blending was almost the same as lying.

When we go to Santa Cruz, we take the big van. I asked Thatcher if I could learn to drive it since I'm sixteen and all, but he said that the government doesn't let people with asthma drive. He said it was considered a danger to society because I might have an attack and pass out. I tried to look it up in the library, but I couldn't find anything about it. I did find something that said they could restrict your license for health reasons, but it wasn't very specific. Do you know if I can drive or not with asthma?

I'm still working the garden, but sometimes it gets hard for me, especially in the spring when the grass gets a little high. Lately, I've been helping my sister out with her baby. She's just a little thing, hardly more than four pounds, and she cries a lot. My sister isn't getting a lot of sleep, so I trade off with her. Thatcher said this was okay, since I'm not much good doing the other things that the boys do. At least I can help.

Thatcher says it's important for each of us to find our calling. My sister has found hers and now maybe I have too, since she needs my help. Maybe this will be enough to let me stay here when I turn twenty-one. Even though I sometimes think I'd like to be part of the world in Santa Cruz, I'm afraid of it too. It seems so big and busy. How did Jeff make the adjustment when he left? Was it hard for him? Looking forward to hearing from you again.

Your friend,
Finn Getter

CHAPTER 3

Monday

Marco could hear voices in the conference room as he walked into the precinct. He let the outer door close behind him and moved toward the half-door, pushing it open, his ears straining to catch the sounds. He recognized Katherine Defino's voice, his past captain, now Deputy Chief of Police, but the other female voice was unfamiliar to him.

His Administrative Assistant Carly wasn't at her desk and he didn't sense anyone else moving about the rest of the precinct. Did they have his entire staff in the conference room with them?

"Inspector Cho," came the unfamiliar voice, "do you have anything to add to this discussion?"

"No, ma'am."

Silence.

Marco knew he shouldn't snoop, but he couldn't help it. If he crossed to his office now, they would see him from the open door. Cho had warned him that Internal Affairs would be at the precinct this morning, but there was nothing he could do about it. He'd had to make his appointment with Dr. Ferguson and that put him at the precinct after Internal Affairs had already arrived.

"Inspector Shotwell?"

"Yes, ma'am."

"You're the newest member of this precinct. You must have a less biased view of the situation. Do you feel your interests are being properly represented at this point? Do you have confidence in the leadership Captain D'Angelo is providing you?"

Marco tightened his grip on his cane. They certainly knew how to divide and conquer. He wasn't entirely sure of

Tag yet. They'd had their run-ins when she'd first come on and she hadn't gotten along with Peyton.

"I have complete faith in Captain D'Angelo," she said.

"No concerns of any kind?"

"Not a one."

Marco released his held breath.

"Well, I can see the blue wall is firmly in place." Marco could hear some shuffling of papers, then the woman gave a heavy sigh. "You all have my card in case you'd like to talk in private. Please feel free to call, but unless you have anything you'd like to add, you are dismissed."

Marco wasn't sure what to do. Did he go back out the door and pretend that he was just coming in, or did he move toward the conference room as if he'd just arrived?

"Mr. Ryder, please stay," came the voice.

Marco went still. *Crap.* His officers might not give him away, but Jake wouldn't feel that same sort of loyalty, and he was pissed because of Peyton. Before Marco could decide what to do, his people began filing out of the conference room. They all came to a halt when they saw him, but they didn't say anything, just gave him significant looks.

Stan was the last to leave and he pulled the conference door shut behind him, staring at Marco with enormous worried eyes.

Tag leaned close to him, dropping her voice. "You need to get in there. They've got Ryder and you know what a wuss he is. They'll have him talking in no time."

Marco gave her a weary shrug. He couldn't do anything about what Jake might tell them.

"She's right, Captain," said Cho. "You need to stop this."

"I can't stop it. I brought it on myself."

"What about Ryder?" demanded Holmes. "Tag's right. He'll spill everything."

"If he does, he does, and if they pull each of you aside individually, you tell them the truth. Do you hear me? No lies. No holding back. You answer their questions."

"The hell you say," grumbled big Bill Simons.

"That's a direct order, Bill. Do you understand me? All of you? You tell them the truth. This isn't just Defino involved now. This is Internal Affairs."

Before they could answer, Marco shifted and walked to his office, disappearing inside.

* * *

A knock sounded at the door half an hour later. Marco blinked, realizing he'd just been sitting behind his desk, doing nothing. Well, that wasn't exactly true, he'd been grappling with the pain in his thigh and thinking about Peyton. God, he missed her almost as much as he'd miss breathing if it were taken from him.

"Come in."

The door opened and Defino poked her head inside. "Can I talk to you for a moment?"

Marco motioned to the chair on the other side of his desk. It seemed strange to welcome Defino into the office that had been hers for so many years, but she came in and looked around, giving him a nod of approval.

Sinking into the chair, she studied him a moment, her hands clasped, her eyes narrowed in concentration.

Marco drummed his fingers on the blotter, then met her gaze. "Am I relieved of duty?"

She tilted her head. "Should you be?"

He held out his hands in a gesture of futility. He couldn't really answer that. Logic dictated that they probably should remove him, but without the job, he'd go crazy. He needed a distraction.

She crossed one leg over the other. "It was hard for me to leave the field. Did I ever tell you that?"

"No, ma'am."

She nodded. "I wasn't sure what the hell I was doing. I felt so unprepared to take the reins and then the thought of sending my people out into potential danger scared me to death. That first year I must have thought about quitting a million times."

"I get that."

"I know you do." She looked around the room. "But gradually, it started making sense, what I was doing, and my people became so loyal to me that I realized what a responsibility I had to them. I started seeing that we were all that stood between chaos and madness, and if we didn't do our job, people got hurt, they died, they didn't get justice. My people are the ones who did the protecting, the serving, the justice, but without me here to guide them, to direct them, chaos would rule."

Marco didn't know how to answer her. He wasn't feeling that at the moment. He was still longing for the street, for the fieldwork, for Peyton as his partner. That's all he'd ever really wanted and now it was gone.

"You have that loyalty, D'Angelo. You have that dedication already." She pointed over her shoulder to the door. "Sam Watson tried and tried to get them to tell her what was going on. She threatened, she cajoled, she pleaded, but they stood by you, every last one of them. They stood fast, declaring their loyalty. Even Jake. *Even Jake.*"

Marco lifted his head and looked at her.

She gave a chuckle. "I thought for sure he was the weak link. She's good, Sam, she zeroed in on him at once, holding him back without the others, but he didn't break, not even for a moment. He gave you his complete trust and devotion."

Marco swallowed hard. He didn't know what to do with that.

"Don't you think such loyalty deserves something in return, D'Angelo? Don't you think your people deserve to know that when you send them out on a call, you are sending them with full confidence in the job they have to do? Don't you think they deserve a captain who is clear headed and focused on their safety?"

Marco nodded, staring at the blotter.

"Don't you think they deserve a captain who's sober and focused and dedicated to his job?"

"Yes, ma'am," he said.

"I don't know what's going on with you, Marco. I don't begin to understand what you're facing, but pull it together, man, because if I have to come out here again…" Her voice trailed away.

Marco met her gaze.

"…it'll be to remove you permanently from duty."

Then she pushed herself to her feet and walked to the door, yanking it open.

Before she left, however, she paused and glanced at him over her shoulder. "If you need anything, you've only to ask."

Marco watched the door close behind her, then he swiveled around and reached blindly for the bottle of Scotch, but the credenza was empty. He stared at the spot, then searched through his desk, looking for anything, but someone had cleaned him out. He figured he could guess who that might be. Damn him. Abe had no right to interfere in this part of his life.

He slumped in the chair and forced himself to draw a deep breath, holding it. His thigh ached horribly, as if someone was using a dull spoon to gouge at the muscles. He rubbed his knuckles against it and deliberately released his held breath.

A knock sounded at the door and Carly poked her head inside. "Tag wants to see you."

"Send her in."

Tag pushed through the door and stood on the other side of his desk.

"Take a seat," said Marco, pointing to the chair.

"If I want to sit, I'll sit."

Marco frowned, but didn't bother rising. Let her stand if she wanted.

"We got a call."

"Okay?"

"Father shot an intruder in his daughter's bedroom last night around 2:00, but the cops who responded think it's strange that there's no sign of forced entry. Do you want me and Holmes to take it?"

"Yeah."

"Fine." She flipped around and moved to the door. Marco sensed tension in her

"Tag?"

She stopped and slowly swiveled to face him. "What?"

"Is there a problem?"

"Nope." She gave a firm shake of her head, but Marco could tell it was a lie.

"Tag, tell me what's wrong."

She took a step back toward his desk. "Permission to speak freely, sir."

"Permission granted."

"Peyton's my friend and I'm having a hard time accepting the way you dealt with her."

Marco leaned back in his chair. Damn it, he wanted a drink. "I see. Well, what happens between Peyton and me is personal and has nothing to do with my job as your captain. Your disappointment in me is noted, but I would expect you to put that aside because when it comes down to it, I am your captain and I deserve your respect."

"As my captain, you are right."

Marco caught the double meaning of her words. She didn't have to respect him as a man. She just had to do her job. "Good, I'm glad we understand one another."

She nodded, then went to the door and exited without a backward glance.

Marco waited a moment, then he went back through the desk again, looking for any booze that Abe might have missed.

* * *

By the time Marco got back to Abe's condo, his leg felt like it was burning from the inside out. He stripped off his suit and gun, forcing himself to hang them up, believing that such a mundane chore might trick him into believing he was okay, but he wasn't. Slipping on a t-shirt and his athletic shorts, he was confronted with the twisted rope of scar tissue that had now become his thigh. In a moment of weakness, he searched through Abe's cupboards for a drink and found nothing. He *knew* there'd be nothing. He'd watched Abe throw the booze away himself. Steeling his resolve, he walked out of the kitchen and went to his room. Sinking down on the bed, he grabbed the thigh with both hands and pressed on it, hoping the pressure would make the burning sensation ease. Nothing was helping.

Leaning back against the headboard, he tried the breathing exercises Dr. Ferguson had taught him, but he could feel panic beginning to edge up inside of him. He couldn't handle the pain. Not on his own. Not without help. He was going to have to go out and get something to dull it. Still, he knew this was a path back into the despair he'd been feeling the last few days. Drinking was a way to dull the other pain he felt, the pain of losing Peyton, but in an ironic twist, he knew that as long as he kept drinking, he couldn't have her. He was in a vicious cycle of self-destruction, but the damn pain was gnawing at his control, making his heart pound.

He didn't even hear the door open, but Abe suddenly loomed at the end of his bed. He knew he was breathing too fast, sweat beading on his temples, but he couldn't slow his heart or stop the panic.

"What's going on, Angel?" Abe said, coming to the side of the bed.

"The pain's making me crazy," he said between clenched teeth. "You threw out all the booze, but I can't do this, Abe. I can't do this without Peyton."

Abe turned on a heel and left.

Marco closed his eyes, fighting the panic, fighting the pain, and knowing he was losing. He couldn't do this. Not without Peyton. She gave him strength to face each day – a reason to get up and keep fighting. So he drank to dull the pain, but at least then he'd been functioning. This wasn't functioning. This was slowly going insane.

Abe was back, holding a pill and a glass of water out to him. "Take this."

"You don't want me to drink, but you want me to take pain pills?"

"It'll take the edge off. Take it."

Marco glared at him, but he grabbed the pill and popped it in his mouth, following it with the water. Abe took the glass from his hand and set it on the nightstand, then he reached for Marco's wrist with his long fingers and felt his pulse, while he studied his watch.

Marco knew his pulse was racing. He could feel his heart pounding in his ears.

Abe released him and sat down on the bed. "You're having a panic attack."

"You think?"

"Look at me. You've got to calm down. I want you to take a deep breath and hold it."

Marco forced himself to comply.

"That's good. Hold it. Now slowly release it."

His breath left him in a shivery pant.

"Good. Now take another and hold it."

Marco kept his eyes fixed on Abe's face, the purple and silver beads on the end of his dreadlocks. He sucked in air and held it.

"Good. Now release."

Marco did what he told him. The pain still raged from his knee to his groin, but it wasn't quite as all-consuming now.

"Close your eyes, Angel."

"Abe."

"Just do it. Close your eyes and imagine the ocean."

"I hate this shit," he said, but he closed his eyes.

"Good. Now imagine the ocean. Can you see the waves? Can you hear the surf?"

Marco tried to pull an image into his mind.

"Hear the surge of the water." Abe's fingers closed over his wrist again. "That's it. Watch the waves rise, recede, back and forth, back and forth."

On and on droned Abe's voice and Marco allowed himself to be lost in the imagery, the imagination, the calm.

"That's good. Keep breathing. Slowly. In and out. Watch the waves. Hear the surf."

The bed shifted as Abe rose to his feet. Marco was vaguely aware that he went to the door and stepped out into the hallway, but he tried to keep the calm folded about him, tried to keep his breathing steady, focusing on the visual picture Abe had given him. The pain had become something he could battle, something he could ignore.

Marco opened his eyes. He could see Abe silhouetted in the doorway, talking on his cell phone.

"Hey, Grey, it's Abe." He chuckled. "Yeah, how's Sarah and the boys? Good, yeah, good. Busy. The dead are always needing their internal organs removed. Yeah, I know, but you smoked me the last time. I'm just not golf material. Can't see any reason to wander around trying to hit a stupid little ball into a metal cup. I think it's a straight man's gig anyway, although I do love the pants."

Who the hell was he talking to?

"Listen, Grey, I'm calling in a favor. Yeah, I know, but I got you a discount on that casket. Come on, man, that beauty was top of the line. Dracula would have loved that casket, right?" He laughed again. "Actually, no, this is for a friend, a very good friend." Abe paused. "Ha, I wish, but my Angel's straight. The entire gay community held a wake over that one, let me tell you. No, look, Greyson, I really need your help with this."

Abe's voice trailed away as he moved toward the kitchen. Marco figured he should probably follow him and find out what the hell he was doing, put up some sort of fight, but whatever Abe had given him was beginning to work and he felt as boneless as gelatin. He couldn't summon up the energy necessary to stand and he wasn't sure he'd be able to stand even if he tried. Closing his eyes again, he brought up the image of the ocean and listened to the rhythmic sound of the waves.

*   *   *

"Hey, Jeff, how you doing?"

Jeff looked up from his mother's letters and smiled at Trevor. "I'm holding it together."

"First day back?"

"Yeah. I needed to get back to work."

"Did you get the paperwork all taken care of?"

"Most of it." He lifted the letter. "This is the last."

"What is it?"

Jeff gave a laugh. "Apparently my mother had a pen pal."

"A pen pal?" Trevor took a seat before his desk, holding out his hand.

Jeff passed the letter over. "Yeah, go figure."

"A pen pal? I haven't heard about that for years."

"I know, but she has stacks of these things. They wrote to each other every week."

"Huh, wild." He passed it back. "Anything interesting?"

"This kid, Finn Getter…"

"Kid? How old?"

"Fifteen when they started writing."

33

"What's a fifteen year old boy want with a pen pal?"

"Seems he was raised in a very secluded family. They didn't have internet or television, and he didn't go to school. He'd go to the library and the librarian would let him get on the computer. That was his only contact with the outside world, that and my mother."

"That's wild. Where's he from?"

"That's also weird. Santa Cruz, California."

"How can that be? Isn't Santa Cruz pretty big?"

"He lives in the mountains above the city."

"Wow, that's crazy stuff." Trevor gave a laugh. "Just think, your mom might have been more technologically advanced than this kid."

"Yeah, can you believe that? My mom, who was afraid of computers, understood how to use them more than a fifteen year old kid."

* * *

Dear Aster,

Thank you for the birthday card. I can't believe I'm seventeen now. I'm still going to the library as often as I can, but it's been hard. Little Gina has to have surgery. She's almost three now, so the doctors thought it was time. Boy, we had to save up a lot of money for that.

In fact, Thatcher let me do some work on the ranch next to us because he said it was my responsibility to get the money needed for Gina's surgery. That's what men do. The work was hard. I'm not much good at mowing and cutting tree branches, but I worked as hard as I could and finally, Gina can get her surgery. My sister, Janice, is really excited. It's been so hard for Gina to eat and she's so skinny. Janice is hoping this will fix everything.

Thatcher won't let Janice stay in the hospital with Gina. He says she's needed back here. He's probably right. Janice does a lot of the cooking and caring for the other children. If she wasn't here, it would make it a lot harder on everyone.

Janice asked if I could go in her place, so I get to stay with Gina in the hospital. That's good. I really love Gina and I know I'd want to be there anyway. Mama says she'll come at night after the work is done, but I told her I didn't mind staying by myself. And I don't. It's nice to be away from the farm. It's nice to be away from the family.

I know I shouldn't say that, but lately Mrs. Elder, the librarian, has been talking to me about going to college. I don't know how that could happen, but she said the community college would take me. All I have to do is show them my grades from home school.

I'd like to do that, but when I told Thatcher, he wasn't happy. I mean, he didn't say no. He just wasn't happy. He said that when I was twenty-one I could do what I wanted, and if I wanted to go to community college then, that was my decision. I agreed. I mean, twenty-one isn't so far away. I might as well stay here until then. Besides, what would Janice and Gina do without me? So, that's that.

How are you? Did you change your heart medicine? I hope you're feeling better. Does Jeff know you had to go to the hospital because your heart was beating too fast? You should tell him. I tell Janice everything.

Your Friend,
Finn Getter

CHAPTER 4

Monday

Peyton sat at her desk, staring at her left hand. This morning she'd forced herself to remove her engagement ring. It was a constant reminder of Marco and she needed to focus on her job. That was all that mattered. Some part of her knew that she wasn't cut out for long term relationships. They'd never worked before. Why would she think it would work now?

Curling her hand into a fist, she grabbed the first burner file in her in-box and threw the cover back, scanning it. She hated this part of the job, looking over other agent's cases, trying to find something they'd missed so the case could be solved. So far, she hadn't found a single case that hadn't been investigated thoroughly, but without new leads, they would never go anywhere.

Margaret, her assistant, stepped into her office. She carried a small box in one hand and a chocolate donut with sprinkles in the other. She set the donut on Peyton's desk and held the box out to her.

"Your business cards arrived. I also got the placard for the door and your locker in the training room."

Peyton tore her eyes from the donut and forced a smile. "Thank you, Margaret," she said, taking the box. "I appreciate everything you do for me."

Margaret smiled and backed from the room. Peyton pulled the donut closer to her. She loved donuts and chocolate and sprinkles, and she especially loved them all jumbled together, but the thought of taking a bite made her feel physically ill.

She pushed it away again and went back to the pile. Tossing the file into the in-box, she thumbed through the stack until she found one with an interesting name. *Operation Iraqi Freedom Lance Corporal Isaac Daws.* She tugged it out and flipped it open.

Lance Corporal Isaac Daws had served three tours of duty in Iraq during the summer of 2004. Upon returning stateside, Daws was diagnosed with PTSD and two years later, he was found dead in a sleazy hotel room in Las Vegas. The coroner ruled it an overdose, but the level of drugs in his system had been far beyond the normal range anyone would inject into himself. His parents hadn't accepted the official report. They put up enough stink to attract the attention of an attorney who got a judge to order another autopsy. This medical examiner, Cecilia Gaston, had ruled his death suspicious.

Peyton flipped through the file. FBI Agent Mark Turner had conducted the initial investigation, but he'd run into a dead end. He couldn't find any sign that anyone else was in the hotel room with the Lance Corporal, there were no phone records indicating he had contact with anyone before he died, and he was found the next morning by the cleaning crew. The only suspicious items Turner had uncovered were a few cryptic notes written on napkins and a single gold coin.

Peyton flipped to the back of the file and located a number of photographs Turner had taken. Three of them showed scraps of napkins with random numbers listed on them. There were four clusters of numbers. The first set consisted of the numbers 42, 45, 50 and 43, 51, 70 on one napkin, then 34, 25, 34 and 34, 05, 13 on another, followed by a cluster of one: 19, 27, 43. The last photo was of a gold coin – on one side, it depicted a pedestal holding a flame and the other, either a king or a god, or so Turner had speculated.

Peyton set down the photos of the napkins, but sat studying the one of the gold coin. The edges were rough, not the perfect circle of a modern coin and the gold had an odd, burnished look to it.

Turning back to the file, she read the rest of Turner's report. Daws had grown up in Daly City, which is why his file ended up in their office. He'd been an average student in high school, enlisted when he graduated, and had been an exemplary soldier. On his second tour of duty in Iraq, he and his convoy had tripped an IED. Two of his fellow marines had died at the scene, another on the way to the field hospital. Daws had suffered a brain injury, been sent home, but three months later, he was returned to Iraq.

Peyton sighed. Shit. The poor guy didn't stand a chance. There had been one arrest for public drunkenness six months before his death, but he'd gotten off with probation. He'd held four different jobs, but he'd been let go from each one. He was too slow or he mouthed off to his supervisor. Once he threatened to beat a customer with a lawn chair. Clearly this was a man struggling to readjust to modern society. Then he'd gone to Vegas. One of the casinos had thrown him out when he got drunk and belligerent at a blackjack table, and the next night he was dead of a drug overdose.

It filled Peyton with sadness. *Serve your country, die in a sleazy hotel, broke and alone.*

She looked at the coin again. What the hell was a soldier doing with something like this? And what was it? Even Turner hadn't been sure what he was looking at when he saw it. Since there had been no real evidence of foul play, Turner had finished off his report, bagged up the evidence, and passed it along.

Lance Corporal Isaac Daws had become a cold case and wound up on Peyton's desk.

Grabbing the photo, Peyton pushed her chair back and went to the door, turning left to circle around the cubicle jungle. She found Margaret at her own desk, typing on the computer. She looked up and gave Peyton a smile, her short brown hair a perfect halo of hairspray around her head.

"Yes, Agent Brooks?"

"I just realized I don't know where Agent Campbell's office is?" Thomas (Tank) Campbell was the third member of the Ghost Squad, built like a truck with a head full to bursting with random knowledge. He'd impressed Peyton on their last case with the wealth of information his crew-cut noggin contained. If anyone might recognize the coin, Tank would be the one.

Margaret rose to her feet and pointed around the arc of the cubicle jungle. "Third door past the conference room."

"Thank you."

"Anytime, Agent Brooks."

Peyton moved briskly toward the indicated door. The gold placard beside it read Special Agent Thomas Campbell. Peyton lifted her hand and knocked.

"Enter."

She turned the doorknob and pushed it open. "Hey, Tank," she began, then stopped short. Tank's office was a veritable library. Every wall was lined with bookshelves and those bookshelves were all filled to bursting with hardbound books. "Oh, my," she breathed.

Tank rose to his feet, crossing around his desk. "Agent Brooks, how nice to see you," he said. "Come in, come in."

Peyton left the door open and stepped forward. As he handed her into a leather armchair before his massive wooden desk, Peyton noticed his office didn't have the requisite grey on grey color scheme that everything else in the building did.

"This is something," she said, looking around. "It's like your own personal library."

He gave a chuckle. "You should see my wife's office. She's an anthropology professor at Cal. She has more books than I do. One of her bookcases slides over the front of another one. Her books are two layers deep."

Peyton smiled. "I didn't know you were married."

He reached for a picture on his desk and showed it to her. Tank and a smiling woman stared back at her, the woman in a white veil and dress, Tank in a tuxedo. The woman was obviously a number of years older than him.

Peyton felt a stab of pain, but forced it down. Tank and his wife looked very happy together. "She's pretty. How long have you been married?"

"Three years." He took his seat again. "I'll tell you a secret. I was her student at Cal."

That explained the age difference.

"Not that we acted on our feelings while I was in her class. It was all very proper. I waited to ask her out until after the final grades were in."

Peyton couldn't help but share his laugh. "That's a great story, Tank. I'm glad someone can make it work." *Shit. Don't go there.* She felt tears prickle in her eyes and bit her bottom lip to stop it.

"You okay, Agent Brooks?" he asked, his expression sobering.

Peyton nodded vigorously. "How 'bout you call me Peyton?"

"Sure. Was there something you wanted or is this just a pleasant visit?"

Peyton passed the wedding picture back to him. "I was going through files and I came across an interesting one." She told him about Lance Corporal Daws, the first autopsy, and the second. Then she looked at the photo in her hand again. "Have you ever seen a coin like this before?"

He took it and gave it a speculative look. "Huh, interesting. The rough edges suggest an ancient coin, and the lack of patina makes me think it's almost pure gold. Gold doesn't really pick up a patina with age the way other metals do. I'm unfamiliar with the markings."

"He had the coin on him when he was found, and three scraps of napkin with numbers written on them."

"Interesting. Do you have the numbers?"

"They're in the file still."

He turned to his computer and lifted the cover on his scanner. "Do you mind if I scan this photo? I'll do some research and see what I can find out."

"Sure. I appreciate the help because I'm drawing a blank."

He placed the photo down on the scanning bed and began clicking on his computer. Peyton watched him for a moment, then shifted in her chair restlessly.

"Tank?"

He glanced over at her as the scanner began to make noise.

"You and your wife, did you ever have doubts before you got married? Cold feet?"

He studied her a moment, then faced forward, clasping his hands on his desk. "No, we didn't."

Peyton nodded. "Thanks."

"That doesn't mean it isn't normal. Every couple's different, Peyton. Everyone goes through different things, but I truly believe if two people are better together than apart, they will make it work somehow, even if it doesn't seem like it at first."

She took in his words. If two people are better together than apart? She'd believed she and Marco were better together, but maybe he didn't. Maybe he felt like he couldn't trust her to stay with him through the bad times. If so, how did she convince him? How did she make him understand she would do anything to keep what they had?

Tank turned back to his computer and clicked some more, then he lifted the lid and gave her back the photo. "Are you sure everything's all right?"

She nodded, not trusting herself to speak.

"Brooks?"

Rosa Alvarez, her boss, poked her head inside Tank's office.

"Yes?"

"A word when you have the time."

"Sure."

Rosa disappeared.

Peyton smiled at Tank. "Thank you for looking at this." She held up the photo. "And for the talk. I appreciate it."

"Anytime. If you want to talk again, I'm here."

"I appreciate that too." With a nod, she stood and headed for the door, trying to figure out what she'd done wrong to make Rosa want a word.

*   *   *

Completely the opposite of Tank's office, Rosa Alvarez didn't believe in anything that would muddy up her image of the consummate professional. There were no personal pictures on her walls and the window coverings had been removed, allowing stark white light to filter into the room. Commendations in heavy wooden frames stood in perfectly spaced rows, interspersed with maps of San Francisco, Washington, D.C. and the FBI compound in Quantico.

She'd not traded up on the standard issue grey desk, but her computer monitor was larger than Peyton's and now showed a GPS map of the City. She motioned Peyton to a seat across from her and slid back her chair, crossing her legs and placing her clasped hands on her knee.

Peyton took the seat, feeling as uncomfortable as she always did. There was something about this woman that intimidated her, made her feel inferior, and she hated that weakness in herself. She hated any weakness in herself.

"Radar informed me you took a few personal days off."

Peyton forced herself to look Rosa in the eyes. "It won't happen again. I'm sorry."

One of the things that intimidated Peyton was the way Rosa probed with her gaze before speaking. Not that she minced words, but she didn't immediately give up what she was thinking. In fact, Peyton had no idea what she thought about her. When Peyton had been a detective with the SFPD, they'd worked a case together. Peyton had surrendered her gun to save Marco's life, something that was apparently a cardinal sin. She still felt like Rosa judged her for that decision.

"Everyone needs personal time, Agent Brooks. You don't have to apologize for it."

"Except I know we were in the middle of a case and I should have stayed to finish it."

"We solved a triple homicide and uncovered the murders of thirty-three other people. We can now give closure to families who never knew what happened to their loved ones. It was a job well done."

Peyton inclined her head. "Thank you, Sarge."

"Radar said you handled yourself well, seeing as this was your first case. You persisted in a line of questioning that eventually led to discovering the actual killer."

Peyton hid her smirk. Go figure. She thought Radar was mostly annoyed by her.

"I appreciate his kind words and confidence in my abilities."

Rosa scrutinized her again. "If you need more time, Agent Brooks, I will grant it to you."

"No, ma'am. I don't need more time."

"I want the best agents in the field. I don't want them distracted by personal problems. If you need more time to work on a personal problem, I would prefer you take it."

"I don't need more time."

"It's important that you understand, your team depends on you having your head in the game. Your teams deserves your complete focus."

"I know…"

"And if you're compromised in anyway, if you have personal issues that you need to confront, I want you to make that priority number one."

"I'm fine…"

"We aren't robots, Agent Brooks. We're still human with the foibles of humanity. We can be compromised by our emotions and…"

"Marco left me."

Silence filled the office.

Peyton closed her eyes and looked down. There, she'd said it. She had to do something to stop Rosa's interrogation, but that hadn't really been what she wanted to say, especially not to Rosa Alvarez.

"I see."

Peyton opened her eyes again, but she avoided looking at her boss. She felt like someone had dropped a weight on her chest and it was difficult to breathe.

"I'm sorry, Peyton."

Peyton's gaze snapped to her face.

"I know how much you both care about each other."

Peyton slid forward in her chair. "I need to work. I need to stay busy. Please don't send me home."

"If there's something you can do…"

"There isn't. He asked me for time to work through some things he's facing and I have to give him that."

"I understand."

"I need this job and I promise you, Rosa, I won't compromise my team, I won't be distracted when you need me. The shock is over, now I've got to process the loss, and the only way for me to do that is to work."

They held each other's gaze, then Rosa broke eye contact and looked at the photo in Peyton's hand. "What's that?"

Peyton glanced down. She'd forgotten she had it. "Um, a photo in a file I was reviewing." She passed it across the desk. "I took it to Tank to see if he recognized it. It was found on the body of a dead marine."

Rosa studied the photo from all angles. "Interesting. Looks old, doesn't it?"

"Yeah. The edges are sort of wonky, not like a modern coin."

Rosa passed it back. "Well, if anyone will be able to figure it out, it'll be Tank."

Peyton nodded.

Rosa folded her hands again. "You've always conducted yourself with dedication, Agent Brooks. I have no doubt that will continue. My door is always open if you need anything."

"Thank you, Sarge."

"You may return to work."

Peyton let out a breath of relief and scrambled to her feet before Rosa could change her mind. She left Rosa's office and wandered back to her own, contemplating what Rosa had said. Radar had praised her in his report and Rosa Alvarez seemed pleased with her work. Usually that would send her over the moon with happiness, but today, it left her feeling hollow and alone.

She paused to study the new placard on the wall beside her door. *Agent Peyton Brooks*. Her daddy would be proud. He'd always told her she was going to do big things. Then why didn't it feel better? Why didn't it feel as wonderful as she'd always hoped?

Because there was no one to share the happiness with, and the only person she wanted there for her had taken himself away.

Squaring her shoulders, she stepped into her office. Emma Redford, or rather Bambi, sat in the chairs before her desk, but she popped to her feet the moment she spotted Peyton, her face awash with anticipation.

As she took Peyton in, her expression shifted to sadness. "You have plans for lunch, don't you?"

Peyton gave a surprised laugh. "No, no I don't have plans. Where do you want to go?"

Bambi clapped her hands together. "What are you feeling like? Cow, pig, chicken?"

Peyton crossed around her and reached for the Daws' file, sliding the photo inside. "How about something without a face?"

Bambi nodded vigorously.

Peyton lifted the file and dropped it on the others. "Then when we're done, let's go to the practice range and shoot the hell out of things."

Bambi looked like she might just burst with joy. "Oh, I like the way you think, girlfriend."

*   *   *

Ruth handed him a glass of iced tea. He sipped at it and settled it on the table, looking out over the backyard. He held one of Finn's letters in his hand, but the night was so nice, the air so warm and sultry, he just felt like sitting for a minute and remembering his mother the way she was when he was younger.

Ruth sat down beside him. "You okay?"

He nodded, giving her a smile. "Just thinking about Mom."

"That's one of those letters?"

"Yeah."

"Why do you keep reading them? They make you sad every time."

"They don't make me sad. It's just…"

"What, Jeff?"

"I wish I'd known she was so lonely. She wrote to this boy for years, every week without fail, and she told him things she never told me. Why didn't she tell me these things? Why didn't she tell me she was afraid at night? That sometimes she felt too weak to make herself dinner."

Ruth reached over and settled her hand on his arm. "She was your mother. She didn't want you to worry. You had your own family you were trying to raise."

Jeff stared at the envelope, the beautiful handwriting. "They were both lonely. They both felt left out, separated by a world they didn't understand."

"What do you mean?"

"Neither one of them understood technology. Remember when I got the cell phone for her."

"I remember."

"She told Finn it worried her all the time. She was afraid people were listening to her or watching her through the camera." He gave a laugh. "When she'd take a shower, she'd hide it in a drawer so the government couldn't spy on her."

Ruth smiled.

"I should have spent more time explaining it to her."

"And it wouldn't have made any difference. Aster was set in her ways. She didn't want to adapt. She liked things the way they were and she hated change. You know that. How many times did we try to get her to leave that house?"

"I know." He gazed at the flowers in bloom, the climbing rose covering the back fence. "I just keep seeing her as that young woman in front of the Washington Monument. Where did that woman go? Why didn't she keep that adventurous spirit?"

"I think it left when your dad died. He was the adventurous one. Remember how he'd get her to go on those cross country trips and she'd complain, but she'd do it for him."

Jeff nodded. "She did pull into herself after he died, but I can't help it, Ruth. I wish I'd tried harder. I wish I would have known. I hate that she was alone."

Her fingers tightened on his arm. "She wasn't alone. She had her friend and they were kindred spirits, Jeff, like souls who comforted each other."

Jeff lifted the letter and read the address for the hundredth time. Kindred spirits? Like souls? God, he hoped that had been enough.

* * *

Dear Aster,

Thank you for asking about Little Gina. She's doing well. She'll always have a scar, but unless you get right in front of her, you hardly notice it. She's gained some weight and that makes Janice happy.

I keep thinking about the hospital. I keep thinking about the doctors and the way they acted. They knew they were helping people. They knew they had power in their hands. I think I'd like to be like them.

I've been researching what it would take to become a doctor. Mrs. Elder is helping me. I think that's what I'd like to do when I leave the family – study medicine. I know it isn't going to be easy, and it's going to take a long time, but I can't imagine anything else making me feel that good.

I'm not sure how I'll pay for it. Once you leave the family at twenty-one, you're expected to make it on your own. You can't come back and ask for help. I get that. It's hard enough for all of us to make it now. There's no way they could help me go to school.

Mrs. Elder says there's a way to accomplish everything. She reminds me a lot of you, Aster. She's so positive, so certain I can do this. I wish

Mama felt the same way. All Mama does is worry about what will happen to me when I leave.

I tell her I'll be okay. I tell her that a lot of men have left before me, but she still worries. The problem is we don't really hear from those that leave. They go out into the world and it swallows them up.

Thatcher says that's normal. That's what men do. They go out and start their own families, but some of the mothers, they still miss their sons. They still wish they could see them.

Honestly, they never say that. Not out loud. It would be bad to say such things out loud. It might jinx the men, it might bring bad things to them, so the mothers don't say it, they just keep it inside, but you can see it sometimes. You can see it in their eyes.

Their eyes say things that their mouths never would. Their eyes say they remember. I know Mama's eyes will say the same thing when I'm gone. I just know it, but I have to go and she has to learn to accept it.

Your friend,
Finn Getter

CHAPTER 5

Tuesday

Marco's entire detective force stood around Carly's desk when he arrived in the morning. Carly sat with her hands in her lap, looking worried. He paused on the other side of the counter, trying to take it all in. He still felt a little fuzzy headed from the pill Abe had given him the previous night, but the pain was manageable.

As always, Tag moved away from the others, grabbing the half-door and pulling it open, so he could address her problem first. "The father of the girl shot *the intruder* in the back as he was climbing out of her bedroom window. There's blood splatter on the curtains, the window sill, and the walls on either side of the window. There's also signs that he was dragged back inside and dumped on her bedroom floor."

Marco moved through the half-door. "So they dragged him back inside to make sure it looked like he was in the room?"

"Right, but you can't hide a shot to the back."

"Meaning he was trying to get away."

"Exactly."

"Did Abe get the body?"

"Yeah, I put a call into him, but he's not there yet."

"Was the girl in the room when he was shot?"

"Yeah, she was."

"What time did this happen?"

"2:00AM."

"Where was she?"

Tag gave him an arch look. "In the room."

Marco drew a breath for patience. He was going to have to do something about Tag's antagonism toward him. Cho and Simons marked it and shifted uncomfortably. "I

51

meant where was she exactly? In the bed asleep or near the window?"

"Oh." She glanced at Holmes.

"By the door," said Holmes.

"The boy a teenager?"

"Yep," answered Holmes.

Marco considered that. "And no sign of forced entry?"

"None."

"Well, in my day, I climbed in a few bedroom windows in the middle of the night." The men gave him knowing laughs, but Carly looked confused and Tag glared at him. "Meaning, the window was probably left open for him to get inside."

"You think the daughter knows him?" said Tag.

"I'll bet she does."

"And she stood there and denied it the whole time? She said she'd never seen him before in her life."

"Well, she didn't want to get in trouble. Let's bring her in and question her without Dad."

"The father lawyered up before the cops even arrived, for both of them."

"Huh, interesting, but we'll deal with that later. I'll bet they go to the same school. Head over to the high school and see if he's a student there. Then find someone who knew the two of them. If we can link them, we might get a shot at interrogating the daughter."

"On it," said Holmes. He and Tag headed for the door.

Marco leaned on his cane and faced Simons and Cho. "Well?"

"The headshop case is stalled," said Cho, crossing his arms over his chest. "We've talked with the wife, the two tenants on either side, we've pulled his records off the cloud and Stan has gone through them, but he doesn't see anything fishy in the transactions. All we've got is the junkie that body slammed you."

"We're still holding him?"

"He assaulted an officer of the law. Yeah, we're still holding him."

"Well, let's get him up here for interrogation."

"Okay."

"Why'd you bring him in anyway?"

"Byrony, the girl that worked in the headshop, said he came in a few days before the owner was torched and demanded weed, but his prescription had run out, so Greer told him to get lost. He threw a stink and they had to call the cops to remove him. He threatened to kill Greer."

"Greer's the headshop owner?"

"Quentin Greer," offered Simons.

Marco felt a wash of guilt. He didn't even know the names of the homicide victims they were investigating. Shit, he had to get himself back on track. "What's the junkie's name?"

"Albie Brighton."

"Okay. Let me know when you get him up here. I want to watch the interrogation."

Simons gave him a salute and Cho nodded, but his eyes traveled over Marco from head to foot. Marco knew he had a lot to repair with his people. He just didn't know how.

After they left, he looked at Carly.

"They were all demanding to talk to you. Did you want me to call your cell?"

"You could have. You also could have told them to go back to their desks until I get in. Then call them up one at a time once I got settled."

"I'm sorry. I didn't think about that."

"Yeah, well, it felt a little like an ambush this morning."

"You're right. I'll do a better job of running interference from now on." She offered him a bright smile.

He forced one in return. She was wearing a sweater that looked like it was two sizes too small, and he could see a lot more thigh than he probably should, but he just wasn't sure how to approach that. Shit. All he needed was a sexual harassment case against him now. Lifting his eyes to her forehead, he drew another of Abe's cleansing breaths. "Can you call Jake Ryder to my office?"

"Yes."

He turned toward his door.

"Captain?"

He stopped and looked back at her.

"Which one's Jake Ryder?"

"The CSI."

"Right. Which button?"

Marco clenched his hand around the head of his cane. "Button number three."

"Thanks."

He eased into his desk chair and positioned his leg, hooking the cane over the chair arm. His phone buzzed in his pocket. He pulled it out, staring at the screen. He realized he was hoping for a text from Peyton, but it was Abe. He thumbed it on.

Grey will see you tomorrow afternoon at 2:00PM. I'll send you the address. Don't be late. Do you want me to come with you? Abe.

No! texted Marco, *just send the address.*

Oh, come on, Angel, I've been dying to see you in your skivvies for years.

Marco let out a laugh and scrubbed a hand across his face. He wasn't even going to grace that with an answer.

A knock came on his open door. He lowered the phone and looked up. Jake leaned in the opening. "You wanted to see me?"

"You want to come inside?"

Jake gave him an aggravated look, but came into the office.

"Take a seat."

He pulled the chair back and sat down.

"Did you get evidence from the case Tag and Holmes are working?"

"Yeah. Took blood samples. Lots of pictures. I was just processing everything when you called for me." The clipped tone of his voice grated at Marco.

"Good. Did you find anything unusual?"

"What? Beyond the fact that the father shot the kid in the back? Or maybe that it was a sixteen or seventeen year old kid? Or maybe the daughter's weird affect when she pretended she didn't know the kid?"

Marco narrowed his eyes on him. "Do you have a problem, Ryder?"

Jake held up a hand and let it fall. "Why would I have a problem?"

"'Cause it seems like I'm getting a whole lot of attitude from you."

Jake scrubbed a hand across his mouth. "Look, Adonis…" Before Marco could correct him, he held up a hand. "Captain, I'm a little pissed."

"Okay."

"I don't know what's going on with you, but you hurt Peyton and that doesn't track with me, then you put me in a position to defend your sorry ass and the truth is, I'm not sure I should have. I lied to them, Adonis. I perjured myself."

"You weren't on trial, Ryder."

"Well, it didn't feel right. I lied to a woman that I respect a lot. I lied to Defino."

"How did you lie?"

"I told her I have faith in your ability to lead this precinct."

"And you don't?"

Jake dropped his hand against his thigh. "No, I don't. You're a hot mess."

"I see."

"And yet, I'm here. And I'll be here, standing by you, even when I shouldn't. Even when I think it's wrong. Even when I think you're an idiot."

Marco didn't answer. He should reprimand Jake for being disrespectful, but he couldn't. Jake was more than an employee. Marco wasn't sure what the hell he was, but he was definitely more than an employee.

"So where do we go from here?"

Jake shook his head. "I don't know, but I just know I don't give my loyalty lightly, Captain. Neither do the rest of your people. So pull it together because I don't know if I'll have your back a second time."

With that, he pushed himself out of his chair and left the office.

*   *   *

Albie Brighton looked like a junkie. His brown hair stood up all over his head, not having been washed for weeks. His eyes were bloodshot and he twitched. His leg jumped up and down as he sat handcuffed in the chair, and his eyes darted about the room. A scraggly beard covered his chin and he had open sores around his mouth. Tattoos ran up and down his arms, but Marco could see scabs where he'd been picking at something on his skin.

Simons stood behind his chair and Brighton kept trying to keep him in sight, but the shackles on his wrist and ankles prevented much mobility. Cho had taken the precaution of chaining him to the floor. Probably a good thing too, because Albie Brighton looked like he wanted to bolt.

Cho took a seat at the table at an angle to him and settled a file on its metal surface. "Albie Brighton, you have priors. Picked up six times for vagrancy, four for drug possession, and once for assault. Now you're in stir for assaulting an officer, our captain." Cho leaned closer to him. "Let's say I don't like you much."

Marco leaned against the table in the viewing room, propping his cane beneath the two-way mirror. It fascinated him to watch the various ways cops went about interrogation, each one different. Tag mocked her suspects. Cho went for intimidation. He himself never knew what approach to take, which is why he'd never been very good at it. But Peyton, Peyton had been the queen. She always knew how to approach a suspect and he'd been amazed at how she usually manipulated them into a full confession. God, he missed her so damn much.

"I want a lawyer."

"We called one. Public defender. He's not much interested in you, but he'll be here. I thought we'd talk while we wait for him."

"I ain't got nothing to say. I'll wait for my lawyer."

"Okay, but with this many priors, you're looking at some serious time. Judges don't like it when you start attacking cops. If you help me, I might be able to help you."

"I'll help you, but you gotta help me first."

"What do you want? I'm not much interested in negotiating with a junkie before I get something first."

"I'm not a junkie. I have a disease."

"You have a disease?" Cho glanced up at Simons. "You hear that?"

"I heard it. It's called being a junkie," said Simons.

Albie contorted his head to look at him. "No, it's called fibermitosis, chronic pain, you know?"

"Fibermitosis? You mean fibromyalgia?"

"Yeah, that's it. I got fibro-algenia."

"Yeah? That's why you shoot up?"

"I don't shoot up. I smoke weed."

Cho gave him a slow, cunning smile. "That you get from a headshop in the Haight run by Quentin Greer?"

Brighton made a disparaging noise. "That mother fu—"

"Uh uh, don't use that language around me."

Brighton leaned forward as far as his shackles would allow. "He's a prick. He cut me off."

"Did he now? Why?"

"He said my prescription wasn't active anymore. I told him I had a new doctor, to call him, but he wouldn't do it. If I don't get my pot, I can't function. I can't even get out of bed. I can't eat. All I got is the pain. It eats at you, it makes you crazy." He touched his temple. "It makes you nuts."

Marco felt a prickle of sweat at his temples. Shit. He knew what that felt like.

"And pot lets you function?" said Cho with a scoffing tone.

"It lets me think. When I got pain, I can't even think straight. I can't do nothing. I can't even be still."

Cho leaned over and looked at his bouncing leg. "You aren't still now."

"I ain't had my medicine for days. Besides that, I had to get other stuff. You know?"

"I know."

"And that stuff isn't the same. It makes me jumpy. It makes me anxious. But weed, man, weed makes everything okay. I'm the nicest guy you'll ever meet when I got my blunts."

Cho opened the folder and looked at it for a moment. "Is that what happened, Albie?"

"What?"

"Greer denied you your blunts, so you poured gasoline on him and lit a match?"

"What?" His face contorted and he looked around at Simons. "What are you talking about?"

"Greer's dead. Someone killed him. Torched him."

"Dead? Bull shit. I just saw him last week."

"That's when he died."

"Bull shit."

Cho picked up a photo out of the file and slid it in front of Brighton. "That's Quentin Greer."

Brighton's eyes went wide and his mouth hung open. "I didn't do that. I didn't do nothing to him."

"Byrony, his assistant, said you came in the headshop and pitched a fit when he wouldn't give you your blunts. Now, here's what I think. You came back that night when he was closing up."

58

"No. I went and got other stuff. I was stoned and I passed out in an alley."

"You and Greer get into another argument when no one was around."

"No."

"Then you tossed gasoline on him. Where'd you get the gasoline, Albie?"

"I didn't go back there."

"Then you lit your lighter. I mean you had one on you when we picked you up. I think you used the same lighter you use for your blunts to make Greer a shish kabob."

Brighton was shaking his head and making strange sobbing sounds. He tried to talk, but he couldn't. Cho swiveled and looked at the two-way mirror. Marco glanced down. He didn't think Albie had enough sense of purpose to carry out this murder. He was exactly what he said, a junkie looking for his next fix. The addiction was so all-consuming that he wouldn't have time to worry about revenge.

"All I wanted was my blunts, all I wanted was the medicine. I'm the nicest guy you'll ever see when I get it. I'm the nicest guy you'll ever know."

Marco tapped on the glass. Cho rose to his feet and left the room, stepping into the viewing room.

"Cut him loose."

Cho sighed. "We got nothing then."

"I know, but he ain't it."

"Yeah. Poor bastard. I almost want to go get him a blunt myself."

Marco nodded, his attention focused on Albie. *All I got is the pain. It eats at you, it makes you crazy. It makes you nuts.* Shit. Marco understood Albie Brighton better than anyone.

* * *

Jeff pressed the glass to the ice dispenser, then filled it with water, taking a sip. He moved out of the dimly lit

kitchen and into the family room, sinking down into his
armchair and settling the glass on the end table.

Picking up his reading glasses, he perched them on
his nose and picked up the stack of letters. Ruth had begun
complaining about the letters, worrying about him reading
them all of the time. She said they made him sad.

They did make him sad. It made him sad to know his
mother had confided things in a stranger that she'd never told
her own son, but it also gave him a glimpse into her life, a
way to learn things about her that she would never have
shared with him.

He didn't want to upset Ruth, so he found himself
waking in the middle of the night and sneaking downstairs to
read in the quiet hours before dawn. He was rationing out
these letters, allowing himself only one or at most two a night
because he was trying to prolong this connection to his
mother.

Once he finished the last letter, he knew she'd be
gone, and he knew he had to accept it. He had to let his
mother rest in peace, but for now, for now he intended to
keep this little part of her with him, treasuring it.

* * *

Dear Aster,

I just turned 18. I'm legally an adult, which means I
have more responsibility now in the family. Janice
is pregnant again. We're hoping for a boy this time.
Little Gina is doing well. Mama has been sick
though. She has this pain in her belly and nothing
we give her seems to help. I'm trying to save up
money to get her to the doctor. I've also been
reading a lot at the library, trying to find medical

books, but Thatcher is starting to limit how much time I can spend there.

He says I'm needed at the ranch. I need to teach the other boys how to do the chores. That's what happens when you turn 18 in the family. You start directing the younger ones on how to do your job because in three years I have to leave, and someone has to take my place.

Since I've never really done the big chores like the other boys, the chopping or the clearing or the building, I've actually been working with the boys like me, the boys who can't do the heavy work.

One little guy named Ezekiel is my favorite. He's so funny. He has the same problem as Gina did, but we don't have the money for his surgery. Anyway he makes jokes all the time. He gets all of us laughing so hard we don't get much work done. Thatcher gets mad, so we tell Ezekiel to stop, but pretty soon he's making jokes again, and we're laughing. I've got to work on him though. Thatcher said if I couldn't get him to take the work seriously, he would have to go do the harder work, but he can't do that. He gets so tired, he has to sit down a lot and he can't stay out in the sun.

Whenever he works with me on the garden, I always set up an umbrella for him, so he can be in the shade. I know the other boys won't do this. They're too busy. They have too much to do.

When I look in the medical books, it says he might have cystic fibrosis. After I told Thatcher that, he started telling me I couldn't go to the library anymore. Janice and Mama pleaded with him for me, but now I can only go for a few hours a week and I'm not supposed to look at medical books.

I do anyway.

I know it's wrong, but I can't help it. I want to be a doctor so badly and I think I could be good at it. Like I found out about Ezekiel, I could find out about Mama and help our family. I think that would be a good thing, don't you? Maybe if I go away and become a doctor, Thatcher will let me come back and be the doctor for the family. That way we wouldn't have to pay outside doctors to take care of us.

What do you think about that? Do you think it would work?

Your friend,
Finn Getter

CHAPTER 6

Tuesday

Peyton read back through Lance Corporal Daws' file, searching for something she or Mark Turner might have missed. The only thing that seemed out of place was the photograph of the coin, but Turner hadn't ventured a guess why a marine would have such a strange item on his person, nor where such a coin had come from.

Margaret entered her office, setting down a cup of coffee. Four packets of sugar rested on the saucer.

Peyton smiled at her. "Thank you."

"Can I get you something for breakfast? Radar likes a slice of bacon on a whole wheat bagel. Maybe you'd like to try that?"

Peyton shook her head. Her appetite had been non-existent lately. She ate only when she realized she was getting light headed. "I'm fine. Coffee's good."

"Sarge called a meeting for 9:00."

"Thank you, Margaret." She went back to reading the file, but Margaret didn't leave. Peyton glanced at her. "Did you need something else?"

She clasped her hands before her. Today she wore a soft yellow sweater buttoned to the neck with her pearls resting just below the collar. Her grey hair was swept away from her face and held in place with spray. Hair did not do unruly things with this woman.

"I may be overstepping my boundaries, Agent Brooks, but I want you to know I'm here if you need to talk. I've worked for the FBI my entire career and I feel it is a fine organization, but sometimes, I worry the agents forget they're human and suffer the same loss and heartache that normal humans do."

"Okay?" Peyton wasn't sure where she was going with this.

"I noticed you removed the picture of you and your young man." She nodded to the empty place on Peyton's desk.

She'd put the picture in a drawer because it hurt her to see it, and it made her want to call Marco and beg him not to do this to them. Biting her bottom lip, she folded her hands on the file. "I see."

"Relationships can be difficult to maintain in this line of work and if you need anything, if there's anything I can get you to make this easier, I'm here for you."

Tears burned in Peyton's eyes, but she blinked furiously to clear them. "Thank—" Her voice caught. She cleared it. "Thank you, Margaret. I appreciate that."

Margaret nodded, then turned and walked out. Peyton sat for a moment, staring at the empty doorway, wondering when any mention of Marco was going to stop being like a shot in the gut.

She tried to concentrate on the file, but by 8:55 she gave up and wandered down to the conference room. Tank and Bambi were already there. Bambi waved furiously at her and patted the open seat to her right, but Tank gave her a lift of his chin.

She nodded at Bambi, but wandered to Tank's side of the table. He rose as she approached. She didn't think that was necessary, especially as it forced her to look up at him, but she wasn't in the mood to say anything.

"I gave my wife the copy of the photo I scanned. She's trying to see if she can place it."

"Good. Let me know if she finds anything. Why would a marine have such a strange coin on him?"

Tank shrugged. "That's the mystery."

"And why didn't Agent Turner think it merited more research when he filed his report?"

"I guess we'll just have to wait and see what the professor has to say."

"The professor?"

"My wife."

"You call her the professor?"

He gave Peyton a sheepish look. "She thinks it's cute."

"It's adorable." And a little weird, but who was Peyton to judge?

He beamed a smile at her.

Peyton patted his rock-hard shoulder. "You should smile more, Tank, it suits you." Then she moved to Bambi's side and took a seat. Immediately Bambi hooked her arm through Peyton's, hugging her and resting her head on Peyton's shoulder.

"Lunch was so much fun yesterday."

"Sure."

"Especially target practice. Who knew you were such a deadly shot?"

Who knew? She hadn't been that good a week ago, but then she hadn't had so much rage bottled up inside of her.

Radar entered the room, his dark eyes sweeping over all of them. He gave a chin nod to Tank. Bambi waved at him, but she got the same chin nod. Peyton didn't even get that much recognition.

He took his seat closest to the head of the table and tucked his sunglasses into the collar of his shirt, leaning back and flattening his hand on the table. Silence settled heavy and awkward over the room. Peyton fidgeted, wishing Bambi would give back her arm.

"So, anyone see the game last night?" she said.

Radar gave her a cool look.

"Which one?" asked Bambi.

Peyton shrugged. She had no freakin' idea. She just knew there had to have been a game on somewhere.

Thankfully, Rosa Alvarez appeared. She gave Bambi a severe frown, causing Bambi to release Peyton. Peyton breathed a sigh of relief. She needed to learn how to deliver one of those looks herself.

Dropping a file on the table, Rosa placed her hands on her hips. "We have a case."

"What is it?" asked Bambi, clasping her hands.

"Mermaids...or mermaid. One mer-uh-person."

She tossed a picture into the middle of the table. Peyton wasn't sure what she was seeing, but it sure as hell didn't look like any mermaid she'd ever seen. In fact, it looked like a...

"Baby?" she said.

Rosa gave an uncomfortable nod.

Radar picked up the photo and took a closer look, passing it to Tank.

Peyton didn't know what to say or do. She hated cases where children were involved, especially babies. Except this didn't look like a normal baby. The lower half of the child's body was fused into a single appendage, tapering to a point like a mermaid's tail. The facial features didn't seem completely formed either.

"Sirenomelia," said Tank, studying the picture.

"What?" asked Bambi, straining to see it.

"Sirenomelia or mermaid syndrome. It's a genetic disorder where the legs are completely fused together. Most cases are fatal, in fact, most babies born with sirenomelia are still born. There are usually abnormalities with kidneys and urinary tract development, which makes it almost impossible for the fetus to survive."

"Where was the child found?" asked Radar.

"Some surfers found her tangled in seaweed at Natural Bridges."

"Santa Cruz?"

"Yes."

"She drowned?" asked Peyton.

"Igor's waiting for the body, but the local M.E. thought she was stillborn, just like Tank said. However, someone dumped her in the surf and we need to find out who."

Tank passed the picture to Bambi. Peyton glanced at it and away. Sometimes the depravity of this job was more than she could handle. Someone threw this baby away, someone hadn't even thought she deserved a proper burial. The poor little thing never had a chance at life, but even in death, no one had wanted to lay claim to her. It was an act of such callousness, such inhumanity, that Peyton felt like someone had draped a lead blanket over her.

"There's a bigger problem, though," continued Rosa.

"Bigger than finding out who dumped a child in the ocean?" asked Radar.

"Oh yeah. We were called in because this is about to blow up all over the airwaves. We need to get out there and get this tamped down because when 6:00PM rolls around, the media's going live with this story and everyone in the nation's gonna know about it."

Peyton exchanged a look with her team members. Yep, finding a baby mermaid floating in the ocean was probably bigger than zombies had been.

*   *   *

Natural Bridges State Beach had once been home to three bridges of stone formed over a million years by the deposit of silt and clay, then eroded away by the Pacific Ocean. Only one bridge remained and it was in danger of collapsing under the constant barrage of the waves. Directly in the path of the monarch butterfly migration, Natural Bridges offered the monarch butterflies a home in the eucalyptus trees along the shore, sheltering them from the wind and cold. Every February the city of Santa Cruz held a migration celebration festival.

The Ghost Squad didn't find hordes of butterflies on the beach, but they did find people, lots and lots of people, and then there were the news vans, so many news vans – both local and out of area.

Radar drove the Suburban through the crowds, honking his horn and showing his badge outside the driver's window. People parted for him, but a number of reporters shoved microphones in his face. When he swiveled his head and glared at them from behind his mirrored sunglasses, they backed off quickly.

They finally made it into the parking lot that jutted up along the beach. A patrol officer blocked it off with a wooden barricade. Radar flashed his badge at him and leaned out the window. "We're looking for Lieutenant Brannon?"

The officer turned and pointed at the beach. "She's over there, talking to the surfer dudes who found the body."

Radar nodded and waited while the officer pulled the barricade away, then he drove into the parking lot and parked closest to the beach. A few other cars occupied the spaces, along with four patrol cars. A handful of people stood leaning on the cars and two women stood by a large passenger van that had the word *Horizon* painted on the side of it.

Peyton climbed out of the passenger seat and followed Radar as he stepped over the roped fence separating the parking lot from beach. The waves gently brushed against the shore, sliding in and out with a calm, almost serene quality. Natural Bridges could be a challenging place to surf when the conditions were right, but most often, it was a great place to paddle out and enjoy the motion of the waves without fighting an undertow.

Peyton had never tried surfing herself, but she could see the attraction if this was where you surfed. With the sun shining on the water, it made a pleasant, picturesque location, if you didn't remember a baby had been tossed into the ocean like so much flotsam.

Lieutenant Brannon had her back to them, talking to the three surfers. They each wore wetsuits, but had the tops pulled down to their waists, exposing their naked, toned chests. Peyton figured they had to be late teens, early twenties, with the rugged sun-kissed looks of a California surfer.

One of them nodded over Brannon's shoulder at the Ghost Squad and she turned, giving Radar a severe look. The look immediately shifted to welcome when Radar held out his badge.

"Lieutenant Brannon?"

"Yes." She shook Radar's hand. "FBI, right?" She stood about 5'6" or 5'7" with dirty blond hair cut into a short bob and brown eyes. Lines around her eyes fanned out into her temples, marking her in her late thirties. She was trim and fit, attractive in a plain, wholesome way.

"Right. I'm Special Agent Carlos Moreno and these are my team members, Agents Thomas Campbell, Emma Redford and Peyton Brooks." He pointed at each of them in turn. "Are these the gentlemen who found the body?"

"Yep. They were surfing when they saw something tangled in the kelp. They paddled over and discovered it was a body. Rather than disturbing it, they paddled to shore and called 911." She nodded at a spot out in the surf, sheltered by an outcrop of rocks. "Before we could secure the place, media started appearing. Someone tweeted about it as soon as the boys got to shore."

Radar tilted his head in understanding.

"We knew what a media frenzy this would become. You know? Mermaid, a discarded baby? God, it's gonna be all over. We figured we better get out ahead of it and call you in sooner rather than later."

"Good," said Radar. "Where's the body now?"

"On its way to San Francisco and your M.E. Our CSI's also a part-time M.E., and based on his initial examination, he feels the baby was stillborn, but that isn't going to be enough for the media. They're going to sensationalize it."

Radar nodded, glancing back at the parking lot and the scrum of people jockeying for a view of the beach from the road. "Anyone see anything?"

"You mean like who threw a baby into the drink? No."

"We saw the pictures. The baby clearly had sireno...uh..." He turned to Tank.

"Sirenomelia," offered Tank. When Brannon gave him a confused look, he amended, "Mermaid syndrome."

"Right. I've never seen anything like it. Bruce, our CSI, said the baby appeared to be no more than a few hours old. He estimated she'd been in the water about 24 to 36 hours. Someone really wanted to get rid of her and fast."

Radar nodded at the three boys. "How often do you surf out here?"

"Every day," said the tallest of the three. He looked to be a mix of Pacific Islander and Caucasian, but his hair was so bleached by the sun and surf it was almost blond.

"High school not a priority?"

"We get out here as soon as school gets out."

"You ever see anyone on those cliffs?" Radar pointed to the rise of rocks and brambles to the right of them.

"All the time. It's a popular hiking trail," said Surfer Dude #1.

Brannon nodded. "We get people up there all the time. We're always pulling someone off those rocks."

Peyton looked back at the parking lot, surveying the cars and the smattering of people who had been here before the police barricaded the beach. Finding the mother of this baby was going to be like finding a needle in a haystack. The baby could belong to anyone. Clearly, the mother had given birth and then panicked when the baby was stillborn, or maybe panicked when she saw the degree of deformity. Rather than toss her in a dumpster as so many new mothers did, she tossed her in the ocean, hiding her shame.

"Sparky?" said Radar. "Any thoughts?"

Peyton glanced back at him. His dark brows were lifted over his mirrored sunglasses. She looked at Bambi and Tank, but they didn't offer anything. "We need to check the local hospitals for patients who recently had babies, but came in without them."

"I already placed a call. My partner's tracking that down," said Brannon.

"Then we need to check the high schools," said Peyton.

"The high schools?" questioned Radar.

"Who else would keep a pregnancy hidden, give birth, and then dispose of the evidence?"

Radar swung back around to look at the surfers. "High school kids," he said. "Can you get us a list of all the high schools in the area?"

Brannon nodded. "Sure can. I'll have that for you by the end of the day."

"Great. I just can't wait to go out and tell the principals we think one of their students gave birth to a mermaid," Radar groused.

*   *   *

Jeff couldn't help but think about the letters. It was almost 11:00PM. Ruth would be headed to bed in a few minutes, then he could get them out. He'd started keeping them in a box in the bottom drawer of his desk because she'd begun suggesting he throw them away. She didn't like how obsessed he was with them.

He didn't think he was obsessed. He just wanted to keep the connection to his mother. They kept her alive for him, at least for a while. He imagined her response, he imagined what questions she asked. He could even imagine her sitting in her favorite armchair in front of the window where the morning sunlight shone through, reading them, smiling as she realized someone in the world was thinking of her.

"Huh, that's so strange," came Ruth's voice.

Jeff blinked and stared at the television. A police officer with dirty blond hair and brown eyes was talking into a microphone. Behind her stood a man in a black suit with mirrored sunglasses and a much smaller woman of mixed ethnicity, also wearing a black suit.

"What?"

Ruth pointed at the television. "The mermaid?"

"What mermaid?" Jeff frowned.

"They found a mermaid in the Pacific ocean. Off Santa Cruz…" Her voice trailed away. "Isn't that where the boy lived who wrote your mother? Phil or something?"

"Finn. Yeah, he lived in the mountains above Santa Cruz. What are you talking about? A mermaid?"

"Weren't you listening? They just gave a report."

Jeff looked at the television. The camera had moved back to the anchors in the studio. "I wasn't paying attention."

Ruth gave him a searching look. "You're doing that more and more. It's those letters. Until you get rid of them, you aren't going to get over your mother's death."

Jeff wasn't sure you ever got over your mother's death, but Ruth had a point. The letters were a distraction. They kept him from facing the truth – that his mother was gone forever.

"Tell me about the mermaid," he said to change the topic.

"Some surfers found a body in the ocean. It looked like a mermaid."

"I don't know what that means?"

"I don't know either. That's all they said. It was a baby."

"A baby? That's horrible."

"I know. Tell me about it." She tilted her head at him. "Isn't it weird that it happened in Santa Cruz?"

"Yeah, but life's funny that way."

"I guess so."

Life sure was funny. Mermaids and isolated farms. And mothers you realized you hardly knew. Life was a damn comedian sometimes.

* * *

Dear Aster,

Janice lost the baby. She was almost five months along when she went into labor. We got her to the hospital, but it was already too late. The baby was completely formed, but he had the same problem as Little Gina and Ezekiel.

I mean the doctors don't think that's what killed the baby because he had other things wrong. His lungs weren't completely developed and he never even cried.

Janice won't get out of bed. Thatcher said she had to get up and get to work again, but I told her to ignore him. Boy, did he get angry. He threatened to send me away early. I said I wouldn't go. Nothing he could do would make me leave Janice now.

I was trembling so bad when I faced him. Even my voice was trembling. I sure wish it hadn't, but I was afraid he was going to hit me. He's never hit anyone on the farm, but he looked so angry, I wasn't sure that I wasn't going to be the first one.

Mrs. Elder says I need to think about leaving. When she says that she means me and Mama, Janice and Gina. There's no way all of us would be able to leave and if we left, where would we go?

Mrs. Elder says she knows of places that might help us, but when I mentioned it to Mama, she got really upset.

Mama is getting worse and now we can't take her to the doctor because we used the money on Janice and the baby. Even worse, Thatcher took the gardening away from me. I don't get to work with the boys like Ezekiel anymore. He says I'm a bad influence.

The only thing I get to do now is stay in the house with Janice. I did sneak away last week and went to the library for a few hours, but Mama and Janice were so scared when I got back that I haven't tried it again. They're really afraid Thatcher is going to send me away early.

What do you think I should do, Aster? Do you think I should talk Mama into leaving? Even as I write this, it scares me. No one has ever left before it was time. It just isn't done. I wish I could talk to you in person. I wish we could see each other. I would like to hear your voice, have you reassure me in person.

Mrs. Elder tries, but she doesn't understand the way you do. She is in control of her life. She isn't dependent on anyone for anything. She understands the world, but you and me, Aster, we're left out. The world has moved past us and I'm not sure if we can ever adapt.

I just don't know what to do. Please give me any advice you have.

Your friend,
Finn Getter

CHAPTER 7

Wednesday

Marco always felt so empty and frustrated after his meetings with Dr. Ferguson. The two of them went over and over the same things, but didn't seem to gain any ground. He didn't have any more idea what to do about his life, how to put it back together again, than he had a week ago, and the group meeting was looming the very next night. Added to that was the doctor's appointment today at 2:00 that Abe had scheduled for him. He had no illusions. There was nothing any doctor could do for him. The leg was as good as it was going to get and it was stupid to hope for anything more.

He took his phone out of his pocket and sat at his desk in his office, staring at the display. It had been more than a week since he'd left Peyton and she hadn't tried to contact him once. He didn't blame her, but he wanted something, anything from her. If she called him, he knew he'd go back even though the logical part of his mind told him it would be a mistake for both of them. He wasn't better. In fact, he was worse than when he'd left her and staying sober was becoming the most difficult part of his day.

"Captain?"

Marco set down the phone and glanced up. Tag stood in the doorway, holding a case file.

"Yeah?"

"They were dating."

It took Marco a moment to process what she said. "The shooting victim and the girl?"

"Yeah. Even the vice principal knew about it. They'd been dating for six months. They just went to prom together."

"So odds are the father also knew."

"That's what I think."

Marco considered for a moment. "Give me the names of the parties involved."

Tag came forward and took a seat across from him. "Father's name is Will Cook, daughter is Amy and the boy's name is Gavin Morris."

"Racial differences?"

"Nope. All white."

"Huh, and the girl actually said she didn't know the boy?"

"Yep." Tag dropped the file on his desk. "Here's Abe's autopsy."

Marco took the file and opened it, glancing over Abe's report. As usual, it was thorough and neatly done. "He was shot four times?"

"Yeah, close range. One severed his spinal cord. Would have paralyzed him instantly. One wound up in his kidney and the other two in both lungs."

"All through the back?" Marco looked at the picture of a skinny, ghostly pale kid, not more than sixteen, with four holes in his back. He rubbed a hand across his forehead. "Have you talked with Morris' parents?"

"Yesterday. The mother couldn't talk to us. She was a basket case. She and the father are divorced, but the father was at the house trying to comfort her. Right now he's in shock too, but once that wears off…"

"They're gonna want something done."

"Yep."

"What about the girl's mother? Where's she?"

"She lives in Vermont. The last time she saw her daughter was at Christmas. She met the boyfriend then herself."

Marco looked at the photo again. "Bring in the father. Let's question him."

"He's got a lawyer."

"He can come. We have a right to question his client."

"You know what the father's gonna say, right?"

"He was standing his ground."

"And you know the NRA's gonna be crawling up our asses the minute we question him."

Marco closed the file. "Bring it on."

Tag gave him a wicked smile, then reached for the folder and rose to her feet. "You got it, Captain."

As she went to the door, Marco called to her, "Tag?"

"Yep?"

"You might call the ADA and warn him though."

Tag chuckled. "Done."

Marco pushed the button on the intercom. "Carly?" When he'd come in a while ago, she wasn't at her desk. In fact, Carly spent less time at her desk than he did. He released the button and waited for an answer. Nothing. He depressed the button again. "Carly?"

She popped her head inside the office. "Yes, Captain?"

"You know you can answer me the same way, right?"

"This just seemed easier."

It was easier to get up and come to his office?

"You know which is the intercom button, right?"

She hesitated.

"The one that says intercom?"

She gave a laugh and shook her head as if to say, *Silly me!* "Of course."

"Are Cho and Simons in yet?"

"Cho and Simons?"

Marco bit his inner lip for patience. "The detectives?"

She tilted up her head, but he could see no recognition in her eyes.

"The big guy whose partner is the little guy?"

"Oh, yes, I think they're here. Do you want me to get them?"

"Yes, and can you call Jake Ryder and tell him I want to talk to him?"

"Right." She dragged the word out. "Jake Ryder."

"The CSI?"

She nodded. "Yes, Jake Ryder. The nice guy?"

"Right."

She started to go, but hesitated.

"Button number 3," he offered.

She pointed an index finger at him. "Button number 3."

Marco buried his head in his hands and tried his breathing exercises. The constant throbbing in his leg put him on edge, made his temper short. Carly was trying hard at this job, but she was so not the right assistant for him.

Giving up, he reached for his desk drawer and yanked it open, grabbing the bottle of aspirin. He dumped four in his hand and dry swallowed them, then picked up the phone and thumbed it on. A picture of Peyton and Pickles dominated his background. He stared at it and fought with himself. Now was definitely not the time to call her.

"You wanted something?"

Marco dropped the phone and motioned Jake inside. Jake moved to the armchairs, but didn't sit.

"I need you to do me a favor and I need you not to give me shit about it."

Jake rolled his eyes. "No conversation has ever gone well that began this way."

"Just listen. I need more suits. I can't keep wearing the same one."

"You *are* beginning to look homeless. Oh, yeah, right, you are. Homeless, that is."

Marco glared at him. "Ryder…"

"What do you want me to do about it? This is Abe's area of expertise."

"I need you to go to Peyton's house and get them for me."

Jake glared back at him. "No."

"No?"

"Look, Adonis, this is stupid. Just go talk to Peyton. Don't keep this up."

"I can't. Not now. Now would be worse than before."

Jake sank into the chair. "The two of you can work it out. You've just got to talk to her."

"Stay out of it, Ryder."

"You're bringing me into it."

"No, I'm asking you to use the key you still have and get me a couple of damn suits. That's all."

"I'm not going in that house without telling Peyton."

"Then tell her. Just…" He forced himself to calm, curling his hand into a fist. "Just please do this one thing for me and don't make me beg."

Jake didn't answer for a moment, then he pushed himself upright. "Pride goeth before a fall, Adonis. This is just plain stupid. You're gonna lose her for good if you don't stop this."

Marco didn't answer.

"I'll bring the damn suits whenever I get them." He gave Marco a final glare, then left the room.

Marco waited for a bit, then he pushed the intercom button again. "Carly?"

No answer.

Muttering a curse and grabbing his cane, he climbed to his feet and limped to the door. Carly's desk was empty. What the hell! Who needed an assistant that couldn't stay put? He might as well do everything himself if this was how flighty she was going to be.

Wandering toward Cho and Simons' desks, he saw no signs of her. Cho and Simons were easy to spot, however, sitting in their chairs and reviewing the case. Marco stopped before them.

"Have you seen Carly?"

"Nope," said Simons.

"I sent her to get you."

"We ain't seen her."

Marco shook his head, then let it go. "Where are we with the case?"

"Completely stalled," said Cho.

"You didn't find any complaints about the business?"

"Not really and most of them are old."

Marco leaned on his cane. "If I've got a business selling something people want badly, I'm gonna have security cameras all over everything."

"The night before Greer was torched, someone smashed the outside security camera with a bat," said Cho.

"Huh? That seems like premeditation to me."

"Yeah."

"Did Greer report it to the police?"

"He did."

"What about security cameras inside the store?"

"There aren't any," said Simons. He rose and grabbed Marco a chair.

Marco sank into it, grateful that Simons didn't make a fuss. "Why aren't there any?"

"According to Byrony, his clerk, a lot of the clientele didn't want to be on surveillance when they picked up their *medicine*. That way there wouldn't be video evidence of what they bought."

"Then how do you know the outside security camera was destroyed by a bat?"

"The tea shop next door caught the guy on their camera."

"Do you have that video?"

Cho nodded, then began clicking on his computer. Marco eased the chair closer to him, so he could see the monitor.

"You can't see anything. The guy wore a hoodie and never looked up." He found the file and opened it.

Marco watched the grainy video.

Sure enough, a hooded figure came into the screen and exited almost immediately. A moment later, the sound of breaking glass was heard and something flew across the camera lens.

"You're right. That does us less than no good."
Marco leaned back and thought for a moment. "Okay, you're going to have to go through all of the clients."

Cho closed his eyes, but Simons gave a grim nod. "That's what I figured."

"Get Jake to help you."

"Ryder?" said Cho, making a face. "Why?"

"Because he picks up things that we miss."

"He's right," said Simons.

"I know he's right, but I hate working with the preacher. He's freakin' annoying."

"He's also smart and observant," said Marco.

"Yeah, he's that too."

"There you are," came Carly's voice behind him.

Marco glanced over his shoulder at her. He knew he should reprimand her for her poor performance, but the last time he did, she burst into tears.

"There's an older woman and a man here to see you."

"What?"

"The man says he's your brother."

Oh shit!

Simons let out a whistle.

Cho gave a laugh.

Marco shot a glare at them, then levered himself to his feet. "Let me know if you find anything."

"We'll do," said Cho with a smirk.

"Hey, Captain, good luck," said Simons.

"Ask your mom if she has anymore chicken parm. I've been dying for some."

Marco ignored him and followed Carly to the front of the precinct.

Vinnie and his mother were waiting inside the half-door, just outside his office. When he appeared, his mother hurried to him and threw her arms around his waist, nearly knocking him over. He looked up at his brother.

"You broke off your engagement to Peyton?" Vinnie said in that accusatory tone of an older brother.

"I asked you and asked you to go to church. This wouldn't happen if you went to church and asked God for help," said his mother, her face pressed against his chest.

Carly gave him a wide eyed look.

He motioned to his office. "Can we talk about this in private?"

Vinnie strode into the office, while Marco detached himself from his mother and led her after him. Vinnie helped his mother into a chair as Marco closed the door and leaned against it.

"You shouldn't have come down here. This is my work," he said.

Vinnie rose to his full height. "I told you not to mess around with this relationship, Marco. Peyton isn't like the other girls you've dated. I was afraid you were going to blow it."

"That isn't any of your business."

"How can it not be?" said their mother, whipping around in the chair. "Peyton was good for you. I was so happy when you and Peyton finally got together. She's a good girl for you. Why would you do this?"

"I had to."

Vinnie narrowed his eyes on him. "You had to?"

"I wasn't good for her. I was jealous all the time and I wanted her to quit her job."

"So, talk it out. Aren't you seeing a shrink or something?" Vinnie made a vague motion with his hand.

Marco drew a breath for patience. "There's nothing to talk out. It's my problem and I have to fix it." A thought occurred to him. "How did you find out anyway?"

"We called Peyton," said his mother.

Marco closed his eyes.

"What did you want us to do? You wouldn't come to Sunday dinners, and you wouldn't go to church. What did you want us to do?"

"Every time I called, you sent me a text saying you were busy." Vinnie leveled a look at him. "Peyton said you left a week ago. Where've you been staying?"

"With Abe."

Vinnie jutted out his chin. "You're coming home with me."

"No, I'm not."

"What?"

"He'll come home with me and your father. He belongs home with us."

"No, I'm not doing that either. I'm staying where I am."

"That's stupid. We're family," protested Vinnie. "You come to family when you have a problem."

Marco knew they weren't going to stop unless he told them exactly what was going on. "I'm struggling with alcoholism, Vinnie. You don't want that around your children."

His mother gasped and made the sign of the cross. "What?"

"That's part of why I had to leave Peyton. When the pain gets bad, I drink."

"How often does the pain get bad?"

"All the time."

Vinnie clamped his mouth closed.

His mother made another sign of the cross.

"I'm getting help and I'm working on it, but I need you both to give me a little space."

"You need to turn to family," said Vinnie.

His mother reached up and curled her fingers around Vinnie's wrist. "Abe's a doctor. He's good. He'll help Marco."

Vinnie glanced at her.

"He'll help," she repeated and rose to her feet.

Marco felt like an ass as she crossed around the chairs and came to him, placing her hand against his cheek. "Seek help from God, my son. Please, seek help from God." He leaned down so she could kiss him, then he moved away from the door and watched her walk out into the precinct.

Vinnie stopped in front of him. "Peyton was the best thing you had going."

Marco nodded. "I know."

"You wait too long and she's gonna move on."

"If I stayed, Vinnie, she would have come to hate me. I couldn't chance that."

Vinnie grabbed him behind the neck and planted a kiss on his forehead. "If you need anything, you know where we are."

Marco nodded.

Vinnie released him and then was gone.

* * *

Marco stood in front of the medical marijuana dispensary and stared at it. It was housed in a well-maintained white building with a wooden door. A small window in the middle of the door allowed him to look inside and see a crystal chandelier hanging from the ceiling. To the left was a wall papered in Victorian era style, a bold black fleur de lis design on a pale pink background. This certainly didn't look like what he expected from a pot house.

He could see a young woman moving around behind the counter. He could just go in and ask questions. No one would even know he was here. Then he could make his decision. His doctor had offered to get him a medical marijuana card, but he'd declined. He just couldn't see how he could do his job if he was stoned all the time. And if the media found out…

Still, he wasn't really doing his job now, was he? Albie Brighton's words kept rolling around in his head, disrupting his thought process. *It lets me think. When I got pain, I can't even think straight. I can't do nothing. I can't even be still.* Maybe if he got rid of the pain, maybe everything would be clear. Maybe he could figure out how to tamp down on his possessiveness with Peyton, maybe he could stop being angry about her job. And maybe rainbows and unicorns would explode from the top of his freakin' head.

He turned away and walked down the street. He wandered around for hours, watching people. He wanted a drink. He passed a few bars and it took every ounce of willpower he had not to go inside.

Finally, he went to Abe's. The moment he walked through the door, Abe confronted him, hands on hips.

"I get you an appointment with the best orthopedic surgeon in the state and you blow him off!"

Marco leaned against the door. His leg throbbed from knee to groin and his temper was frayed. He had a moment's thought of just going back out the door and finding the first drug store that sold liquor.

"Not now, Abe."

"Not now? Why did you miss your appointment? Greyson Chamberlain is the most sought after orthopedic surgeon in Northern California and he doesn't have room in his schedule for the patients he has. He made a special appointment for you!"

Marco tightened his fingers on the cane. He could feel the edge of panic starting to rise inside of him. He'd taken almost fifteen aspirin today, but all it did was take the edge off.

Abe's gaze raked over him, then his expression changed, softened. He reached out and grabbed Marco's elbow. "Sit down. You're hyperventilating again."

Marco hadn't realized how fast his breathing was until Abe did. He limped to the couch and threw himself down, then braced his elbow on the arm and covered his eyes with his hand. Black spots were starting to appear in his peripheral vision and he felt a cold sweat sliding over him.

Abe left and Marco could hear him rummaging around in the kitchen.

The pain raged in his leg, creeping up into his hip. He ground his teeth, trying to control it, but it was winning. A moment later Abe took a seat on the coffee table in front of him and placed a glass of water in his hand.

"Take this."

Marco didn't even protest as he took the pill and swallowed it, following it with a gulp of water. Abe took the glass and placed it on the table, folding his hands before him.

"We've got to get more help, Angel," he said. "Why didn't you go to the appointment?"

Marco opened his eyes, lowering his hand. "I just couldn't hear another doctor say there wasn't anything more that can be done."

"I don't think that's what Grey would have said."

Marco clenched his fist. "What about medical marijuana, Abe? You could write me a prescription."

Abe leaned back. "What?"

"I went to a dispensary today. What if it would let me work? Let me get back some sort of normalcy? Maybe it would let me calm down enough that Peyton and I…"

Abe shook his head.

Marco slumped in defeat.

"Don't get me wrong, Angel. I think it's an answer for a lot of people. I'm not against it, but for you, for a man in your line of work, I can't recommend it. You carry a gun, Marco. You can't be compromised, you can't have your reflexes dulled. You have to think and react in an instant. If you were smoking pot, it would make you vulnerable."

"Then there's no hope." Marco had never felt so bleak, so alone in his life. There just didn't seem to be anyway out of this nightmare.

"You've got to trust me, Angel. Trust Dr. Chamberlain. There's something that can be done."

Marco looked down, then he pushed himself to his feet, gritting his teeth as his leg nearly buckled. "I'm going to bed."

"Angel, please."

"I just need to sleep, Abe. I just want to sleep." He couldn't face another round of disappointment right now.

*   *   *

Jeff glanced out the door of his office. No one was around. He pulled up the search engine on his computer and typed in *mermaid found off coast of California*. A number of stories popped up on his screen. He clicked on the first one that looked like it was from a reputable news source. Something about the coincidence between his mother's letters and this finding were too significant to ignore. His knowledge of Santa Cruz was limited. He thought of it mostly as a surf hangout and a college town. Now, in the span of a week, he'd heard about it twice.

Scanning the news article, he found only sketchy information. Not much more than what the television news source had reported the previous night. The baby had been found by surfers, it had severe birth defects, in particular both legs had been fused into a sort of mermaid tail, and the coroner believed it had been stillborn.

The police and now the FBI had no idea who disposed of the body or why, but they were asking the public for help. Special Agent Carlos Moreno of the FBI requested that anyone with information contact his office. According to Agent Moreno, "This may be a young woman who was trying to hide her pregnancy. She may be afraid to come forward, but we need to identify the baby's mother and give the mother any help she may need. Please contact us."

Jeff leaned back. He had a daughter. Josephine had turned twenty-one two months ago. How could any parent not know his daughter was pregnant? Not offer to help her? There was nothing either of his children could do that would make him turn away from them. Nothing.

So why hadn't this young woman gotten the help she so desperately needed?

Oh, the things people did to each other. The neglect, the disinterest – even he was guilty of it. Before he judged anyone else, maybe he needed to atone for his own failings.

* * *

Dear Aster,

Things only seem to be getting worse. I had my 19th birthday the other day, but we didn't celebrate. Mama is vomiting blood. We don't have the money to take her to the doctor and Thatcher said it wouldn't do any good anyway. He said he's seen this before and it's probably stomach cancer.

I snuck off the farm and went to see Mrs. Elder. She helped me look up medical stuff on the computer. I know I'm not supposed to do that, but I don't have any other choice. If we can't take Mama to the doctor, I have to do something.

But I'm afraid Thatcher may be right. It sounds like cancer. Mrs. Elder said she wanted to call the authorities and send them to get Mama, but I wouldn't let her. It would cause so much trouble. You have no idea, Aster.

The older boys guard the farm and there would be problems if the cops show up. Once a hiker got lost on our land. He asked us for help. Thatcher had some of the boys drive him into Santa Cruz, we were trying to help him, but he told the cops something weird was going on at the farm.

A cop showed up at the gate. Some of the boys wanted to get their weapons and show him that we weren't going to be intimidated by the government, but Thatcher talked them out of it. He met the cop and let him come on the farm.

The cop couldn't find anything wrong, but he still talked to a lot of us. Thatcher didn't try stop him, but it didn't matter, no one had anything bad to say anyway. Mostly the cop wanted to know if we went to school. We showed him our school books and our work, and he didn't find anything wrong with that. Sure, we don't have a lot of money, or fancy clothes, or computers and stuff, but we do fine for ourselves and we don't have to answer to anyone.

The cop went away, and we haven't had anyone else come out. I know Thatcher would let the cops take Mama to the hospital, but Mama already said she wouldn't go and I don't want trouble. I mean, Thatcher wouldn't want trouble either, but some of the older boys, well, they say things, scary things.

I probably shouldn't have told you that, but I trust you, Aster, just like I trust Mrs. Elder. We really do fine for the most part, and really, there's nothing that could be done to save Mama now. She's in the hands of the savior and that's all there is.

Your friend,
Finn Getter

CHAPTER 8

Wednesday

Margaret waited at the door to Peyton's office when she arrived the next morning. She smiled at the older woman. Margaret wore a pale blue sweater, buttoned to the top, with her pearls resting along the braided collar.

"What's up?" Peyton said, turning into her office. A cup of coffee, four packets of sugar, and a bagel with cream cheese waited for her. Peyton settled her briefcase on the desk and reached for the first sugar packet. It did no good to fight it. Margaret was determined to mother her.

"Radar wants you to see Igor first thing this morning."

Peyton straightened, dropping the empty sugar packet into the garbage. There went breakfast. "Me?"

Margaret nodded. "He wants to talk about the case."

"Why me?"

"Radar asked for you specifically. He's in a meeting with Sarge."

Peyton made a face. "I hate going into Igor's lair. Why can't Tank or Bambi go? Bambi loves it up there."

"I'll call her and have her go with you."

That was worse. "It's okay. I'll go. Is Tank in yet?"

"No, he worked late last night researching sireno...sirenomeg..."

"Sireno-something or other. I got you."

"He knows so many things, I feel stupid next to him."

"Tell me about it."

"Have you met his wife?"

"The professor?"

Margaret gave a laugh. "Cute, aren't they?"

"I haven't met her, but I bet they are all sorts of adorable."

Margaret leaned closer to Peyton. "She's older than he is."

Peyton smiled. "I know."

Margaret straightened, touching her perfectly coifed hair. "I'm sorry, that's wasn't very professional. I shouldn't gossip."

Peyton placed her finger over her lips. "I won't tell anyone," she said with a wink.

Margaret laughed. "I'll go call Bambi for you."

Peyton started to protest, but Margaret was gone before she could say anything. She eyed the bagel a moment more, then decided she'd have less to lose if she got sick after visiting with Igor.

She wandered down to the elevator, smiling at the people as she went. They hardly glanced at her. She'd never seen a place more focused and determined than this one. People came here to work and that was all.

Pressing the button on the elevator, she rocked on her heels. She'd been here about a month now and besides her immediate team and Margaret, she knew no one. At the precinct, everyone had been friends – closer than friends, family. She forced thoughts of the precinct from her mind because that made her think of Marco. Truth be told, everything made her think of Marco, but after tossing and turning last night, unable to sleep, she'd determined that the quickest way to get over this loss was to stop thinking about him altogether. If only her damn heart would take that advice.

The elevator opened and she stepped inside, pressing the button for Igor's floor.

"Hold the door," came a familiar voice.

Peyton gritted her teeth, but caught the door before it could close. Bambi jumped inside a moment later, looking like a runway model in a black suit. She beamed at Peyton and clasped her arm.

"I thought I wasn't going to make it for a moment."

Peyton gave a short nod.

"I'm so glad you asked me to go with you. I know how you hate going to Igor's lab."

Peyton nodded again.

Hooking her arm through Peyton's, she faced the door. "Just you and me, the dynamic duo. We could be like a superhero team or something."

"Or something," said Peyton.

The elevator dinged and the doors slid back. They stepped out into the sterile lobby with its heavily reinforced doors and glistening white walls. Peyton reached for her keycard and swiped it against the reader. The glass doors hissed open and she started down the hallway toward Igor's lair.

"Does anyone else work in these labs?" she asked Bambi, pointing at the heavy doors on either side of them.

"Of course they do."

"I've never seen anyone else up here when I come."

Bambi shrugged. "Lab rats keep to themselves. That's why we always have to come to Igor, he never comes to us."

"He went out to the cemetery when we dug up Old Man Harwood."

"That was special. He usually doesn't do that."

"He could call us on the phone and spare us…" She caught herself as she looked into Bambi's gleaming eyes. "Spare me the horrors of his lab."

"That's not how Igor works."

"He could change."

"He's brilliant at what he does, so we make concessions. Besides, I love coming here."

And Peyton didn't, so why the hell did Radar make her do it?

They came to Igor's door and Peyton pressed the intercom button. "Igor, it's Peyton."

A crackle, then Igor's pleasant voice floated out to them. "Agent Brooks, what a delightful pleasure!" The door buzz and Peyton steeled herself as she pulled it open. Igor met them in the middle of the room, his gloved hands clasped before him, his bald head gleaming in the fluorescent lights. "And Agent Redford, a double delight."

Bambi grabbed his arm and hugged it. "How are you, Igor?"

"Me, I'm fantastic. And you?"

"Just perfect." She glanced over her shoulder at his autopsy table. "Oh, my, this is so fascinating." She released him and moved to the table, her attention completely captured.

Peyton tried to avoid looking directly at it, but she couldn't mistake the tiny form lying so lost and forlorn on the stainless steel. Igor gave her a sympathetic look.

"I'm sorry, Agent Brooks, I know how squeamish you are."

Peyton focused on his myopic eyes behind his round glasses. "Did you find anything?"

"The child was stillborn, but I believe she was full term."

"She?" Peyton inadvertently glanced at the body.

"Yes, I found an ovary in autopsy."

Peyton closed her eyes. She wondered if the mother had known she gave birth to a daughter. "Anything else?"

Igor turned and went to a tray set up next to the autopsy table. He picked up a sample dish and carried it back to Peyton, holding it out. Peyton took it and studied the few fibers resting on the bottom of the dish.

"Fibers?"

"Cloth, tangled in the baby's nails. I think it's from a blanket. She was swaddled before she was tossed into the ocean."

Peyton looked up. "Swaddled? Where's the rest of the blanket?"

Igor tapped a blunt finger against the dish. "The fibers are natural, undyed. I think the blanket came apart in the violence of the surf and the only reason we have these is they snagged on the baby's nails."

Peyton looked at the table. She couldn't believe how tiny the body was, but maybe someone had cared for her, if only enough to wrap her in a blanket. Something Igor said finally sank in. "Natural fibers? What do you mean exactly?"

"This didn't come from a commercial manufacturer. Santa Cruz used to be a hippy enclave, so you can probably find a lot of stores that sell natural clothing, maybe even hemp."

"Hemp?"

"It makes excellent fiber, which can be weaved into cloth or some of the strongest rope known to man."

"Is this hemp?"

"I need to run a few more tests, but I'll get back to you as soon as I have the results."

"But you're sure it's natural fiber?"

"Sure? I'm not sure of many things, Agent Brooks, but I can tell you this…" He tapped the dish again. "…this was not mass produced."

"Okay. We'll look for natural clothing stores then. Thank you, Igor."

"My pleasure, Agent Brooks, and might I say, it's been delightful having you visit me here."

Peyton smiled, despite the fact that she'd rather be anywhere else. "Emma?"

Bambi hadn't moved. She stood at the side of the autopsy table, just staring at the tiny body. Peyton didn't want to go to her, she didn't want to get near that table, but Bambi didn't seem to hear her.

"Emma?" she called again.

Bambi's blond head lifted and she looked over her shoulder.

"Ready?"

She gave a distracted nod and moved toward Peyton. Peyton turned and walked to the lab door, pushing the button. "Bye, Igor," she called over her shoulder. Igor waved.

Once in the hallway, Peyton glanced at the other woman. "You okay?"

Bambi's expression was troubled and she gave a vague shrug. "She was so small, so tiny."

"I know."

"I felt so…" She held out her hands helplessly. "…bad. She's all alone. She has no one, no one to care about her. Who discards a baby?"

"I don't know, Emma," said Peyton, sliding her card across the reader. "Maybe the mother didn't know what else to do. Igor thinks she tried to swaddle her. Maybe that's all she could give her."

"It still makes me sad."

They fell silent as they waited for the elevator. Peyton found this part of the job the most unbearable. The depravity of humanity had long ago ceased to shock her, unless children were the victims. She'd never been able to accept the loss of a child, no matter how it happened. It didn't make it any easier that this baby hadn't been killed, but had died naturally, it still hurt. She had no name, no identity, no one to mourn her passing. Such callousness made her sometimes wonder what the hell she was doing in this line of work.

"You know what we need?" said Bambi, turning toward her.

"What?"

The elevator arrived and the doors opened. Bambi stepped inside and turned to face her. "Men."

"Men?"

"Yep." She grabbed Peyton's hands, pulling her onto the elevator. "Let's go on a double date. There's this guy that I see off and on, and he has this really cute friend. I could call him and set it up for tonight. They could take us for dinner and drinks, and oh, dancing."

Peyton squeezed Bambi's hands and gently pulled away. "I appreciate it, Emma, but I'm not going on a double date."

"Why not? There's nothing like a cute guy to take your mind off sad things."

"Because I can't even think about dating right now."

"It doesn't have to be dating. It can just be sex."

Peyton sighed and pushed the button for their floor. "I'll pass, but thank you."

"Fine." She slumped against the back of the elevator, but a moment later, she sprang forward again. "A girl's night out, then?"

Peyton couldn't help but smile at her enthusiasm. "Another time, okay?"

Bambi released her breath. "Okay, but now I'm sad again."

"We could go target practice this afternoon."

Clapping her hands, Bambi hugged Peyton. "Yes! I'd love that."

* * *

Peyton had hardly gotten back to her desk, when Tank poked his head inside. "Hey?"

"Hey," she said, smiling at him.

"The professor's still working on that coin. Really a puzzle."

"I know. Tell her I appreciate it."

"You think we could locate the actual article? I mean it has to be in evidence, right?"

"Right. I'll put in a request."

Tank nodded.

Peyton's phone buzzed and she reached for it. "Brooks?"

"Sarge wants to see you in her office," came Margaret's voice.

"I'm on my way." She hung up and headed toward the door. "I'll let you know as soon as I get clearance," she said to Tank.

He gave her a salute.

Arriving at Rosa's office, Peyton could see Radar sitting in a chair before her desk. Rosa motioned her inside. Peyton opened the door and moved to the grey chair next to him. He gave her a lift of his chin, nothing more. Peyton returned it with a mocking half-smile. *Men.*

"You wanted to see me?"

Rosa reached for a newspaper on her desk and dropped it in front of Peyton. A bold black headline raged across the front page, *FBI Recovers the Little Mermaid From the Pacific*, followed by a picture of Natural Bridges.

Peyton blew out air.

"What did Igor have for us?" Rosa asked.

"The child's a girl, she was stillborn and most likely full-term. And she was swaddled."

"Swaddled?"

"Igor found fibers tangled in the baby's fingernails. Natural fibers. He's going to run more test and find out exactly what, but he's certain they weren't manufactured commercially. He suggested we look at stores that sell natural clothes, maybe even made from hemp."

"Good, that's something."

"Lieutenant Brannon's partner, Sergeant Reynolds, contacted the hospitals," said Radar, "but no one showed up needing medical attention after a delivery. Tank has the list of high schools and he's calling the principals to see if any of their students were pregnant. I'll have Bambi look up stores that sell natural clothing and we can do a little footwork, see if anyone remembers a pregnant woman purchasing a blanket."

"Sounds good," said Rosa, then she focused on Peyton again. "Here's the thing. We need to control the media on this. The local police are doing their best, but now that the reporters know we're involved this is gonna take off. Especially since they've coined a cute name for it."

"Her," corrected Peyton.

Rosa narrowed her eyes and Radar gave her a look that said she shouldn't be correcting her superiors.

Peyton didn't back down. "She was a person, Sarge. I think she deserves some respect."

"Fine, *her.*" Rosa held out a hand to Peyton and gave Radar a pointed look.

Radar nodded.

"What?"

"Just this, we need someone to handle media when we're in the field. Radar and I think you'd be perfect."

"What? You mean go on camera and answer questions?"

"That's right. He's willing to train you, but I think you'd do well as our spokesperson."

"No." Peyton shook her head. "I don't do well on camera." Once Captain Defino had made her address the media at a press conference when they were hunting the Janitor. While she'd handled it well, it made her feel sick to her stomach. She'd been terrified she was going to say something wrong.

"No?" The way Rosa said *no* clearly indicated that wasn't an option.

"No, ma'am."

Radar made a grunt.

"Are you suggesting Bambi would be a better choice?"

Peyton knew this game. Name a rival and her competitive nature would take over, but Rosa didn't understand she didn't feel competitive with Bambi. "She might be very good at it. She's certainly pretty enough."

Rosa's expression grew grim.

Radar rolled his head on his neck and stared at her. "Are you difficult just for the sake of being difficult?"

"No, I'm difficult…" She caught herself. She wasn't difficult. "I'm just being practical. I'm not good at double speak."

"You'll learn," said Radar.

"I don't look good in front of cameras."

"Wear makeup."

Peyton shot a venomous look at him, then she leaned forward in her chair. "Why me, Sarge?"

"Because," said Rosa, folding her hands, "you have charisma and you can think on your feet. The public will love you."

Peyton looked over at Radar.

He gave her a big, fake smile. "Own it, Sparky. You were born for this."

And Peyton knew she'd been had.

*   *   *

"Whatever you do, never answer a direct question."

Peyton braced her chin on her hand, watching the Coast Highway roll by outside the window.

"You can always get around it by being vague." Radar glanced over at her. She didn't bother to return the look. It didn't do any good anyway. He had his mirrored sunglasses in place. "Are you listening to me?"

"I'm listening."

"You don't seem to be listening."

"What do you want me to say?"

"Let's practice."

"Practice what?"

"Is it true the FBI recovered a mermaid from the surf around Natural Bridges?"

Peyton slumped back in the passenger seat. "I hate roleplaying, Radar."

"And I hate when you sulk."

"I'm not sulking."

"The hell you say. You've been sulking for over a week now and it's getting boring."

She gave him a glare, but he didn't notice it.

"Is it true the FBI recovered a mermaid from the surf around Natural Bridges?"

Peyton drummed her fingers on the armrest. "We recovered the body of a child. If anyone has any information about the child or the child's parents, please contact blah-de-blah-blah."

"But is it true the child was a mermaid?"

"The child was female, born with distinctive physical anomalies. Anyone with information about the child's parents should contact our office immediately. The person or persons responsible may need medical attention and we want to make sure they receive the care they need."

"Good." Radar eased the big Suburban up to a traffic light and stopped. "So, before we get there, I should probably ask how you're feeling?"

Peyton gave him a suspicious look. "How I'm feeling?"

"You know, emotionally. I know it's been hard on you, what with everything…"

Peyton continued to stare at him. "Hard on me what with everything?"

"Look, Sparky, I'm trying to be…compassionate. Can't you just accept it?"

"Sure."

"Well?"

"I am investigating the demise of my personal life at this time, but any information you have that might be pertinent to this situation should be relayed to my office in a timely fashion. Any assistance the public can give toward easing this difficulty will be appreciated."

Radar gave a wry shake of his head and started moving again. "Smart ass," he muttered under his breath, but Peyton could see the corners of his mouth twitching.

They pulled into the parking lot of the police station and came to a manned gate. Camera crews and news reporters blocked the front sidewalk, immediately surrounding the Suburban and shining their cameras inside. Peyton turned her head away, trying to avoid them. Radar pulled out his badge and showed it to the officer at the gatehouse.

"We're here to see Lieutenant Brannon."

The officer nodded, then stepped up into the gatehouse and pressed a button. The gate arm lifted and

Radar drove the Suburban through, pulling around the back of the station and parking. As they climbed out, Peyton could hear the murmur of the media from the front of the building. There must be at least a hundred people gathered there, and a billion more that would receive the news feed into their televisions and computer screens in a few minutes. She felt a little nauseous at the thought.

"Chin up, Sparky. You're looking green."

Peyton didn't bother to answer him, following him to the back door. Another officer opened it for them and ushered them inside. Radar showed his badge again and asked for Brannon. They were led into a wide open squad room with partitions separating the various teams from one another. The officer led them to the front of the precinct where Lieutenant Brannon and a tall, thin cop stood, watching the spectacle.

Brannon turned as soon as they arrived, holding out her hand to Radar. "Glad you're here." She offered her hand to Peyton. Peyton absently took it, focused on the people outside. A podium had been set up on the top step and microphones lined the surface. "This is my partner Sergeant Henry Reynolds. Hank, these fine people are Special Agents Moreno and Brooks."

The tall, thin officer shook hands with both of them. He was younger than Brannon with thinning brown hair and a long face with a prominent chin. "Nice to meet you."

Radar gave him his ubiquitous chin lift.

"Nice to meet you," said Peyton.

"Our captain's meeting with the mayor, so he isn't here right now, but he wanted us to address the media when you arrived," offered Brannon.

Radar put a hand in the middle of Peyton's back and urged her forward. "Brooks here is your man."

Peyton shot a look at him and shrugged off his hand.

"Good," said Brannon. "We checked all the hospitals. No one entered for postpartum treatment."

"Our colleague is calling the principals of the high schools now, looking for any pregnant students," offered Radar.

Brannon and Reynolds nodded.

"Our M.E. found natural fibers tangled in the baby's nails. He thought it might have come from a blanket or something," said Peyton, trying not to look out the windows. "Are there any natural clothing stores in Santa Cruz?"

Brannon and Reynolds exchanged a look. "I think there's four or five," said Reynolds. He had a deep baritone voice that rumbled when he spoke. "But you'll want one that sells children's clothes, right?"

"Right."

"The Natural Child on Soquel."

Radar reached for his notebook and wrote the name inside. "We'll check it out tomorrow. Now…" He gave Peyton a wicked smile. "We deal with them."

"Okay. Ready?" said Brannon.

Peyton shook her head.

"Don't screw this up, Sparky," said Radar as Brannon led the way to the front door.

Peyton muttered a curse under her breath and followed the other woman out into the late afternoon sunlight. She could hear the mechanical sound of digital cameras snapping picture after picture and the crowd surged forward, spilling onto the stairs.

Brannon made a straight line for the podium. "Good afternoon, everyone," she said. "We're here to give you an update on the case and answer a few questions. Please understand that when the press conference is over, we ask that you vacate the premises." She motioned Peyton up beside her, then stepped back.

Peyton drew a deep breath and walked to the podium. She looked over her shoulder at Radar, but he was watching the crowd, his expression hidden behind his mirrored sunglasses. Peyton could feel her heart pounding beneath her ribs and her palms were suddenly damp with sweat. She lifted on tiptoes and adjusted the microphone.

"You might need to get her a box," muttered Radar behind her.

That did it. She was so not going to let this intimidate her, and damned if she wasn't going to show Radar she was made of sterner stuff. Squaring her shoulders, she tilted back her head. "Good afternoon, I'm Special Agent Peyton Brooks with the FBI," she said into the microphone, careful not to speak too closely. She'd learned that lesson the first time she addressed the media. "Yesterday, a newborn child was found in the surf near Natural Bridges State Beach. Currently, we do not have an identity for the child and are asking for the media's help in locating the mother. We are concerned she may need medical attention or psychological counseling. Any assistance the public can give us in locating this woman would be appreciated. Lieutenant Brannon of the Santa Cruz Police Department will give you her contact information."

"Why is the FBI involved?" asked a reporter in the front, a man wearing a dark business suit in the warm Santa Cruz sun.

"Due to the delicate nature of this case, we were asked to lend our resources and assistance. Any time children are involved we may be called in to assist the local police."

"Was the child a mermaid?" shouted another reporter she couldn't see. A few more shouted the same question.

"The child displayed a number of physical anomalies, but I can't comment further on that at this time."

"Was she murdered?"

Peyton shook her head. "She was not."

"What was the cause of death?"

"The Medical Examiner believes she was stillborn. Our job at this point is locating the child's mother and offering her any assistance we can. Again, I stress that the mother may need medical attention."

"She tossed her child into the ocean. Surely you're going to arrest her for that?" shouted another.

"At this point in our investigation, we are concentrating on finding the mother."

"Tell us if she was a mermaid!"

"Can you provide us with pictures?"

"Did she have fins?"

Peyton glanced at Lieutenant Brannon. She returned a disgusted look. "Lieutenant Brannon will give the hotline number for the public to call if they've seen anything or know of any information pertinent to this case."

"Agent Brooks?" shouted a number of voices. "Agent Brooks!"

Peyton ignored them and stepped away from the podium. Lieutenant Brannon read the hotline number into the microphone and Peyton watched a number of reporters scribble it down, but many others kept calling Peyton's name.

As Lieutenant Brannon finished, the four of them turned and walked back to the glass doors, pulling them open. The reporters continued to shout questions at Peyton's back until she was safely inside the precinct again.

Peyton's heart still pounded and she ran a shaking hand over her hair to smooth it. Radar gave her a half-smile. "Well?" she asked him.

He shrugged. "Well, you didn't suck."

Peyton lifted her hands and let them fall. Damn Radar and his backhanded praise.

* * *

"Good afternoon, I'm Special Agent Peyton Brooks with the FBI."

Ruth gave a snort. "You'd think they'd at least give her a stepstool or something. She barely reaches the microphone."

Jeff glanced up. A young African American woman stood in front of the Santa Cruz police department, addressing a crowd of reporters. The microphone came somewhere in the middle of her nose.

"Yesterday, a newborn child was found in the surf near Natural Bridges State Beach. Currently, we do not have an identity for the child and we're asking for the media's help in locating the mother. We're concerned she may need medical attention or psychological counseling. Any assistance the public can give us in locating this woman would be appreciated."

"Is this about the mermaid?" he asked.

Ruth nodded without taking her eyes from the television. "Such a sad thing. I can't understand how any mother could just dispose of her child that way."

"Maybe she didn't know what else to do."

The reporters were shouting questions at the FBI agent and she was deftly deflecting them without really giving away any important information.

Ruth clicked her tongue against the roof of her mouth. "I just can't figure it out. How in the world would anyone be pregnant, give birth, dispose of the body and just disappear? I've given birth twice and let me tell you, you don't just get up and walk away. And somebody had to see her throw the body in the ocean." She glanced over at him. "Why does this crazy stuff always happen in California? You never hear of someone in Reno throwing a baby into the ocean."

Jeff shrugged. "Maybe because we don't have an ocean."

She frowned at him, but she went back to watching the television.

Jeff shifted in the chair. The FBI agent backed away from the podium and another woman in a police uniform took her place, rattling off a number for people to call. Jeff's thoughts turned to Finn Getter and his mother. He supposed Finn wouldn't know anything about the excitement in his hometown, not as isolated as he was. Poor kid, he probably would have been fascinated by it.

*   *   *

Dear Aster,

Mama went to sit with our Lord in Heaven last week. We finally got her to the doctor, but it was too late. All they could do for her was give her medicine so she wasn't in so much pain. We didn't have enough left over to bury her, so we had to ask the state for help. They agreed to cremate her.

Thatcher really hated to do that. He said it interfered with our independence, but there was nothing else we could do. Still it makes me sad. Mama doesn't have a headstone or a marker, nothing to indicate she was ever in the world. I wish I could have done more for her, but it's difficult when I can't work like the others. Janice tried to put a little aside. She hopes to save enough to get Mama a marker someday, but I'll be long gone before that happens.

Janice is doing better. She misses Mama same as I do, but she looks stronger than she did. After she lost the baby, I was worried about her. She looked pale and weak. Little Gina didn't understand why her mama wouldn't get out of bed. Once Mama was gone, though, it's like Janice knew how much we both needed her to get better.

There's another good thing that happened, but I'm embarrassed to tell you about it. I met someone. Actually, she's been here for years, but recently we've started talking. She helped me take care of the little ones when Janice wasn't well. Her name is Molly. She's so pretty, Aster, like sunlight on rose petals. She's my age, nineteen, and she wants to be a doctor too.

Thatcher won't let the girls go to town, unless they have a chaperone. Mama used to chaperone for Janice. It's usually one of the older women. Molly talked her chaperone, Susan, into taking her to town the other day. She asked to go to the library so she could get some books to read to the little ones.

I snuck off the farm and met her there. I know we shouldn't have done it, but it was a lot of fun to hide in the big aisles of books and spend some time together surrounded by them. We sat on the floor and held hands. I've never held hands with a girl before, but it was everything I dreamed it would be.

Susan came back too soon, but at least we got a few minutes to ourselves and I got to show her all of the books on medicine. She wanted to stay longer, but we couldn't risk it.

I know nothing can come of this because I'm leaving in less than two years, but having Molly around makes the loss of Mama just a little bit less painful. Thatcher says we can have sweethearts when we go into the world at twenty-one, but I see a lot of the kids at the library and they hold hands all the time. Most of them are younger than I am, and they do more than hold hands, Aster. They kiss in public.

Thatcher says that's why the rest of the world is such a mess and he's probably right, but I can't help but wonder what it would be like to kiss Molly. I hope that doesn't make you think bad thoughts about me.

Your friend,
Finn Getter

CHAPTER 9

Thursday

Marco's hand shook as he poured himself a cup of coffee. He'd been almost a week without a drink, but in some ways the mornings were worse than the nights. Of course, at night the physical pain was worse, but in the mornings, everything seemed so bleak and hopeless, and he missed Peyton then most of all.

Waking up in a strange bed, waking up without her, was beginning to make him wonder what the point of waking up was anymore. He'd never really thought himself the relationship sort, but since he and Peyton had started living together, he'd changed his mind. He even missed her silly little dog.

"Captain?"

Marco quickly replaced the coffee pot with the mug only half full. He didn't want everyone else knowing how bad he was, how much he wasn't sure if he could keep this up. "Yeah?" He picked up the mug, taking a sip.

Stan and Jake stood just inside the break-room doorway. Stan peered at him from behind his coke-bottle glasses, giving him that same half-preoccupied look. Marco wondered if Stan's mind wasn't always divided between the present and some distant future no one could fathom except for those of superior intelligence.

Marco knew exactly what was on Jake's mind. Jake's expressive face could never hide any of his emotions. He zeroed in on Marco's hand, forcing Marco to put down the coffee cup and shove his hands in the pockets of his suit jacket.

Stan carried a sheaf of papers. He moved over to the table and began spreading them out. "We wanted to show you what we've got."

Marco grabbed the cane from where it leaned against the counter and moved over to him, leaving the coffee behind. Jake eyed him as they passed each other, but Marco refused to make eye contact. He didn't need a lecture from Jake Ryder right now.

"Great. Show me." He grabbed a chair and sank into it, letting Stan loom over him.

"These are all the clients Quentin Greer's had over the last six years."

"Why six?"

"He's only been in business that long."

"Okay, go on."

"As you can see, it's a massive list."

Marco nodded.

"Jake had the idea to cull it."

"How?"

Jake came back to the table, carrying two coffee cups, the one Marco had attempted to fill and another. He placed the cup in front of Marco. "You want something, Stan?"

"No, I'm trying to cut back."

Marco and Jake looked at him. Marco had ever seen Stan drink coffee. "How did you cull the list?" he said, reaching for the mug and taking another sip.

Jake sat down across from him. "I figured we could eliminate people who were dead."

"Dead?"

Jake lifted his own mug and took a sip, giving Marco a nod over the lip. "Think about it. People who are prescribed marijuana are usually prescribed it for very specific illnesses."

"Cancer, AIDs," offered Stan.

"Terminal," said Marco. "What'd that bring the list down to?"

"Still a lot, so we broke the living list down to those who were still customers and those who were not, meaning they hadn't purchased anything from Greer in the last two months."

"Okay, and that number?"

Stan held up a couple of sheets stapled together. "A fair number, but a reasonable amount for Cho and Simons to track down. Still, I did one better. I eliminated people that moved out of the area, I mean far enough away that they couldn't make it back for a casual visit."

"Good."

"That's not all," said Jake. "I got to thinking that it probably wasn't the current customers who wanted to torch Greer, since that would disrupt their supplier. Or the customers that moved out of the area."

"Or the dead, because...well...they're dead," said Stan with a shrug.

Marco frowned at him.

He shrugged again. For the first time, Marco noticed his t-shirt. It had a number of blue and red balls squished together in the middle with a line arcing around and around it. The caption read *Never trust an atom. They make up everything.* "You know, dead men tell no tales."

"Stan," he said to focus him.

Jake gave that stupid grin of his.

"I was wrong," said Stan.

"Wrong?"

"Jake pointed out there might be a connection with someone who died."

Marco shifted his attention to Jake. "Can we just cut to the chase?"

"I broke the dead into two categories – those that died from a terminal disease, and those that didn't." He reached over and picked up a single sheet of paper. "The names on this paper all died from other causes."

Marco accepted it and scanned the list of seven names. "Do we know how they died?"

"Two died in car accidents. One died in a murder/suicide situation. One overdosed on meth, but the other three all died in violent shootouts, either gang related or in a skirmish with police."

"So you think that their violent deaths connect to Greer somehow?"

"No, they all died before Greer, so they didn't have anything to do with his death, but maybe someone connected to them did. Maybe it was a gang that planned to break into the headshop and he stopped them. Maybe they wanted the drugs to sell on the streets and he refused, but all three of these customers were killed during the commission of some crime. Crime breeds crime," said Jake.

"Let's start there. Give the three names to Simons and Cho, and let them track down any contacts." Marco stared at the names. "Stan, see if any of them have a record in the system. Maybe we pulled them in on another crime, or maybe this isn't the first thing they've torched."

"Serial arsonists?"

Marco shrugged. "It's worth a shot." He glanced over the bulk of their work. "Keep your other lists. We may have to go back to the list of customers who stopped coming but didn't move out of the area."

"Done," said Stan, bending to gather them up.

Marco pushed himself to his feet, reaching for his cane. "Good work, you two. I'm impressed."

Stan gave him a delighted smile, but Jake simply leaned back in his chair, his eyes following Marco's hand as he reached for his cup of coffee. "Adonis," he said.

"Not now. I've got work to do."

"Adonis?"

Marco gave him a glare. "It's captain, Ryder. Damn it, it's captain."

Jake held up a hand and let it fall against the table, but he didn't say anything else. Thank God for small favors.

*　*　*

Will Cook wasn't a physically imposing man. He stood about five seven, five eight, weighing around 180 lbs. His hair had receded to a ring of brown around the crown of his head and he wore a goatee with a mustache.

Marco watched him through the two-way mirror as he sat at the table, whispering to his lawyer. The lawyer, Derek Renshaw, had represented Claire Harper in her trial. Claire had poisoned her adoptive daughter, Jake's wife Zoë, and was now serving three consecutive life sentences at the Central California Women's Facility in Chowchilla. Derek Renshaw was about thirty-five, knew his law, and didn't give up. He'd never met a murderer he didn't think he could get off.

Jake stepped into the room and stood for a moment, watching Renshaw. Marco glanced at him, then leaned against the metal table, crossing his arms over his chest. Jake pointed at the two-way glass.

"That's Renshaw," he said.

Marco nodded. "He's representing Cook."

"The father who shot the kid?"

"Same one."

Jake made a disgusted face. "There was blood all over that room, Adonis. He shot that kid four times, then dragged his body through the window and back into the room."

Marco glanced at the glass. "The NRA says it's self-defense."

"Have they called the precinct?"

"They got him a lawyer."

Jake looked back at Renshaw. "God, I hate seeing him."

"Yeah, well, defense attorneys are no friends of cops, so…"

Tag and Holmes entered the room, Tag carrying a file. "How do you want us to play this?"

Marco studied Renshaw and Cook. "Renshaw isn't going to let him say much. The only thing you can do is get him to say something out of anger or frustration. Go after his manhood. Keep reminding him he shot an unarmed kid in the back."

"Who do you want questioning him?"

Marco looked over at them – the tough-as-nails Tag Shotwell with her tattoos and leather, or the kick-ass, military look of Drew Holmes? He gave them a slow smile. "Let Drew have a go at him. Get him on your side, make him think you're one of the boys. Men defending their women folk."

Tag returned Marco's smile, then handed the file to Holmes. Holmes gave them both a worried look, tapping it against his palm, then he squared his shoulders and they left the room.

"You sure about that?" asked Jake.

"He's ready. Besides, this guy isn't gonna respond to a woman."

"Bet he'd respond to Peyton. She was the best damn interrogator I've ever seen."

Marco glanced at him, then looked away. He didn't want to talk about Peyton.

A moment later, Tag and Holmes appeared on the other side of the glass. Jake leaned against the table next to Marco, curling his fingers around the table's edge.

Holmes grabbed a chair, then took a seat. The suspect leaned away from him as Tag wandered around behind him, drawing Renshaw's attention.

"So," said Holmes, laying the file on the table. "We were hoping we could have a little chat."

"My lawyer says I don't have to answer anything."

Holmes nodded his head. "He's right. You don't have to talk to us at all. Besides, we already know what happened."

Cook looked to Renshaw. Renshaw laid his hand on the man's arm, using his other to unbutton his suit jacket.

"They're trying to get at you. Ignore it," Renshaw said.

Holmes gave Renshaw a crooked smile. "That's right. Ignore us. We got all the evidence we need here. Blood splatter, autopsy, ballistics report. You don't need to tell us a damn thing."

Renshaw gave Holmes a sarcastic look. "I've seen it all too and it's clear that Mr. Cook was protecting his home and his daughter. We are allowed to protect our homes in this state, aren't we?"

"Oh, yeah, I got no problem with that," said Holmes. "Someone breaks into my house and I won't hesitate to fire on their ass. What about you, Tag?"

Tag stood with her feet braced, her hands on her hips. "Hell yeah, I would. You don't go messing in my house."

Holmes nodded. "I get it. If I had a daughter, if anyone even tried to do anything to her, broke in my house and threatened her in any way, he'd be dead too."

Cook relaxed, flattened his hands on the table.

Holmes expression shifted, his eyes narrowing. "Thing is, I wouldn't be shooting him in the back."

Cook visibly reacted, his shoulders tensing, his jaw clenching. Renshaw tightened his hold on his arm.

"Don't listen to them," he warned.

"He's right. Don't listen to us. Still, it was cowardly, wasn't it? Shooting a kid. He was, what? Seventeen? *Seventeen?* Man, hardly past puberty."

Cook glared at him.

Holmes chuckled. "Well, I guess he was past puberty, wasn't he? I mean, your daughter did invite him in. I mean, your daughter was...uh, entertaining him, so to speak."

Cook lunged for Holmes, but Tag had moved up behind him and grabbed his shoulder, slamming him back into the chair. Renshaw threw an arm across his chest to hold him back.

Holmes gave a belligerent chuckle. "Wow! A woman just checked you, bud. No wonder you had to shoot the kid in the back."

"You sonovabitch! Don't talk about my daughter like that!" shouted Cook, rising to his feet. Both Renshaw and Tag held on to him, keeping him from attacking Holmes.

"She invited him into her bedroom. You shot the kid because he was giving it to your daughter, not because he invaded your home."

"You sonovabitch!" Cook strained against their hold. "He raped her! He was raping my girl!"

"No, he wasn't. She invited him in."

Cook reared against their hold as Holmes calmly walked to the wall and picked up a phone, calling for backup.

"For God's sakes, Will, shut up!!" said Renshaw, throwing his body against Cook. "Don't say another thing!"

"Yeah, don't tell us anything else. We got it. Your daughter wanted sex and you couldn't handle it. You shot the kid because he was giving your daughter what she wanted," said Holmes, holding the receiver to his ear.

"You bastard, you're damn right I shot him! You're damn right I did! And I'd do it again too! Piss-ass kid messing with my daughter!"

"Shut up!" shouted Renshaw, struggling to control his client. "Just shut the hell up!"

Holmes faced him again and crossed his arms as officers flooded into the room, taking Cook down.

Jake gave a low laugh and shook his head. "That was brilliant, Adonis. You knew Holmes would act like the arrogant prick he is, didn't you? He couldn't resist goading the guy."

Marco gave Jake a wink, then reached for his cane. "It's Captain, Ryder, *Cap-tain*."

* * *

Devan met him just beyond Carly's desk, his jacket open, his left hand on his hip. "The NRA, D'Angelo? The freakin' NRA?"

Marco kept walking, giving Carly a smile as he passed her desk, headed for his office. "How's your wife feeling? She had the baby yet?"

Devan trailed after him. "Are you freakin' kidding me?" He followed him into his office, bracing a hand on one of the armchairs. "I got a call from Charlton Heston himself."

Marco paused before taking his seat. "Charlton Heston? Isn't he dead?"

Devan lifted his hand and let it fall. "Does it matter? It's the NRA."

"I'm familiar with them."

"They're all over this case. They even paid for this Cook bastard's lawyer."

"I'm aware of that." Marco reached for the file in his in-box and opened it on his desk, shifting through until he found a picture of a pimply faced kid in a pale blue tuxedo. He held it out to Devan.

"What's this?" asked Devan, taking the photo.

"Gavin Morris."

"Gavin Morris?"

"The kid your buddy Cook shot in the back as he was fleeing out the window."

Devan stared at the picture.

"That's a picture from his high school prom, a prom he went to with Amy Cook, Will Cook's daughter."

"They were dating?"

"A little more than dating. They were having sex. Near as we can figure, Daddy Cook caught them in the act."

Devan sighed and handed the photo back. "You're gonna ask me to go before a Grand Jury, aren't you?"

"As soon as we gather all the evidence. We still need to interview the girl." Marco placed the photo in the file and closed it, then he took his seat.

Devan slumped into the chair across from him. "You know I have political aspirations, right, D'Angelo?"

"You've made that clear."

"And you don't give a damn about that?'

"Not even half-a-damn."

Devan studied him, then shook his head. "I thought you'd be different."

"What does that mean?"

"I thought you'd be more like Defino. She knew what cases she could win and which ones weren't worth the trouble." He pointed out into the precinct. "This guy isn't a threat to society. He's a threat to his daughter's boyfriends. Odds are he never kills anyone else again."

Marco leaned back in his chair. "I'm certain Gavin Morris' parents aren't comforted by that."

Devan shook his head, staring at the file. "I really thought you'd be different."

"Different how? You thought I wouldn't do my job?"

"I thought you'd be malleable, pliable. I didn't think you'd view every damn case as a crusade. That was the shit that Peyton pulled. That was her method, not yours."

"Maybe she rubbed off on me. For the better."

Devan met his look. "I have political aspirations, D'Angelo."

"You have a daughter about to make her debut in the world. What sort of world do you want to give her, Adams?"

Devan pushed himself to his feet. "You're not Gotham City's superhero, D'Angelo, and I'm not your Goddamn sidekick."

Marco shrugged. "I don't know. You wouldn't look bad in tights."

Devan choked out a laugh. "You have no idea how good I'd look in tights."

Marco smiled.

"Fine. Put together your evidence and get it to me. I'll take it to the Grand Jury."

"Appreciate it."

Devan walked to the door and pulled it open.

"Give Rani my regards."

Devan made a wry face. "Thanks. That's gonna comfort her tons when I tell her we're never gonna see the inside of the governor's mansion." Then he was gone.

*   *   *

The group meeting was held in a boxy shaped office on the first floor of Dr. Ferguson's building. Marco entered the room apprehensively. There were six people gathered around a table, placing cookies on paper plates and filling paper cups with different fruit juices – three were male and three female, their ages ranging from late twenties to mid-fifties.

One of the women, an Asian woman with her dark hair pulled back in a bun, detached herself from the group and approached him, holding out her hand. "Welcome, I'm Tricia Tran. I run the group here, and you must be Captain D'Angelo." She was dressed in a smart jacket and skirt, her expression warm and welcoming.

He shook hands with her. "Marco, please."

"Welcome, Marco. Dr. Ferguson said you'd be joining us tonight." She motioned over her shoulder at the table. "Please feel free to help yourself. We'll be starting in a few minutes."

Marco glanced around at the circle of chairs in the middle of the room and shifted weight. God, he'd give anything to be anywhere else. "Look, Ms. Tran, Dr. Ferguson insisted on this, but I have to be honest with you. I'm not sure it's gonna work."

She gave him a patient smile. "Call me Tricia, please, and I understand. A lot of people are skeptical their first time at meeting, but I'm glad you're here. Why don't we get started, so we can put your fears to rest?"

He started to tell her he wasn't afraid, but decided against it.

"Please sit anywhere," she instructed and moved toward the circle. As soon as she did, the other people meandered away from the table and began taking seats.

A middle aged woman in jeans and a blue t-shirt grabbed the seat next to Marco, offering him her hand. "I'm Barb Harris."

"Marco D'Angelo."

She gave him a smile and sat down. Transferring the cane to his right hand, he wedged his bulk into the unforgiving folding chair and stretched out his leg, absently rubbing his thigh. A younger man with a crew cut sat down next to him. He wore a jeans jacket and Doc Marten boots like Marco used to wear when he was a street cop. He gave Marco a lift of his chin, but nothing more. Marco returned the gesture.

"Okay, since we have a new member, I thought we could go around the group and introduce ourselves today," said Tricia. "State your name and your occupation." She touched the hand of a woman in her mid-thirties sitting next to her. "Would you go first, Linda?"

The woman had brown hair that came to her shoulders, large, droopy brown eyes, and a mouth that turned down at the corners. She wore a light skirt and a pink sweater with brown penny loafers.

"I'm Linda Hill," she said, looking right at Marco, "and I'm a librarian."

Marco wasn't sure what he was supposed to do, so he just gave her a nod. Linda looked to her right at an African American man in his mid-fifties. He leaned forward in his chair, his arms braced on his thigh, his hands clasped before him. He wore a button-up shirt and jeans with sneakers. His head was completely bald and he had deep sunk dark eyes.

"I'm Rodney Hughes." He scrubbed a hand under his nose, his leg bouncing. "I sell insurance."

Next to him was a white guy about the same age. He also wore a button-up shirt, but it was buttoned to the top with a pair of black slacks and dress shoes. His pale blond hair was cut close to his scalp and his blue eyes were watery.

"Hey," he said to Marco, giving him a tight smile.

"Hey," Marco answered.

"I'm...uh...Mitch Walker. I'm an engineer for the city of San Francisco." He gave another tight smile and scratched at his hair. He reached over and clapped the young guy next to Marco on the shoulder. "Your turn, pal."

The kid gave him a nod. "I'm Kurt Foster. I'm on leave from the army." He looked up at Marco with haunted brown eyes, then glanced away.

Marco looked over at Barb, then at Tricia. Tricia gave him an understanding smile, indicating it was his turn.

"Uh…" Marco glanced around the group. Shit, he didn't even want to tell these people his name. "I'm...uh, Marco D'Angelo." He glanced at Barb again.

"What's your occupation, Marco?" asked Barb.

"Cop," he said, but when Tricia raised her brows, he added, "um, Captain."

"We're glad you're here, Marco," said Tricia.

Marco dropped his eyes to his cane. He was so not glad he was there.

"I'm Barb Harris, retired teacher," said the woman next to him, crossing one leg over the other.

"And I'm Tricia Tran, psychologist. I'm very glad to see everyone tonight and very honored to have a new member to share with us."

Marco glanced up at her.

"The way this works, Marco, is we meet every Thursday night for as long as necessary. Participation is voluntary." *Not for him.* "So whenever you'd like to join in, simply raise your hand. If you want to observe until you feel more comfortable, that's okay too. We try to be low pressure, although I do have to ask that anything that's revealed in this room never leave it. We want to create an atmosphere of trust and kinship, and we can't maintain that if we fear our confidences will be violated."

Marco chewed on his inner lip. Sure, he wasn't going to tell anyone a damn thing about this. He sure as hell didn't need anyone knowing he was here.

"Marco?"

"Hm?"

"Can I get your verbal agreement to keep our meetings secret?"

"Yeah, of course." Like they had any secrets he wanted to divulge anyway. "I won't say a word."

"Good." Tricia clasped her hands. "Does anyone want to share?"

Marco immediately dropped his eyes again, running his thumb over the silver head of his cane. He could see everyone else avoiding eye contact in his peripheral vision, or shifting uncomfortably in their chairs.

Finally the engineer raised his hand.

"Mitch?" said Tricia.

"I moved. I finally did it. I got a place of my own in the Sunset."

"Good for you," said Tricia and many of the others also praised him.

"It was hard. I've been with Brian for ten years, but I just couldn't take the abuse any longer."

Marco glanced over at him, frowning.

"Even as I was leaving, he wouldn't let me take hardly anything. He kept the television, the microwave, but they're just things, right? I mean, my self-worth is more important."

"Yes, it is," said Tricia.

"That was brave of you," offered Barb. "It's hard to start over."

"It is. It's hard, but I feel liberated. I'm not going to lie. I feel like there's hope."

"I'm proud of you, Mitch. I know how you've struggled with this decision," said Tricia. "It can be very hard to realize a relationship isn't giving you what you deserve. Humans are communal animals. We want to be with other humans, but if that person isn't bringing positive energy into our lives, we have to cut them loose."

Marco exhaled. He was in psychobabble hell.

Across from him, the librarian raised a shaky hand.

"Yes, Linda," said Tricia, turning toward her.

"Bob died."

The entire group gasped, including the young guy next to Marco.

Linda's eyes welled with tears and her shoulders shook. "I came home from work and found him under the coffee table."

Found him under the coffee table? What the hell!

"Oh, goodness," said Tricia, reaching for a box of tissues behind her chair. She handed it to Linda and wrapped her arm around the other woman's shoulder.

"I just feel so empty. I didn't want to get up this morning. No one understands. No one gets what I'm feeling."

"We understand," said Tricia.

Barb left her seat and knelt in front of Linda, wrapping her in her arms. "I'm so sorry, sweetheart, that's just horrible."

"You should have seen him! His tongue was hanging out of his mouth."

Marco found his own mouth hanging open. What the hell happened to this poor fool?

"He looked so small and shrunken. I just can't believe he's gone. And I'd just bought him his favorite tuna."

Marco's brow furrowed. He turned to the kid next to him. "Her husband?"

The kid gave a sad, sorrowful shake of his head. "Her cat."

It took another fifteen minutes for everyone to comfort Linda. She sobbed into her tissues and blathered on about the cat, while the rest of them shook their heads and muttered consoling words, including the men. They seemed genuinely distressed for her. Marco thought he was going to crawl out of his skin.

Finally Tricia called for a break so Linda could wash her face and pull herself together. Marco made his escape, ducking out into the hall while everyone else went after refreshments. He'd almost made it to the lobby of the building when he heard heels on the marble floor behind him.

"Captain D'Angelo?" called Tricia.

He stopped, closing his eyes, and slowly turned around.

"We're not finished."

Marco let her come up to him. "I am."

"Why?"

Marco tried to draw in his thoughts, tried to think of some way to put it so he wouldn't hurt her, but there just wasn't any soft way to say it. "This isn't for me."

"You haven't given it a chance."

He held up a hand, indicating the room. "A cat? Really?" When Tricia's expression shifted to disapproval, he extended his hand to her. "Look, I like animals just as much as the next person. Hell, I'm a vegetarian, but a cat?" He drew a deep breath and released it. "It's not your fault. There was no way this would work anyway. I'm just not the kind of guy that goes around spilling his guts to strangers. I'm sure it works just fine for them, but…a cat?"

"Are you prioritizing levels of grief, Captain D'Angelo?"

He didn't know how to answer that.

"That's a dangerous thought process. Each person experiences grief in a different way. For Linda, that cat was the reason she got up in the morning. He was her constant companion. He gave her unconditional love, and when she came home at night, he was there for her. Does that really seem like an insignificant contribution to you?"

Marco didn't know how to answer that. Put that way, it didn't seem insignificant at all. "I'm sorry, but this is why this doesn't work for me. These people deserve better than what I can give, and I don't want to mess up what you've already got going here. It's really not you, it's me."

She folded her hands before her. "You have to do what you feel is best for you, of course."

"Thank you." He started to turn.

"But before you make your decision, ask yourself why a man who carries a gun, who faces life or death every day, doesn't have the courage to face a room of grieving people."

Marco's eyes whipped to her face.

She gave him that speculative look of hers, then turned and walked back the way she'd come, disappearing into the meeting room.

* * *

Ask yourself why a man who carries a gun, who faces life or death every day, doesn't have the courage to face a room of grieving people.

The hell with that! Marco threw open the front door of the building and stomped out onto the street, then turned around and glared at the empty lobby. What the hell! He didn't need another half-baked psychologist using his head for her playground. Shit!

He paced back and forth, curling his hand into a fist on the top of the cane. Who the hell did they think they were anyway? Ferguson demanded he attend these meetings or he'd lose his job, then this Tran woman put on this superior air when he told her, as nicely as he could, that her group was bullshit! Who the hell did she think she was!

He started walking toward the garage where he'd parked the Charger, but stopped and turned around. Furious energy zipped and zinged inside of him and he had to work it off before going back to Abe's. Abe was going to grill him and he just couldn't face it right now.

Walking down Market in the opposite direction, he kept going over and over her words in his mind. *Ask yourself why a man who carries a gun, who faces life or death every day, doesn't have the courage to face a room of grieving people.* Bitch! Who did she think she was? She didn't know shit about him. She didn't know a damn thing he was feeling!

He found himself in front of a bar. He knew he should turn around and walk back to the Charger, but he didn't. His hand shook and he felt a fluttery feeling in his belly. Not to mention his damn leg was throbbing with every beat of his freakin' heart.

Just one drink. Just one shot before going back to Abe's. He could face anything if he could just have one drink.

Reaching for the handle, he pulled the door open and went inside. He found a booth on the side of the room, deep and dark with only a candle flickering in the center of the table. He slid into the seat and rested the cane against the table.

A young waiter approached. "What can I get you?"

Marco stared at him a moment, telling himself he should walk out again, but he lifted a hand and swiped it across his mouth, finding his upper lip damp with perspiration. He needed something to steady his nerves. "Shot of Jack."

The waiter nodded and walked away.

An hour later, Marco stared into the amber fluid filling yet another shot. He'd forgotten how many, but the pain in his leg was bearable again. Suddenly someone stopped beside him, laying a hand on his shoulder.

"Hey, handsome, want some company?"

He glanced up at a large breasted woman with a tiny waist and bottle-blond hair. Fake eyelashes made her eyes seems enormous and mysterious. He motioned with the shot-glass to the seat across from him and she slid into it, her curves straining the lines of her tight blue sheath dress.

"I'm April."

"Marco," he said, giving her a slow perusal.

She smiled, showing him even white teeth behind full red lips. "Nice to meet you, Marco."

"Can I buy you a drink?"

"Sure. I'll have white zin."

Marco motioned the waiter over and tossed back his own shot. "White zin for the lady and another one for me."

The waiter nodded and walked away.

"So, why is a man who looks like you drinking all alone?"

Marco smiled. "Why is a woman who looks like you coming up to a stranger in a bar?"

She returned his smile. "Curious, and lonely." She licked her lips. "Are you lonely, Marco?"

His gaze swept over her again and he couldn't deny she made him want to not be lonely anymore.

*   *   *

"Are you still reading your mother's letters?" came Ruth's voice.

Jeff's first instinct was to hide them, but that was silly. He wasn't doing anything wrong. "Yeah, I can't get over the connection between Mama's pen pal and this case in California."

"You mean the mermaid thing?"

"Yeah."

"Jeff, it's the middle of the night."

"I know."

Ruth came and took a seat on the footstool before him. "What's going on, honey?"

"Nothing. Really, Ruth, it's nothing."

"It's something if it has you up in the middle of the night going over old letters. They weren't even written by your mother. That I could understand, but this...what is this, Jeff?"

"This kid, Finn Getter, wrote religiously to my mother, every week without fail. His life was difficult, Ruth, so difficult. He lived in isolation. He didn't even really understand how the internet worked, but he made a connection with my mother, a connection I didn't have."

"So that's what this is? Guilt?"

"Maybe, I don't know. I wish I'd spent more time with her. I wish I hadn't always been so preoccupied. I keep wondering what things she told Finn in her letters. Did she tell him how disappointed she was that I didn't spend more time with her? That I didn't make more of an effort?"

"I don't think Aster would have said that. She wouldn't have criticized you to anyone. She adored you, Jeff."

He nodded and reached out, squeezing her hand. "Don't worry, okay? I'll come to bed in a little while. I just want to sit here for a moment and remember her."

Ruth gave him a smile and leaned forward, kissing him, then she rose to her feet and went back to bed.

* * *

Dear Aster,

Molly and I snuck off the farm and tried to go to a movie. It was an old movie, I can't remember the name, but it doesn't matter. We sat in the dark and held hands the whole time.

We were practically the only people in the theatre, so we could whisper to each other. We talked a lot about the future. I turn twenty in just a few weeks, which means I have only a year left before I have to go. Molly turns twenty in a month.

I can't believe I did this, but I asked Molly to come with me when I have to leave. And you know what, Aster, she said yes. She said yes. I'm so scared and excited. I don't know how I'll provide for us, but I have to do something because I don't want to go without Molly.

I also asked Janice and Little Gina to come with me. And know what else, Janice agreed. She said she'd start putting away a few dollars every time she sells something at the farmer's market in town. She and the other women take the extra vegetables we grow and some of the clothes they weave and sell them at the market.

Thatcher lets them keep a few dollars for themselves, for things girls need, you know? Janice said she'd start putting aside a few dollars every market day for us to leave. It's a secret. Molly agreed to add some of her money to it whenever she can.

Sometimes I think we're making a huge mistake, but Janice says that since the three of us are nearly adults, we should be able to find work. She keeps telling me not to worry so much, but I'm just not sure Thatcher's going to let us go when it's time.

Janice says he can't keep us, but I know a lot of the boys have left at twenty-one and not a single one ever tried to take anyone else with them.

Keep me in your thoughts, Aster, and maybe someday I can come to Reno and meet you in person.

Your friend,
Finn Getter

CHAPTER 10

Thursday

Peyton pulled open the door to a smiling Jake. "Hey."

"Hey, ex-roomie." He came inside and bussed a kiss across her cheek. "Hate the hair."

She touched a hand to her matronly bun and shut the door behind him. "It's regulation."

Jake gave a nod and bent, scooping Pickles up. "Regulation sucks."

She moved around him and went into the kitchen. Early morning sun was trying to fight its way through the cloud cover. "You want some coffee?"

"Sure." He climbed on a barstool at the counter and settled Pickles on his lap. Peyton poured them both a cup and passed his across to him. He picked it up and took a sip. "Mm, good."

"Yeah, well, you spoiled me for cheap coffee when you were living here."

He smiled. "I wish I'd had an effect on the precinct."

Peyton's eyes went beyond him to the garment bag slung over the couch. "His suits are in there."

Jake glanced over his shoulder. "Thanks."

Peyton leaned on the counter. She was so damn tired. She kept waking up in the middle of the night, her heart in her throat. It was just like it had been after she'd been kidnapped by the Janitor. The PTSD was back in full force. She'd forgotten what it was to wake up in a panic, as long as Marco slept beside her.

"How is he?"

Jake lowered the coffee mug. He started to answer, but nothing came out.

"Jake?"

"He's complicated, Mighty Mouse. One minute he's this brilliant captain who knows how to utilize his people to everyone's advantage. I mean he's better than Defino ever was. The next, he's on a drunken binge, sitting in a filthy motel."

"He's still drinking?"

"Who knows? I can't figure him out. Abe said he's been having panic attacks. He's had to give him tranquilizers twice in the last week. And he won't go see this orthopedic surgeon Abe knows. Abe even made an appointment for him, but he blew it off."

Peyton looked down in her coffee.

"Maybe you should call him..."

"No!" Her eyes snapped back to Jake's face. "He wants space and I'm going to give it to him. He walked out on me. Not the other way around."

Jake's expression grew grim. "Peyton, he doesn't know what he's doing."

"He did then. He did when he asked you to pick up suits for him. I'm not going to be a fool for him or anyone else, Jake."

"This is Marco, Peyton. This isn't anyone else."

"It doesn't matter." She took another sip of her coffee and tossed the remainder in the sink. "He made the decision without me, so that says it all." She went around the counter and grabbed her gun off the peg by the door. "Now, I'm sorry, but I'm late for work."

Jake sighed and climbed off the stool, setting Pickles on the couch. "You know where to find me if you need me, Mighty Mouse."

"I know, Jake. Thank you."

* * *

Radar pulled the Suburban to the curb on Soquel and set the brake. Peyton looked out at the bright banner flying over the doorway of the Natural Child. The window displays showed a number of toys – a wooden rocking horse, a stuffed bear, and some fuzzy yellow ducks. Pairs of tiny shoes stood in a line at the base of a bookshelf filled to bursting with children's picture books.

Radar shifted in the driver's seat, looking back at Tank and Bambi. "You two take the other natural clothing store down the block. Sparky and I will handle this one."

Bambi and Tank nodded, then exited the vehicle. Radar studied Peyton from behind his mirrored sunglasses, but she refused to look at him. She was getting tired of Radar's speculative looks.

"You ready?"

"Yep," she said, reaching for the handle on the SUV's door and shoving it open. She stepped up on the sidewalk and waited while Radar came around the front of the vehicle. As he pulled the door of the shop open, a bell tinkled above the transom. He removed his sunglasses and tucked them into the neck of his shirt, then motioned Peyton in front of him.

The smell of lavender wafted over them. Dried sprigs of it sat in a basket on the top of a display shelf. Below it were a number of handmade soaps and shampoos, all wrapped in brown paper. A rack of children's clothes stood to the right.

Peyton fingered the natural fibers, the small shirts and tiny pants, the sundresses woven with bright embroidery thread. Marco had mentioned wanting children. She'd never given it much thought. The entire time they'd been partners, he'd always said he never wanted children, he didn't believe cops should procreate, but just before he'd left her, he flipped the switch.

She hadn't given it much thought when she'd accepted his proposal. He'd always been enough for her. She'd just wanted him in her life, but that didn't mean she wasn't willing to talk about children. That didn't mean she wouldn't have considered it with him.

"Sparky?"

Peyton rested her hand on her belly, wondering what it would be like to know life was growing inside of her. To know that her body was making another person, someone who combined both she and Marco.

The woman they were trying to find now had known. She had felt life growing inside of her. She'd known she was going to become a mother. What shock had she felt when the baby was born so badly deformed? When she held her in her arms and knew she wasn't breathing? Peyton couldn't imagine the shock, the pain of that. It overwhelmed her, made her ache inside.

"Sparky?" Radar touched her shoulder.

Peyton jumped, stepping away from him, her eyes whipping to his face. He held out his hands. "It's okay," he said in a steady voice.

She brushed a hand across her mouth. "I'm sorry. I haven't been getting much sleep lately."

Radar nodded, giving her that searching look of his. "You okay now?"

"Yeah." She straightened her suit jacket. "I'm fine." He still eyed her warily. "Don't look at me like that. I didn't pull my gun or anything."

"Right."

She rolled her eyes. "What did you want?"

He motioned over his shoulder at a rattan basket overflowing with naturally dyed fabrics shaped into baby blankets. Peyton moved past him and ran her hand over the top of one, then picked it up and shook it out.

"Can I help you?" A woman in a flowing skirt and a peasant blouse came out from behind a curtain along the back wall. "I'm sorry. I was just trying to catalogue our latest order."

Radar reached for his badge and showed it to her. "Special Agents Carlos Moreno and Peyton Brooks, ma'am. Do you own this store?"

"My husband and I do." She glanced toward the front. Her long brown hair fell nearly to her butt, straight and unadorned. She had a number of bracelets on her wrists made out of twined thread. "You're investigating the mermaid case, aren't you?"

"Yes, ma'am," said Radar, reaching for a business card and handing it to her. "We understand you sell only natural fibers."

"Right. Wool, cotton, alpaca, flax."

"What about hemp?" asked Peyton.

She smiled. "I haven't ventured into the hemp craze like some. I don't know what it is but people shy away from using it in baby clothes. Silly really, there's no reason not to use it. It's amazingly strong and resilient."

Peyton held up the blanket. "What's this made from?"

She took it, running it through her hands. "Flax."

"Have you sold any of these blankets lately?"

The woman narrowed her eyes. "I can look it up on my sales record, but maybe one or two over the last six month. It's mostly the clothes that get snapped up. I do a lot of consignment sales." She handed back the blanket. "Do you want me to look?"

"Please."

"I'll be just a moment," she said and moved toward the curtain, disappearing behind it.

"We should call Igor and find out if he's sure the fibers were hemp," Peyton said to Radar.

"I'll do that." He reached for his phone. "You okay in here?"

Peyton gave him a scowl. "I'm fine, Radar. Geez. Go make the call."

He walked to the door and stepped out onto the sidewalk. Peyton wandered around the store, looking at the handmade wooden toys, then stopped by a pile of books and began leafing through them. Cartoon animals and bright colors flooded the pages, the animals engaging in all sorts of silly antics. Peyton flipped to the back of one and found a stamp. *Santa Cruz Public Library*. Hm, why were library books sitting on a shelf in a baby's clothing store?

She picked one up and carried it to the counter, waiting for the woman to reappear. The bell over the door tinkled again as Radar stepped back inside. He shoved his phone in his jacket pocket as he moved toward her.

"Catching up on your reading, Sparky?" he said with a mischievous grin.

"Actually, I was looking for something to keep you occupied on the ride back to the City."

"Driving keeps me occupied."

"I can drive too."

"So you say."

"Did you get a hold of Igor?"

"Yep, he said the fibers were definitely hemp, so we're wasting our time here."

Peyton turned the book over. "Why would they have library books in a clothing store?"

Radar shrugged. "What does that have to do with our case? You think you've uncovered a great library theft ring or something?"

Peyton frowned at him and settled the book on the counter. "You're sure ornery today."

He stretched out his arms. "I love being on a case."

Peyton gave him a nod, then turned when the woman stepped out from behind the curtain. "I sold three blankets in the last six months. Two to women from out of town, here on vacation, and one to a grandmother for her granddaughter."

"You're sure the material on the blankets is flax, not hemp?" asked Peyton.

"Yes. If you want to find clothes made from hemp, try Margy at the Naturama."

"Naturama?"

"Yep, it's a health food restaurant further down Soquel. She also has a gift shop in front where she sells clothes made from natural fibers. She carries hemp."

"Thanks." Peyton pushed the book toward her. "Why do you sell library books?"

"Oh, Mrs. Elder at the library gives me old books when she gets new ones. There's only so much room on library shelves, you know? I sell them for pennies on the dollar and give the proceeds to her for her library fund."

"Thanks," said Peyton again, then she slapped the back of her hand against Radar's flat belly. "Come on, boss. Wanna get your beansprouts on?"

He gave a grunt and followed her from the store.

* * *

Peyton texted Bambi their next location and they walked down the street, leaving the Suburban where it was parked. The sun was out and the day was warm, the hint of an ocean breeze keeping everything pleasant.

They walked up three blue tiled stairs into the Naturama. The interior floor was also tiled, a long rectangle lined on both sides with tables and chairs, and in between the tables were plants, tropical plants spilling out of their brightly colored pots. To the left of the entrance was a small alcove choked with bric-a-brac and the same natural soaps they'd found at the Natural Child. A few ponchos and natural fiber t-shirts made up the clothing assortment.

Radar glanced over everything, then held up his hands and let them fall. "I don't see blankets."

A teenaged girl approached them. "Two for lunch?"

Peyton smiled at her. "Is Margy here?"

"Oh, she's making her famous gazpacho. Can I tell her who's asking for her?"

Peyton removed her badge and held it up. "We just want to ask her a few questions."

"Do you want me to interrupt her?"

Peyton glanced into the restaurant. They were the only ones here, but it was almost noon and she hadn't eaten anything today. "No, just tell her we're here. We'll grab lunch while we wait."

"Great." The girl snagged two paper menus off the counter and motioned them to a table.

Radar grumbled as he took a seat, flipping open his menu. "I guess I won't be getting bacon here."

"You don't need bacon at your age."

He gave her a severe look. "What does that mean?"

She smiled and opened her own menu. A few minutes later the teenager returned with two waters. "I told Margy. She said she'd be out in a few minutes."

"Great. Thank you."

"Do you know what you want?"

"I'll have the avocado and sprout sandwich on whole grain bread," said Peyton, handing back the menu. "And a side of the quinoa salad."

The girl smiled and scribbled something on a pad of paper, then turned to Radar. "And you?"

Radar made a face. "A bowl of the gazpacho, I guess."

She took his menu and left.

"Should we order something for Bambi and Tank?" Peyton asked him.

"How should I know?"

Peyton grabbed her phone and texted Bambi, then she reached for her water and took a sip. "Can I ask you something?"

Radar leaned back in his chair, unbuttoning his jacket. She could see the handle of his gun poking out beneath his arm. "Shoot."

Interesting choice of words. "Whenever we pair up, you always keep me with you. Why?"

He gave her that searching look with his dark eyes again. "Does that bother you?"

"No, I just want to know why."

"It's training, Sparky. I run point, therefore, it falls to me to make sure you're properly trained."

Well, that made sense. She'd hoped it was because he thought she was brilliant, but that was probably hoping for too much, especially from him.

"Can I ask *you* something?" he said.

"Can't promise I'll answer," she said, giving him a broad smile.

He grunted. "You still seeing a shrink for the PTSD?"

"Nope. I was cleared."

"Is that a good idea with everything that's happened lately?"

"I'm fine, Radar. You don't have anything to be worried about."

"If you say so."

Peyton looked at her water glass. She didn't think she wanted to talk about this, but something about packing up Marco's suits had upset her more than she wanted to admit. It meant the separation was more permanent than she'd thought it would be.

"You and Mrs. Radar ever have trouble?"

Radar drummed his fingers on the table. "Trouble? Marital trouble?"

Peyton nodded.

"Everyone has marital trouble, Sparky."

"You ever separate?"

"Nope, but we almost did after Arthur died." Arthur had been Radar's partner before Peyton came on the team. He took a bullet for Radar. "I was messed up and I took it out on her."

"How did you work it out?"

Radar shrugged. "We just did. I went to counseling and she forgave a shit-load of crap. It wouldn't have worked if she hadn't been willing to forgive me."

Peyton swallowed hard and nodded.

A woman with long grey hair approached their table, carrying a plate and a bowl of soup. "Jenny says you wanted to talk to me," she said as she set the food down in front of them.

Peyton showed her her badge. "I'm Special Agent Peyton Brooks, and this is my partner, Special Agent Moreno. The woman at the Natural Child suggested we talk to you."

"This is about the mermaid thing, right?"

Lord, news traveled fast. "Yep."

"What can I help you with?"

"We discovered the baby was swaddled in a blanket made from natural fibers, specifically hemp. We understand you carry clothing made from hemp?"

"T-shirts, a few skirts. No blankets." She thought for a moment, looking out the windows. "You know who you might ask?"

Peyton shook her head.

"We have a farmer's market downtown on Center and Lincoln Street every Saturday. A few women usually come from Horizon and sell vegetables and stuff. They always have clothes, blankets and such, made from hemp."

Peyton considered that. Horizon? Why was that name familiar to her?

"What time on Saturday?" asked Radar.

"Uh, it starts about 10:00."

"Do they come every Saturday?"

"Most of the time. At least one or two of them show up."

Peyton's phone buzzed and she pulled it out. Bambi had responded to her text. "Can we get two more sandwiches like mine with the quinoa salad?"

"Coming right up," Margy said, moving toward the back.

Radar picked up his spoon and aimlessly trailed it through the red liquid in his bowl. "I really like bacon."

Peyton pushed her sandwich aside. "Radar, that Horizon thing's familiar. Where have I see it before?"

Radar shook his head, lifting a spoonful and letting it spill back into the bowl. "Building or something?"

"No." Peyton chewed her lower lip, trying to remember. "It was somewhere around here."

"At the press conference yesterday?"

"No."

"In the shop?"

"No…" Peyton's head lifted. "It was on a van in the parking lot when we first came out here."

"Parking lot?"

"Yeah. Remember at Natural Bridges? They'd closed off the road to keep the media away."

"Right."

"But there were a few cars still in the lot. One of them was a van and on the side it said Horizon."

Radar looked up at her. "You sure?"

Peyton nodded.

Radar leaned over the bowl and lifted the spoon to his lips. "Well, I guess I know what we're doing on our Saturday then." He took a sip, then made a surprised face. "Hm, that's good."

"Even without bacon?"

He gave her an arch look. "Nothing's that good, Sparky."

* * *

Peyton's phone rang. It was after 9:00PM and something about a ringing phone that late at night set her heart to pounding. She snatched it off the coffee table and looked at the display. *Her mother.* Great. Just what she needed. She reached for the remote and turned off the television as she pressed the icon for the call.

"Hey, Mama," she said into the receiver.

"Hey, baby, I haven't seen you in a few weeks. I thought you and Marco could come to dinner. I know you usually have dinner at his folks on Sunday, but if you're free I'd love a turn at Sunday dinner myself."

Peyton closed her eyes. She hadn't known how to tell her mother that Marco left her. Alice wasn't sure marrying a cop was a good idea. She couldn't get over her own loss of Peyton's father.

"Sunday works fine, Mama. I'll be there."

Alice hesitated. Peyton should have known that she couldn't slip anything past her mother. Mothers were trained to pick up on those little shifts in language. "Is everything all right?"

She tucked her knees under Marco's jersey and wrapped her arm around them. Pickles rolled over on his back next to her. Once her house had been teeming with people, living in every room, sleeping on every available surface. Now she was alone. She hated alone. Tears stung her eyes.

"Everything's fine, Mama," she said brightly. Too brightly. Even she heard how strange her voice sounded.

"Peyton?"

Peyton started to tell her, but a knock sounded at the door, setting Pickles to barking. She felt her heart kick against her ribs. Who the hell was coming over this late at night?

"Someone's here, Mama, I've got to go."

"Who's there? Peyton, what's going on?"

"Everything's fine. I'll see you on Sunday, okay?"

"Peyton, I don't like you answering the door at night. Let Marco get it."

"Mama, I have a gun." The knock came again, loud and demanding. Peyton climbed off the couch.

"Still, let Marco get it."

"Okay, Mama, I will. See you Sunday around six?"

"Six is good. Cliff can't wait to see you, honey."

Sure, he couldn't. Cliff Martin was her mother's live-in boyfriend, who wasn't exactly thrilled she had a mixed race daughter.

"Bye, Mama."

"Bye, darlin'."

Peyton set the phone on the coffee table and walked to the peg by the door, drawing her gun. She pointed a finger at Pickles and he sat, falling silent. Then she eased to the door and peered out the peephole. Her breath caught and she quickly replaced the gun as the person on the other side knocked yet again.

Unlocking the door, she yanked it open. "What the hell are you doing here?" she demanded.

He gave her an unfocused look, then slowly licked his lips, his eyes lowering down her body. Emotions warred in Peyton – she wanted to strike him, she wanted to slam the door in his face, she wanted to scream at him, but she did none of those things.

"I had to see you," he said, looming in the entrance. He reached out and cupped her cheek, then slid his hand around to the back of her neck under her heavy hair, pulling her toward him. Peyton braced her hands on his chest to hold him off, but when he lowered his head toward her, she found herself lifting on tiptoes to meet him.

He tasted smoky and dark – Jack Daniels. She pushed against his chest, but he simply lifted his mouth a hair's breadth from hers.

"You've been drinking," she accused.

He nodded and started to kiss her again, but she held him off.

"How the hell did you get here? Did you drive?"

"Took a cab." She heard a clatter, but didn't bother to look down. He'd dropped his cane, so he could slide his free arm around her waist and haul her up against him, even as he captured her mouth again.

Peyton knew she should break his hold, pummel him with her fists, but she found her hands curling into the lapels on his suit, pulling him into the house with her as she met his demanding kiss.

"This is wrong," she said, feeling her back come up against the sofa table.

He slid his mouth along her face to her ear, then slid it lower to her throat. With his other hand, he swept her keys and wallet onto the floor, then lifted her and set her on the table. She was breathing hard as he drew back and looked her in the eyes.

"This is the only thing that's gone right in days," he answered before molding her to him again.

*   *   *

Jeff folded the letter and put it back in the envelope, then added it to the pile. He wasn't sure what to do. It wasn't like Finn Getter's situation had anything to do with him. He'd written to Jeff's mother, not Jeff.

Still, he couldn't deny this kid seemed to be in trouble.

He reached for the letter again and pulled it out, folding it open. He stared at the date. Six months ago. *Six months.* It was probably too late to do anything now. Finn would have turned twenty-one by this date and he'd have been forced to leave the farm, set out on his own somewhere else.

Jeff didn't begin to know how you tracked someone down who didn't seem to have an actual identity. The kid didn't really have any sort of education. He'd never held down a real job. He puttered about taking care of kids and messing in a garden.

He would have been turned out into the world with very little money, no prospects, and no real idea how to survive on his own. His life had been sheltered and the only experience he had with the *real* world was what he got from outdated computers at a public library.

Jeff paced his study, wracking his brain. Why was he getting so mixed up in this kid's life? He couldn't do anything to help him now. It was six months ago. He'd either found a way to survive or he hadn't. And he hadn't written to his mother since then.

That's what worried Jeff most of all. The desperation in the last letter, the hurt and betrayal, the fury – it was impossible to deny. This kid needed help. He might have found a way to survive on his own, but he still needed help.

He'd been friends with his mother. Jeff owed her that much. She would want him to find this kid. She would want him to track him down and make sure he was all right. At the very least, she would want him to let Finn know that she was dead.

His eyes landed on the newspaper he'd bought just the day before. Ruth had clicked her tongue against the roof of her mouth, thinking he'd finally lost his mind, but she hadn't said anything. He went back to his desk and scanned the letter, then looked up at the newspaper.

The young FBI agent was featured on the front, addressing the media about the mermaid case. She was stationed in San Francisco and this time the papers had listed her phone number as well as the phone number of the local police station. The FBI would have a better chance of finding a missing person.

He traced his finger down the letter. *There are too many deformities for it to be coincidence. I read that in the medical books. I know it's true. Something has to be done to stop him.* There are too many deformities? Jeff looked back at the FBI agent's picture. Too many? Like a mermaid?

* * *

Dear Aster,

I want to die. I'm so sorry to start a letter this way, but I don't know how else to express myself. I've lost Molly for good. I can't tell you how, but I just don't know what I'm going to do.

I haven't told you everything about our lives. If I told you everything, you'd be shocked. You'd think it was strange, and I'm afraid you wouldn't want to be friends with me anymore.

I'm almost twenty-one. Six months, Aster, and I have to leave. I don't know where to go or what I'm going to do. Mrs. Elder said she'd help me, but what can she do? I can read and write, but I don't really have any other skills. I can't do physical labor because of the asthma and I'm not skilled at anything.

We had such plans, Janice, Molly and me, but it's all ruined now. And I don't understand why. Thatcher says it's the way things work here, but it doesn't make sense. It doesn't have to work this way.

And it just keeps getting worse. Two more babies were born with Little Gina's problem and there are worse ones. Babies that don't make it like Janice's second. The women give birth too early or when they do give birth, the babies won't breathe.

I know this isn't normal. I know there shouldn't be this many children born with problems. There are too many deformities for it to be coincidence. I read that in the medical books. I know it's true. Something has to be done to stop him. Something has to be done.

And I have to do it. I have to stop him, Aster. For Molly and my sister, for Little Gina, he has to be stopped.

I'm sorry this letter is so bleak, but I have no one else to talk to.

Your friend,
Finn Getter

CHAPTER 11

Friday

Marco woke up as Peyton threw back the covers and climbed out of bed. He reached for her, but she'd already disappeared into the bathroom, locking the door behind her. Sunlight filtered through her window, making the hammering in his head more pronounced. He rolled to his back and covered his eyes with his arm. He could hear the shower start and knew he had to get up.

Grabbing the covers, he threw them back and sat up, scrubbing his hands over his face. He could feel stubble on his jaw and his eyes felt gritty. He swung his legs to the floor and levered himself upright. He wasn't sure where he'd left his cane, but his leg screamed in protest when he put weight on it.

Looking around the bedroom, he didn't find any of his clothes. *Shit.* Most of last night was a blur, punctuated by distinct memories of Peyton. He wasn't sure how she was going to feel about him this morning, but last night, she hadn't pushed him away. Not once.

He limped into the living room, finding clothing strewn across the floor. Pickles padded after him and sat in the entrance to the kitchen, watching him gather up his things and dress. He found his cane on the floor by the door.

By the time Peyton emerged from the bedroom, he'd walked Pickles, fed him, and put on a pot of coffee. He was just pouring them both a cup when she appeared on the other side of the counter in a conservative black suit with her hair pulled back tight in a bun. Certainly not the wildly passionate woman he remembered from the previous night.

He stared at her, emotion overwhelming him. It would be so easy to slip back into this with her, so easy just to take up where they left off as if nothing had happened. He wanted it more than he wanted his next breath.

"What the hell was last night?" she said, her eyes hardening.

He didn't know how to answer that. He just wanted her to forget everything that had come before and let him back into her life.

"Marco?"

He leaned on the counter to take some pressure off his leg. "I don't know."

"You don't know? Well, figure it out because I deserve an explanation."

He held up a hand. "Sweetheart."

She flinched. That took him aback. So did her demeanor. This wasn't his lover of last night. This woman was pissed. "That's not going to work. I want answers." She tossed his phone onto the counter and it slid over to him. "So does Abe, by the way."

He glanced at the phone. Okay, now what? If he told her why he'd shown up here last night, she'd be even angrier.

"Peyton, please."

She turned away, starting for the door.

He straightened, moving around the counter toward her. "Peyton!"

She whipped around. "Don't come near me. Don't touch me. Don't take another step. You're not getting me to back down this time."

"Okay." He held out his hands. "Please, sweetheart, just listen to me."

She crossed her arms over her chest. "I'm listening. Start talking."

"It isn't like you think."

"You came over here last night drunk. Is that not like I think?"

No, that was pretty much it.

"Why were you drunk?"

"I went to the group meeting Dr. Ferguson recommended, but it wasn't for me. It just wasn't right, so I left."

"You left?"

"Before it was over."

"I see, and went straight to a bar?"

He sighed. "I didn't plan on that."

"No? You didn't? What? You just stumbled into one?"

"Peyton."

"I'm sorry, but I asked for an explanation and you're making me drag it out of you. I think I deserve more than that."

"Okay, here it is. I went into the bar and I drank too much." He rubbed the back of his neck. "A woman came up to me..."

"A woman?"

"You wanted the truth."

"So, that's what last night was? You wanted sex, so you thought you'd just pop by?"

"I wanted you. That's all I wanted. When she came up to me, all I could think about was you."

Her face shut down. He could see it happen and he didn't know how to stop it. "If you want to work on our relationship, I'm all for that." She pointed a finger at him. "But don't you ever, ever come over here again looking for sex! Do you understand me, D'Angelo?"

He didn't know how to respond to that.

"I'm not your whore!" Then she turned and grabbed her gun off the peg, wrenching the door open and walking out.

Marco jumped when the door slammed shut behind her. He knew it wouldn't do any good to go after her. She'd never looked at him with such hate, such venom before and it staggered him. He sat down hard on the barstool and stared at the floor.

His heart was pounding so hard, he wasn't sure if he was having a heart attack or not. Closing his eyes, he tried to calm his breathing. Shit. He'd done it now. He'd probably lost her for good.

* * *

"Fix me!"

Dr. Ferguson gave him that slow placid look, his fingers steepled before his mouth. Marco leaned on the other side of his desk, his hand curled into a fist around the head of his cane.

"Good morning, Captain D'Angelo."

"No, no more of that. I want answers and I want them now. Tell me what I need to do. Tell me how to fix this and let's get it done. I'm sick of sitting here talking about nothing. I want you to fix this!"

Dr. Ferguson lowered his hands and reached for his pen. "Can you be more specific?"

Marco banged his fist on the desk and paced away. He couldn't believe how much rage he had inside. He was so close to punching someone...something. A psychiatrist, most likely.

"Something's happened, obviously."

Marco looked over his shoulder at him. Was he shitting him? "Really? Didn't your spy report on me?"

"My spy?"

"The psychologist…" He waved his hand. "Tran or Trang or something."

"Tricia? Yes, she mentioned that you left before the meeting was over. Very disappointing."

Marco moved back to the desk and leaned over it. "Disappointing? A woman sobbed for fifteen minutes about a dead cat!"

Dr. Ferguson pursed his lips. "Do you dislike cats in general or did you object to the female tears? I know you have a problem with that."

"What?"

Dr. Ferguson held out a hand, indicating the chair across from him. "Please sit down, Captain D'Angelo. I find your looming presence intimidating."

If he knew Marco's thoughts at the moment, he'd be more than intimidated.

Marco slumped into the chair, gripping the cane with both hands.

"What happened after you left the meeting?"

"I got drunk in a bar." He realized he felt exhausted. All morning he'd zipped around in a near panic, but now every ounce of energy he had seemed to have leached out of him.

"Ah, that is unfortunate."

"It gets worse."

"How?"

"I met a woman."

"Oh, goodness."

"No." Marco shut his eyes. "I didn't go home with her. I went to Peyton."

Dr. Ferguson didn't respond. Marco glanced up at him. God, he hated that still, observing psychiatrist expression. Ferguson's quick mind had already reached a number of conclusion and he was just waiting for him to reveal more. Marco always felt like a bug under a magnifying glass, expecting the cruel little boy to pluck off his wings.

"Go on."

"She hates me. I've lost her for good. I don't know what to do. How to make it better. Nothing is right without her, but I ruined it. I made her hate me."

"Dear God, what happened?"

Marco blinked at him. "What?"

"You didn't…"

"Didn't what?"

Dr. Ferguson started to respond, but stopped himself. Marco suddenly got where he was going.

"No. No! *Jesus.*"

"Okay, okay, that's good. That's very good."

"What sort of monster do you think I am?"

"I think you're a man on the edge and the way you were talking I was afraid she might have rejected you."

Marco gave a shivery exhalation. "It would have been better if she did."

"Okay, so you had intercourse."

"Right."

"And?"

"And this morning, she accused me of only coming over for sex."

"Which is what you did?"

"Yes, no...I don't know. All I know is she told me never to come back again."

"Were those her words exactly? Never come back again."

"Unless I wanted to work on the relationship." Marco braced his arms on his thighs and rubbed his hands over his face. "I screwed up. I shouldn't have gone over there. Not that way. Now she'll never talk to me again."

Dr. Ferguson didn't answer.

Marco looked up through his hands at him. "Tell me how to get her back."

"You don't. Not like this."

"What?"

"You need to leave it alone for a while. You were right to begin with. You need to work on you. You need to stop the drinking, you need to attend group and not leave in the middle of it, and you need to figure out how to be happy with who you are before you can ever be any good for Peyton."

This was so not what Marco wanted to hear. "What about last night?"

Dr. Ferguson shrugged. "Stop beating yourself up over it. It happened. It's over and now you move on."

"She hates me."

"That's ridiculous. She's angry with herself."

"What?"

"If she hated you, she wouldn't have slept with you, Captain D'Angelo. She's a grown woman who can make her own decisions and last night, she made the decision to have sex with you. This morning, she's pissed at herself about it, but she'll get over that."

"How do we ever get back to where we were?"

"You may not be able to, but right now, you've got to figure out how to fix you. Then and only then, when you're in a better place, can you think about working on the relationship with Peyton."

"But you do think we'll get there again?"

"I'm not saying that at all. I'm not sure it can be salvaged, but hopping into bed with each other is not the way to build a sustainable relationship. If and when you go back to Agent Brooks, you're going to have to woo her."

"Woo her?" *What the hell!*

"Yes, woo her."

"Woo her? What are you, Shakespeare?"

Dr. Ferguson smiled. "Not at all. All I mean is that rather than jumping right for the intimacy of sex, maybe you need to date her. Take it slowly. Show her she can trust you again."

Trust him again? Shit. With Peyton, that was going to take a miracle.

* * *

Jake, Tag and Holmes were standing by Carly's desk when he arrived at the precinct. He damn near turned around and walked out again. Immediately Jake's eyes swept over his suit and Marco knew the moment he opened his mouth what he was going to say.

"Hold on. I went and got you suits yesterday."

Marco pointed a finger at him as he shoved open the half-door. "Don't say a word."

Jake frowned. "But I took the suits over to Abe's."

"Ryder!" The half-door swung back violently and hit the counter. Jake and Carly jumped.

They all shared a look, then Tag cleared her throat. "I've got Amy Cook and her lawyer in interrogation."

"Okay?" Did he have to supervise everything that went on here?

"Ryder had an idea."

Freakin' wonderful. Jake with an idea was all bad. "Yeah?"

Tag slapped Jake on the shoulder.

Jake continued to frown at Marco's clothes, but he shook himself. "You should question the girl."

"Me?" He never did interrogation as a street cop. Why would he do it now as a captain? "Why?"

"You've been shot."

"Thanks for reminding me. I almost forgot for thirty seconds."

"Even more charming than usual," said Jake.

"Just tell him," demanded Tag, slapping his shoulder again.

Jake gave her hand an arch look. "Your finger tattoos might say happy, but that doesn't mean it's a freakin' celebration whenever you hit me." He rubbed his upper arm.

Marco made a growling noise in his throat.

"Okay. Tag said the girl's traumatized by what happened. She won't talk with anyone, not even her lawyer. I thought maybe you could be sympathetic and get her to open up."

It wasn't a bad idea. He scratched at his stubble. "Okay. Who's the lawyer? Renshaw?"

"It was," said Holmes, "but the mother came out from Vermont with the grandparents and they got her a different lawyer." Holmes lifted a piece of paper and looked at it. "The girl's lawyer is Laura Crawford."

"Not familiar with her."

"She's from Redwood City," offered Tag.

"Are the mother and grandparents here?"

157

"Waiting across the street at the coffee shop."

"Well, let's get this done then."

Tag and Holmes, followed by Jake, wandered toward the interrogation room. Marco paused by Carly's desk. "In my top drawer is a bottle of aspirin. Can you get it and some water, and bring it to me?"

"Of course." She scrambled to do what he asked.

Marco entered the interrogation room behind the others and looked at the young girl sitting at the table. She was about seventeen with long, straight brown hair, brown eyes, and a fresh, cleanly scrubbed face. She wore a hoodie over a floral print t-shirt and jeans. Laura Crawford sat next to her in a navy skirt and pale blue blouse, her blond hair cascading in loose curls down her back, her features pretty and youthful, although she had to be older than she looked to have this sort of job.

Holmes handed him the file and he opened it, glancing over the report, grimacing as he saw the photos from the crime scene. Blood blanketed the room, splattered on the window and the walls on either side and pooled on the carpet. The bed, a pink pile of blankets and sheets, lay directly to the right of the window.

"Did they do a rape kit on her?"

Tag reached over his arm and flipped a few pages, pointing. "Evidence of intercourse, no sign of trauma."

"They weren't using protection?"

"Apparently not."

"Could she be pregnant?'

"Too soon to tell."

Marco sighed. This is what happened when teenagers tried to grow up too quick. Carly stepped into the room, holding a glass and the aspirin bottle. He handed the file back to Tag and took the bottle, shaking four pills into his palm, then reached for the water. He tossed the pills into his mouth and chased them with the water, draining the entire glass.

He felt everyone's eyes on him, but he ignored them. He was captain. He didn't have to explain a damn thing to them. He gave Carly the glass again. "Thank you."

She smiled and retreated.

Marco smoothed down his hair and adjusted his jacket. It really needed a good pressing at the drycleaners. Tucking his shirt into his belt, he turned toward the door. As he opened the inner one, the girl and Laura looked up at him. The girl's eyes immediately focused on the cane and watched him as he limped to the table and sat down, stretching out his leg.

"Hello, Amy," he said, reaching into his jacket pocket and taking out his business card. He slid it across the table to her, but the lawyer picked it up, studying it. "I'm Captain D'Angelo."

Laura frowned as he held out his hand first to Amy and then to her. They both shook and then Amy clasped her hands in her lap again.

"Captain?" said the lawyer. "Why do we merit such attention?"

He smiled at her. He wished he'd had time to shave this morning. He probably still had shaving equipment at Peyton's house, but he'd felt like he should get out of there as quick as he could once she left.

"No special reason."

Amy's eyes lowered to his cane as he shifted it to the side.

"I know you've been through a lot lately, Amy. You must wish things would go back to normal."

She gave him a nod, her eyes wary.

"School's almost out for the year and then summer, right?'

"Right. Finals are next week."

"I see. Must be hard to concentrate."

She met his gaze, then looked away.

"What's this about, Captain D'Angelo? Amy doesn't have anything to say."

Marco nodded. "That's okay. I get that. We're just hoping maybe she can clear up some stuff for us."

"Like what?" asked the girl.

"You don't have to answer any of his questions," said Laura.

"My questions aren't that bad, Amy. For instance, you live with your dad, right?"

"Right."

"And your mom lives in Vermont?"

"Right."

"That's pretty far away. You must miss her."

"I do."

"How come you live with your dad?"

"You don't have to answer…" began Laura.

"I get that," said Amy to her lawyer. "I heard you the last fifty times."

Marco smiled at that. Nothing like a little teenage attitude. Laura leaned back in her chair, giving him a *whatever* look.

The girl shifted back toward him. "My mom used to drink. A lot. The judge decided it was best if I live with my dad."

"I see." Here was his opening, but he hated to admit this to anyone, especially the people standing on the other side of the two way mirror. Still, he wouldn't get another chance like this. "I know what that's like."

"You do?"

"Yeah, I have a drinking problem too."

Her attention focused on him. "Mom doesn't drink anymore. She got help, but they won't let her take me to Vermont. That's where Grandma and Grandpa live. She lives with them."

"Is it hard living with your dad?"

"He's protective, you know?"

"Yeah, I'd be protective of my daughter if I had one, but…is he too protective, Amy?"

She shut down, looking away from him. He could see her shoulders hunch.

He shifted in the chair, trying to ease the pressure on his leg. "It's loud, isn't it?"

"What?"

"A gun going off, especially in a small space."

She chewed on her lower lip.

"The sounds, the smell, the flash – it stays with you, doesn't it? You can't get it out of your head. You can't forget it. You close your eyes and there it is again, yanking you awake. The roar, the smell of gunpowder, the smell of blood."

"That's enough, Captain D'Angelo."

Tears spilled over Amy's eyes, running down her cheeks. She swiped at them with the back of her hand.

He looked down at his leg, remembering the taste of blood in his mouth, the sound of the shot echoing back at him, the way he was suddenly on his back, staring up at the metal crossbeams overhead. Peyton screaming, *NO!*

"Someone shot you?" came Amy's voice.

He blinked and looked up at her. For a moment, he couldn't process where he was, then he wiped a hand across his mouth. His hand shook. "Yeah. Yeah, about seven months ago."

She reached up and began twisting the tie on her hood around her finger. "I begged him to stop. I tried to stop him. Gavin didn't even know he had a gun. I didn't tell him."

Marco leaned on the table. "You tried to stop your dad?"

Amy nodded. "I screamed at him that it was Gavin, but he wouldn't listen. Everything happened so fast. Gavin was trying to put on his clothes and I grabbed my robe, but my arms got stuck in the belt and then…"

"Then?"

"Amy," said Laura, placing her arm around her shoulders.

Amy shrugged her off and grasped Marco's hand. "He shot. I screamed and screamed and…"

"And?"

"He shot again."

"Where were you when he shot, Amy?"

"I was standing right next to him, I was grabbing his arm. I begged him to stop."

"You grabbed his arm? Which arm?"

"Amy, don't say anything," said Laura.

Amy's grip tightened and she shook her head. "I can't remember…it happened so fast. I can't…"

"Amy?" Marco moved into her line of sight. "Which arm did you grab?"

She lifted her head, her eyes fixed on his. "I grabbed the gun. I grabbed the gun and tried to push it up. It burned me." She held out her hand.

Marco turned it into the light. A faint red welt ran along the top of her palm below her fingers. Cupping her cheek in his hand, he wiped a tear away. "You did good, Amy. You did real good."

"What's gonna happen to my dad?"

"I don't know, but you did the right thing. You did right by Gavin, Amy, and that's what matters."

She nodded and closed her eyes, then Laura folded her in her arms and looked at Marco over her head. "Can we go now?"

"In a minute," he said, reaching for his cane and levering himself to his feet.

Tag and Holmes met him at the door to the interrogation room. Tag gave him a smile. "Good job, Captain."

"Get ballistics to check for fingerprints on the barrel of the gun. Match them to Amy's."

"On it."

They both hurried away.

Jake remained in the room, watching Amy as she was comforted by her lawyer. "That girl's gonna need serious counseling."

Marco moved to stand beside him. "Yeah. The things we do to each other."

Jake looked over at him, eyeing him up and down. "That took a lot of courage, Adonis."

"What?"

"Admitting your drinking problem."

Marco stared at the girl, all of seventeen, her whole life ahead of her. "Not as much as she showed. Not nearly that much."

*　*　*

Late that afternoon, Marco went back to Abe's house, showered, shaved, put on clean clothes, and searched for one of Abe's magical pain pills. He popped one in his mouth and downed it with another glass of water. He couldn't believe how dehydrated he was from his binge drinking the previous night.

Just as he was placing the glass in the kitchen sink, he heard the front door open, followed by male laughter and voices. He wandered into the living room where Abe and two other men were clearing off the dining room table and setting out a deck of cards and poker chips.

One of the men, a short Hispanic man in an impeccable silver suit, caught sight of him and stopped moving. "Well, hello Dolly!" he said, his dark eyes widening.

Abe looked up. He wore a hot pink silk shirt and black slacks with hot pink cowboy boots. "If it isn't the prodigal son returning home. Your phone must be broken, otherwise I can't imagine why you couldn't even send a text."

Okay, he deserved that. Abe gave him a dismissive look and went back to setting up the table.

The third man, an African American of medium height with a bit of a paunch, wandered over to him, circling around behind Marco's back. He trailed his fingers across the width of Marco's shoulders. "How tall are you, darlin'?" he purred.

"Six four," said Marco, stepping away from him and moving toward the table. "Abe?"

Abe refused to look at him. "I have a lovely crudité in the fridge and the little Japanese restaurant on the corner is sending over a platter of sashimi."

The Hispanic man clapped his hands. "I love sashimi. What about you, dreamboat?" he said to Marco, giving him a wink.

"Sure." Marco turned to Abe. "Abe?"

Abe fussed with the poker chips, counting them out. "Abe?"

"I have nothing to say to you, Angel."

"Lover's spat," stage-whispered the Hispanic man to the other one.

Marco glanced at him, then reached across the table and caught Abe's elbow, stopping him. "Abe, I'm trying to apologize."

Abe went still, lifting his eyes to his face.

"I'm sorry about last night."

"Oh," said the African American man, "forgive him already!"

Abe's smile lit up his face and he laid his hand against Marco's cheek. "You are always forgiven, Angel." He pointed at the two men. "These are my friends, Misha and Serge."

Serge, the shorter man, held out his hand. When Marco offered his own, Serge clapped his free hand over the top. "I would forgive you anything, darlin'."

"Thanks." He turned to Misha.

Misha gave him another wink. "That goes double for me."

"Awesome." Just as he tried to take his hand back, the door opened and Jake appeared in the opening with his German shepherd Tater in tow.

"Okay, I thought we'd try raspberry pomegranate vodka tonight." He held up a clear bottle with a pink label, then focused on Marco. "Oh, sorry, Adonis. I didn't know you'd be here." He gave Abe a worried look. "Should I throw it away?"

"Nope," said Marco, easing around the table. "I'll just be in my room." He gave Jake a confused look, but before he could make his escape, Serge clamped a hand on his shoulder and shoved him toward a chair.

"Oh no you don't. You're staying!"

His leg gave and he found himself sitting down hard.

"Easy on the goods, man," said Abe, coming over to him and helping him right himself. "You okay, Angel?"

Marco nodded.

"I'm sorry, Abe. It's just we don't often have so much eye candy at our monthly poker games."

Everything coalesced in his head, except Jake. Why the hell was Jake here?

"So, break out the glasses and the crudité, and let's get our gambling on," said Misha, rubbing his hands together.

Before Marco could escape, Serge and Misha took seats on either side of him and Jake dealt the first hand, while Abe distributed drinks and set out his crudité, or whatever the hell it was. Abe made a point of giving him a large glass of water, glaring at Serge when he protested that Marco should share his vodka.

Marco knew about male poker nights. After all, he had three brothers, so the drinking and the card playing weren't unusual, but the company was. After nearly every hand, Serge suggested they play strip poker. Every time he said it, he gave Marco a lurid look. Since Marco was the only one sober, and therefore, the only one actually winning, he wasn't sure what Serge hoped to accomplish.

On his left, Misha kept him entertained with off-color jokes. "What do you call a gay cowboy?"

"No idea."

"A jolly rancher."

"What do you call a gay boxer?"

Marco shook his head, giving Abe a pained look.

"A fruit punch."

Abe chuckled and dealt another hand.

A little after midnight, Abe called his friends a cab and they tumbled out of the door, giggling and trying to hold each other up. Abe set about gathering the plates and glasses, waving Marco off when he moved to help. Jake gathered up the poker chips and tried to put them back in the container, his aim hampered by vodka. Tater snored softly under the table, his head on Jake's foot.

"Did you see the way Misha cheats?" said Abe, rolling his eyes. "A full house, my ass. He had that second ace in his lap."

Jake laughed. "He always cheats, but it doesn't get him anything. He's the worst poker player I've ever seen."

Abe nodded, then he gave Marco a beaming smile. "You upped my reputation tonight, Angel. They both think you're my new boy toy. Hell, Serge didn't think I could get a younger man."

Marco gave him an uncomfortable smile. "Glad I could help."

"You and Tater are gonna have to take the couch tonight, Jakey," said Abe, lifting an arm-load of dishes. "I have an Angel in my guest room."

"Not a problem," said Jake, giving him a drunken wave of his hand.

Abe smiled at Marco again and headed toward the kitchen, whistling some show tune. Marco watched Jake as he tried to match up the colors on the chips.

"You play poker with them every month?" he asked, reaching for the cards and knocking them into a stack.

"Yep."

"Hm."

Jake gave him a lazy look. "I'm not gay, Adonis."

Marco held out a hand. "Doesn't matter to me if you are."

Jake shook his head with a wry laugh. "See, here's your problem."

Marco set down the cards and leaned back. "Enlighten me."

Jake shifted in the chair, leaning an arm on the table. "You can't allow yourself to enjoy anything."

"That's not true."

"Isn't it?" Jake tapped a finger on the table. "Listen, when my wife died, I had two paths in front of me. I could curl up in the fetal position and give up. That's what I wanted to do. Or I could live the way she did, not worrying about what everyone else thought about me, just having fun and experiencing new things. Like this. Like the poker game tonight. Those guys are really good guys."

"I didn't say they weren't."

"And they're fun. I like spending time with them. So what if we're not from the same background or the same sexual orientation. They're fun and that's all that matters." Jake pointed a finger at him. "Peyton gets this. Peyton knows that you gotta be open to new experiences, new adventures, not worry about what's..." He made quotation marks with his fingers. "...*right* all the time."

He slapped at Marco's arm and missed. "That's why she'd be better off with me than you."

Marco's expression sobered. *She'd be better off with me than you.* He pushed himself to his feet and started toward his room. Abe came out of the kitchen and Jake struggled to stand up.

"I didn't mean it, Adonis."

"What's wrong?" asked Abe.

Marco didn't answer, just brushed by Abe and went to his room, slamming the door behind him.

CHAPTER 12

Friday

Peyton slammed the door behind her and stormed down the ramp, using her remote to unlock the Prius. She tossed her gun in its holster onto the passenger seat and threw herself behind the wheel. The silent start of the Prius just wasn't satisfying this morning. She wanted the roar of the Charger to match her furious mood.

Slamming her open palm on the steering wheel, she let fall a string of curses. Damn him! Damn him again and again and again! She should never have let him in the house last night. She should never have let him touch her.

She had no restraint where he was concerned. He touched her and that was it. She was putty in his hands, wanting nothing more than to completely give herself to him. Every time. Every damn time!

Well, no more! She wasn't kidding. She wasn't going to be used by him or any other man. Never again. Never, ever again!

Especially not by him.

Tears burned in her eyes, but she fought them back. No more crying. No more wallowing in misery over him. It was over and that was best. He made her weak. He made her forget who she was and what she intended to do with her life.

She didn't need this. She didn't need any man making her into a sniveling fool for him. Not Marco, not anyone. She was done with men. She was done with Marco. She would stay celibate and single and alone for the rest of her life and she would be happy with that. Damn it, she would be happy with it!

She forced herself to pull out of the driveway and turn down the street. A part of her wanted to run back into the house, but she buried that part as deep inside as she could. She'd faced her father's death. She could face this. She could learn to accept a life of self-fulfillment, of self-actualization, of self-realization, of...of...nothing.

Tilting back her head, she drew deep, deliberate breaths until the desire to cry left her. Women didn't need men anymore. They could take care of themselves. And if they wanted sex, well, they could find a way to have that too without attachments. If Marco could go to a bar and find a one night stand, so could she. She could use men the way they usually used women. Marco had contented himself with such encounters for most of his adult life. So could she. And she was going to start this weekend.

She was going to take Bambi up on her offer of a double date and she was going to get on with her life. And she was going to do it tonight.

Arriving at the FBI office, she parked the Prius and punched the button for the elevator. Once she got to her floor, she wandered around until she found Bambi's office, located a few doors down from Tank.

Peyton poked her head inside, but Bambi wasn't there. Her office wasn't much better than Peyton's. On the wall opposite her desk, she'd hung her degrees. She had an impressive education, bachelor's degree from Stanford and a master's degree from USC, plus her FBI certification. Peyton moved to her desk and picked up a photo. Bambi, wearing a cap and gown, smiled for the camera, and behind her were a man and a woman, the woman looking like an older version of Bambi.

A strange desk calendar caught her eyes. She leaned on the desk and pulled it to her. On one side were the traditional pages with the year and the day of the month, but the other side were prints of shadowy figures wielding knives and machetes and evil looking swords with hooked ends.

Peyton's mouth fell open as she flipped through the disturbing pictures. Men with masks, men with dark robes and hoods pulled over their heads hiding their faces, men with blood dripping from their weaponry.

"Peyton?" came a cheerful voice, causing her to jump.

The little metal clasp holding the calendar together separated from the base and the dates spilled out onto Bambi's desk. Peyton's eyes widened and she frantically tried to gather everything up.

"God, I'm so sorry, Emma," she said, but the more she tried to arrange the pages, the more they spilled out of the clip.

Bambi came around the desk, laughing. "It's okay. I do that all the time. The hook on the other side broke in March, so I have to use a pair of tweezers to shift each day."

Peyton gave her a miserable look as Bambi gathered the loose dates in her hands and began putting them back on the clasp. "I didn't mean to come in here and break things."

Bambi waved her off. "Are you kidding? I don't care. I'm just happy you were looking for me."

Peyton's gaze shifted to the photo. "Are those your parents?"

"Yep. Ma and Pa Redford." She gave a high, tinkling laugh. "Actually, Shannon and Bruce."

"They seem very nice."

Bambi smiled at them. "They are. Mom's an Ob/Gyn and Dad's a heart surgeon."

"Wow! Did they want you to go into medicine?"

"Probably, but they've always encouraged me to do what I want."

"Do you have any siblings?"

"An older brother, Pete. He's a brain surgeon."

Peyton felt insignificant and unaccomplished next to her. "Wow," she said again. *Spectacular. Keep up the brilliant conversation, why don't you, Peyton.* "So…" She dragged it out, clasping her hands before her. "I was thinking that maybe you could set me up."

"Set you up?" Bambi's eyes widened and she dropped the calendar dates on the desk. "Oh, my God, that would be perfect. You would love Pete."

"Pete?"

"My brother."

"No, oh, no, Emma, I didn't mean your brother, I meant…" She drew a deep breath. What the hell was she doing? She didn't want to date someone and she didn't want a one-night stand.

Bambi's eyes got even bigger. "Oh, you mean you and me go out and get a hook up?"

Lord, that sounded even worse than she thought it would. "You know what, forget it." She waved her off. "I don't know what I was thinking."

Bambi grabbed her hands. "No, it's perfect. Don't you back out on me now. We're going tonight. I know this great dance club. It's a total meat market."

Peyton felt panic move through her. This was a mistake. This wasn't what she wanted at all. She wanted Marco and she wanted her life back. "Look, Emma, I…"

"Agent Brooks?"

Peyton glanced over her shoulder. Margaret leaned in the doorway. "There's a man here to see you, a Jeff King."

"I don't know anyone by that name, Margaret."

"He says he saw you on the news conference. Security vetted him and let him up. What do you want me to tell him?"

"I'll be right there."

Margaret gave her a smile and then dropped her voice. "I also have a nice chocolate donut with red and gold sprinkles."

Now that sounded more tempting than a meat market of men. She moved toward the doorway, lured by the promise of sweet chocolate bliss.

"I'll pick you up at your place at 9:00PM tonight," said Bambi at her back. "Just text me your address. That way you can drink and I'll be the designated driver."

Peyton gripped the door jamb, staring back at her.
Oh, shit, what had she gotten herself into now?

*   *   *

Peyton walked around the cubicle jungle with
Margaret in silence, but halfway to her office, Margaret
cleared her throat and reached out a hand, stopping Peyton.
Peyton looked over at her.

"I don't mean to pry and it's none of my business, but
you should be careful going out with Agent Redford."

Peyton knew she should tell the woman it really
wasn't any of her business, but she kind of felt the same way.
"Why do you say that, Margaret?"

"She's...um..." She glanced over her shoulder. "She's
different than you are."

"How so?"

Margaret clasped her hands before her, giving Peyton
a miserable look.

"It's okay. You know I won't tell anyone anything."

"She devours men."

Peyton started to respond, then stopped herself,
holding up a finger. Considering their last case was
cannibalism, she couldn't be any too careful. "When you say
devours..."

"She has sex with them and leaves them."

Peyton let out her breath in relief. "Good."

"Good?"

"No, not good, but I thought..." She motioned back
toward Bambi's office.

"Oh..." Margaret's eyes widened. "Oh, I see. No, no,
not like that. I mean I can see how you got there, what with
all the horrifying pictures and the interest in the dead, but..."

They both laughed.

Peyton squeezed Margaret's arm. "I appreciate the
warning. I'm probably not going to go anyway. I just feel a

little confused and lonely right now, but I'm not the one-night stand sort."

"You need to give yourself time, dear." Margaret patted her arm. "You need to let your heart heal, and you need to know that you really are over your young man."

Peyton blew out air. Good advice that, considering that last night proved she wasn't over her young man at all. "Well, I've got another man waiting for me."

"I'll just bring you that donut as soon as he's gone."

"Thank you, Margaret, I appreciate it." She moved away, walking briskly to her office.

Jeff King was a middle aged Caucasian man with a stocky build. He rose as she entered and Peyton marked that he wasn't more than five six or five seven, brown hair shot through with grey, and hazel eyes. He wore a button up checked shirt that was tucked into his jeans and black sneakers of a non-descript brand.

"Mr. King?"

"Yes, ma'am," he said, nodding.

She offered him her hand. "I'm Special Agent Peyton Brooks."

"Yes, ma'am," he said, his shake firm without trying to break her fingers. "Thank you for seeing me."

"Of course. I'm not sure how I can help, but I'll do my best. Please have a seat." She motioned to the chair he'd been sitting in and he sank into it as she went around her desk and sat down in her own chair. "What can I do for you, sir?"

He gave a wry shake of his head. "Probably nothing, but I had to try. I saw you on the news conference the other day in Santa Cruz."

Peyton made a face. "Yeah, they kinda threw me out there unprepared."

"No, it was good."

Peyton laughed. "You're too kind, Mr. King, but I don't have a lot of experience talking in front of so many people."

"No, really, it was good." He gave a careless shrug. "My wife did mention that they might have given you a box or something to stand on." He held up a hand. "Meaning no offense."

Peyton laughed again. "None taken. She's right. They always place the microphone so far above me I look like a little girl trying to sneak cookies out of the cookie jar."

He smiled and relaxed a little.

Peyton rested her arms on her desk. "How can I help you, sir?"

He gave her a sheepish look and reached for a leather briefcase sitting by his chair. Setting it on his lap, he opened the top flap and reached in, pulling out a stack of letters. "My mother died a few weeks ago, Agent Brooks."

"I'm very sorry for your loss."

"Thank you, ma'am. I appreciate it." He set the stack of letters on Peyton's desk. "After she died, I was cleaning out her study when I found these."

Peyton picked up the first one, looking at the neat script. "Your mother was Aster King."

"Yes, ma'am."

"I see."

"I was missing my mother, so I started reading the letters. They're all from a young man. They were pen pals."

"Really? I didn't know people did that anymore."

"Well, my mother would be one to keep such traditions alive, Agent Brooks."

Peyton glanced at the letter again. "You found something in these letters that concerns you?"

"Yes, the boy, Finn Getter, lives in the Santa Cruz mountains on something he calls a farm."

"A farm?"

"I think it's a commune of sorts. There seems to be a lot of people living there. It's run by a man that Finn only calls Thatcher, but he definitely seems to be the head of things."

"The Santa Cruz mountains have a lot of people living off the grid, so to speak, Mr. King. Vietnam veterans, others who find modern society difficult, but that's not illegal, per se."

Jeff nodded, clasping his hands before him. "I know that, ma'am, but something's not right at this farm place. When the young men turn twenty-one, they're forced to leave, go out into the world. The only education they get is homeschooling, some reading and writing, simple arithmetic. Then they're shoved out with no skills, no work experience, no true education."

"Again, not illegal."

"The women stay. They're never allowed to leave. They get very little health care. Finn's mother died of stomach cancer and no one did anything to help her until it was too late."

That made Peyton stop for a moment. "What do you mean they can't leave?"

"I mean they can't leave. Finn had plans to leave with another girl and his sister, but something happened in his final letter. He tells my mother that their plans were ruined and he wanted to…" Jeff stopped, staring at the stack in front of him.

"To what, Mr. King?"

"Kill Thatcher."

Peyton took her notepad out of her jacket pocket and began jotting some notes. "Do you know where this commune is located exactly, Mr. King?"

"No, but there's more."

Peyton stopped writing. "Go on."

"I know this sounds coincidental and weird."

She was investigating the disposal of a mermaid. Did he think she didn't know weird? "Tell me anyway." She forced a smile for him.

"There's something genetically wrong on that farm."

"Genetically wrong?" The way he said it made the hairs on the back of Peyton's neck rise. "What do you mean genetically wrong?"

"The children born there have birth defects, a lot of them. Finn doesn't say what it is, but his sister gave birth to a little girl that needed surgery to eat and there were five or six others that had the same birth defect if I counted right. Then Janice, Finn's sister, lost a baby. In the final letter, Finn realizes that so many birth anomalies just aren't right. He spends as much time as he can at the local library with a Mrs. Elder."

Peyton frowned. *Mrs. Elder.* That name was familiar. Where had she heard it before?

"He had an interest in medicine, so she'd get him medical journals to research. He realized that something wasn't right. Then I heard the report on the mermaid in Santa Cruz. That seemed more than coincidental."

Peyton stared down at the letter. "We'll look into it, Mr. King." She reached for the stack. "May I keep these until we have a chance to do more research?"

"Of course, but you don't have much time, Agent Brooks."

"Why not?"

"In the last letter, Finn Getter was almost twenty-one. He had six months left on the farm." He paused, then leaned forward and tapped the date on the stamp. "Last week that six months was up."

* * *

Peyton punched the button on Igor's lab door and Radar walked through. He gave her an arch look.

"Sparky, you better have something good because you interrupted lunch with my wife."

Peyton released the button. "How is Mrs. Radar? Gosh, I can't remember her first name."

"Because I never told you."

"Oh, right. But the cats again? Fluffy? Mittens?"

He glared at her. "Why did you bother me at lunch?"

Igor leaned on his autopsy table, the letters spread around him. Tank sat on his right side with a computer tablet. He was making notes on the tablet with a stylus.

"Hello, Radar. I think our lovely Agent Brooks has found something very interesting here," said Igor.

Peyton gave Radar a smug grin.

Radar ignored it and moved to the autopsy table. "What is it?"

"These, Radar, are letters from a young man living in the Santa Cruz mountains on what I believe to be a commune."

"A commune? Like in the sixties?"

"Precisely. They're not uncommon. Well, they may be uncommon, but they're not unheard of now."

"Actually," said Tank, "since the 1990's the number of people living in communes has increased. The attraction is easy to see, a group of like-minded people working and living together toward one goal. Recently, the move has been toward clean living, attempting to impact the environment as little as possible. They believe in clean energy, government independence and…"

"And the point?" demanded Radar.

"I'll let Agent Brooks fill you in," said Igor, pointing at her.

Peyton launched into a brief explanation of her meeting with Jeff King, the last letter in the batch, and the strange, possible connection with their Baby Jane Doe. Radar listened with his arms crossed over his chest.

"And you think these two very random occurrences are somehow connected, Sparky?"

Peyton started to answer, but Igor held up a hand. "Actually, I do too." He picked up a letter and held it out to Radar. "This young man, Finn Getter, describes a birth anomaly in his young niece that I feel must be cleft palate."

"Cleft palate? That's a common thing, right?" said Radar.

"Actually, cleft palate is rarer than cleft lip. Cleft palate happens about 1 in 1,500 births," said Tank.

Radar gave him a disbelieving look. "You have that number just swimming around in your brain?"

"No." He held up the tablet. "CDC website."

Peyton smiled at him. She liked Tank.

"According to a quick scan of the letters, Finn describes at least four children on this commune with cleft palate."

"Well, it's a long way from cleft palate to a mermaid," said Radar.

"Sirenomelia," said Tank.

"Whatever," snapped Radar. "How are the two related?"

"I can't tell you that until we get some tissue samples, DNA."

"On the basis of what?" said Radar. "I can't just march onto a commune and tell those people, hey, you got some birth defects, so we're gonna start taking DNA."

"Of course not," said Igor. "That would be a violation of their civil rights."

"Of course it would, so why am I here?"

Peyton took the last letter from Igor. "It sounds like these women are being held against their will. We're trying to find the mother of the baby and this is the only lead we have."

"No, we have the hemp fibers. That's solid evidence I have in my hands. If you find any real evidence in those letters, any actual claim of a crime being done, I'm all over it, but right now we have to pursue what's in front of us, and that's the fibers found on the body." He shook his head. "If we start poking fingers in a commune, you know what the media is going to do with that? I don't need a Ruby Ridge or Waco on my hands, Sparky. We stick to what we have."

"What about the letters?" she asked.

178

"They're just letters. Get someone to read through them that doesn't have a case, but you, you have a case to work. Tomorrow we go to the farmer's market and look for your Horizon van, and that's all."

Peyton sighed and glanced over at Igor and Tank. Tank dropped the letters on the autopsy table and gave her a helpless shrug.

* * *

Peyton hurried to catch up to Bambi as they left the parking garage and headed for the nightclub. She wasn't as used to walking in high heels as Bambi and she wasn't sure her enthusiasm level for tonight came anywhere close to the other woman's.

Bambi stopped and hooked her arm through Peyton's. "Come on, this is the hottest new club in North Beach and we look smokin'."

Peyton gave her a forced smile and tried to quicken her shorter stride. The red sequins dress rode high on her thighs. Coupled with the red stiletto pumps and her curls loose around her shoulders, she felt completely out of place. Standing next to Bambi, who looked like sex walking in a virginal white mini-dress with spaghetti straps and black five inch heels, she was afraid they might need the guns they'd stashed in the trunk of the Prius before the night was over.

"I wish you'd let me drive," Bambi complained. "Then you could get drunk."

"I don't mind being the designated driver."

A line stretched across the front of the club, circling around the side of the building. Raucous laughter escaped whenever the door was opened by a bouncer clad in a black t-shirt and black jeans. Peyton could feel the bass of the music pulsing through the brick walls of the building and onto the sidewalk.

She pulled back as Bambi led them to the front of the line. She could tell the inside was crowded by the glimpse she got through the open door – bodies bumping and grinding into one another, surging with every pulse of the strobe lights and the heavy bass of the DJ.

"Emma, I don't think I can do this."

"Yes, you can."

"Shouldn't we go back there?" She pointed to where the line disappeared around the corner.

"Just watch," said Bambi and she adjusted her dress, as if that were necessary to highlight her abundant curves. Walking up to the bouncer, she reached into her handbag and pulled out her FBI badge, then said something to him.

His eyes tracked over her, then did the same to Peyton. Peyton didn't like the look and wanted to sock him in the face, but he unhooked the rope over the door and motioned them inside. Bambi grabbed Peyton's hand and dragged her into the building.

The second the door closed behind them, Peyton knew this was a mistake. Booths in brown leather hugged the walls, but the entire middle of the building was a dance floor where people ground against each other.

"Come on, let's dance," shouted Bambi in her ear.

Peyton shook her head. "I need a drink first."

Bambi led her to the bar, pushing into the crowd trying to get the bartender's attention, but Peyton took her elbow and pointed to the far corner near the wall where there were two open stools. They took a seat and Bambi waved the bartender over. He was a handsome man with black hair and goatee, dressed in an old-time western get-up, complete with garters on his shirtsleeves.

"What can I get you, ladies?" he said, flashing a bright smile at Bambi.

"Screwdriver," said Bambi and motioned to Peyton.

"Water."

Bambi frowned at her, but the bartender left to make their drinks. "What gives?"

"I don't drink anymore."

"Why?"

"Long story."

Bambi bounced on the stool to the beat of the music. Leaning close, she pointed out a couple of men at the other end of the bar. They were giving Bambi sultry looks. "What about them?"

Peyton followed her pointing finger. "What about them?"

"They look promising."

"Do you do this a lot?"

"What's a lot?"

"Frequently. Do you pick up men in bars frequently?"

"No." She made a waving motion with her hand. "I pick them up in grocery stores, the laundromat. Oh, once in a hospital emergency room."

Peyton laughed. "No long term romances?"

"Who needs them. Look around you, Peyton. There's just oodles of men to pick from, why would you ever settle for one?"

Peyton could think of a few good reasons to settle for one, if he was the right one.

The bartender returned with their drinks. "On the house," he said, giving Bambi a wink.

She blew him a kiss, then picked up the drink and put the straw to her full, red lips. A moment later, the drink was gone. Peyton's brows rose.

"Come on, let's go dance," she begged Peyton.

"Let me work my way up to that, okay? You go."

"Are you sure?"

"Yes."

"Watch my purse," she said, shoving the bag across the bar at her, then she was gone, disappearing into the crowd on the dance floor. Peyton noticed the two guys at the end of the bar followed her.

She picked up her water and took a sip. God, she didn't want to be here. She would give anything to leave. This was such a mistake.

"Hey." A very young man sat down next to her. He was Hispanic, pretty with just a hint of stubble on his jaw. His eyes were like dark velvet.

"Hey," said Peyton.

"Can I buy you something?"

"No, thank you. I'm good." She held up her water.

"This place is off the hook, huh?"

"I guess."

"You wanna dance or something?"

"Not right now."

"Why not?" His gaze swept over her. "That dress was made for the boogie, baby!"

Peyton laughed. "I'm just observing right now."

"Ah, that's no fun. You gotta get in there. Do the bump and grind, get the sweats."

"You go. I'll just wait here."

"Naw. I'll sit with you. I don't mind. I can dance any day." His eyes lowered to Peyton's breast. "I don't mind."

Peyton leaned her elbow on the bar and placed her chin on her hand. "Look, this isn't gonna happen. I'm just getting out of a relationship."

"Whoa! I know what that's like. I just got out of one myself."

"Really?"

"Yeah, me and my girlfriend, we been together for like years. All through high school and stuff. Then a month ago, she just tell me we over, man! Just like that."

Peyton's expression sobered. "High school? How long ago was that?"

"Oh, man, three years. Can you believe it? I been outta high school three whole freakin' years."

Three years? Peyton felt ancient all of a sudden.

"Can you believe it?"

"No," she said.

"So, wanna dance?"

"No."

"Aw, come on, chica! I like older women."

Peyton didn't know how to respond to that.

"She said no," came a voice behind the young stud. "Why don't you find another chica, bud?"

A man with light blond hair had come up behind the boy. He had to be Peyton's age or older, nearly six feet with broad shoulders – clean shaven, not exactly handsome, but not ugly, a face filled with character.

The boy took the measure of him and Peyton wondered if he'd be stupid enough to try something. The blond guy had him by a good fifty pounds. "Whatever, dude!" he said, sliding off the barstool and pushing past him. He gave Peyton a look over his shoulder, then slipped onto the dance floor.

"Thanks," she said as he took a seat beside her.

"My pleasure."

Peyton lifted her water glass and took a sip. She wanted to tell him she didn't need a man coming to her rescue, but figured it wasn't worth the effort.

"Mike Edwards," he said, holding out his hand.

Peyton accepted it. "Peyton Brooks."

"Nice to meet you, Peyton." He gave her an appreciative look, then released her. "So, can I get you another drink?"

"No, thank you."

He drummed his fingers on the bar. "So what's a classy lady like yourself doing in a dive like this?"

"Oh, that is the most ancient pick-up line I've ever heard."

He laughed. "Did it work?"

"Not even a little."

He smiled. He had a nice smile. It softened the lines around his mouth and eyes. "Sorry. That was my best one." He held out his hand. Peyton noticed he didn't have a wedding ring. "Still, I'm serious. This doesn't seem like your scene."

"Oh, I like this scene just fine." Before the Janitor she'd enjoyed coming to such places with Abe, but now… "I'm just tired. Long day."

"Got it. What's say we go over to Foleys? They've got dueling pianos. It's a lot quieter and we can talk."

Peyton frowned at him. "No, I'm gonna stay here."

He held out his hands again. "Worth a shot, right?"

"I guess."

Bambi appeared out of the crowd, throwing her arms around Peyton's shoulders. "Come on, please dance with me," she said in Peyton's ear. "Please."

Before Peyton could protest, she pulled her off the barstool and toward the dance floor. Peyton just had time to snag Bambi's purse before she found herself thrust into the middle of flashing colored lights, banging rhythms, and people…so many people all jostling against her. She felt a hand slide over her ass and she didn't know if it was the man or the woman behind her. Then a man pushed up against her, grinding his crotch into her backside.

She spun to face him, but Bambi yanked on her arm, dragging her deeper into the crowd and farther away from the edge. More bodies surged against her and the hammering of the beat drowned out all other sound.

Peyton felt panic edge up inside of her. People surged against her, rubbing their bodies on hers, pushing her this way and that. The lights swept over the faces, contorting them. The smell of sweat and booze and perfume tickled the back of her throat.

She couldn't do this. She couldn't stand it.

She shoved one guy off and broke into the hole his body created, then she shoved and pushed to make it to the outside. Stumbling off the dance floor, she placed a hand against her chest, her heart hammering violently.

She staggered to an open booth and sank onto the seat, closing her eyes and fighting for composure. Sweat trickled down her back, ran between her breasts, her heart was thudding so hard, she could feel it in her temples. Her head buzzed and she knew if she opened her eyes, she'd see black spots.

"Here," came a male voice.

She opened her eyes and looked up into Mike's weathered face. He held a damp napkin out to her. She took it and placed it against her throat. He held a glass of water for her. "Take a drink."

She grabbed it with her free hand and downed half the glass. "Thank you."

He nodded and slid into the booth across from her. "Better?"

"Yes."

"PTSD's a bitch."

Peyton frowned at him. "How the hell do you know?"

"I'm an ex-soldier. Army rangers. I fought in both Iraq and Afghanistan."

She nodded and forced herself to take a deep breath. "I knew this wasn't a good idea."

He leaned closer, staring into her eyes. "Your pupils are contracting again. Good sign." Peyton noticed he had green eyes.

"How long were you in the army?"

"Twenty years. Went in at 18, right out of high school."

She took another breath and finished the water. "So, you asked me why I came to a nightclub like this. Why are you here?"

He looked around. "I love the music."

Peyton laughed.

He gave a shrug. "I don't know. It gets lonely, you know? Just trying to fill the time."

"Never married?"

"Divorced. You?"

Peyton looked away. "Engaged, but...no more."

"Ah, I'm sorry."

"It happens."

"Because of the PTSD?"

"What?"

"Your engagement ended because you have PTSD?"

"No." She wasn't going to tell a stranger what happened between her and Marco. "It just ended."

"Fair enough. Look, I was out of line earlier, Peyton. I shouldn't have asked you to go to a different bar with me, but I just felt a connection, you know?"

"No, I don't know."

He smiled. "I saw you and I thought, now there's a real woman." When Peyton frowned, he held out his hands. "Honestly, no line. You're not like the other paper-dolls here."

Paper-dolls? Interesting assessment.

He extended his hand to her. Peyton reluctantly accepted it. "I'd just like a chance to get to know you better. That's all. So let's start over." He shook her hand. "I'm Mike."

"Peyton."

"Nice to meet you, Peyton. What do you do for a living?"

Peyton opened her mouth to respond and stopped. Now there was a loaded question. "I'm in public relations," she said.

He smiled. "Beautiful and mysterious. You just proved my point. You, my dear, are a real, three-dimensional woman and I would be so honored if you'd give me your number."

Peyton went still, carefully extricating her hand. Give him her number? Boy, this guy moved fast. "Tell you what, Mike. Why don't you tell me more about yourself first?"

"Fine. We'll play this your way." He laughed and leaned back in the booth. "Let's see. I was born under the given name of Michael Barnabas Edwards."

"Barnabas?"

"I know. My grandfather's name, but it just shows you the lengths I'll go to to get your number."

Peyton couldn't help but laugh.

An hour later, she knew he'd gotten married right out of high school, but two years later, they'd divorced. His wife had remarried and had three children. He'd been stationed all over the country, a true nomad, and now he lived in South San Francisco. He'd taken a job in security, but he was itching to move. He just couldn't stay in one place for long, unless of course, he met the right woman.

Peyton steered the conversation away from that angle, asking him about his military service. He seemed more than willing to tell her whatever she wanted to know. He told her he volunteered at the VA hospital, which is how he knew about PTSD, and then wanted to know about her.

She kept it clinical. She told him about her father and mother, but she didn't talk about her career. She told him about Abe, but she avoided all talk of Marco. And finally, she spent a few minutes talking about Pickles. All safe subjects. All guaranteed to tell him less than nothing about her.

He accepted her reluctance to talk and instead regaled her with stories from his days in the army. Bambi found her just when Mike had gotten up the courage to ask her for her number again.

She slumped into the seat next to Peyton. Sweat glistened on her chest and forehead, her pupils dilated. She gave Mike a critical look.

"This is my friend, Emma," said Peyton, motioning to Bambi. "This is Mike Edwards."

"Please to meet you," he said, offering his hand.

Bambi continued to eye him. "Same here." She shifted on the bench and dropped her voice so only Peyton could hear, but she was drunk, so pretty much everyone in their area heard. "Are you ready to go? The guys here suck."

Peyton nodded and passed her her purse.

"Wait. Emma, I was just trying to get your friend's phone number."

Bambi rose to her feet and pulled Peyton up with her. "She's not giving out her phone number tonight, Mike. So

sorry." She pushed Peyton in front of her. "Good luck
though." She pointed across the dance floor to a redhead
grinding against a brunette. "They look like they'll give you
their numbers."

As soon as they got outside, Peyton pulled Bambi to a
stop. "What was that about?"

"What?"

"You were rude to him."

Bambi put her hands on Peyton's shoulders. "Listen,
girlfriend, he's not right for you."

"Why?"

Sliding her arm around Peyton's waist, she steered her
toward the parking garage. "He wants a relationship. You just
need sex, so unless you're going to take him home for that,
he's not your type."

Peyton didn't need sex, but Bambi was right, she
didn't need Mike Edwards either.

CHAPTER 13

Saturday/Sunday

"I have a memory of Serge asking you to dance on the table," said Jake, entering the kitchen and slumping into a chair. Tater padded after him, laying his head on Jake's thigh.

Marco looked over, then poured him a cup of coffee and brought it to the table, scratching Tater's ears. Jake gave a nod and took the mug, just breathing in the steam. Marco sat across from him with his own coffee.

"Did that happen?" asked Jake, peering at him through one eye.

"The request or the dancing?"

"Either."

"The request yes, the dancing not so much. Since I can hardly walk with a cane, climbing on the table seemed a bad idea."

Jake pointed a finger at him and took a sip of the coffee. "You're showered and shaved. Why? It's Saturday."

"I'm going to the precinct."

"Why?"

"We have two cases to work."

"The Cook case is almost wrapped up. We just gotta get the ballistics report and give the evidence to Devan."

"But the headshop case still has no answers, no suspect, nothing."

Jake nodded, bracing his head with his hand. "Raspberry pomegranate vodka seemed like such a good idea before we actually started drinking it."

Marco chuckled. "Most things do."

Jake chewed on his bottom lip. "I also vaguely remember saying something really stupid to you."

"You always say something really stupid."

"Yeah, but this was more stupid than usual."

Marco shifted in the chair, rubbing his thigh. "It doesn't matter."

"It does. I didn't mean it."

Marco shrugged. "Whatever. You were drunk."

"Why can't you ever just loosen up for a minute?"

"Ryder."

"No, I'm serious. I'm trying to apologize to you for something stupid I said and you can't accept it. You can't even let me get to the damn apology."

"You don't have to apologize. You're entitled to say whatever you want. Last night we weren't at work where I'm your boss, so let it go."

"No, we weren't. So what are we? You and me when we're not at work?"

Marco leaned on the table, lowering his voice. "You've gotta stop hanging out with gay guys."

"I'm not asking you for a love declaration, Adonis, I just wanna know what we are. Are we friends?"

"Ryder." Marco ground his teeth. He hated this shit. Picking up his coffee cup, he pointed it at him. "You're right. No more raspberry pomegranate vodka for you. It makes you…" He made a face. "…squishy."

"Squishy?"

"Emotional. Men aren't supposed to go around saying their feelings."

"That's not true."

"It is."

"So if I love a woman, I'm not supposed to tell her. I'm not supposed to tell my friends they mean something to me. I can't tell Tater he's my widdle baby doggy." He made smooching noises at the dog. The dog's tail thumped.

Marco rolled his eyes.

"Fine. Want some flapjacks?"

"What?"

"I make flapjacks after a drinking binge. It soaks up the alcohol."

"No, it doesn't."

"Well, I think it does." He started to push himself to his feet.

"Do you mean it?"

Jake stopped and sat back down again. "Mean what?"

Marco looked him straight in the eyes. "The things you say about Peyton. You've always said them. You've always remarked on how she looks or commented that you'd like to take my place. Do you have feelings like that for her?"

"I think this is a dangerous conversation to have and you're right, we should just keep it professional."

"I'm not going to get mad at you, Ryder. We're grown men here. Just tell me the damn truth."

Jake held up a hand. "I have a little crush on her. Who wouldn't? She's great. You know, like Stan Neumann has."

"Stan Neumann has puppy love. He worships her. She could never live up to the fantasy he's created about her, but you...you're different."

"How am I different?"

"She cares about you."

"She cares about Stan too. In fact, she cares about everyone on the planet."

Marco leveled a look on him. "You told me last night she'd be better off with you."

"I was drunk."

"What if you're right?"

Jake exhaled and looked away. "This is why I don't want to have this conversation. You and me, we're friends, Adonis. Whether you want to admit it or not, we are. We've been through a shit storm together and when she was in Quantico, you relied on me. Whatever I said last night was drunken babbling and it meant nothing. You and Peyton belong together. You've always belonged together and I don't know why you waited so long to tell her that. Then I don't know why you were such an idiot to run away when the situation got real, but you did. I'm not going to step in and interfere with that."

"But if I had died on Treasure Island?"

"You didn't."

"But if I had, Ryder, would you pursue something with her?"

Jake scratched at his hair. "Shit, Adonis, this isn't a good idea."

"Just answer me, okay?"

Jake leaned forward, glancing toward the other part of the condo to make sure they weren't being overheard. "Peyton's awesome. I care about her deeply, and I'm not going to lie, I think she's sexy as hell."

Marco's hand curled into a fist on the table.

"But it would never work and we both know it. She's crazy in love with you and that isn't something that is going to change, no matter what stupid, brain-dead things you pull. But here's a little advice, D'Angelo. Pull your shit together and then spend the rest of your damn life doing everything in your power to make her happy. I got four years and then Zoë was gone. Four years is nothing."

Marco sighed.

"So about the flapjacks? You in or not?"

Marco nodded, staring into the depths of his coffee cup.

*　*　*

Sitting at Cho's desk, Marco played the recording over and over again, watching the figure in the hood cross the screen, then the sound of smashing glass, followed by an object flying past the camera lens. Something about the video bothered him, but he couldn't put his finger on it.

He took it back to the beginning, concentrating on the figure in the hood. Maybe there was some way to get his height from the angle of the camera. It would give them more than they had now.

"Cameras on every corner, in every store, and yet they still don't show you much," came a voice behind him.

Marco glanced over his shoulder at Frank Smith, the beat cop with the thick head of hair and bushy mustache the envy of most men. He leaned back and scrubbed his hands over his eyes. "You're right. This case has got me stumped."

"Cho and Simons asked me to update you on it. They ran down a few leads yesterday."

"Great. What you got?"

"I went with Cho and Simons to check out some dead guy who got shot holding up a liquor store for cash. The cops shot him as he tried to get away."

"Name?"

"Alvin Lefty Bennett."

"Lefty Bennett, huh?"

Smith laughed and grabbed a chair. "Yeah, lost his left hand in some sort of accident. I need a name like that."

"We all need a name like that." He considered a moment. "I'd probably be Gimp D'Angelo."

Smith laughed. "You're Italian. You'd probably be The Gimp. I hate to think what mine would be."

"Big 'Stache Smith." He motioned at his upper lip.

Smith laughed again.

"You want a good Italian name, my brother Vinnie's got one. We used to call him Vinnie the Juice."

"Vinnie the Juice? Why?"

Marco shrugged. "He liked juice."

They laughed again.

"Did Cho and Simons tell you their next move?"

"Well, Lefty ain't their man. All his priors were for knocking off stop-n-robs. He was dead a good two months before Greer bought it. Now they're trying to track down the other two guys on Ryder's list."

"I thought those guys were dead before Greer too?"

"Yeah, but they're trying to get something on them. Family, girlfriends, you know? Lefty was what you'd call a loner."

"Do the other two have records?"

"One does. One doesn't."

"The one that doesn't, what's his name?"

"Calvin Delacruz."

"He was a client of the headshop?"

"Yeah, AIDS."

"But he didn't die from it?"

"Nope. He was shot real close to the headshop, three blocks away."

"By who?"

"Gang bangers. Robbed him and then put a plug in his skull. Right between the eyes."

"We didn't get that case?"

"Nope. The bangers were arrested a few blocks away, trying to use his credit card."

Marco reached over and started the video again. "What about our third guy?"

"Emilio Velasquez. He's promising."

"How?"

"His girlfriend was picked up for assaulting an officer a week ago. She's a real hot head, long list of priors. Assaults, gun violence. And get this, Emilio was picked up for arson when he was seventeen. Burned down the neighbor's garage."

Marco stopped the video. "Huh, we should haul the girlfriend in. How was he killed?"

"Drive-by. Someone sprayed the house with bullets and he caught two in the chest. Killed him instantly."

"They get a suspect?"

"The Gang Task Force asked to run point on that one. They've been trying to get access to this gang for years now."

"Tell Cho and Simons to bring in the girlfriend. The arson angle's our best bet."

"I'll let them know."

"Thanks, Frank. I wish I didn't think this was a red herring."

"What do you mean?"

"I mean we're looking at guys who were dead before Greer got torched. I'm not seeing a motive for anyone surrounding them to do this."

"The list of current customers is long, Captain. I think they're just trying to eliminate what they can."

"Yeah, but I think we need to go back to the original list. Ryder's theory is that no one would do this if they were a current customer because they wouldn't want to stop their source, but that's pretty weak logic to me. We got drugs, we got desperate people, and one thing I know, desperate people do desperate things."

"I'll let Cho and Simons know you want them to start on the other list."

"After they bring in Velasquez's girlfriend."

"Got it."

Smith pushed himself to his feet as Marco started the video again. He watched, then hit the pause button, staring at the screen. Backing it up, he let it play….again and again and again. Reaching for the phone in his pocket, he thumbed it on and pulled up his contact list, pressing the icon for Cho.

"What's up, Captain?" came Cho's voice after the third ring.

"Where are you?"

"Home. Just getting ready to come in."

"Grab Simons and hurry up."

"What's up, boss?"

"I may have found an image of the killer."

Cho went quiet for a moment. "We're on our way."

*   *   *

Cho and Simons crowded around the desk as Marco played the video again. He paused it, pointing to the window of the teashop. "Look there. It's a partial reflection of our guy."

Cho leaned closer, squinting at it. "I'll be damned, but it's blurry as hell."

Marco nodded, studying it. "That's why I called Stan."

Simons placed a beefy hand next to him and leaned on his shoulder. Marco tried not to move away, but having such a big guy hovering over him made him anxious. "I don't see nothing."

Marco swiveled the chair around, forcing both of them to back up. "I'll show it to Stan and see if he can do anything. What else do you have for me?"

"Bartlet and Smith are bringing in Emilio Velasquez's girlfriend now. Calvin Delacruz is the last guy on the list. He had AIDs, so he was getting pot from the headshop, but he was shot by a couple of gang bangers who took his wallet. He has a father here in the City. I thought we'd ask the father to come in, but beyond that, we're still at ground zero," said Cho.

"You're going to have to go back to the longer list of current clients."

"That's gonna take weeks to go through."

"Tag and Holmes almost have their case wrapped up. I'll put them on the headshop case as soon as they're finished."

Cho nodded.

"What about the girl that works at the headshop? Brittany or whatever?"

"Byrony Kenning? Nope, she's got an alibi."

"She was at a rave up north," said Simons. "We got pictures of her with the stage behind her."

"And the wife?"

"She'd gone to Arizona to visit her sister. We have the plane tickets."

Stan bustled around the corner of the precinct. "What you got for me, Captain?"

Marco motioned at the computer screen. "See that reflection there. Can you enhance it, so we can get a possible ID?"

Stan leaned over Marco and clicked with the mouse. Marco again tried not to shy away. He knew what Ryder would say, that he was too damn uptight, but he hated feeling people looming over the top of him, especially when he couldn't easily put distance between them.

Stan clicked and clicked and clicked, his tongue caught between his teeth. He smelled like some sugary candy cereal Marco remembered eating as a kid. Glancing down, he noticed that Stan wore another silly t-shirt with a cartoon character and the saying *Trek Yourself Before You Wreck Yourself* emblazoned across his chest. And as always, his favorite converse sneakers.

He envied Stan a little. He was so unafraid to be whoever the hell he wanted to be. Like Jake. Like Abe. Like Peyton. Marco frowned. He'd surrounded himself with free-spirited people, but why? He knew what Dr. Ferguson would say. He wanted to be like them, so he thought they might rub off on him, but he didn't think that was what it was.

He didn't want to be them, but having them in his life made his existence less boring. Well, in all fairness, Peyton had brought them all into his life, so having her in his life made his existence less boring. He was no better than Devan. Everything always came back to Peyton.

"I think I can clean it up." Stan motioned to the screen. "We've only got half the face, but I'm pretty sure I can do a mirror image on the other half and give us a rough approximation. Then I've got some software that will help unpixelate the image." He peered at Marco through his thick lens. "This is gonna take some time."

"Whatever it takes, Stan. I trust you."

Stan went still, then he ducked his head. "Thanks, Captain. If you let me get to the computer, I'll send the video to myself."

Marco wheeled the chair back and grabbed his cane, standing up. Maybe he was getting the hang of this supervision thing after all. Tell your people you trust them, then they worked harder for you. Hm.

"Tell me when Bartlet and Smith return with Velasquez's girlfriend," he said to Cho and Simons, then moved toward his office.

* * *

Luana Cooper was young, mixed race, and had a mouth on her like a truck driver. From the moment Cho escorted her into the interrogation room, she'd been using the f-word for every part of speech known to man. Marco watched through the two-way glass as Cho and Simons loomed over her. The entire time she swore at them, twisting her head around to see Simons behind her. She definitely had a temper, but he just wasn't seeing how she could be linked to Quentin Greer.

Finally Cho slammed a hand down on the table. "Enough. Say that word again and I'll put you in lock up for indecency."

"Indecency? What the fu—"

Cho pointed a finger at her and she clapped her mouth shut.

"Why you got me here? What you think I do this time?"

"We want to talk about Emilio Velasquez, your boyfriend."

She gave a short laugh. "My dead boyfriend. Besides that, he was a loser. I was fixin' to get rid of the douchebag myself."

Cho took a seat across from her. "He get shot in your house or his?"

"Our house. We rented it together."

"You know a place called the House of Weed."

"Yeah, that's where Emilio got his ganja. He went there ever week. No doubt."

"What he need the ganja for?"

198

"He had the glaucoma, you know?" She shook her head wryly. "He smoke from the time he roll his lazy ass out of bed until he pass out in front of the TV."

"Not a working man, eh?"

She made a rude noise.

"He ever tell you he had problems with Quentin Greer?"

"Who?"

"Quentin Greer, the ganja store owner?"

"No." She leaned forward and pointed at Cho. "I heard he got hisself burnt up. For real."

"Yeah, he's dead." Cho reached for the file. "Turns out Emilio liked to set fires for fun?"

She made another noise. "He done that shit when he was a kid. He don't do that stuff no more."

"He don't do nothing no more?" said Cho.

She gave a laugh. "No doubt."

"You don't seem all that choked up about Emilio's death?"

"What you want me to do? He sit at home, smoking the ganja, and eatin' my food. Ain't nothing to get choked up over."

"Didn't like the smoking, huh?"

She shrugged. "I don't care if you gonna be smokin', so's you go to work too. Emilio, he didn't do nothing but the smokin'."

"Bet that pissed you off?"

"Damn skippy!"

"Enough to want to cut off his supply?"

Luana leaned back, giving Cho a slow smile. "You mean you wanna know if I made the ganja dude a crispy critter?"

Cho sighed, sharing a look with Simons. "Yep, I wanna know if you made him a crispy critter."

"I got an alibi. I was working at the Metreon Cinema 16. My boss is Danny Yang." She gave him another cunning smile. "Anyways, I'm Buddhist."

"You're Buddhist?"

"Yep."

Cho picked up a paper and scanned it over. "I got a long list of priors here, Luana – assault, assault with a deadly weapon…" He glanced at Simons over her shoulder. "A waffle iron on that one."

"Ooowee!" said Simons.

"Assault with a knife."

"That was a steak knife," she said, waving her hand airily.

"Illegal gun possession."

"I was holding it for a friend."

"Attacking an officer."

"Now that wasn't my fault."

Cho gave a wry shake of his head. "I'm all ears."

"He grabbed my boob."

"He was trying to subdue you."

"By feeling me up? Shee-et."

"Still say you're a Buddhist?"

"Yeah. My shrink say I got anger management issues, on account of I weren't breastfed or nothing, so I turn Buddhist."

Cho closed the file and rose to his feet. "Sit tight, Dalai Lama."

"Who you calling a llama, pig!" she said, giving him a disgusted face.

Cho just shook his head and left the room, stepping across to viewing. "She ain't it, Captain."

Marco laughed. "No, but I like her."

"Yeah, she grows on you like mold."

"Cut her loose and go to the other list. I didn't think this was gonna get us anything."

Cho nodded and turned to go.

* * *

Marco hesitated in the doorway of his office. Tag, Jake and Cho were making their way to the precinct door. He glanced outside, marking that dusk had fallen and cast long shadows over the back parking lot.

"Thanks for coming in today," he said to them.

They came to an abrupt halt and looked over at him, then they shared a strange look.

"Night, Captain," said Cho, forcing a tense, awkward smile.

Marco frowned.

Tag held up a hand, giving him a half-hearted salute.

"Enjoy the rest of your weekend," he added. Something was definitely up. Jake wouldn't make eye contact.

"We will," said Tag, pushing open the half door and nodding her head toward the outside. Cho pushed past her, but Jake hesitated, his face twisting into a troubled expression. With an exhalation, he turned to face Marco.

"We're going to dinner at Peyton's."

Tag slapped him with the back of her hand, but he didn't back down, rubbing the spot as surreptitiously as he could.

Marco tilted back his head, his fingers tightening on the head of his cane. "Okay?" He tried to sound as casual as he could.

"See you Monday, Captain," said Tag, but Cho turned away from the door.

"We can stay if there's something else you need us to do."

Tag rolled her eyes.

"No, go. It's fine. Everything will wait until Monday. We're stuck until Stan cleans up the video and ballistics won't come back on the Cook gun before Monday at the earliest."

Jake shifted weight. "We could go get dinner or something."

Marco shook his head. "Go. I'm fine. I've got plans anyway."

Tag glanced over at him. "You do?"

"Yeah. No worries."

She tried to slap Jake again, but he sidled away from her. "He's got plans, idiot," she hissed at him.

"I heard him," but he gave Marco one of those searching Jake looks.

"Night, Captain," Cho said, pushing open the door. Tag followed him.

Still Jake lingered. "We could catch a movie?"

Marco sighed. "Go to Peyton's, Ryder. I'm not going to a movie with you. You'd want to hold hands or something."

Jake gave him a faint smile. "Fine, but I'm free tomorrow. We could get a pedicure or a wax."

Marco laughed. "Get out of here."

With a final backward glance, Jake followed the other two out of the precinct. Marco moved to the counter, watching them go. He'd never been excluded from dinner at Peyton's before. Even when he was trying to keep distance between them, he'd always been first on her guest list.

Closing his eyes, he fought himself. He wanted a drink. He wanted to dive into a Jack Daniels bottle and search for oblivion. He wanted to forget for just a few minutes.

And because he wanted it so bad, he pulled out his phone and thumbed it on, but he hesitated, looking at his contact list. His finger hovered over his brother's name. He could call Vinnie and Vinnie would be there for him, but that would mean taking him from his family, his wife and kids. He didn't need a younger brother pulling him down.

Marco's fingers closed over the phone. A bottle of Jack Daniels would be less trouble. There wouldn't be any questions or demands. There wouldn't be any guilt, until tomorrow. But knowing that everyone was going to Peyton's house made drinking a really bad idea. The last thing he needed was to show up there and plead for entrance.

He pressed the icon for Vinnie's number.

"Hey, little brother," came Vinnie's enthusiastic voice. "I'm so glad you called."

"I was wondering…" His voice trailed away as he thought of Peyton's house filled with all the people who meant most to him in the world. And there she'd be in the midst of them, drawing them together with that unconscious charisma she possessed. "I was wondering if you had a few hours to kill."

"Name it and I'm there."

Marco thought. Where could they go that wouldn't put him at a disadvantage, tempt him with alcohol?

"Remember when we used to hang out at Ocean Beach?"

"Yeah, I'll meet you there in half an hour."

Marco reconsidered. He didn't need Vinnie of all people grilling him for answers. "Look, forget…"

"I'll see you at Ocean Beach in half an hour. Make sure you're there." Then he was gone.

Marco stared at the display, thinking to call him back and cancel, but he knew that come hell or high water, Vinnie would go to Ocean Beach.

* * *

All three of his brothers were waiting for him when he arrived. They'd picked a spot above the beach, perching themselves on boulders that lined the parking lot. Marco limped over to them and allowed them to give him rough hugs. Bernardo shoved a can of soda in his hand.

Marco looked at it wryly. Once they'd meet out here, sneaking beers from their father's stash in the garage. Leo always commented that someone was filching his beers, but he never accused his sons. Later, Marco realized he knew what they were doing all along.

He awkwardly propped himself on a boulder, wedging the cane next to him, and popped open the can. The roar of the waves, the damp of the ocean air, and the smell of seaweed brought back so many memories for him.

He could see gulls wheeling over the surf and out a little farther he spotted the laborious pump of a pelican's wings before it tucked them into its body and dropped out of the sky into the ocean like a stone. He smiled.

He liked it out here.

People strolled up and down the beach, bundled against the late day chill, walking dogs, following small children who darted in and out of the surf. Some of them held hands. One couple stopped to look at the horizon, then turned toward each other and the woman lifted on tiptoes to kiss the man. Marco looked away. He and Peyton had spent days wandering the beach when they took their trip to the islands. Mostly they sat in the sand, his arms wrapped around her, his cheek resting on her shoulder.

"Do you remember Brad Peterson?" asked Franco, looking back at him.

"Captain of the football team?"

"Yeah, when you were a freshman and he was a senior?"

Marco nodded. He remembered him. Because of his size, Marco had been moved to varsity his first year, playing guard for Brad. Marco hated Brad. He was always snapping his towel at Marco's ass in the locker room, calling him Pretty Boy, and making kissing sounds whenever he was around.

"Didn't he play for the Bills?" asked Bernardo.

"Yeah, for a number of years. He was dating that Carol...um…"

"Carol Talone," Marco said. He also remembered Carol. Carol had taken it upon herself to educate him in all things female. Senior girl, freshman boy, he hadn't been in a position to complain, especially because whenever Brad pulled his shit, Marco knew he had something over him.

"They got married, didn't they?" said Vinnie.

"Yeah, still are. They just moved back to the Bay Area. I ran into Brad at the grocery store." Franco leaned closer. "He's bald." He motioned to his own thick, black hair. "He has this horrible comb-over."

The brothers laughed.

"Just shoot me if I ever do that," said Bernardo.

"Same here," said Vinnie, clicking his soda can against his brother's.

"You remember Wendell Williams?" said Bernardo.

"Weasel Williams?" said Vinnie and Franco together.

Marco smiled.

"Yeah, the little guy who'd wet his pants at school."

"I remember him picking his nose and eating it," said Franco with a shudder.

"He's a millionaire."

"No?" said Vinnie. "He used to come by the house, looking for you guys."

"He's the reason I passed Calculus," said Bernardo with a laugh. "Yeah, he's a millionaire. He got in with one of these startups in San Jose, and bam, he made it big."

"Shit. Weasel Williams a millionaire. I'm definitely doing something wrong," said Franco with a sigh.

Marco gave him a nod of agreement.

"Would you look at that sunset?" breathed Bernardo.

Marco looked out. A ray of sunlight had pierced through the cloud cover and shown down on the blue-grey of the ocean, painting the undersides of the clouds a brilliant pink fading to pale orange. The sound of gulls carried to him over the pulsation of the waves and a dog barked.

Vinnie draped an arm across his upper chest, pulling him back against him for a moment and kissing his temple. "It's gonna be okay, baby brother," he said in his ear.

CHAPTER 14

Saturday/Sunday

Peyton grabbed the paper out of her printer and hurried from her office, turning left to circle around to Tank's overflowing space. Few people were in on a Saturday, but a smattering of agents milled around the cubicle jungle and talked on phones.

Tank stood by the window, a book in hand, studying something on a page. He looked over at Peyton as she rounded the corner and stopped before his desk. "Peyton, nice to see you. Is Radar ready to go?"

Peyton held up the paper. "Not yet, but Lance Corporal Daw's evidence box arrived downstairs. You wanna look at it with me?"

He closed the book and moved to the shelf replacing it. "Of course I do. Do we have time?"

Peyton shrugged. "We can stall. If Radar can't find us, what's he gonna do?"

"Get angry. Have you seen the way that vein bulges in his forehead? I'm always afraid it's going to blow."

"Vein?" Peyton considered that. She hadn't noticed it before. Hm.

Tank grabbed his suit jacket and swung it on, moving around the desk. "Lately, I've seen it a lot. When Arthur was alive, it didn't happen so much, but after he died, Radar's jaw was so tight it looked like a rope running across his forehead. We were all glad when he got therapy." Tank led the way out of the office and they circled toward the elevator. "But the last few weeks, it's been back again."

Peyton stopped walking. The last few weeks? Since she'd come on-board? Shit, was she giving Radar an aneurysm?

Tank glanced back at her. "You coming?"

She jogged to catch up, watching as he punched the button for the elevator. Studying the paper, she wondered if they should leave the evidence box until they returned from Santa Cruz, but she quickly stuffed that thought away. It didn't hurt Radar to wait. He could do his meditation crap for a few minutes.

The evidence room was in the basement, which seemed a bit of a cliché to Peyton. It reminded her of those obligatory scenes in movies when a clerk takes a box of important evidence and begins walking down long aisles of storage as the camera pans out to reveal the vast horde of stuff being ignored by some government agency.

A very short man with wispy grey hair stood on a platform behind the counter. He wore a bowtie and his white shirt sleeves had been rolled up to his elbows. He had a small face, small eyes, button nose, and a tight, small mouth. He looked like an elf. Peyton fought a smile as she produced her writ of access to look at the box.

He eyed it, then eyed her, then reached for a pair of half-glasses, perched them on his button nose and eyed the paper again. Then without a word, he hopped off his platform and disappeared into the aisles behind him.

Peyton smiled up at Tank, rocking on her heels. "So…he's friendly."

Tank gave her a wry smile in return. "He doesn't deal with people very often."

"I got that," she said, tucking her hands into the pockets of her suit trousers. "Lots of boxes. LOTS of boxes."

"Shhh," hissed the little man, appearing at the end of the aisle. He glared at Peyton as he carried the box to the counter.

Peyton gave him a sheepish look and reached for it as he hopped up on his platform again. He yanked it away, settling it on a counter to the right of him. Grabbing a clipboard, he slapped it down in front of Peyton and pointed at a line.

"Sign."

Peyton reached for the pen attached to the top of the clipboard. It was chained to the hole in the clip. "Does it run away a lot?"

He cocked his head at her and gave her a piercing look. His eyes were a summery green. "What?"

"The pen. Does it run away? Is that why it's on a leash?"

Tank made a choking sound, drawing the little guy's attention.

"People are always walking off with it."

Peyton nodded and signed her name. He grabbed the clipboard and turned it around, studying her signature. While he did that, Peyton shoved her hand under his nose. "Peyton Brooks. I'm new here. It's nice to meet you."

He studied her hand a moment as if it might bite him.

She kept it extended, giving him a beaming smile. "I'm sure we're going to work together a lot and personally, I'm looking forward to it."

He hugged the evidence box with his right arm, but he grasped her hand with the fingers on his left hand and gave her a little squeeze. "Myron Hammersmith."

"Myron Hammersmith? Now that's a heroic name, to be sure. Like a Viking or something."

"It's British," he said.

"Technically," answered Tank, "it means one who smiths hammers. In medieval times, names often designated a man's trade or some such."

"Exactly."

Peyton smiled. These two were perfect for each other. "Good to know." She reached for the box and Myron finally relinquished it. Carrying it to a table perpendicular to the wall with the door, she settled it and peeled off the lid.

A pair of jeans and a t-shirt in a sealed plastic bag lay on top, followed by a run-down set of sneakers in another bag. Peyton lifted them out and looked them over, while Tank loomed behind her. Setting them aside, she picked up three more bags. Inside each was a napkin with numbers written on it. Two napkins had six numbers and one had only a single set of three.

"What are those?"

"I don't know, but they were in Mark Turner's file too."

"Mark Turner was the first investigating agent?"

"Yep."

"What did he think they were?"

"He didn't know."

"Combinations?"

"Probably, but to what?"

Tank shrugged, taking one of them from her hand and turning it over to look at the back.

Peyton settled the other two bags to the side and rose on tiptoes to look into the bottom of the box. It was empty.

"What the hell!"

Tank glanced into it as well. "Where's the coin?"

"I don't know." She tilted the box and looked at the label on the front of it. The clothes, the shoes, and the three bags with napkins were listed, but the coin was not. "It's not listed on here either."

She picked up the clothes and turned the bag over, trying to see if the coin had wound up inside of it by accident, but nothing shook loose. She did the same with the shoe bag, then she went back to the clothes and pressed them against the table, trying to feel for the coin hiding in the fabric.

Tank laid the napkins out on the table in a line and studied them. "What would these be a combination for? A safe? But where?"

Peyton distractedly shook her head. She could feel nothing in the clothes except the stitching where the jeans had been sewn together. She turned to Myron. "There's something missing from the box."

"Is it listed on the manifest?"

"No, but I know it was in here. Agent Turner took a picture of it and included it in his file."

"What was it?"

"A gold coin."

"If it isn't on the manifest, it wasn't in the evidence box. Evidence is handled with extreme care and is never out of the sight of a sworn evidence clerk at all times, once it leaves the chain of custody."

"But I'm telling you it was here. He had a picture of it in the file."

"Maybe it belonged in another file."

"No, it had the case number stamped on the back of it."

"If the coin is not on the manifest, it was never part of the evidence for this case," persisted Myron.

Peyton opened her mouth to protest, but her cell phone rang. Myron gave her an arch look and put a finger to his lips, indicating silence. Peyton snatched the phone out of her pocket and thumbed it on, glaring at him. She'd give him silence!

"Yeah!" she barked into the phone.

"Just what I need on my Saturday morning, Sparky, attitude."

Radar. "Sorry, what's up?" She forced false brightness into her voice.

"I thought we were heading out to Santa Cruz. Bambi's here, but you're not, and I wouldn't want to go anywhere without your sunny disposition beside me."

"Okay, we're coming."

"We're?"

"Me and Tank."

"You have Tank with you? Where are you?"

"Evidence."

"Evidence? What are you doing down there?"

"Researching a cold case."

"Well, we have a live case right here. You wanna give that some of your attention?"

"Okay, just give us a minute. Do some of your meditation or something? Tank's worried about that vein in your head."

"What vein in my head?"

Tank gave her a frantic shake of his own head.

Peyton patted his shoulder. "We're coming now, Radar. Sit tight."

"What vein in my head?"

"See you soon, buddy," she cooed into the phone and disconnected. Putting everything back in the evidence box, she smoothed her hands over the clothes Lance Corporal Daws had worn just before he died. Such a small amount of nothing to leave behind. *Such a small amount of nothing.* What the hell.

*   *   *

"What's this cold case you're so fixated on?" asked Radar as he drove down the coast toward Santa Cruz.

Peyton stared out the window. She liked this drive. The ocean glimmered blue-green in the morning sunlight and cypress trees twisted their way along the bluffs. Green valleys appeared before them, rolling into the harsh lines of the cliffs where the surf had eroded away the land.

"Lance Corporal Isaac Daws. He died in a sleazy motel room of a drug overdose two years after being discharged. He had a purple heart and numerous commendations for service and bravery."

"Who had the case first?"

"Mark Turner." She looked over at Radar, but she couldn't see anything behind his mirrored glasses. "You know him?"

"Nope. He's not in our office."

"Las Vegas."

"Ah, is that where Daws was found?"

"Yep."

"Why do we have it?"

"He grew up here. His parents didn't accept the medical examiner's conclusion, so another autopsy was done. That one turned up some troubling results."

"Who did the second autopsy?"

Peyton tried to remember.

"Cecelia Gaston," said Tank behind her.

Peyton held up a hand to indicate he was right.

"He was found with a strange coin in his pocket, but when we looked at the evidence box, it wasn't in there. Turner took a picture of it and put it in the file, but I felt everything in that box and looked at the manifest, but it was gone."

"What kind of coin?"

"Not sure."

"The professor's doing research on it," offered Tank.

Radar gave a short nod.

"Ooh, I like a mystery," said Bambi. "You need my help on this?"

Peyton started to answer, but Radar held up a hand. "We have a case. We need to focus on that. Put the Daws case away until we're done with this, then we can all take a look at it."

Peyton gave Bambi a smile and turned back to the front. "How can evidence go missing, Radar?" she asked.

"Many reasons. Let it go for now."

Peyton relinquished, sliding down in her seat and watching the countryside speed past the window. When they arrived in Santa Cruz, Lieutenant Brannon met them at the entrance to the farmer's market. Peyton climbed out of the Suburban and closed the door, watching as Radar crossed to Brannon's side and shook her hand.

"Reynolds is keeping an eye on the Horizon women. They're at the other end of the market with a table, selling vegetables and some cloth. We didn't approach them, but the cloth looks like natural fibers," said Brannon.

Radar turned to his team. "Sparky, you're with me. Tank, Bambi, spread out and search for anyone else selling natural clothing. Approach cautiously. We're just asking questions right now." His voice trailed away and his attention went beyond them. "Shit."

Peyton looked over her shoulder to see a news van pull up in front of the market.

Brannon reached for her radio. "Hank, we got a news crew here. I'm gonna head them off. You wanna make sure there isn't another crew coming in on your end of the street."

"Got it," came the response.

Radar motioned Peyton to follow him. Bambi gave her a wave of her fingers as she moved off with Tank in the opposite direction.

"Radar," Peyton said, falling into step beside him. "What exactly are we going to do if we locate the baby's mother? Are we going to arrest her for something?"

"There are a number of things we could arrest her for, Sparky. Let's cross that bridge when we find it, okay? Right now, I just want an explanation of why she did it."

"What if she's just a scared kid? What if she didn't know what else to do?"

"Then we'll question her and decide how to proceed." He placed a hand on her arm and stopped her. "You don't think it's okay to just toss a baby away like garbage, do you?"

"Of course not, but I also don't know that a crime was committed here either."

"We'll let judges and lawyers decide that, okay? Let's just focus on our job."

Peyton nodded and continued beside him. He was right, of course, but it seemed a whole lot of effort for something that was a questionable crime, when Lance Corporal Daws had died under truly suspicious circumstances.

As they meandered through the crowds, Peyton found herself enchanted with the market. People sold vegetables and fruit. They crafted dishes and knick-knacks. They raised bees and gathered honey. They made candles and soaps and shampoos and perfumes. And some made clothing.

Every place they stopped, they asked the people what the material was and every time they got different answers, but none were made of hemp. A woman sold rag dolls made from cotton. Another had beanies out of wool, and a third knitted stuffed animals from mohair. Peyton wasn't sure what mohair was, so the woman produced a photo of her angora goats, beaming proudly at them as if they were her own children.

Finally, they worked their way to the end and Peyton spotted the Horizon van. Two women in plain, brown dresses greeted customers from behind a wooden table. A round sun was painted on the side of the van with the word Horizon slashing across it.

Fingering the wooden handle of a boar's bristle brush, Peyton watched the women interact with the people around them. One was young, about sixteen or seventeen, the other in her mid to late forties. They had their hair pulled away from their faces and wound in a bun, no makeup or jewelry to adorn them.

"Well?" said Radar beside her.

"I'm not sure what to do."

The women barely spoke with their customers, keeping their eyes downcast, their heads bowed.

Slipping off her suit jacket, Peyton handed it to Radar. "Hold this."

"Why?"

"I look like a fed in it." She unbuttoned her white shirt sleeves and rolled them up to her elbows, then unbuttoned the first couple of buttons at her throat. Reaching up, she pulled the clips out of her hair and shook her head to let it spill around her shoulders.

"You planning to seduce them?"

She gave Radar a pointed look. "Whatever works, buddy."

"You've called me that twice. Stop it. I'm not your buddy."

She blew a kiss at him. "Of course you are."

He clenched his jaw and Peyton saw the vein in his forehead.

"Calm down. Your vein is showing. Mrs. Radar wouldn't like that." Running her fingers through her mane of hair, she left him standing at the display of wooden utensils and sauntered over to the Horizon table.

She caught sight of Reynolds, his tall, spare frame looming over the people at the end of the market, leaning against the barricade. She gave him a nod and picked up a tomato, rolling it in her hand.

"How much?" she asked the younger girl.

She glanced at her through her lashes. She had brown hair, a plain face scrubbed free of all makeup, and pale brown eyes. "How many do you want?"

"A couple of pounds."

The girl reached for a paper bag and began putting tomatoes into it.

Peyton glanced at the other woman, but she was helping a man choose squash. Next to her sat a display of brown cloth with embroidered edges.

"Are those blankets?" she said, nodding at the end of the table.

"Yes," said the girl.

"What are they made from?"

The girl glanced up at her again. Peyton gave her a disarming smile.

"I love natural fibers," she said, but the girl's eyes lowered to Peyton's polyester suit. "When I can find them," she added.

The girl continued to pick out tomatoes. "They're all natural."

"But from what? Flax, cotton?"

The girl glanced over at the older woman, catching her attention. She gave the man his squash and dropped the money in a wooden box, then came to the girl's side.

"Can I help you?" she asked Peyton, meeting her eye. She also had pale brown eyes and brown hair.

"I was just wanting to know what the blankets are made from?"

"Natural fibers."

"Right. But which?"

The girl settled the bag of tomatoes on a rusty scale and weighed it.

The older woman gave her a forced smile. "Hemp."

"How much for a blanket?" Peyton moved down the table and fingered it. It was surprisingly soft.

"They're not for sale."

"Why are they out here then?"

"Display," said the older woman.

She lifted her eyes to the van. "What does Horizon mean?"

"It's the name of our farm."

Farm. Finn Getter had mentioned the farm in his letters to Aster King.

"How fascinating. Where is it?"

The woman grabbed the bag of tomatoes from the girl and held it out to Peyton. Her eyes swept over Peyton's clothing. "That'll be $6.00."

Peyton reached for her wallet and took the money out, passing it to the woman. "I only have a twenty. Can you give me change?"

Snatching the bill from Peyton's hand, she opened the wooden box and began searching through the money. Peyton moved back to the girl. "You might know my friend. He's about your age."

The woman stopped moving. The girl took a step away from the table.

"He lives on a farm around here too. He told me he helps keep the vegetable garden, grows tomatoes and squash."

The girl refused to meet her eye.

"He has a funny name. He was named for a character in a book."

The girl's gaze snapped to her face.

"Finn. Finn Getter? You wouldn't know him, would you?"

The older woman moved in front of the girl, holding out the twenty. "Take the tomatoes. They're yours."

Peyton looked around her at the girl, then she reached into her pocket and pulled out a business card, settling it on the table. "We can help you," she said, meeting the woman's eyes. "We can get you to a shelter."

"We don't need help."

"Okay, but if anyone on the farm needs medical attention, we can get that for you too. We can…" She leaned toward the girl. "We can bring doctors, medicine, counselors."

"We don't need help from outsiders." The older woman made an impatient motion with the twenty.

Picking up the business card, Peyton reached out and closed her hand around the woman's, folding the twenty and the card into her fingers. Holding her eyes, she squeezed her hand. "Keep it." Then she opened her fingers and took a step away.

The woman didn't drop her gaze nor did she release the card.

Peyton backed from the table slowly, then turned and strode back to Radar.

"Well?"

"Something's wrong."

Radar nodded. "Looked that way from here."

"We need to get on that farm."

"Under what grounds, Sparky?"

"A mermaid being tossed in the ocean."

"Can't prove it came from there."

"The blanket was hemp, but they wouldn't sell me one. Can we get a warrant for that?"

"I don't see how. We had a few fibers at most."

Peyton looked back at the van. The two women were packing up, the blankets had already disappeared. Shit. She knew something was wrong with those women, but she had no way to prove it. She knew they recognized Finn Getter's name. She'd seen the light in the younger girl's eyes.

Finn Getter. He was the answer. He was the way to get onto that farm.

She whipped back to face Radar. "Finn Getter spent as much time as he could at the library."

"Yeah?"

"The librarian was Mrs. Elder. I knew I'd heard that name before. Maybe if we go see her, we can get to Finn. And if we get to Finn…"

"Maybe we get to the farm."

"Right."

"Why do you think this connects to the mermaid?"

"Something's not right there, Radar," she said, motioning to the van. "I'm telling you. Finn talked about birth defects on the farm and those women act scared. The older woman told me the blankets were made of hemp. Come on. This isn't coincidence. This is all connected."

Radar exhaled and rubbed at his forehead. Peyton noticed his vein was bulging again. "Goddamn it, Sparky, you're going to get me mixed up in a cult thingy."

"A cult thingy?"

"Ruby Ridge, Waco? Either of those ring a bell?"

"Yes, but what choice do we have? The younger girl? She's maybe fourteen or fifteen. Who knows what's going on at that farm, Radar?"

"We go in there and guns get pulled."

Peyton glanced back at the van. The younger girl was watching them surreptitiously as she boxed up produce. "Since when is the FBI afraid to do what's right? Since when is the FBI afraid to help people in trouble?"

Radar whipped off his glasses and glared at her. "Since innocent people die in these things. This is still America and if you want to live in a bloody damn cult, you have the right to do it."

"Well, the part of that I heard was *if.* What if you don't want it? What if you have rampant inbreeding causing birth defects? What if young girls are being forced to bear children before they're old enough, leaving them with the only option of throwing the bodies into the ocean?"

Radar held her gaze. "You're trouble, you know that, Sparky?"

She didn't respond.

"The minute I saw you, I said that one's trouble. She's going to make my life hell."

Still Peyton didn't respond.

"You aren't a superhero. That badge doesn't give you the right to interfere in people's lives. You need to know when you have something and when to walk away. You were right before. What are we going to prosecute? There was no murder, there was simply a bad decision of disposing of a body improperly. Then because the media got involved, we got dragged into it, but there's no case here. There's just a weird cult, some weird letters, and…" His gaze went beyond her to the van. "…and a baby who was tossed away like garbage."

Peyton crossed her arms in front of her.

Radar's eyes whipped back to her face and he lifted a finger, pointing it at her. "Fine. We'll come back on Monday and talk to Mrs. Elder. We'll see if she can locate Finn Getter and then we'll ask him what goes on at the farm."

Peyton smiled.

Radar shook his head, clenching his jaw. "No, don't you smile at me. You're trouble. The minute I saw you, I knew you were trouble. And they went and gave you to me. Shit." Turning on his heel, he began walking the way they came.

Peyton glanced over her shoulder. The girl was climbing into the passenger seat of the van, but she looked back, making eye contact with Peyton before she disappeared inside. Peyton shifted her attention to the painted sun and the lettering on the side of the van. *Horizon, my ass,* she thought.

* * *

Walking up the ramp to her door, Peyton reached for her gun. She could hear voices on the other side, music playing, and laughter. Without drawing it, she reached for the handle and eased the door open, peering into the house.

Abe wheeled into her line of sight, carrying a tray with tall, thin glasses on it, sporting a sprig of mint at the top. She breathed out and eased her hand away from the gun, stepping inside. As soon as they saw her, all motion ceased.

Peyton catalogued everyone instantly: Abe, Jake, Cho, Maria and Tag. Their faces burst into smiles and "Peyton!" rang out over the thump of the base. Pickles raced for her and she scooped him up, closing the door behind her.

"Nice of you to break-in," she said.

Jake was the first to approach, kissing her on the cheek and taking the dog. She removed her suit jacket and gun, hanging them on the peg by the door. She couldn't help but search the room a second time, looking for Marco. She knew he wouldn't be there, but she couldn't help herself.

Abe bounced over, extending the tray. "How about a mojito, sweets? You only get one, so sip it slowly."

Peyton took a drink and gave him a smile. He planted a kiss on her forehead. "You might have told me you were planning a break-in."

"And spoil the surprise? Silly girl."

Silly girl, indeed.

Maria stopped in front of her. "I won't even ask what you've got going on here." She motioned down Peyton's body. "But go get changed and come see what we have for dinner. We've got a taco bar going."

Peyton nodded and wended her way through the living room, waving to Tag and giving Cho a quick hug. She slipped into a pair of shorts and a loose tank top, releasing her curls from the bun she'd hastily tied after they left the farmer's market. Picking up her drink, she returned to the living room and Maria pounced on her, dragging her into the kitchen.

All the fixings for tacos had been laid out on her counters, among Abe's paraphernalia for drinks. "Grab a plate. You look thin," Maria tsked. "You're not going to have any ass at all if you keep this up. You look like a prepubescent boy."

Peyton opened her mouth to respond, but decided it wasn't worth it. There was no win with Maria. Either she had the ass of a hippo, or she had no ass at all. Before she could dish up a plate, Maria began piling things on it, shoving it into her hand and pushing her out of her own kitchen.

Peyton retreated to the couch and sat down next to Tag. "Hey, partner," she said.

Tag offered her a chin lift. "What's shaking, Fluffy?"

"Not much. How are you?"

"I got saddled with Holmes as a partner. How do you think I am?"

Peyton lifted a taco and took a bite, giving Tag an understanding nod. "He's all sorts of pleasant, isn't it?"

"If I have to hear how many women he bangs in a month again, I'm gonna castrate him."

Peyton laughed. "You eating?"

"As soon as Betty freakin' Crocker gets out of the kitchen." Tag leaned close to Peyton. "She said my face was looking fat."

Peyton smiled. "Usually she compares my ass to large animals, but today she said I looked like a boy."

Tag shook her head, then pushed herself off the couch when Maria came into the living room and took a seat in Marco's chair. "So I bought some new product for your hair. You can't go around looking like Bozo the clown."

Tag halted as she passed behind Maria's chair and made a stabbing motion with her hand. Peyton hid her smile, reaching for her mojito instead. As soon as she finished her plate, Maria pounced on her, taking it from her hand. Peyton eased back on the couch and watched Jake and Cho argue about which opera was the best.

Her house was filled with people again and it made her happy.

Abe carried his drink over to the couch and dropped down beside her. She snuggled against him, resting her head on his shoulder.

"How you doing, my sweet girl?"

"Better now that you're here."

He nodded, pressing his cheek to her hair. "You sleeping all right?"

"Not so good."

"Nightmares?"

"Yeah. Thank you for coming over." She leaned back and looked into his face. "What's Marco doing?"

Abe shrugged. "I left him to his own devices, sweets. He needs to get his ducks in a row and I can't do it for him."

"Is he still drinking?"

"Off and on. He won't see my friend Grey, so the pain is eating at him, but you can't force someone to do something they won't."

She played with a bead on the end of Abe's dreadlock. "He say anything about us?"

"I haven't had much time to talk to him. Although, the other night, he played poker with Serge and Misha."

Peyton gave him a disbelieving look. "Marco? My Marco?"

Abe pealed off into laughter. "Yep. Serge and Misha loooved him. And they told me I couldn't get a younger man."

"You didn't get a younger man."

Abe placed a finger against his lips. "Shh, little soul sista. What they don't know can't hurt them."

Peyton laughed and laid her head on his shoulder. "I love you, Abe."

"Right back at you, sweeting."

Commotion broke out in the kitchen. Peyton glanced over and watched as Maria carried a cutting board into the living room. On it was a line of peppers and a knife. Cho carried four glasses and a carton of milk.

Maria settled the cutting board on the coffee table and motioned everyone around. Jake gave Peyton a nervous look, sinking onto the couch beside her.

"What's going on?"

"We're having a little competition," offered Maria. "Tag here says she can eat a ghost pepper. I informed her that due to my Mexican heritage, I can eat a far hotter pepper than she can." Resting a hand on Cho's shoulder, she gave him a condescending smile. "And darlin' Nathan here thinks that because of his Chinese heritage and male parts, he can best both of us."

"What about Jake?"

They all looked at Jake. Jake was staring at the peppers as if he expected them to sprout heads and talk to him. Laughter erupted.

"Hey! I've eaten peppers before."

"When? Just before you went out to tip cows?" asked Cho.

Jake glared at him.

"We'll start here and work our way up." Maria pointed at each as she named it. "Bell pepper, pablano, guajillo, jalapeno, and finally the hottest we could find, habanero. You wanna try it with us?" she asked Peyton.

Peyton vigorously shook her head. "No thank you. I like my stomach lining just fine."

Maria gave Abe a sultry look.

"Flirt with me all you want, baby," he said, waving her off. "I save my internal organ damage for alcohol."

"Okay. Everyone pour a glass of milk and take your first bite," she instructed.

Jake gave Peyton a tense smile and popped a bell pepper in his mouth. He made a face as he chewed.

Peyton shook her head in amusement. "That can't be hot, Jake."

"It tastes waxy."

Peyton laughed and watched everyone else down their bell pepper. Tag had perched herself on the edge of Marco's chair, giving the contest her full attention, but Peyton noticed Pickles had managed to ease himself halfway onto her lap. So much for not liking dogs.

"Okay, now the pablano."

Jake stared at the small slice of pepper, then resolved, he popped it in his mouth and chewed. After a few seconds, he stopped chewing and gave Peyton a frantic look before reaching for the milk. Cho rolled his eyes and swallowed. Maria and Tag didn't seem to notice any effect.

"Are you out, Jake?" Maria asked with just a hint of disgust.

"No. I'm still in."

Peyton squeezed his arm. "Don't hurt yourself."

"I'm in," he said, motioning at the cutting board. "You guys out?"

They reached for the third pepper. The guajillo. Jake chewed and his face contorted into a grimace, then his eyes started to water and his ears turned red. He bolted from the couch and ran into the kitchen, spitting into the sink.

Abe chuckled beside her.

Cho made a face, but he managed to swallow, reaching for his milk.

Tag and Maria glared at each other, but they downed their bite without noticeable discomfort.

"I'm out," moaned Jake from the kitchen.

"No shit," grumbled Cho.

"Well?" challenged Maria to Tag.

"Bring it on, sister!" snarled Tag.

They reached for the jalapeno. Cho picked his up with more reluctance. Jake returned to the couch, wiping a napkin across his tongue.

"I feel like my mouth's blistered," he moaned. Peyton rubbed his shoulders and watched the others.

Suddenly Cho grabbed for the milk, gulping it down. Tag and Maria stared at each other as they chewed and swallowed. Waving his hand, Cho continued to gulp milk. "I'm out. Jesus H. Christ, I'm out."

Maria ran her fingers over his cheek. "It's all right, baby."

"It's all right, baby?" gasped Jake. "With me, I get *you're a stupid wimp*, but he gets *it's all right, baby*."

"He carries a gun," said Maria.

Cho gave him a mock glare.

Turning to Tag, Maria motioned to the habanero. "You wanna continue?"

"Damn straight, I do." She drummed her fingers on the table, making the happy tattoo dance. "You wanna continue?"

"No problemo," said Maria, reaching for the bite.

Tag grabbed hers as well and they popped them in their mouths at the same time. Peyton shook her head as she watched them. Maria's expression never changed, but Tag's eyes started to water and she shuddered as she continued to chew.

"You're both nuts," she commented, but she loved this. This was what she'd missed since Marco left. She liked chaos and people breaking into her house for a taco party. She liked having the room filled to overflowing. If only he was here. If only she could curl up in his chair with him and feel his arms enfold her.

"Give?" said Maria, smiling.

Tag closed her eyes and continued to chew, her hand curling into a fist.

"Give!" demanded Maria.

Tag shook her head, but her face had gone red and sweat beaded on her brow. With supreme effort she swallowed. "Never!"

Maria's face grew crafty. She reached into her pocket and pulled out a baggy. A bright red pepper lay in the bottom of it. "This is a red savina. Let's make a little wager."

Tag breathed with her mouth open, but she didn't reach for the milk. "Name it."

Maria smiled, but it wasn't a happy smile. "If I win, you let me do your hair."

Tag glanced at Peyton and Peyton grimaced. "My hair?" She brushed a hand over her short locks.

"Yep. Color, cut and style."

"Style?"

"Curls."

Tag reared away.

Jake gave a low whistle.

Peyton felt sure she'd cry defeat, but she firmed her jaw. "Fine, but if I win…"

"Yes…"

Tag's gaze shifted to Cho. "If I win, Cho takes Holmes as his partner for a case."

Cho shook his head frantically. "No, no that's not fair."

Tag held out her hand to Maria, but her eyes were on Cho. "Do we have a deal?"

"Maria?" begged Cho. "Don't do this. Please, don't do this to me."

"It's okay, baby," she said, stroking his cheek, then she took Tag's hand. "You have a deal." Thrusting the baggy at Abe, she shook it. "Do the honors."

Abe took the pepper from the bag and laid it on the cutting board. When he placed the knife against it, Maria tsked in protest. "Don't be a wuss. Cut a good slice."

"I'll give you wuss, sister," grumbled Abe, hacking off a large chunk.

Tag made a whimpering noise.

"You wanna cry defeat?" asked Maria, reaching for her own slice.

Abe punched Cho in the shoulder. "Did she put your balls in a baggy and carry them in her pocket?"

Cho glared at him, but returned his concentration to the game.

"Straight woman calling me a wuss, she-et!" Abe groused.

Peyton smoothed a hand down his arm.

"I'll tell you who's a wuss." He pointed a finger at Maria.

Peyton shook her head at him.

He grumbled and sat back against the couch. "And I can get me a younger man whenever I damn well please, too."

Peyton hugged his arm and laid her head on his shoulder.

"And women, if I wanted them. If I liked all those squishy parts." He slashed a hand at Maria and looked out the window.

"Ready?" said Maria to Tag.

"Ready," said Tag, tilting up her chin. She reached for her piece and popped it in her mouth. For a moment, she just sat, gripping the arms of the chair, her expression urgent. Maria casually bit into her pepper and began chewing, but Tag didn't do anything except sit and hold it in her mouth.

Cho wrung his hands, watching them, but Maria seemed unfazed.

Suddenly Tag leaped from the chair and raced to the kitchen, retching into the sink. Jake and Abe groaned, but Maria and Cho surged to their feet, leaping about in triumph.

"You did it!" shouted Cho, swinging her around in a hug. "Holy shit, you did it!"

Maria threw back her head and laughed.

Peyton smiled, watching their exuberance. Then Cho pulled her back to him and planted a kiss on her mouth.

Everyone shouted "NO!", but it was too late. Releasing her, he fumbled for the milk and tried to wipe the pepper oil from his lips.

CHAPTER 15

Monday

Marco turned as the precinct door opened and Jake stepped through, followed by Tag...and yet not Tag. Her hair was a honey blond color, not shocking white, and it lay in soft waves around her face, making the skull tattoo on her neck stand out even more.

He gaped at her as she gave him a wounded look, pushing open the half-door and slumping past him toward the inner part of the precinct. "Wha—" he said, following her with his eyes, but she never stopped, just slowly walked away without speaking.

He turned to Jake.

"Red savina."

"What?"

"You don't want to know. I used to have taste buds..." His eyes drifted away like he was looking into the abyss. "...but they died."

Marco opened his mouth to respond, then decided it did him no good.

Shaking his head, Jake followed the path Tag had made toward the break-room.

Marco frowned, his gaze coming to rest on Carly's empty desk. Of course. Why would he expect his assistant to be in before him on a Monday?

"D'Angelo!" came a loud voice as the outer door flew open. "Let's talk NRA." Devan loomed on the other side of the counter, vibrating with hostility.

Marco drew a breath and released it. Well, hello Monday!

He motioned into his office and Devan followed him inside. As he crossed around his desk, Devan took a seat.

"The NRA wants the case against Will Cook dropped. They want him released without charge and the shooting declared self-defense."

Marco hesitated before taking his own seat. "No."

Devan glanced up at him. "No? I need something more than that."

"Hell no." He sat down.

Devan scooted forward in his chair, unbuttoning his suit jacket. "Rani wants a house on Nob Hill. With a yard, and a swing-set and gates. Do you know how much swing-sets cost on Nob Hill?"

Marco shrugged.

"And five kids. Five kids!" He gave a frantic shake of his head. "She wants five kids, D'Angelo."

"And Gavin Morris' parents want their son back."

Devan slumped in his chair. He held up a hand and let it fall. "The NRA are very persuasive."

"Because they carry guns."

"There's that. And other things."

"The only thing necessary for the triumph of evil is for good men to do nothing."

Devan lifted his head. "Edmund Burke."

Marco shrugged.

"I don't need a conscience."

"Are you sure of that?"

Devan clenched his jaw. "Well, I sure as hell don't need you to be it."

"I'll have the ballistics report on the gun today. If Amy Cooks' epithelials are on the barrel of that gun, you have to take it to the Grand Jury. If her skin is on that gun, if her fingerprint is there, Cook knew who he was shooting, Adams. He knew and he shot four times."

"And what about the NRA?"

"Ignore them."

Devan shook his head. "That's easier said than done."

"Then stand up to them. Look, Devan, I believe in the second amendment. I carry a gun, but I'll be damned if

I'm going to be held hostage by them. They have the right to fight for what they believe in. So do I, and I believe that Gavin Morris was murdered."

"Okay. Okay. You win, D'Angelo, but I wish this case never came across your desk. I wish I never heard of it."

Marco shrugged. "We can wish for many things, Adams, but it's what we do with the things that lay before us that matter."

Devan pushed himself to his feet and leaned on the desk. "I hate it when you're deep."

Marco smiled and watched him walk from the room.

He knew Devan faced a battle, but it was the right battle and it had to be fought. Will Cook had shot an unarmed boy in his house, a boy who had been invited there by his girlfriend. This wasn't a gun rights issue. This was murder.

If Cook had used the gun to scare him, or warn him, they wouldn't be here, but he'd shot to kill. The kid never had a chance. He never had a chance to defend himself. He'd tried to flee and he'd been shot in the back.

It might be different if he'd faced Cook. If he'd been trying to defend himself. If he'd done anything that remotely looked like an attack, but he hadn't. Of all the cases Marco had seen, there were two things humans did. They fought back and they ran. Gavin Morris ran.

Marco's thoughts came into focus. Humans fought back. They didn't stand around and let you douse them with gasoline and they didn't let you set them on fire. They fought back, but Quentin Greer hadn't fought. He hadn't put up a struggle. He'd allowed someone to torch him and he hadn't done anything about it.

Marco punched the intercom button. "Carly?"

No answer.

Grabbing his cane, he climbed to his feet and limped into the precinct. Carly's desk was empty, so he made his way through the precinct to Cho and Simon's desk. Simons rocked forward in his chair when Marco appeared, and Cho sauntered over, carrying coffee from the break-room.

"Quentin Greer didn't fight back."

"What?" asked Cho, handing Simons a mug.

"He didn't fight back. He let someone douse him with gasoline and set him on fire, but he didn't fight back. How does that happen?"

Cho exchanged a look with Simons. "I'm not sure."

"I want to see the crime scene photos."

"Now?" asked Simons, sipping at his coffee.

"Yes, now."

"Sure thing, Captain," he said, rising to his feet. "I'll get Ryder."

Marco nodded. It felt good to have someone do what he wanted for a change.

* * *

The crime scene photos were a horror show. The charred remains of Greer sat in the middle of the shop and around it the wooden floors, plaster and counter had all been burnt to cinders. Greer's hands were raised, the fingers clawed, what remained of his mouth open in a scream.

Marco picked up the photo and looked closer at it. Greer's hands weren't raised, they were pressed against his upper stomach between his pectoral muscles. Marco frowned, reaching for the magnifying glass Jake had laid out on the conference room table by his evidence bag.

Greer was on his back, his hands pressed to his sternum.

Marco lifted his gaze to Cho and Simons. "He's on his back."

They exchanged a look with each other. "Right?"

"He must have been on his back when he was doused with gasoline."

Cho sat forward, holding out his hand for the picture. Jake hopped off the table at the back of the room and looked over his shoulder. "Shit."

"Look where his hands are. They're not in a defensive posture, they're pressed to his chest."

Simons leaned over and looked as well. "Damn it. How did we miss that?"

"Where's Abe's autopsy report?"

Cho passed Simons the photo and reached for the file, locating it and sliding it across to Marco. Marco searched the report, but Abe had concluded Quentin Greer had been killed by the fire.

"He was facing his attacker," said Jake, taking the photo out of Simons' hand. "He must have known him."

"Or he wasn't threatened by him. If someone brings a gasoline can into my store, I'm going to feel threatened."

"Which is why the torching happened after Greer was dead, or almost dead. It was an attempt to hide the crime," said Marco. "Get Abe on the phone and tell him to redo the autopsy. He needs to look for a stabbing wound somewhere around here." He pressed his fingers to his own chest.

Cho jumped to his feet and hurried out of the conference room.

Jake looked up at Marco. "I'm sorry I missed this."

"You?" said Simons. "I'm a seasoned investigator. I shouldn't have missed it."

"Everyone missed it, including Abe, and Abe doesn't miss anything." Marco drew a deep breath. "This is my fault. I caused a distraction for all of you and this is the result." He held out his hand, indicating the photo. "Let's go back over the current customer files. This is looking more like a crime of passion than premeditation. And Ryder, see how Stan is coming with that image in the glass. I'm not sure we have the right time of death."

Simons leaned forward in his chair. "We have Calvin Delacruz's father coming in this afternoon. Delacruz is the last on our list of dead. He's the kid who was shot by gang bangers and robbed."

"He had AIDS?"

"Right. Do you want us to call the father and tell him to forget coming in?"

"Yeah. That's not gonna get us anything."

Simons rose to his feet and moved past Jake into the precinct. Jake gave Marco a piercing look as he gathered his things. "You know, you're a good captain, Adonis. This job suits you."

Marco turned toward the door. "Just see what Stan has, okay?"

"Why can't you just accept a compliment when you get one?"

Marco looked over his shoulder at him. "I don't want approval, Ryder. I just want people to do their job and come back safe. They don't need distractions in this line of work, and I caused one. What the hell good does a compliment do? What does it mean? Nothing."

Jake gave him an unyielding stare. "It means you have people at your back, Captain. It means that when you send them out into danger, they trust that you are doing the right thing. It lets you know that you are."

Marco didn't answer, but damn it all, Jake had him yet again.

* * *

"Jake Ryder keeps telling me I'm a good captain. Like he thinks my self-worth is tied to what he thinks."

"Is it?"

Marco looked up at Dr. Ferguson. As always, he had his hands steepled before his mouth, his hair mussed, his suit rumpled, his glasses just slightly askew. "No."

"And yet what he says frequently bothers you. Why?"

"He says things that are true." Marco held up a hand. "Sometimes. Sometimes he's just full of shit."

"What else has he said that's true?"

"What?"

"What truths has he told you?"

Marco shifted in the chair. "That Peyton would be better off with him than me."

"And you believe this?"

"She adores him. She fought so damn hard to get him off that murder charge and then she got him a job, let him live in her house."

"But she chose you?"

"Peyton doesn't always do the most logical thing."

"Why would Jake Ryder be better for her than you? You said the things she did for him. What does he do for her?"

Marco looked out the window. He hated talking about other men like this. He especially hated talking about Jake because if Jake knew, he'd love it. And that annoyed the hell out of Marco. "Jake is...Jake is good. Jake's a good person."

"And you're not?"

"I'm…" Marco met Dr. Ferguson's gaze. "I'm a lot of things, but that's not a word I've ever heard about myself."

"And why do you feel that way?"

"I'm a cop. I've seen things. I've done things." Marco drummed his fingers on the arms of his chair. "I've killed."

"So has Peyton. Is she a good person?"

"Peyton?" Marco laughed. "Peyton's the best person I know. *I* made Peyton kill."

"How?"

"She killed the Janitor to save me."

Ferguson picked up his pen and wrote on his pad, then he settled it on the table again. "You accept responsibility for many things, Captain D'Angelo. Do you realize that?"

"Isn't that what a captain's supposed to do?"

"Yes, and it's a rare quality when so many people, CEO's, politicians, celebrities, refuse to take any responsibility at all. Which is why, perhaps, that Mr. Ryder feels the need to tell you you're doing a good job. Accepting a compliment doesn't make you vain or weak or less of a man. It's a validation that you are a man."

*   *   *

It's a validation that you are a man. Marco climbed out of the Charger and pressed the lock on the door. Shit. He had to finish this therapy, so he could stop having to spend so damn much time thinking about this shit. It was messing with his head. It was making him question everything he knew and if he wasn't careful, it was going to make him sensitive.

That's what annoyed him so damn much about Ryder. Ryder was so freakin' sensitive. He always saw things, sensed things that a man shouldn't. A man should just boldly plow through life without stopping to analyze every damn thing, but Ryder did and now, freakin' hell, Marco found himself doing the same thing.

"Captain D'Angelo?"

Marco's heart kicked against his ribs and his hand gripped the cane violently. A man had stepped out from between two parked cars in the parking lot. "Yes?"

"Your secretary said you'd be coming back soon, so I thought I'd wait."

Marco tried to center his weight. He was never sure if his damn leg was going to hold him and the last assault by Albie Brighton had sent him sprawling on his ass. This man wasn't overly large, five seven or so, 180lbs. He looked to be in his mid-forties with a bit of a paunch. "Who are you?"

The man took a hesitant step forward. "I'm Gavin's father. Ryan Morris."

Marco relaxed. "Why don't you come in, sir?"

"No." He glanced at the precinct, then back to Marco, his hands tightening into fists. "I saw the news article about my son, how the NRA's involved." His face contorted. "How they bought that murdering bastard Cook a lawyer."

"I can't talk about an on-going case, Mr. Morris, but know we are doing everything in our power to…"

"To what? I read that they want Cook released, that they're demanding it." He took a step toward Marco, jabbing his fist into the air. "They're saying it was self-defense. He shot my son in the back and it was self-defense!"

Marco glanced toward the precinct. He didn't want to draw his gun on a grieving father, but this man was clearly over-wrought. "Mr. Morris, let me assure you we are taking this case very seriously. I've spoken with the ADA twice about it. We don't believe it was self-defense."

"They're powerful. The NRA. If they drum up enough public opinion…"

"Mr. Morris…"

"You'll let them have what they want. I know how it works. My son is an acceptable death. He's collateral damage just so they can keep their guns. So they can have a false feeling of safety. My son is a sacrificial lamb!"

"No!" said Marco, holding up a hand. "That's not what I think at all, sir, but this isn't helping anything. You need to go home and let my people finish their case. I'm following it closely myself and I promise you we will do everything in our power to get your son justice."

"And what good will that do? What the hell good will that do me or his mother or the other parents who are going to be facing the same thing a week from now, a day, the next hour!"

The precinct door opened and Smith stepped out, followed by Bartlet. Marco held up a hand to stop them. They waited on the top of the stairs, their hands near their guns, but Morris didn't notice them.

"Answer me!"

Marco took a step closer to him. Morris' attention fixated on his leg. "You have to trust me, Mr. Morris. You have to believe me when I say that I intend to fight for your son. I can't promise we'll win, but I can promise you I will go down swinging."

Morris' gaze rose to Marco's face and the fire seemed to leach out of him. "He was my only son."

"I know that, sir."

"He was all I had."

"I know."

"They can't win this. They can't use him this way."

"They won't. I won't let them."

Morris nodded, his eyes dropping to Marco's leg again.

"Go home, Mr. Morris. Go home and let me work this case."

Morris nodded once more, half turning away. He still didn't notice Smith and Bartlet on the stairs. "He was my only son."

"I know, sir."

"He was all I had."

Marco waited until the man got in the car and started it, then he release his held breath.

*   *   *

Returning from the break-room, Marco saw a large man standing on the other side of the counter, ball cap on his head, glancing around nervously. Of course, Carly was nowhere to be found.

"Can I help you?" Marco settled his mug on the edge of Carly's desk.

"I'm Al Delacruz. An Inspector Simons asked me to come in today to answer some questions about my son." He took the ball cap off and passed it through his fingers. Marco noticed his hands were large and calloused. He had a deep scar right in the middle of his chin. It looked like someone had tried to cut the man's face in two. The scar was broad and pink and shiny.

"Inspector Simons was supposed to call you and cancel the appointment, Mr. Delacruz. He didn't call?"

Delacruz shrugged massive shoulders. "If he did, I didn't get it. I've lost my cell phone and I haven't been home to check the landline. I've been at work all day. Man, I wish I'd got that call. I'm backed up at work and I can't really afford the time."

Marco moved to the half-door and opened it. "Come in and let's talk for a moment." He motioned to the conference room. Delacruz forced his bulk past him. He didn't reach Marco's six four, but he was well over six and built like a truck.

He entered the conference room and sat down. Marco looked at his coffee on Carly's desk and decided to leave it there. His leg was hurting him too much to walk all the way back to the break-room for a second mug and Carly wasn't around.

Entering the conference room, he left the door open and took a seat across from the other man.

"What happened to your leg?"

Marco hooked the cane over the chair arm. "Gunshot."

Delacruz gave a nod. "In the line of duty?"

"Yep." He held out his hand. "I'm Captain Marco D'Angelo, Mr. Delacruz."

Delacruz accepted his hand in a crushing grip. "I don't want to bother the captain," he said. "I should probably go."

"It's fine. Since you're here, why don't we talk about your son?"

"Calvin?"

"Right. See, we're investigating the murder of Quentin Greer. He was the owner of the headshop where your son bought his medicine."

"Medicine?" snorted Delacruz, leaning back in the chair and folding his hands on his belly. "That medicine got him killed."

Marco marked the short burst of temper. "I'm sorry for your loss, Mr. Delacruz."

Delacruz rubbed a hand over his face. Marco noticed the dirt under his fingernails. "Don't listen to me, Captain D'Angelo. I'm just bitter. It's been hard."

"I can imagine."

"He was a good kid, my son. Smart, smarter than his old man. His mom died when he was five. I raised him and his sister by myself."

"That must have been difficult."

He shrugged. "Calvin was a good kid."

"What do you do for a living, Mr. Delacruz?"

"I repair heating and air conditioning." He gave a faint laugh. "Not much use for air conditioning here, but when I was in Sacramento, shit, I was always busy."

"I'll bet. Why'd you move here?"

"Calvin got sick. He needed help."

Marco nodded.

"I couldn't help him. He'd let his sister do things for him, but me...me he kept at arm's length."

"He wanted his independence?"

Delacruz's dark eyes fixed on Marco. "No. When my son told me he was gay, I threw him out of the house."

Marco leaned back in his chair.

"I will never live it down. I will carry that guilt with me forever. He left Sacramento and came here where he felt accepted."

Marco didn't know how to respond. What did you say to comfort someone who'd turned his back on his own blood?

"Then he got sick."

"He needed the medicine to help him with the treatment, didn't he?"

Delacruz shook his head. "Don't call it medicine. It's a drug and it killed my son."

"How do you figure?"

"He was getting better. The AIDs drugs were working, but he kept going and getting the pot. He wouldn't stop. He said it helped him eat, but when I went to see him, he'd just be stoned out of his head. You couldn't talk to him, you couldn't get him to do anything. He just wanted to sit in front of the television and...and do nothing."

"I see."

"My son was a brilliant piano teacher." He closed his eyes and leaned his head back, his grief palpable. "You should have heard him play, but when he started smoking, the piano went quiet. The music stopped." He opened his eyes and looked at Marco. "I'm starting to forget what it sounded like."

"Did you know Quentin Greer?"

Delacruz just stared at Marco as if he could hear music Marco couldn't. "No, I didn't know him. I'm sure he thought he was helping people. I'm sure he believed in what he was doing, but his *medicine* made the music go away and then it got Calvin killed."

"Calvin was robbed for his wallet."

"Sure, they took his credit cards, but they also took the dope. That's what they really wanted. That's what the other cops told me."

"Other cops?"

"Who first had the case. They found the gangbangers who killed Calvin and they still had the dope on them. They were buying stuff to have a party and smoke it."

"You must be angry about Calvin's death, Mr. Delacruz."

"I am angry."

"At a lot of people."

Delacruz's gaze lowered to the table and he wrung the hat in his hands. "No, Captain D'Angelo, I'm angry at me."

Marco waited.

"I threw my son out for being gay. Now all I can think of is I lost three years of his life. If I had known it'd be so short...if I'd had any idea, I would have spent every moment with him. I would have sat with him and just listened to him play. I would have done anything to keep him with me."

Marco gave a nod. "Again, I'm sorry for your loss, sir."

Delacruz just stared at things unseen. "Thank you, Captain."

"I won't detain you further. I know you have work to do." He rose to his feet.

Delacruz rose as well. "Sure." They shook hands. "Take care of that leg."

"Thank you, sir."

Walking into the precinct, Delacruz let himself beyond the half-door. Marco watched him as he wended his way into the parking lot, his head bowed, the ball cap back in place, hiding a devastating grief that would never go away.

"There you are. I've been looking all over for you," came Carly's voice. "I made chocolate chip cookies. Do you want me to get you some?"

Marco glanced over at her. Was she freakin' serious? Chocolate chip cookies? She beamed happiness at him. He turned away and went to his office, shutting the door behind him. God, he needed a drink.

*   *   *

Abe opened the door to his condo as Marco placed his plate on the dining room table. Abe's face lit into a smile. "You made me dinner, Angel?"

"Nope. Mama D'Angelo did. She sent me a care package when I left last night."

Abe slung his leather bag onto the couch and moved toward the table. He wore a violet silk shirt with pinstripes running through it and pale lavender pants. Matching violet wingtip shoes covered his feet. Marco hid a wry smile as Abe sank into the chair across from him.

"This looks amazing."

"Yep. Tastes even better."

"What is it?"

"Polenta pasticciata."

"Vegetarian?"

"Yep."

Abe lifted his fork and cut into the dish, carrying a bite to his mouth. Closing his eyes as he chewed, he made a moaning sound. "This would be so good with a glass of pinot noir."

Marco hesitated with the fork almost to his mouth.

Abe's eyes popped open. "Sorry, Angel."

Marco waved him off. "No worries."

"How's the leg today?"

"Can we talk about something else?"

Abe gave him a searching look. Marco dished up another bite. Finally Abe relented, "Okey dokey. Let's talk dead bodies then."

Marco swallowed and reached for his water glass. "So much better. Did you look at Quentin Greer again?"

"I did. Ran a new set of x-rays and tomorrow, I'm gonna take that sucker apart ligament by ligament."

"Awesome." Marco set down his fork. He was so often grateful that he was a vegetarian now.

"I found a hole in the xiphoid process."

"Xiphoid process?"

"Lower part of the sternum." He leaned back and pressed his finger to the spot. It was very near where Quentin Greer had placed his own hands when he died. "The body was so desiccated from the fire when I did the last autopsy, but still I shouldn't have missed it. I've been pissed at myself all day over it."

"You've been a little distracted."

"That's no excuse. I'm always distracted. Brilliant people are. It's a curse of having too much of the mind at work all the time."

"Right. What do you think caused it?"

"Something was shoved in there with a lot of force. I won't know completely until I take him apart, but on x-ray it looks round."

"So not a knife?"

"No." He began eating again. "I hope that whatever the weapon is left something behind in the wound."

"Call with the results as soon as you get them."

"What are you thinking, Angel D'?"

"I think Quentin Greer was stabbed, then torched. Otherwise, I can't see how he would let anyone douse him in gas and set him on fire."

"Maybe it was a lover."

"A lover? Why would he let a lover do that?"

"I'm just trying to be helpful. That's a pretty passionate crime, don't you think? I mean think about it, Angel. A jilted lover comes into the headshop, confronts Greer about his indiscretions, then in a fit of passion, pours a gallon of gasoline over his head. Greer, realizing what he's lost, holds out his arms and accepts his own demise because he realizes he can't live without him."

"Him?"

"Of course."

"Why him?"

"In case you've forgotten, Angel, I'm gay."

"I haven't forgotten."

"Besides, violent passion like that could only come from a man."

"I don't think you're right."

"I think I am. I've been in some passionate relationships in my time, Angel."

"I'm sure you have, but you don't need to relive them right now."

Abe pealed off into laughter. "You're such a prude."

"Sure."

"If you knew about some of my affairs…"

"Abe."

"Well, it just seems like everyone in our little group thinks I'm this asexual being and that I haven't had my share of romance."

"No one thinks that."

"Thinks what?"

"Either thing."

"I'm not following you, Angel."

Marco exhaled in frustration. This is why it was dangerous to get into a discussion with Abe. "No one thinks you're asexual or haven't had...um, romances."

"You should have heard Maria the other night."

"She said you were asexual?"

"She said I didn't know how to cut a pepper."

Marco leaned back in the chair. He wasn't sure he wanted to continue this talk, but he was so damn curious about what happened that night. "Is that a euphemism?"

"A what?"

"Cut a pepper."

"A euphemism for what?"

Marco shook his head vehemently.

"Oh," said Abe, placing a hand against his chest. Then he collapsed in another fit of laughter. "I like it. I'm going to use that from now on."

"Great."

"Serge and Misha will love it."

"Glad to help. What were you saying about Maria?"

"She can be a bitch, you know?"

"Right. Abe?"

"They were having a pepper eating contest and Jake was out first. He couldn't get past the guajillo."

"Not surprising."

"Then Cho dropped out, so it left Tag and Maria. Maria produced a red savina."

Marco gave an understanding exhalation. That's what Jake was talking about.

"And then, she proceeded…" Abe looked away, waving his hand. "It's hard for me to say it. It was so insulting."

Marco waited.

"She called me a wuss."

Marco caught a burst of laughter, clamping his mouth shut.

"It wasn't funny, Angel."

"Of course not." He picked up his fork and started eating again. "How was Peyton?" He tried to sound casual, but it was impossible where she was concerned.

Abe sighed. "The two of you make me so sad."

Marco looked up at him. "Why?"

"Look, straight romance doesn't really do it for me, but you two, you had something. There was real passion there and that doesn't come around very often. So much of the time we just settle."

"I destroyed her trust, Abe."

"So build it back."

"How?" He took a sip of his water and held it up. "I've been clean since last Thursday. Not a drop to drink, but every minute of that time, I've wanted to. I've thought of it obsessively."

"Because you're in constant pain. You need to see Grey, Angel."

"So he can tell me this is all the better it gets."

"What if he doesn't? What if there's something he can do?"

"Can you promise me that, Abe? Can you promise?"

"No, I can't."

"Right." He set the glass down hard. "So right now, I have hope it'll get better. I can trick myself into believing that someday there won't be this pain. If I go to him and he says this is it…I think that will destroy me."

Abe sighed.

Marco stared at him a moment more, then went back to eating.

"She's not sleeping."

Marco paused, but he didn't look up.

"The nightmares are back. She said you were the only one who could keep them away."

"What do you want me to do with that?"

"Think about it. Realize that if this is all the better it's gonna get, is it really better without her?"

"It's better for her. I don't know how much longer I can keep this up, how much longer I can stay away from the booze, so yeah, it's better."

Abe didn't answer for a moment, then he leaned forward on the table. "Here's what I don't get, Angel. You're holding out hope that some miracle's going to happen, that someday you're going to wake up and your leg will magically be better."

Marco met his gaze.

"But you won't go to church, where you might get some real comfort."

"I don't believe in miracles anymore, Abe. Church won't help."

"And you won't go to group where you can share your loss with others."

"To wallow in it? To moan and complain about my sorry life?"

Abe leaned forward. "Then wouldn't it be better to go see Grey and know there's nothing more that can be done, instead of sit around hoping for something to fall on you. You're a man of action, Angel, a man unafraid to face the darkest heart of mankind, but right now, right here, in this, you're being a wuss. Man up, D'Angelo, and face what you fear most."

CHAPTER 16

Monday

The library in Santa Cruz was housed in a two story building that stretched for nearly a block. As Peyton and her team entered, she felt the hush of the place descend on her.

Not that she'd been in a talkative mood on the way down here. Dinner at her mother's had been filled with questions and snide comments from Cliff about her ability to hold a man. He remarked on more than one occasion that she might rethink her sexuality. Peyton had resisted the impulse to tell him he might rethink his face, but she knew it would only hurt her mother. She'd left early and returned home to Pickles and an empty house. She hated the empty house and if Pickles hadn't been there, needing her, she wasn't sure what she would have done.

"Get your head in the game, Sparky."

She glanced over at Radar, pulling herself out of her distraction. He removed his sunglasses and glared at her, then lifted his eyes to Tank. "You stay with us, but Bambi, you go see what you can find out about Horizon. Ask around. See if anyone knows anything."

"Can Peyton come with me?" she asked, rubbing a hand along Peyton's arm. Peyton actually would have preferred that. She was tired of Radar's disapproval.

"Nope, Sparky's with me. She's gotta charm this Elder broad."

Peyton gave him an arch look. "Someone has to since that's clearly not in your skill set."

"You wanna dance, little girl, I'll dance."

She held up her hands in a motion of surrender, but she never released his gaze. "I'm just stating the obvious."

Tank and Bambi exchanged anxious looks. Radar marked it and pulled in a deep breath, holding it. Gradually he exhaled, then forced a tight smile. "Let's just get what we came to get, okay?"

Peyton gave him a nod.

Bambi squeezed her arm, then wandered off, looking back at Peyton. Peyton turned and surveyed the room. Directly before them was a long, curving counter, circa 1970, dotted in regular intervals with a computer. One woman manned the counter, her long brown hair falling to her shoulders in a blanket of loose curls. She appeared to be about 30 or so with a pretty face and stylish clothes. Definitely not what Peyton thought of as a librarian.

Striding up to the desk, she plastered a bright smile on her lips. "Good morning."

"Good morning," the woman said, eyeing the two men behind Peyton. "How can I help you?"

Peyton reached for her badge and laid it on the counter. She didn't have the patience this morning to do small talk. "I'm Special Agent Peyton Brooks with the FBI."

"And you're investigating the mermaid."

Wow! Everyone in this town kept themselves well informed. Except to be fair, the media had been hounding this case nearly 24 hours a day.

"Right. We're looking for Mrs. Elder."

The woman nodded and went to a phone, picking up the receiver. She pressed a few buttons and listened. "Lois? The FBI would like to talk to you." She listened some more, then she nodded. "Okay, bye."

Replacing the phone on the cradle, she motioned to a set of stairs tucked away behind her, leading to the second floor. "Go up the stairs, turn left and walk through the Young Reader's lounge area. Lois Elders is in her office next to the bathrooms."

"Thank you. And you are?"

"Cheryl Watts."

Peyton passed her a card. "Cheryl, if you have any information on the case we're working, I'd appreciate a call."

She picked up the card. "Special Agent Brooks, I spend most of my time here, or with my kids. I have four of them. Between soccer and ballet, I don't really have time to watch TV or keep up with the local news."

"But you work in a library. People must talk to you."

"Only to find something they want. It's a library. Silence is sort of the norm."

Peyton sighed. This case didn't have to be this slippery. If only Radar would follow her instincts and get a warrant for the Horizon farm. "Thank you, anyway."

They walked to the stairs. Tank's longer stride took him to the top quicker than she and Radar, but Peyton suspected Radar hung back just so he could hiss instructions at her. "Keep focused on why we're here. We're investigating a mermaid disposal, nothing else. We aren't here about a cult or trying to get involved where we don't belong."

"I've got it, Radar," she said through clenched teeth. "But you do understand that investigating the mermaid disposal might at some point take us to Horizon."

"I don't understand that and neither do you. You have no proof the two are connected. Leave it at that. Work with what's in front of you. You've got to stop making speculations and inferences. Use only what evidence you have and don't go searching for unrelated links."

Peyton rolled her eyes as they topped the stairs. The Young Reader's Lounge was a set of brightly colored mats with the letters of the alphabet on them, hooked together like puzzle pieces. Scattered over the mats were overstuffed pillows and beanbag chairs. Children lounged around the room, reading silently or whispering to their parents. Peyton smiled at a dark haired boy who glanced up at her. He returned the smile, then went back to his book.

Tank waited on the other side of the room with a small woman whose grey hair and cat-eye spectacles screamed librarian. She wore a cardigan sweater, a long plaid skirt, and sensible shoes. She exuded a grandmotherly aura that Peyton found immediately disarming.

She held out her hand when they stopped before her. "Special Agent Brooks, ma'am, and you must be Mrs. Elder."

"I am. Thomas has been filling me in on your case." She motioned behind her to her office. "Won't you come in?"

The office was pleasant – the walls pine paneling, the floor carpeted in quiet-enhancing brown Berber. She had a small wooden desk, but a circle of armchairs took up most of the space. The desk and the chairs overlooked the wall of windows that allowed Mrs. Elder to survey her charges in the Young Readers' lounge.

"Please have a seat."

Peyton and Tank sat down in the nearest chair, but Radar stood, waiting for Mrs. Elder to work her way into the circle. Then he produced his badge and offered it to her. "I'm Carlos Moreno, ma'am. I run point on this team."

Her eyes shifted from the badge to his face and back again, then she took her seat. "I'm aware of that, Agent Moreno. Thomas filled me in on all of your names while we waited for you."

Radar shot a look at Peyton and Tank, then sank into the chair, leaving a gap between him and everyone else. Peyton frowned at him. What the hell was up his ass today?

"Mrs. Elder, thank you for seeing us."

"It's my pleasure. The media have been here, searching through our archives, asking my staff ridiculous questions. I know you're doing everything you can, but the faster you get this case solved, the quicker our lives return to normal."

Peyton nodded. "Understood. I'm sure the media have asked you this, but do you have any idea who might have given birth to the baby we found?"

"I'm afraid not. It's a big city and there are a lot of tourists who come through."

"Right." Peyton glanced at Radar, but he was watching out the windows at the kids. "Mrs. Elder, a few days ago a man came to see me. His name was Jeff King. He had some letters that were written to his mother by a young man named Finn Getter."

Recognition lit in Mrs. Elder's eyes. Radar shifted around and studied her.

"In the letters, Finn mentioned you. He said you helped him use the computers, look things up, gave him advice."

"Yes, I did." She clasped her hands in her lap. "I knew Finn very well."

"I need to find Finn, Mrs. Elder."

"That's going to be hard, Agent Brooks. Finn lived on a very secluded farm."

"Horizon?"

"Yes."

"When you say farm, do you mean commune?"

"I do." She glanced at the two men, then shifted weight. "I know how that sounds to law enforcement, but there are a number of communes in the Santa Cruz mountains. Mostly they're people who for various reasons want to live off the grid. I can understand that desire when I see my city overrun with news crews, let me tell you."

Peyton gave her an understanding smile. "Are you familiar with Horizon?"

"Only from what Finn told me. He struggled a bit with the rules there, but for the most part, he felt it was a very positive way to live."

"You said it would be hard to find Finn now. What did you mean?"

"Finn turned twenty-one. In his *family*, for want of a better word, young men are encouraged to leave at twenty-one to make their own lives."

"And where did Finn leave to?"

"San Francisco."

"He told you this?"

"He came to see me the day before his birthday. He told me that was his plan. I asked him to write, but well...you know how it is with young people. They get so involved in their lives they forget."

Peyton looked at her own clasped hands. "I read all of the letters Finn wrote to Aster King, Jeff's mother. In the last letter, he was pretty bitter. Did he mention that to you?"

Mrs. Elder sighed. "Yes. He thought he'd fallen in love with a young lady, Molly as I remember it. He asked her to leave with him and at the time, she agreed, but she changed her mind. Finn was devastated, especially since his own sister, Janice changed her mind too. He'd planned to take Janice, Janice's daughter, and Molly with him. When the women backed out, he felt lost and alone."

"He blamed a man named Thatcher."

"Yes, well, we all blame our father figures, don't we? I'm not saying Thatcher doesn't run a tight ship, but for everything I've heard of him, he's fair and accepting of his people's decisions. If the girls had decided to leave, Thatcher wouldn't have prevented it."

"He denied Finn's mother medical attention."

Mrs. Elder held out her hands. "You have to look at it from their perspective, Agent Brooks. Those people chose to live off the grid, they chose to give up the trapping of modern society for ill or good. Who am I to judge their choices? Who are you?"

Peyton sat back in her chair. "If young women are being held against their will, if they're being forced into inbreeding..."

"Who said anything about inbreeding, Agent Brooks?"

"A mermaid was found floating at Natural Bridges."

"But you have no proof it came from Horizon, now, do you?"

Peyton glanced over at Tank. He shrugged.

"I was raised as a Jehovah Witness, Agent Brooks. Are you familiar with that religion?"

"I am."

"It wasn't so long ago that we had to contend with people calling us a cult because of our belief system. I think it's a dangerous practice when outsiders choose to label others based on their mores, don't you, Agent Moreno?"

Radar sat up straight. "Yes, ma'am," he said.

Peyton ground her teeth, slowly rising to her feet. "And I think it's dangerous when people turn a blind eye to abuses just because someone slips the mantle of religion around himself. I guess we'll just have to disagree on this point, Mrs. Elder. So, San Francisco, huh?"

"What, Agent Brooks?"

"Finn Getter went to San Francisco?"

"That's right."

"Excellent. Then I'll just track him down and see how he feels about Thatcher and Horizon. It'll be better to get it from the horse's mouth anyway."

With that she turned and walked to the door, yanking it open. Without looking back, she headed for the stairs, and a moment later, Tank caught up with her. They met Bambi at the bottom.

"Anything?" Bambi asked.

"Finn Getter went to the City. We need to locate him. Did you get anything?"

"I talked with some teenagers who knew of Horizon. Some of the Horizon people came to their school, distributing fliers and asking them if they were tired of being infected by modern society."

"What does that mean? What were they trying to do?"

"The fliers apparently invited them to a prayer meeting in a field near the Horizon farm. None of them went to it. Their parents forbade them."

"Huh?" said Tank, glancing back as Radar came down the stairs.

"Well, that's the very image we want to project, Sparky. Rudeness and intolerance."

"Are you serious? Did you hear her defend a cult?"

"I heard her give a very reasoned response to your concerns."

Peyton gaped at him.

"Radar, something's not right with this Horizon place," said Tank.

Radar's eyes whipped to his face. "You too? You heard her say those women chose to stay. Why would they do that if they were being abused?"

"Stockholm syndrome?" said Tank.

Peyton held up a hand.

"Bull shit. Show me the proof."

"I don't have proof, Radar. I just have a bad feeling about this."

"A feeling? You have a feeling? Since when do *you* have feelings, Tank?"

"Hold on a minute," said Peyton, stepping between the two of them.

Bambi moved to her side. "That was uncalled for, Radar. Besides, they're right. This just isn't adding up."

Radar's angry gaze passed over the three of them, then he threw up his hands. "I don't need this shit right now, Goddamn it!" And he turned, storming across the library.

Tank started after him, but Peyton pressed a hand to his chest, stopping him. "Let me. I think this is about me anyway. We'll meet you at the Suburban."

Tank and Bambi started to protest, but Peyton walked away from them, hurrying after Radar. She found him on the street, pacing up and down. He had his sunglasses on and his hands shoved into the pockets on his trousers.

"What's going on, Radar?" she said.

"What's going on?" He stopped in front of her and she could see the vein bulging in his forehead. "What's going on? You're turning my people against me. You're trying to take over."

She took a step back, shocked. "I am not."

"Aren't you? You come in here all charming and sweet. Bambi falls all over herself for any crumb you toss her

way and now Tank. You've got Tank ignoring my orders to
follow you on a wild goose chase." He pointed at the library.
"In all the years we've worked together, Tank has never once
contradicted me. Not once."

"Radar, I'm not trying to take over. I don't even
know what the hell I'm doing half the time. You're our leader
and I'm happy for you to take that role. If I've overstepped
my boundaries, I'm sorry. It was an innocent mistake on my
part. I'm used to working with a partner, not a team. With my
partner, it got so we could read each other's thoughts.
This...this is hard for me."

His look softened. "There will come a time for you to
lead, Sparky."

"I don't want that. I just want to solve this case. And
to be honest with you, I only think this is marginally about
me pushing my limits. I think this is about you. You're scared
of getting in the middle of this cult thing."

He looked away.

"Am I right?"

"You're not wrong."

"What's freaking you out, Radar? Tell me."

"These things always go bad, Sparky. I've seen it a
hundred times. Waco, Ruby Ridge, Jonestown. They go
horribly wrong and a lot of innocent people die." He paced
away and came back, removing his sunglasses. "The case
when Arthur died?"

"Yeah."

"We were breaking up a dog fighting ring in
Petaluma, but actually the participants we were after lived in a
mobile home park in Guerneville. They were all supporting
each other, buying groceries together, paying the rent with
proceeds from the dog fighting."

"They were like a commune."

"Yeah." He looked away, shaking his head. "We
didn't know what the hell we were walking into. They were
armed to the teeth and high. Arthur, as always, was first one
in. They opened fire. They riddled him with bullets." His

voice trailed off and he swiped a hand across his nose. "He never knew what hit him."

"How many people died?"

Radar blinked and glanced up at her. "Seven perps and three of our guys. One took a bullet in the spine. Been in a wheelchair ever since. We had to shoot fifteen dogs that day. *Fifteen.* They just came at us, crazy from abuse and neglect. I can still hear them crying."

Peyton blinked back tears. "I'm so sorry, Radar."

He gave a laugh and swiped at his nose again. "So when you say we've got to go on that farm, my guts twist inside and I think I'm gonna vomit. It always goes bad, Sparky. It always goes wrong on these things."

"Okay." She ran a hand down his arm. "Okay, Radar. So what do you want us to do? What's our next move?"

He stared at her hand a moment, then he blinked hard a few times. "We need to find Finn Getter. Let's find that kid and ask him what the hell we face if we go in there. If we're gonna do it, let's at least go in there knowing exactly what we're doing."

* * *

Radar's words haunted Peyton as she drove to the grocery store on her way home. *It always goes wrong on these things.* He wanted them to find Finn Getter. Even with the prodigious resources of the FBI at her fingertips, that was a tall order. How many people came to San Francisco every single day and disappeared on her streets?

God, she wanted to call Marco and ask his advice. He'd have some idea how to begin the search, but she couldn't do that. Marco would so not welcome a call about work from her. So what would he suggest? He'd tell her to check shelters, employment offices, churches. That was a start.

She parked the Prius and got out, walking toward the grocery store. She hadn't bothered to remove her gun, but it was hidden under her suit jacket and her badge hung from her belt. She could show that in an instant if anyone questioned her. She just needed a few things, then she was going home to soak in the bathtub in lilac scented oil. Maybe it would relax her enough where she could sleep.

Snagging a grocery cart, she wandered down the aisles, grabbing what she needed. The cabinets were getting bare and Pickles was starting to feel neglected without his regular doggy biscuits. Scraps from her plate were fine for a few days, but Pickles was a dog who liked his cookies. Marco had gotten him hooked on this particular brand and as long as Marco had been at the house, Pickles had never done without. Since he'd left, Peyton hadn't been much in the mood to get food. She knew that was wrong. The one constant in her life, the one person who never left her, was Pickles and here she was letting him down.

She grabbed the box and threw it in the grocery cart. Shit. She was feeling maudlin tonight, missing Marco more than she wanted to admit, but she hated herself when she was maudlin. Straightening from her slump over the cart, she picked up the pace.

Pretend you're up and full of fire and maybe you'd trick yourself into believing it.

Turning the corner, she nearly ran her cart into another shopper. He pulled up at the last minute just before impact.

"Whoa!"

Peyton blinked at him in surprise. She recognized the weathered face and blond hair, the piercing green eyes.

"Mike?"

"Peyton?" He gave a delighted laugh. "Wow!"

"What are you doing here?"

He looked at his shopping cart. "Oh, shit. I'm doing it again. Sleep shopping."

She laughed. "I'm sorry. Stupid question."

"Not at all. So, what's a classy lady like you doing in a place like this?"

She lifted the doggy biscuits. "Trying to keep the longest relationship I've ever had."

"Ah, I see." He smiled, lighting up his eyes, then he looked her over. "Hm. Does the generic black suit give me a clue as to your employment?"

Peyton fingered her badge. "FBI."

He reared back. "No shit." Leaning closer, he dropped his voice. "Do you have a gun?"

She opened her suit jacket and showed the butt of her gun.

He gave her a sultry look. "Now that's hot, lady."

She laughed. "Great. Look, why are you shopping here? I thought you lived in South City."

"That's my mom's place. I finally got a flat in the Avenues. Moved in yesterday." He glanced down and fingered the corner on one of his boxes. "Look, Peyton, I really had a nice time with you the other night."

She nodded.

"I wasn't lying. I felt a connection."

"Mike."

"No, let me finish, please. I get that you're just leaving a relationship, but I thought maybe we could spend some time together. No pressure. No expectations. What do you say?"

Peyton crossed her arms on the handle of the grocery cart, leaning on it. God, she was tired. "I say no. It wouldn't be fair to you. I'm not over my fiancé and I'm not sure I'll ever be. That was sort of the problem before we got together, and I don't think it's ended."

"What do you mean?"

"I mean I measured every man by him and they always came up wanting in my eyes. You deserve better than that."

He gave a wry nod. "I see."

"I'm sorry, Mike."

"No, I get it. He must be something, huh?"

She shrugged.

"But we can be friends, right? You can never have too many friends."

Peyton offered him a gentle smile. "I don't think that would work either. I'm sorry."

He held up a hand. "No problem. Well, it was worth a try. I mean, come on, girl. You're the total package. Smart, funny, sexy and…you carry a gun."

A laugh slipped out of Peyton. "You're not making this easy, Barnabas."

He chuckled at her use of his middle name and moved his cart close to hers. Leaning toward her, he winked. "That's the point, baby. See you around."

She gave him a nod and he pushed his cart down the aisle she'd just left. Peyton quickly finished up the rest of her shopping and moved to the check-out. He waved to her from a checker a few rows down. She held up a hand.

Shit. Would she ever feel like dating again? Did she even want to try? Every single time, it ended and it ended badly. She didn't seem able to hold a man's interest for more than a few months. Marco had been her longest relationship.

She watched the checker pass the groceries over the scanner, thinking of Marco. Marco hadn't been like any of the others. She'd seen a future with him, she'd seen them growing old together. How did she just give up on that? How did she move on from the one man she'd loved more than anyone else?

She wasn't aware of Mike leaving the store, but as she paid for her purchases, a commotion outside the store drew her out of her thoughts. A few workers ran to the entrance and out the automatic doors. Some customers walked to the windows, looking out, trying to see past bags of charcoal and barbecue paraphernalia.

Peyton thanked the checker, then grabbed her cart, wheeling it for the exit. Moving past the automatic doors, she came to a halt. A bicycle lay on its side in front of a blue pickup truck, groceries strewn in the parking lot. The driver's door on the pickup was open and a crowd had formed to the left of the truck, just before its bumper. Peyton could see a man's body between the legs of the crowd.

She grabbed her badge and pushed into the circle. "FBI," she said, then came to a halt.

Mike sat on the ground, his head braced in his hands, a little blood trickling from a wound in his scalp. His shirt was torn and he had a few abrasions on his upper arms and shoulders. Peyton knelt beside him.

"Mike, what the hell happened?"

He glanced over at her with squinted eyes. "I wasn't paying attention and I rode my bike into the pickup."

"I didn't even see him!" said a middle aged man. "Suddenly he was there."

"Did you hit your head?" she asked.

"I'm not sure."

"Did anyone call an ambulance?" she said, looking at the crowd. They refused to meet her gaze. "Did anyone—?"

"I told them not to."

"What? You could have internal injuries, a concussion."

He reached for her arm and gripped it. "I don't have insurance yet, Peyton."

"What about the VA? You were a soldier."

He gave her an arch look.

"You've got to be seen by a doctor."

"No, I'm okay. Nothing's broken. Help me get to my feet."

"I don't think that's a good idea, Mike."

"No, really, I'm okay. It just rung my bell, but I'm feeling better. Help me get up, please."

She braced him as he pushed himself to his feet. Doubling over, he rubbed at his scrapes. "See, just a little banged up."

Peyton shook her head. "I still think we need to go to the hospital."

"Naw. I've been through worse. This is nothing compared to an IED going off beneath your tank." He stretched his back, then his attention focused on his bike. The front tire was bent. "Oh shit."

"I didn't see him," said the man in the pick-up.

Peyton pushed him back as Mike stumbled over to the bike. "Oh shit," he repeated, grasping his head.

"Mike, we need to have you checked by a doctor."

He leaned on the pickup. "I can't go to the emergency room. I'll wait all night and I can't afford it. If I go to the VA, well, either I'll be better or dead before I get to see a doctor." He pressed his hands against his head. "How the hell will I get home?"

Peyton didn't know what to do. She was sure he needed a doctor, but he was refusing to go to the hospital. She could order the pickup guy to take him home, but that seemed like the coward's way out of this mess. With a sigh, she knew she had no other choice.

"I'll take you, but I don't have room for the bike." She turned to the pickup driver. "Can you take it?"

"I didn't see him. He just came out of nowhere."

"You said that. Can you drive his bike to his house? Can you follow me?"

"Yeah." He paced away and came back again.

Peyton pulled a card out of her pocket and handed it to him. "Write your information on the back of this." She passed him a pen.

He went to the pickup and began writing. Peyton retrieved her cart and started picking up Mike's fallen groceries. A number of people helped her. The pickup driver returned with her card and hoisted the bike to his shoulder, carrying it to the bed. Peyton pointed at the Prius.

"That's my car. Just follow me."

Pickup guy nodded and climbed into his truck.

Peyton grabbed Mike's arm. "Come on. Hold onto the cart."

He grimaced as he straightened, but they made it to the car. Peyton opened the passenger side and helped him sit down, then she went to the back and popped the trunk, shoving all of the groceries inside. As she did so, she reached for her phone and called Abe.

He picked up on the second ring. "Hey, little soul sista, how are you?"

"Fine. Look, Abe, are you busy?"

"Busy having a fine dining experience with an angel."

Peyton fought the wash of regret that swamped her, slamming the trunk shut. "Look, if you've got a few minutes, I need your help."

"Is something wrong, sweets?"

"No, just a friend of mine took a tumble and I want you to look at him."

"Him?"

Peyton pulled open the driver's door and sank into the seat. "Yeah, I'll explain later. Look, meet me at this address." She nudged Mike and he rattled off the address, his arm braced on the window, his head resting against his hand. Peyton gave Abe the address, then started the Prius.

"What's going on, Peyton?"

"Just come to that address, okay, Abe? Please, for me."

"I'm on my way. Do I need backup?"

"God no!" she said breathlessly. "Whatever you do, don't do that. Just you. Alone."

Abe didn't respond for a moment and she used the silence to back the Prius out of the parking space. Glancing in the rearview mirror, she marked that the pickup had pulled up behind her.

"I'll be there in two shakes," said Abe and disconnected.

Peyton glanced over at Mike. He had his eyes closed, his fingers splayed across his forehead. "How you holding up?"

"Jim Dandy. So who's Abe?"

"My best friend. He's a coroner for the City."

"I'm not dead yet, Peyton."

She laughed. "He's a doctor, he's free, and he's what you get unless you'll let me take you to the hospital."

"I'll take it. Especially if you play nurse."

Peyton rolled her eyes and pulled into traffic.

Mike's flat wasn't far from her house on 19th. She pulled into the driveway and glanced in the rearview mirror as the pickup eased up to the curb. Climbing out, she hurried around and helped Mike out of the passenger side. He handed her his keys.

"First door at the bottom of the stairs," he said.

She unlocked the outer gate and helped him to the door, sliding the key into the lock. Pickup guy followed her, carrying the bike. "Just set it down anywhere," she said, motioning to a spot beneath the stairs. He set the bike down and waited, while she unlocked the door.

"Can you get the loose groceries out of my trunk?" she ordered, pushing the button to release the trunk.

He gave a grunt, but moved to do what she asked.

Peyton helped Mike into the flat. They had to sidestep a number of boxes stacked along the walls. She found a light switch by the door and flipped it on as Mike moved to the couch and gingerly took a seat.

Peyton wasn't sure what to do now, so she turned left and found a small kitchen with a door that led to a bathroom. Entering the bathroom, she searched through a couple of boxes on the floor until she found towels and washcloths. Rinsing one in cold water, she carried it into the other room and handed it to Mike.

He was stretched out on the brown sofa, his feet on one arm, his head on another. He took the cloth and pressed it to the wound in his scalp. "Thanks. Any aspirin?"

"Let's wait until my friend gets here."

Pickup guy entered, carrying the groceries. "Where you want these?"

"Kitchen," said Peyton, pointing over her shoulder. She shoved a box aside and took a seat on the coffee table next to Mike. "Are you sure we shouldn't go to the hospital?"

"I'm fine, Peyton. Just a little bump." He patted the space next to him. "I'd be better if you'd sit next to me."

"I'm good."

Pickup guy came out of the kitchen. "Anything else?"

"No," said Peyton. "I've got your information if I need to get ahold of you."

He gave Mike a worried look, then went to the door, but came to an abrupt halt when Abe suddenly loomed in the entrance. He looked like a giant eggplant in his lavender get-up and wild dreadlocks.

Pickup guy sidestepped him, giving him a bewildered once over, but Abe didn't notice, coming into the flat with his medical bag in hand. He came around the couch and stared down at Mike with a critical look on his face.

"Mike, this is Abe," she said.

"Hey," answered Abe.

"Hey," said Mike. "I think I'm hallucinating."

Peyton laughed and rose to her feet, hugging Abe, then she relinquished her spot and let Abe get to work. While Abe examined his patient, she wandered around the flat. A picture of Mike in an army ranger's uniform with his fellow servicemen had been propped on a built-in bookcase. Next to it was a wooden box, open, showing a purple heart. Peyton touched the velvet lining the box and moved over to a picture of an older woman and Mike at a picnic. It must be his mother.

There were few other personal effects. She figured they must be in boxes still. Turning, she watched as Abe examined Mike's pupils and checked his reflexes. "Looks like just bumps and bruises," he said, returning his stethoscope to his bag. "No sign of concussion."

"Thanks, Doc," said Mike, offering Abe his winning smile. "See, I told you I was fine."

Peyton gave a grateful nod. "I'm glad." She motioned to the door. "We should go and let you rest."

Abe snapped the bag closed and rose to his feet, moving toward the door. "Nice to meet you."

"Same here." Mike sat up, groaning as he did so. "Peyton?"

Peyton turned and looked back at him. He waved her over. Reluctantly she eased past Abe and went to his side.

"You don't have to leave."

"I do. I have a dog to get home to and you need your rest."

He caught her hand. "Can I have your card?"

"Mike."

"Please?" He gave her such a pleading look with the dried blood along his scalp and his scrapes and bruises. "I promise I won't abuse the privilege. I'll just call to let you know how I am."

Peyton glanced over at Abe, who was frowning at her, but she reached into her pocket and pulled out her card, passing it to him. "Only to tell me how you are."

"Right." He smiled at her, then he lifted her hand and kissed the back of it. "Thank you for rescuing me tonight."

She disengaged gently and walked back to the door. "Get some rest, Mike," she said, then motioned Abe through in front of her and closed the door at her back. Abe didn't say anything until they were out in front of the flat, standing by her Prius.

"Who the hell is he?"

"A guy that got hit in front of the grocery store."

"Seemed like he knew you from more than that."

"I met him the other night."

"Where?"

"What are you, my father?"

"No, I'm your best friend and I came all the way over here tonight to examine a strange man that you *rescued*."

"Don't say it like that."

"Like what?"

"All judgy."

Abe placed a hand on his hip. "Look here, little sister, it's my job to judge. Where did you meet this guy?"

"A nightclub."

"A nightclub?"

"Abe."

"Why were you in a nightclub? Especially without me."

"I went there with Bambi."

"To do what?"

"To do what?"

"Stop answering me with my own questions. Why were you in a nightclub?"

"To have fun."

"You're engaged."

Peyton gave a violent shake of her head. "No, I'm not. Not anymore."

"Peyton."

"No, Abe. He broke it off. He left me."

"He's struggling with some life altering changes, sweets. You gotta give him time, not pick up the very next stray to cross your path."

"I didn't pick him up."

"Excuse me." Abe took a step away from her. "I came over here to give some stranger a physical based on your telephone call."

"I ran into him at the grocery store. He wanted my number, but I told him I wasn't over Marco yet. That's all."

"Then how did you wind up taking him home?"

"He got hit by a pickup in the parking lot."

Abe gave her a skeptical look.

"On his bike."

His frown deepened.

"Look, nothing happened. Nothing's going to happen. I just…"

"You just?"

"I hate being alone."

Abe cupped her chin and lifted her face, so she had to meet his gaze. "I know that, sweets, but this guy isn't right for you. You've got a guy who loves you."

Tears filled Peyton's eyes. "Does he, Abe? Does he really? If he does, how can he do this to me?" She pressed her fist between her breasts. "How can he hurt me like this?"

"He's doing it because he loves you. He's trying to protect you from himself."

Peyton tore her face out of his hold.

Abe tugged her into his arms, resting his chin on the top of her head. "I'm working on him, sweets. I'm working on him. Just give me a little time, okay? Just give me time."

Peyton clung to Abe and nodded, but inside it felt like she was suffocating.

CHAPTER 17

Tuesday

Marco pressed the button on the automatic doors and stepped into Abe's laboratory. Abe was bent over the burnt corpse of Quentin Greer, but he glanced up and flashed a toothy smile for Marco, returning immediately to his work.

"Hey, there, Angel."

"Hey. You left early this morning."

"The hunky captain of the precinct I work for demanded a second autopsy. Clever fellow found something I missed." He gave Marco a wink. "Let me tell you, if he wasn't so gorgeous, I just might be offended that he doubted me."

"What do you have?"

"There appears to be particles in the wound. I'm trying to get a sample and see what the weapon was."

"Is that what killed him?"

"The fire didn't help."

Marco looked down at the charcoal face of the victim, the white of his teeth showing stark through the gaping hole that remained of his lips. "Jesus."

"Yep. Pretty horrifying."

"Did he die from the stab wound, Abe?"

Abe gave him a grim look. "I can't be sure. It certainly immobilized him and he would have bled out, but whether he was dead before he was torched is hard to prove. The contractions of the hands, the grimace all lead me to believe he was partially aware when he was set on fire."

"So, someone stabbed him, then figured that wasn't enough. They burnt him alive for good measure."

"Actually, they were probably trying to get rid of the evidence with the fire, but didn't realize it can take awhile to bleed out."

Marco shook his head, looking away. Sometimes he thought he just couldn't face one more dead body, smell anymore rotting flesh, agonize over one more victim. What the hell was wrong with him that he'd made homicide his life?

Deliberately changing the subject – mostly because it was the one he wanted to discuss anyway – he drummed his fingers on the metal table. "So, where did you go last night when Peyton called?"

Abe shrugged, continuing to prod the body with his tools. "She asked me to come over, so I did."

"It was late. You seemed intent to stay home, until she called."

Abe glanced up at him. "If there's something you want to know, Angel, just come out and ask it. You and I don't need games…well, games like this. There are other games that I'd personally like to play."

"Okay." Marco held up a hand to stop him.

"With whipped cream."

"Okay!"

Abe chuckled.

"Why did Peyton call you last night?"

"To ask me for help."

"With what?"

"Someone who needed medical assistance."

"Who?"

"Mike."

"Mike?"

Abe set down his tools and pulled off his gloves. "Do you want this autopsy report today?"

"Yeah. I also want to know who Mike is."

"Well, then you're going to have to ask Peyton."

"I'm asking you."

Abe picked up a petri dish and carried it to the microscope, lowering his head to look. "I think you should trust Peyton."

"Trust her? Why wouldn't I trust her?"

"I hate it when you go all investigator on me, Angel. It's so anal retentive." He fiddled with the lens.

"If you'd tell me what I want to know, I wouldn't have to go investigator on you. Who the hell is Mike?"

"A guy she met…well, hello!"

Marco huffed in frustration. "Abe?"

"There's an oil based lubricant in the wound."

"What?"

"I'm going to have to run more tests, but it looks like a machine oil of some kind."

"Abe, I want to know about Mike."

Abe glanced over at him, straightening from his crouch over the microscope. "Angel…"

Marco's phone went off. He dug it out of his pocket and pressed it to his ear. "D'Angelo."

"I got an arraignment hearing at 10:00AM this morning. How bad do you want this Cook clown?" came Devan's voice on the other line.

"Bad."

"Then you need to get down to the courthouse. Amy Cook says she can't testify against her father unless you're there."

Marco met Abe's eyes. "I'll be there."

"Great," said Devan. "Don't be late." Then he disconnected.

"I've gotta go."

Abe gave a relieved nod.

"We're not done."

Clapping his hands excitedly, Abe turned toward him. "So you are considering the whipped cream?"

Marco stated to protest, then stopped himself. It did absolutely no good where Abe was concerned. "Hold on. What do you mean there's lubricant in the wound?"

"Like I said, it appears to be some sort of machine oil."

"And the wound is round?"

"Yep."

"So, definitely not a knife?"

"Not a knife."

"How much force would it take to shove something round into him and through his sternum?"

"A lot. And more so to pull it back out again. There's fragmenting along the hole where it was yanked out, but it didn't have to go in very far and it couldn't have or the xiphoid process would show more damage. If the superior epigastric artery was severed, there's your cause of death. The puncture of the xiphoid process is secondary."

"But it could give us the murder weapon."

"That it could."

"I want to know if there are any other injuries."

"That's what I plan to do, Angel, take this poor sucker apart."

"Call me if you get anything."

"I will."

Marco gave him a last searching look, then turned and limped out of the lab.

* * *

Amy Cook and a woman, who could only be her mother, sat outside the courtroom. Devan was nowhere to be seen. Amy's brown hair was pulled back in a ponytail and she wore a skirt and a button up blouse in pink. She looked all of her seventeen years. Her eyes rose to his and she gave him a pleading look.

He offered her a comforting smile and then extended his hand to the other woman. She was the spitting image of Amy, same brown hair, same brown eyes, if just a little older. "Captain Marco D'Angelo," he said to her.

She gave his hand a quick grasp. "Angela Cook, Amy's mother. Look, does she have to do this?"

Marco took a seat next to Amy. "How you holding up?"

"I feel like I'm going to be sick." She nodded at a knot of men in business suits on the other side of the courtroom door, standing in a circle, talking and glancing over their shoulders at her. "Why are they here?"

Marco studied them.

"It's the NRA," whispered Angela, leaning close to him.

"They're just here to protect their interest. Have they said anything to you?" he asked Amy.

"No, they just stare at me."

"It's okay. Where's Ms. Crawford?"

Amy wrung her hands in her lap, shaking her head.

"The lawyers were all called in to talk with the judge," said Angela. "Does she have to do this? I don't want her on the news."

"I'm sure the ADA is working to keep her out of it. After the hearing, I'll take you out the back and drive you home myself, okay?"

Amy gave a tense nod, then offered him those pleading eyes again. "How can I testify against my father? How can I say things about him?"

Marco shifted toward her. "You aren't testifying against your father, Amy. You're just telling what happened. That's all."

"But he's going to prison."

"You don't know that."

She hunched over, curling her arms around her stomach. "I can't do this. I can't put my father in prison."

Angela rubbed her back. "We need to leave. This is too hard."

Marco felt panic edge to the surface. Amy Cook was their only chance at making Will Cook pay for Gavin Morris' death. His eyes shifted to the courtroom door and he wondered if he should tell Devan what was happening.

Angela got her daughter to her feet and Marco rose beside them. As he did so, his eyes fell on Ryan Morris, sitting with a woman in chairs across from the courtroom door. Morris was watching him intently.

"Amy, just listen to me a minute," he said, putting a hand on her arm.

She stopped and looked up at him, still clutching her stomach, but she slowly sank into the seat again, her mother beside her.

He sat down and drew a deep breath. "I know what I'm asking you to do is the hardest thing you've ever done in your life, in anyone's life."

"You're asking me to send my father to prison."

"No, I'm asking you to tell the truth. That's all. Go in that courtroom, face those lawyers and the judge, and tell the truth."

"He's my father."

"I know, and I know how hard this is, but right now, you've got to think about Gavin."

"Over my father?"

"Yes, Amy, over your father." He drew a deep breath. God, he hated what he was about to do. "Hear me out, okay?"

Amy nodded.

"During Greek times, there weren't hotels for people to stay in, so when someone came to your house, it was expected they would be welcomed, given food, shelter, and most of all, protection."

Amy and Angela frowned at him. Marco bit his lip. It had sounded so much more reasonable when Jake told him this. Why couldn't he say it just the way he had? Pushing through, Marco glanced at Ryan Morris. His eyes were empty, his expression bleak. The woman beside him cried into a tissue.

"We still hold to those ideals, Amy. When people come into our homes, they expect to be treated well. They expect us to shelter them, feed them…protect them." Angela glared at him, but he ignored her. "You invited Gavin into your house. He thought he'd be safe there."

"Are you blaming her for what happened?"

"No." Marco shook his head, focusing on Amy. "I know you tried to save him. We have your fingerprints, your skin on the barrel of that gun. You tried to stop the shot even at risk to yourself." He leaned toward her. "That took courage, Amy. That took guts. You stood up to your father and you tried to protect Gavin."

She stared at him.

"I need you to do that again. I need you to walk into that courtroom and answer the lawyer's questions and tell the truth."

A tear rolled down her cheek. "I'm scared."

"I know. Brave people always are, Amy."

"He's my father."

"I know, but this isn't about him. This is about Gavin."

The door open. Devan and Laura Crawford walked out. Devan glanced at the huddle of men in suits, then walked over to the Morrises, while Laura came to Amy.

She gave Marco a nod, but focused on the girl. "They're ready for you."

Amy frantically clasped his hand.

"I'll be right there with you," he said, squeezing her fingers lightly.

She gave a jerky nod and rose to her feet, her mother and Laura supporting her as she walked down that hallway to the courtroom door. Marco rose to follow, but came to a stop as Devan turned toward him.

"You sure about this?" Devan asked, watching as Amy, followed by the Morrises, entered the courtroom.

Marco glanced at the huddle of men in suits. "Yeah."

Devan glanced at them as well. "You're asking a girl to testify against her father."

"I'm asking her to tell the truth."

Devan considered him a moment. "I liked you better before you got all deep."

"You never liked me and you know it."

"True, but this new D'Angelo is a pain in my backside."

Marco smiled.

"Come on." He grasped Marco's elbow and started for the courtroom, but as Marco moved to follow, one of the men in suits stepped between them. Devan stopped immediately and gave Marco an anxious look.

"How can you do this?" said the man, pushing his face as close to Marco's as he could. He wasn't as tall, but they weren't off by much.

"How can I do my job?"

"Arrest a man who was protecting his home. His daughter."

"Move out of my way before I arrest you."

"For what?"

"Obstruction." Marco stared him down.

"You carry a gun yourself."

"And I know when to use it. Now move."

The man glared at him a moment more, then he stepped away, allowing Marco to pass.

Devan held the courtroom door open, breathing out a sigh. "Nothing like that would happen if I was in the legislature."

Marco moved through the door. "You'd just have a whole new set of sharks to swim through, that's all."

* * *

Marco sank into the seat behind his desk, folded his arms on its surface, and dropped his head on them. He was exhausted, the pain raged from his hip to his foot, and he couldn't get Amy Cook off his mind. She done exactly what he'd asked her to do. She'd answered the lawyers' questions, even the ones that directly pointed guilt at her father, but what had it cost her? What were the permanent scars left on a child who not only witnessed her father kill, but then had to testify against him?

"Let's go, Adonis."

Marco looked up from his arms. Jake stood in the doorway. Shit, he didn't need this right now.

"What?"

"Let's go." Jake pointed into the precinct.

"Where?"

"Out."

"I'm gonna need more than that."

"Out of the building."

"Ryder, I'm hanging by a thread here."

"I know. Please, just get up and come with me."

"Where?" he growled.

"Dr. Chamberlain."

"No."

"Abe said I had to take you, so let's go."

"Abe doesn't carry a gun, I do. Abe isn't your captain, I am. You might want to rethink who you take orders from."

"Abe said to take you and that's what I'm doing. He said to ask you if you wanted your autopsy on Quentin Greer."

"Abe has to give me the autopsy no matter what, so…that argument is weak sauce, Ryder."

Jake shrugged. "He can drag his heels on it."

"Not for long." He put his head down again.

He heard Jake come into the room and take a seat in the chair across from him. "How did it go with Amy Cook?"

Marco looked up again. "What?"

"How did it go? Did she testify?"

Marco ground his teeth. "Yeah, she testified. She did exactly what I asked her to do."

Jake leveled a look on him. "Amy Cook faced a room of lawyers and judges…"

"And the NRA."

"Damn! So that little girl faced all that and gave testimony about her own father, but you…you can't face going to the doctor."

Marco didn't move for a moment, but when he did, he grabbed his cane so violently, Jake jumped. "Fine. Let's go."

"We're taking the Daisy."

"We are not taking the Daisy."

"I get to drive."

"You do not get to drive."

Jake rose and faced him as he came around the desk. "Then I call shotgun."

Marco fought the laugh that sprang to the surface and glared him down. "Fine. You get shotgun."

*   *   *

He finished buttoning his pants, tucking his shirt into the waistband. Taking a seat, he grabbed his shoes and socks and began tugging them on, feeling edgy and angry and wanting a drink so bad he could almost taste the Jack Daniels on his tongue.

Just as he finished, Dr. Chamberlain came into the room, carrying a sleeve for x-rays. He hooked a stool and pulled it over in front of him, sitting down and pressing his hands together on the x-ray sleeve. Marco stared at those hands instead of the man who possessed them. He didn't want to hear what Chamberlain had to say.

Greyson Chamberlain was of average height with a full head of grey hair, a long clean-shaven face, and a prominent brow-ridge with deep-set pale brown eyes. Caucasian with a slight hint of a Bostonian accent.

"I'm glad you came in, Captain D'Angelo."

"But…" He shot a glance at him.

Chamberlain's thick brows rose. "But?"

"I heard a but in there." Marco leaned back in the chair, running his hands up his thighs. "Look, I know there's nothing you can do."

"That's not true."

Marco hesitated. He didn't want to believe it. He didn't want to hope for anything. "Okay?"

"Our first priority is pain management. The degree of pain you're feeling must be unbearable. We're going to work to control it, but eventually, I want to fix it."

"Fix it?"

"I'll talk about that in a minute." He pulled out an x-ray and held it up. Marco almost couldn't look at the metal and bone fragment mess that was his own thigh. "The second thing is to give you more stability. I'm not certain you'll ever be without the cane, but at least we can give you more strength in that bone."

Black spots danced in Marco's field of vision and he lowered his head, closing his eyes.

Chamberlain put a hand on his shoulder. "Are you all right, Captain D'Angelo?"

"Give me a minute."

He heard the stool roll away, then running water. The hand returned to his shoulder. "Here. Drink this."

He opened his eyes to see a small paper cup before him. He grabbed it and gulped it down as Chamberlain took his seat again.

"I understand how you feel. Abe told me you'd pretty much given up hope."

Marco nodded, wiping the sweat from his upper lip.

"I'm not telling you I can give you the leg you once had, but I can improve it."

"If you can even take away a little of the pain, I'll manage the rest of it."

Chamberlain smiled. "We can do more. So like I said, first is pain management. I want to try a TENS."

"Tens?"

"Transcutaneous Electric Nerve Stimulation. We'll get you set up with one today before you leave. It's a battery operated unit with electrodes applied to the skin to send electrical pulses into the nerves. I've had good short-term results with it. It's non-invasive, so that's a good first step."

Marco could only nod. His throat felt too tight to speak.

"Then I want to send you back to physical therapy. I want you to start water therapy and add in ultrasound. This will also help with strengthening the leg. Finally, you need another surgery."

"Surgery?"

"The TENS isn't going to permanently solve your pain, and it isn't going to answer the instability of the bone. You need a bone graft and I think you need a nerve-block. I'm recommending a three-in-one nerve block of the femoral, obturator, and sciatic nerves."

"How long is recovery?"

"It'll be much the same as it was before, but without the pain, you'll be able to do physical rehabilitation with better results."

Marco rubbed a hand over his forehead. He couldn't process everything the doctor was saying. "I'm never going to remember all of this."

Chamberlain laughed. "With your permission, I'll explain it to Abe, then he can discuss it with you when you're over the shock."

Marco nodded, staring at the x-ray in Chamberlain's hand. He felt tears threaten in his eyes. "I didn't think there was hope."

"I'm aware of that."

He looked up at the doctor, blinking hard. "I don't know how much Abe has told you."

Dr. Chamberlain smiled. "Let's say Abe's not a man who believes in secrets."

Marco laughed. "Let's say that."

"I know you've been drinking."

"I haven't drank in nearly a week, but it's a daily battle."

"And that may still be a battle, but hopefully by the end of this, you won't be reaching for the bottle because of pain."

"I left my fiancée because of this, because I didn't feel like I was the same person anymore."

Chamberlain sighed. "Like I said before, Captain D'Angelo, I'm not able to give you back the leg you once had, but I've found that people get a lot of clarity once the pain is managed. Pain makes us lose ourselves. It becomes so consuming that we can't focus on what's important in life." He gave a short chuckle. "I'm not a marriage counselor, but I am proud to say I've saved a few marriages in my time just by eliminating someone's pain."

Marco smiled. "Thank you, Dr. Chamberlain. Thank you for seeing me."

"It's my pleasure, Captain D'Angelo. Besides, seeing Abe Jefferson in my office always gives me and my staff endless pleasure."

"Is he out there now?"

"Yeah. He has the office staff rolling on the floor."

"What's he wearing today?"

"It looks like parachute pants in red, blue and yellow bands of color going down his legs and a sky blue colored shirt with hot air balloons all over it."

Marco burst into laughter. "That's new."

"I'll bet."

"Here's the really sad part. Every morning before I leave for work, I hang back just long enough to see his latest outfit."

Chamberlain laughed as well. "It must be like living in a carnival."

"A circus."

"Mardi Gras."

Marco looked down, trying to contain the sudden emotion filling him. Dr. Chamberlain rose to his feet and placed a hand on his shoulder. "Let's get you fitted with the TENS and help you take your life back."

Marco couldn't answer, just nod.

CHAPTER 18

Tuesday

Peyton bolted awake, her heart crowding her throat, her body drenched in sweat. She tented her knees and raked her fingers into the hair at her temples. The dream was always the same. She found herself locked in a box of some kind, the walls closing in on her, the heat stifling. Bang, kick, punch with all her might and she could never escape. Gradually breathing would become difficult and she'd find herself giving up. Always she reach the point of giving up, but just when she did, Marco would rescue her. Not tonight. Tonight she'd hit that point where she lay down on the ground, curling into a fetal position, but no one came. No one opened the door.

Angry with herself, she tossed back the covers and swung her legs to the floor. The bedside clock said 5:30AM. Might as well give up on sleep for tonight. Pickles looked over at her from the comfort of his bed, but with a groan of doggy suffering, he rolled onto his back and went to sleep again.

"Typical man," she said to him as she walked into the bathroom. He didn't respond.

Splashing water on her face, she fixed her ponytail and stripped off her tank top and sleeping shorts. Then she forced herself to tug on her jogging clothes. As she was lowering the shirt, she caught sight of the two scars in the mirror from where she'd been tasered. A shiver raced over her, but she fought it off and returned to the bedroom, grabbing her sneakers. Tugging them on, she realized she was angry. And Marco was the target.

He'd left her to fend for herself. After all the years they spent together, he left her to focus on himself. She depended on him. She needed him. He was her rock, her stability, her center, and now that center had removed himself, leaving her behind.

She viciously tugged on her shoelaces. She hated weak women. She hated women who said they couldn't live without a man, so why wasn't she getting over this loss? Why wasn't she moving on?

Rising to her feet, she walked into the living room and forced herself to cross to the door. She hesitated with her hand on the doorknob, then reached over and grabbed her gun, strapping it on. As an added precaution, she picked up her badge and tucked it into her waistband, then opened the door.

The San Francisco fog met her. It was a welcome friend that curled around her and enveloped her in its familiarity. She jogged down the ramp and paused at the bottom, stretching. Memories of Marco came back to her. How many times had they done this very thing together? Well, until he'd been hurt. Then the jogging had stopped.

Anger bled away, replaced by sadness. An ache bloomed in her chest whenever she thought of all he'd lost, of all he'd been forced to give up. Marco was a man who depended on his physical size and prowess, but he'd been robbed of it. And she'd hadn't realized how much he was hurting because she'd started her new job.

She didn't want to think about that, so she forced herself to start running. Still the thoughts wouldn't be banished so easily. She'd left him struggling, so she could work the job with the FBI. Shit, she'd left him to train at Quantico when he'd just started his physical therapy. Had she stayed with him would things be different? Had she been there when he needed her most, would he have chosen to stay with her when he felt himself slipping? Maybe this was all her fault. Maybe he couldn't trust her to stay with him during the most difficult times because she hadn't been there before. Maybe he had to leave because he knew she couldn't handle it.

She made him into her rock, but she hadn't been a rock for him.

Running harder, she tamped the thought down as deep as she could, but it kept pushing its way to the surface, until the cadence of her run almost seemed like an accusatory voice whispering that *she'd* left him over and over in her mind.

Returning to the house, she fed Pickles, took him on his customary one block walk (he refused to go farther unless he was carried), and returned to take a shower. As she was applying a quick swipe of mascara, her cell phone rang.

Missing Marco had become a weight in her chest, so she didn't even look at the display as she answered it, hoping it was him. Maria's voice filled the line.

"Hey, girlfriend."

"Hey, Maria."

"What you doing tonight?"

"Probably working."

"You gots to eat at some point, right?"

"Sure."

"Cho and me want you to meet us at Dosa on Valencia for dinner."

"Dosa?"

"Indian restaurant. You like Indian food?"

"Sure." When she'd dated Devan, he took her to a different ethnic restaurant almost every night. They'd eaten more than their share of Indian food. "Can I ask why?"

"We want to see you."

"You saw me on Saturday, Maria."

"So I gotta make an appointment or something?"

"Well...you did call to ask me to clear my schedule for dinner."

"Why you do this to me, Brooks? I'm your best friend. Best friends go to dinner. Will you meet us or not? We got reservations at 6:30."

"Okay! Okay. I'll be there. Shesh. Does anyone ever say no to you, Maria?"

"Not twice. Later, Brooks." Then she hung up.

Peyton gave a little laugh and shook her head, returning to the bedroom to change into her suit. Before she had her shirt buttoned, the phone rang again. She looked at the display this time to avoid the stab of disappointment she felt when it wasn't Marco.

"Hey, Abe."

"Hey, little soul sista, how are you this beautiful, foggy San Francisco morning?"

"I'm fine. Just trying to get ready for work." She hesitated, then blurted out what she wanted to know. "How's Marco?"

"Oh, so you do remember him."

"Abe!"

"I just wasn't sure, seeing as you were already moving onto a new dressed-up dude."

"Abe!"

"Come on, sweets, what are you thinking?"

"Nothing. I told you he's just a friend."

"Um hm. I know how you collect them strays, sugar, and that particular stray isn't feeling the friend zone with you."

"It's fine, Abe."

"No, it's not. Think about it, sweets. The damn fool fell off a bicycle. He's a full grown man, sugar. What full grown man falls off a bicycle and gets hit by a car in a grocery store parking lot?"

Peyton laughed. It was a bit ridiculous. "He wasn't paying attention."

"Really? He got Alzheimer's or something?"

"That's not very nice."

"I'm not the one who's gotta be nice, sugar. That's your job. That's why you collect all us strays."

"You're terrible."

"Now you listen to me, little girl. Even the SPCA gets full sometimes. You gotta stop doing this. You don't need any more sad-eyed puppies following you around. Cut this one loose."

"Abe."

"I'm not playing, sugar. This Mike guy isn't all there. I didn't say a word when you took in Jake. I love me some Jakey. And Maria's my girl. Tag was a bit of a stretch, but her happy tattoo makes up for a lot of crimes. But this guy...this guy..."

"Is what?"

"He fell off his bike in a grocery store parking lot, Peyton!"

A laugh bubbled out of Peyton again. Damn, Abe always knew how to cheer her up. "Okay, okay, I get it. I won't see him again."

"Whew! Damn it, girl, you don't have to make it so hard. Between you and Angel, I'm a busy man."

"Yes, you are."

"You take care and I'll call you later, okay?"

"Okay."

"Love you, sweets."

"Love you too, Abe."

Then he was gone.

* * *

Peyton scrubbed a hand across her face and grabbed for the coffee Margaret had left them all, taking a sip. Hers had four packets of sugar in it, but Margaret had added the sugar in the break-room so the others couldn't see. Peyton was becoming more and more attached to Margaret.

"Okay, what else? He hasn't shown up at shelters, he hasn't gone to any of the churches we've called."

"I'll look in the police database and see if he was picked up for vagrancy," offered Bambi, clicking away on her laptop.

"Good."

Tank scratched at his crew-cut. "What about unemployment offices? I'll check and see if he filed a claim."

"Better." Peyton chewed on her bottom lip. "What if he didn't stay in San Francisco?"

They glanced over at her.

"What if he had to leave? Or what if he's still in Santa Cruz? What else does a person need to become a full-fledged member of society no matter where they are?"

"Driver's license," said Bambi.

"Social Security Card," offered Tank.

"I'll look those up." Peyton began clicking away. The Driver's license turned up nothing, but she decided to try his birth certificate where she finally got a hit. He'd been born in Ogden, Utah to Susan and Henry Getter. Upon his birth, his parents had applied for a Social Security card. Peyton followed that to see if maybe Finn had applied for Social Security benefits. Nothing.

His letter said his mother died. She went searching for a death certificate. She found the record from the County Coroner's office about her cremation. She searched for Finn himself, but with a sigh of relief, didn't find a death certificate.

"I got nothing in the police database," said Bambi.

"And the unemployment office is a bust."

"No death certificate, so that's something. I have a social security number and a birth certificate. Let me see if I can locate his father. He was born in Utah. Maybe Finn went there." She clicked on the website and searched for Henry Getter. A death record appeared on the screen, showing he died when Finn was three. He wouldn't have even remembered his father. "His father's dead too."

"What about grandparents? Aunts? Uncles?"

"That's going to take a lot more searching."

"I'll try Facebook," offered Bambi and she went back to clicking.

"I'll try the other social media sites that young people go on. Maybe once he was away from this Thatcher guy, he decided to enter the modern world as a full-fledged member," said Tank.

Peyton nodded and reached for her coffee. She could call Stan Neumann at the precinct. If anyone was able to find a trace of this kid, Stan would be the man...she grimaced at her own rhyme. But calling Stan meant he'd have to tell Marco and Marco would probably get angry that she was using his people to do her job.

She braced her head with her hands. Why was everything leading back to Marco today? Why the hell couldn't she get him out of her mind?

"Peyton?"

Peyton glanced over her shoulder at the door. Margaret was leaning inside.

"You have a visitor?"

"A visitor?" She rose to her feet. "Who?"

"He says to tell you Barnabas is here. He was cleared downstairs."

Peyton's expression hardened. Okay, now this was going too far. She gave him her card out of guilt and sympathy, but she didn't expect him to use it the very next day. She felt Bambi and Tank's eyes on her, but she ignored them, walking to the door.

"Who's Barnabas?" asked Bambi, but Peyton waved over her shoulder and kept going.

When she turned the corner into her office, she found him fingering things on her desk, in particular the cold files she'd been working on. When he saw her, he took a step back, throwing up his hands. She pushed the files back into her in-box and glared at him.

"What are you doing?"

"I'm sorry," he said, his face filled with regret. "I was looking for a picture of your ex-fiancé. I just wanted to see my competition."

Peyton straightened, but her expression didn't soften. "Why are you here?"

He reached for something on the corner of her desk and held it up. It was Pickles' dog cookies. "I thought Pickles might like these back. They got mixed in with my groceries when that guy with the pickup truck carried them in." He pressed his hands together in a gesture of supplication. "I'm sorry, Peyton. I really didn't mean to snoop or anything. It's just you won't give me the time of day and I figured this guy must be a god or something."

Peyton's expression softened. "He's mortal." She reached for the cookies. "Look, Mike, I'm flattered by this attention. I really am, but I'm just not in a good place right now. Marco was a part of my life for nearly nine years. It's just not that easy to get over him and I don't want to make you think differently. This just isn't going to happen. I'm sorry."

He started to say something, but Radar appeared in the doorway. He took in the scene – Mike standing on the inner part of Peyton's desk, Peyton on the outside. "What's going on?" he demanded in that Radar tone of his.

Mike's face shifted to panic. "Uh, I, uh…"

"This is Mike Edwards, Radar. He just came to give me cookies."

Radar frowned at the box. "What?"

"For my dog."

"Why?"

"It's a long story."

Radar crossed his arms over his chest. One hand held a file. "I'm all ears."

Peyton gave him a bewildered look. "It's a long story."

"Do I look like I've got some place to be?"

Mike acted like he wanted to bolt.

"Well, you'll have to hear it another time. Mike was just leaving." Peyton crossed around the desk and placed her hand on Mike's shoulder, urging him to the door. He circled around Radar, but Radar didn't budge. Peyton pushed him in the back and he squeezed out into the hallway.

He hesitated on the other side. "If you change your mind, you know how to reach me."

Peyton smiled. "I appreciate it."

"Bye, Peyton," he said, offering her a lift of his hand.

"Bye, Barnabas," she answered, watching as he headed toward the elevator, then she turned back to Radar. "What was that about?"

"I don't like civilians on our floor."

"He was cleared."

"I don't care."

"He's ex-army."

Radar narrowed his eyes. "Does it look like that matters to me, Sparky?"

Peyton sighed. "We can't find anything on Finn Getter, except a social and a birth certificate. The good news is there's no death certificate, so he's still out there somewhere. He was born in Ogden, Utah. Bambi and Tank are trying to find traces of him on social media."

"Social media?"

"Facebook, etc. It's what the youngin' do nowadays."

"Is that a shot at my age?"

Peyton held up a hand.

He jerked his chin toward the door. "Close it."

Peyton eased it shut. "What's up?"

He held out the file to her. "Look at this." His features grew even grimmer.

Peyton took the file and opened it. The name at the top was Franklin Thatcher. She scanned the various reports, feeling her stomach knot. Arrested for statutory rape at age eighteen for having sex with a minor who was thirteen at the time. Arrested again for molestation at age twenty-four for having sex with a fifteen year old. There were no more arrests, but a probation officer had found him with a sixteen year old when he was thirty-three. The girl claimed they were married, produced a marriage license with permission signed by her mother, and the probation officer hadn't been able to do a thing about it.

Peyton flipped back to the first arrest and searched for the city of record. Her breath caught. Ogden, Utah. The next time he was arrested, he'd set up shop in Santa Cruz.

Peyton lifted her eyes to Radar. A muscle ticked in his jaw. "This guy's a predator, Radar."

Radar nodded.

Peyton searched through the file and found a picture of him. Franklin Thatcher was a tall, spare man, even in his youth, with an unruly mass of wavy brown hair, large brown eyes, a long chin, and a scar running through the middle of his upper lip. Peyton looked closer.

"He had a cleft lip."

Dropping the file on the corner of her desk, Peyton grabbed the box of letters from Finn out of her bottom drawer. She thumbed through them until she found the ones she wanted. "Read this." She thrust one of them at Radar.

He took it and read, while she continued searching.

"Little Gina, Ezekiel, two more children he doesn't name. They had trouble eating. They had to have surgery."

"He never says what's wrong with them, Sparky."

"It doesn't matter. Isn't it obvious? They had cleft lips."

"You don't know that. You're speculating."

"Am I, Radar? Am I really? Franklin Thatcher is the father of these children." She slapped a hand on the file. "He's raping these girls on that ranch, Radar."

Radar finished reading the letter. A light knock sounded at the door and Margaret poked her head inside. "Sarge wants to see you, Radar."

Radar looked up at Peyton, carefully folding the letters. "Tell her I'll be right there."

Peyton could feel her heart beating faster. She knew what Radar feared, but something horrible was happening on that farm and they needed to investigate it. Finn knew something was wrong. *There are too many deformities for it to be coincidence.* Peyton felt sure the mermaid had been born on Horizon.

Radar reached for the file on Thatcher and opened it, sliding the letters he held into it. Closing his eyes, he let out a heavy sigh. "Let's go talk to Sarge," he said.

* * *

Rosa studied the file, her forehead braced on a hand, her fingers spread across her brow. As she read, she twisted her lips to the side and pursed them. It was a contemplative pose, but Peyton wasn't good at sitting still. She shifted on the armchair, crossing one leg over the other, then shifted the other way, re-crossing her legs.

Beside her, Radar sat, his hands gripping the arms, his head tilted back – his meditation pose. Peyton hated him for it, her eyes roving over Rosa's desk. She started to reach for a business card holder on the corner, but Rosa beat her to it, moving it out of the way.

Gripping the arms the way Radar did, she found a string dangling from the fabric on the arm of the chair. She started to pull it with the fingers on her left hand, sliding her fingers up to the top when it got too long. Unfortunately, it wasn't coming to the end like she thought it would, but it was making a small pile in her hand. Peyton's eyes widened and she wasn't sure what to do.

She tried to glance over the side of the chair to look at it, but she couldn't see anything. Bending forward as if she were going to tie her boots, she tried to peer under the chair, but that didn't do much good. It looked like the whole arm was coming unraveled.

She straightened and tried to shove the thread back into the fabric, but the minute she started to pull her hand away, it pooled against her fingers again. Swallowing hard, she tried to break it, but it was too strong. Shifting in the chair, she brought her other hand over and tried to snap it between both hands, but that didn't work.

Twining it around her index finger, she caught the end at the arm of the chair and yanked quick – once, twice, three times, but it didn't break. She was going to have to use her teeth.

Someone made a coughing sound.

Peyton glanced over and found both Rosa and Radar staring at her with raised brows. She gave an anxious smile, nodding at Rosa's desk. "Do you have scissors?"

Without removing her hand from her forehead, Rosa grabbed the scissors and held them out to her. Peyton cut the string, passing them back, then she didn't know what to do with it. She balled it up and on a whim, shoved it in her pocket.

Rosa and Radar continued to stare at her.

Peyton shrugged and sank back on the chair, folding her hands in her lap and gripping them tightly.

"This is troubling," said Rosa, lowering her arm.

"Trouble would be a step up from what I fear," answered Radar.

"I don't like cult things."

"Me either."

Her eyes shifted to Peyton. "Why do you think the mermaid came from here?"

"The birth defects. I think either they're interbreeding on that farm, or Thatcher's messing with every woman there and passing his genes on like gangbusters."

Radar made a grunt of disapproval at her colloquialism, but Rosa smiled.

"Still, we can't definitively link the mermaid to Horizon," Rosa said.

"No, but we can go to Horizon and look for Finn. We need to question him."

Rosa considered that.

"I'm certain they have guns," said Radar. "And based on the use of hemp, I'm thinking they grow pot illegally too."

"Have Tank see if they have a grower's license."

"We did. They don't."

"But we don't have proof they're growing pot?"

"We have the fibers from the baby's blanket," said Radar. "The ones Igor found. He's verified it as hemp."

"But we can't prove it came from Horizon."

"We have witnesses who told us to look at the Horizon women," offered Peyton.

"Circumstantial at best."

"But enough to get a warrant."

Rosa studied her. "Okay, Brooks. If you can get a warrant, we'll give it a shot."

Peyton started to rise, but Radar cleared his throat again. "With all due respect, Sarge…"

"Go on."

"If we go in there hot, they'll come at us hot. We don't have enough evidence to get a full search warrant. We need something more. I need something more."

"Meaning what?"

"I need to know the weapons we face, the numbers – we don't have any of that."

"So what are you suggesting, Radar?"

Radar glanced at Peyton. "I think we should go in there just the four of us."

"That makes me nervous," said Rosa.

Radar shrugged. "I'm not saying we don't have the full fire power of the FBI behind us, but I think if we go in there in full force, there's gonna be shooting."

"How are you going to get on that property without a warrant?"

"We go to the gate and we ask to speak to Thatcher. Tell him we're trying to find Finn for questioning on a crime," offered Peyton.

"And if they won't let you on the property?"

"They let a patrol officer on the property before."

Rosa turned back to the file and studied it. "I wish you could have gotten those women to talk to you. Maybe we go that route again."

"That's a week away. I can't stand the thought of those girls enduring another week of torment."

Rosa picked up Finn's letters, reading.

Radar drew a breath, held it, then released. "Sparky's right, Sarge. Something's not right on that farm. I'm convinced of that after talking to the librarian. She knows more than she's letting on."

"If there are guns on that farm and things get chippy, you and your team could be dead in seconds."

"I'm aware of that."

"But you still think this is the way to go?"

"I think it's the only way to go. Maybe I'm the only one who needs to go on that farm at first."

"No!" said Peyton, turning toward him. "You? You're the one who doesn't want to go."

"Sarge is right. There's a risk."

"Well, you're not taking it alone." She looked away from him, crossing her arms on her chest. "You and me can go in."

"That's comforting. You're my backup?"

"I'm good backup."

Rosa smiled. "I think you need to ask the rest of your team, Radar. I want our guys stationed just outside this Horizon place and I want you wired. If things get chippy, they go in hot like you said."

"Done," said Radar, pushing himself to his feet. "We'll get set up today and go in tomorrow bright and early."

"And if they don't let you on the property, Brooks here is gonna sweet talk a warrant out of a judge, right, Brooks?"

"Right, Sarge."

Radar made a derisive grunt.

Peyton rose also. "You know I'm all kinds of sweet," she told him, following him to the door.

"The hell you are. You're prickly as a cactus."

"Which happens to be all sorts of sweet inside."

"Brooks?" said Rosa.

Peyton paused in the doorway and looked back. "Sarge?"

"Be careful out there. Radar's right. These things go south in a hurry. Don't drop your guard for a moment. And whatever you do, Brooks, damn it, don't surrender your gun."

Peyton gave her a nod, but her stomach felt like it was in knots.

* * *

Peyton found Maria and Cho already sitting at a table, sipping some wine. They rose when she hurried over to them. She was glad she'd taken the time to go home and change into a little black sheath dress with heels. The interior of Dosa was filled with elegant woods, rich scents, and low lighting.

Maria kissed her on the cheek and Cho gave her a hug, then he reached over and filled a wine glass for her. While he did that, Maria gave her a critical once over. "You're too thin."

Peyton lifted her wine glass. "You're always telling me I'm too fat."

"I've never said that."

"You've always compared my ass to a large animal of some kind. Water buffalo, I think, was the last one."

"That's not calling you fat."

Peyton gave Cho a wild-eyed look. He smiled and shrugged.

"You need a new black dress. Abe and me gotta take you shopping."

"I'm still paying off the last shopping trip you and Abe took me on."

"That was for work clothes. We need other things now."

"What other things?"

Maria stared hard at Peyton's breasts. "A new bra for one thing. You lost so much weight, you don't got nothing up there anymore."

Cho made a choking sound and lowered his wine. Peyton gave Maria another wild-eyed stare.

A waiter approached the table, passing out a single sheet of paper. "Have you dined with us before?" he asked.

Peyton shook her head.

"Pick one thing from each course."

"Wow! I'm not sure what to pick."

"May I make recommendations for you?"

"Certainly."

"The kale and mung salad is a wonderful starter. Opens the palate. I particularly like the summer uttapam with caramelized onions and sweet peppers. And for the third course, I recommend the lamb."

"No, no lamb. I'll take the lotus root kofta. Everything else you suggested is great."

"Excellent selection."

He turned to Cho and Maria. Cho ordered for the two of them, while Maria shot daggers at Peyton. After the waiter walked away, Maria leaned toward Peyton. "Why are you still eating vegetarian? That's why you're so thin."

"Maria," pleaded Cho, but she ignored him.

"You could have gotten the lamb. We're buying."

"I don't want lamb. I've never been big on lamb. Besides, I'm not that thin. Why are you carping at me? Is this why you asked me to dinner?"

"No." Maria glanced around the room, then narrowed her eyes on Peyton. "You're still eating vegetarian because of *him*."

Cho slumped back in his chair, grabbing for his wine glass.

Peyton swallowed hard and looked away. Today had been particularly difficult for her. She'd missed Marco all day and she didn't need Maria poking her finger in it.

"Answer me, Brooks."

Tears stung Peyton's eyes and she reached for the napkin, twisting it in her hands.

Cho glanced over at her, putting a hand on Maria's back. "Go easy, okay?"

Maria left her seat and popped over into the seat next to Peyton, pulling her into her arms. "I want you to be happy, Brooks. I hate seeing you like this."

Peyton pressed her forehead to Maria's shoulder, fighting for composure. "I just miss him so much, Maria."

"I know." Maria rubbed her hands down her back. "I know you do, but you've got to pull it together. You've got to get that fight back in you. That's why I give you a bad time."

Peyton let out a watery laugh, easing away to look in her face. "That's why?"

"Yeah, I love you. I'm your best friend." She kissed Peyton on the forehead. "Come on, honey, you gotta pull yourself together."

Peyton pressed the napkin under her eyes and forced a smile. "You're right."

"You know I'm right." She picked up Peyton's wine glass and put it in her hand. "Now drink up. I'm gonna hit the little girl's room, then we're gonna have some fun."

Peyton nodded and took a sip as Maria grabbed her purse and flounced away to the bathroom. Settling the glass on the table, Peyton met Cho's look. "How are things at the precinct?"

Cho shrugged. "We've got two cases, both are a bitch. One has the NRA breathing down our backs."

"Ouch."

"Yep."

"And the other?"

"Somebody toasted the owner of a marijuana dispensary. We don't have a viable suspect and it's one of those slippery ones where the evidence isn't adding up."

"Sorry. How's Marco handling it?"

"When he focuses, he's good, Brooks. Real good. Problem is getting him to focus."

"Jake says he's better than Defino."

"He knows his shit. He knows how to work people and he's different than her."

"How so?"

"He isn't afraid. Take this NRA case. It's got us all jumpy, but he's determined to prosecute it. He's got Adams in fits."

Peyton smiled.

"Adams wanders around the precinct grumbling that he's never going to see the inside of the governor's mansion."

"And that just makes me all sorts of sad."

Cho laughed with her, then he sobered. "He'll be a good captain, if he ever pulls his shit together."

Peyton looked down at the table. She didn't know what to say. Marco clearly didn't want her help in doing that.

Maria bounced back to the table, settling her napkin on her lap. "So, what are we talking about?"

Peyton and Cho exchanged a look. Peyton didn't want to get another scolding from Maria.

"Um, whether we should get a dog or not," said Cho quickly. "And what kind. Peyton thought we should get a...what was that again?"

"Lab."

"Lab, right."

Maria frowned at them.

"They're the most popular dogs in America," said Peyton, holding out her hand.

"And I thought we'd name him Relish, in honor of Pickles."

"Relish?"

Peyton gave her a bright smile. "I think it's perfect."

"Relish." Maria rolled her eyes and reached for her wine. "Honestly."

Cho nudged her with his arm. Maria settled the glass on the table again and gave him a simpering look, then she faced Peyton. "We actually asked you to dinner for a reason."

Peyton frowned. "Okay?"

Maria held out her left hand. On it winked a massive diamond with a circle of smaller diamonds. "Nathan asked me to marry him."

Peyton's mouth fell open as she looked at the ring. Then she gave a startled laugh and grabbed Maria's hand, tilting the ring into the candlelight on the table. "Oh, my God, that's gorgeous, Maria."

Maria squeezed her fingers. "Isn't it?"

Peyton smiled at them, then rose and leaned over the table, kissing Maria's cheek and hugging Cho. "I'm so happy for both of you."

Maria kept hold of Peyton's hand. "Are you sure?"

"What do you mean?"

"I mean are you sure you're okay with this?"

"Of course I am." Peyton sank into her seat. "I can't imagine anything better than two people I care about as much as you getting married."

"I want you to be a bridesmaid."

"A bridesmaid?"

"Actually I want you to be maid of honor, but my stupid sister insisted it be her."

"Bridesmaid? Wow. Uh…"

"Please say you will," said Maria, tightening her grip.

"Of course, I will. I'd be honored."

Maria glanced at Cho.

"Simons is my best man, but I planned to ask Marco to stand up with me too," said Cho, wincing.

Peyton forced her smile to remain bright. "Of course. Yeah."

"Are you okay with that?" asked Maria.

"I'm great. Really, Maria. I'm so happy for the two of you. Everything else is unimportant. So, when's the wedding?"

"July 10th."

"July 10th of this year?"

"Yep. We want to keep it small. Just immediate family and friends."

"July 10th's just two months away."

"I know. Abe's offered to help me."

Peyton knew her mouth hung open and nothing came out. Abe? If Abe was helping and *she* was a bridesmaid, oh God, what the hell sort of dress would the two of them pick out for her? She could see herself lost in a froth of pink taffeta with capped sleeves and a hoop skirt with bows. *Bows.* Oh, so many bows. Dear God.

"Peyton?"

Peyton blinked and reached for her wine, draining it. Then she looked around for the waiter. "We need champagne," she said.

CHAPTER 19

Wednesday

"I saw the orthopedic surgeon Abe recommended."

Dr. Ferguson lowered his hands. "And?"

"He gave me this device called a TENS."

"I'm familiar with it. Is it working?"

Marco rubbed a hand on his thigh. "It seems to be doing something. The pain's there, but it doesn't feel like I'm on a razor's edge anymore."

"That's good."

"He wants me to have another surgery. Bone graft and nerve block. More rehabilitation."

"Are you going to do it?"

Marco nodded. "I have to. I have to try anything." He shifted in the chair and scratched the back of his neck. "I think Peyton's seeing someone," he blurted out.

"Okay?"

Marco tried to maintain a neutral expression, but he hadn't really thought he was going to bring this up. Still, it had been on his mind constantly for days now. "She called Abe the other night to help her with something. Abe won't come out and tell me what it was, just that some guy named Mike got hurt."

"How does this make you feel?"

"How does it make me feel?" Marco bit down on his bottom lip, trying to keep control, but his hand curled into a fist. "It doesn't make me feel good."

"Does it make you want to drink?"

"Everything makes me want to drink. My job, my leg, Peyton." Marco cleared his throat. "I can't stand the thought of her with anyone else."

"Did you think this wouldn't happen?"

"I didn't think it would happen this fast."

"Are you sure it's what you think it is?"

Marco hesitated. He didn't want to believe it. He didn't want to think she would start dating again this quickly. They had something special. Or he'd thought they did, but he knew Peyton. "She hates being alone. She hates it."

"And you think she'd enter a relationship so soon just to get away from being alone?"

"I don't know."

"So what are you going to do about it?"

"What can I do? I left her. She has every right to replace me." He realized his fingers were aching where he clenched them so tightly. Deliberately, he forced himself to open them, flatten them on his thigh. "I don't know."

"Are you going to group tomorrow?"

"What?"

"Group is tomorrow. Are you going?"

"You told me I had to go."

"I did. I want to make sure you carry through with it."

Marco started to respond, but his phone rang in his pocket. Dr. Ferguson gave him an aggravated look, but he reached for it anyway. "D'Angelo?"

"Hey, there, Angel, hope I'm not interrupting anything important?" came Abe's voice.

"Not a thing," said Marco, giving Ferguson a wry look.

"The residue I found in the wound on Quentin Greer?"

"Yeah?"

"I thought it was a machine oil?"

"Right."

"It's an ester oil."

"An ester oil?"

"Yep. A synthetic oil used in industrial applications."

"Like what?"

"Refrigeration, car air conditioning units, usually used in extreme temperatures."

"Can you email me your report?"

"On it."

"Thanks, Abe."

"Anytime, Angel."

Marco disconnected the call and reached for his cane. "I'm sorry. I'm gonna have to cut this short."

"We've just begun, Captain D'Angelo."

"I know, but there's a murderer out there and we just got our first lead."

Dr. Ferguson's expression twisted into a frown. "Group tomorrow night, Captain D'Angelo. No excuses and I'll see you again on Friday. Clear your calendar because we're using the entire hour."

Marco ignored the warnings as he headed for the door.

* * *

Cho had Abe's autopsy printed by the time Marco made it back to the precinct. He and Simons were at their desks reading it over. Jake sat on a chair between them, searching for something on his computer tablet.

"Well?" Marco demanded.

"Good morning to you too, Captain Adonis. I'd love a cup of coffee."

"Then make it two. I'd like one myself."

Jake grumbled, but he settled the tablet on the desk and rose to his feet, wandering toward the break-room.

"We're going over the autopsy. I just checked with Stan on the partial from the video and he's still working on it. He thinks he might have something by the end of the day," offered Cho.

"Good."

"Ryder's going through the current customers to see if any work in a blue collar job with heavy machinery or automotives," said Simons.

"That's a lot of files, isn't it?"

"Yeah, I'm gonna start hitting them myself."

Marco looked over Cho's shoulder at the picture Abe had taken of the wound in Greer's sternum. "What would make that hole?"

"Screwdriver?" said Jake, returning with the coffee. He passed a mug to Marco.

"Maybe, but that's a lot of force. How much force would be necessary to create that wound and yet not fracture the bone?" asked Marco, taking a sip.

Cho turned pages. "Abe estimates the assailant had to be at least six feet, 200 to 225lb."

"Cross reference the customer list with driver's license records," Marco said to Jake. "That'll be a quicker way to eliminate possibilities. We're looking for a big man."

"Good thinking. I'm on it."

Marco looked around. "Anyone seen Carly today?"

"Who's Carly?" asked Simons.

"My secretary."

"Administrative Assistant," said Jake, fussing with the tablet.

"Whatever."

"Haven't seen her," said Cho. "Didn't think she worked here anymore."

"She wasn't in the break-room?" he asked Jake.

"Nope."

Marco shifted back toward the front of the precinct. "Let me know if you get a hit."

"We'll do," said Jake, waving him away.

Marco wandered toward his office, carrying his coffee. Something was bothering him about Abe's autopsy, but he couldn't place what it was. As he reached the front of the precinct, Carly rushed through the outer door, skidding on the tiles in her ridiculously high heels.

"I'm so sorry I'm late. I couldn't find my car keys."

Settling his coffee mug on her desk, he glanced at the clock over the conference room. 9:30AM. "You're an hour and a half late."

She pushed through the half door and brushed back her blond hair. "Whew! That's good news. I thought it was closer to two. I left you a message."

"Where?"

"On your voicemail."

"What voicemail?"

"Here at the precinct."

"I don't have voicemail at the precinct."

She chewed on her inner lip. "Then who did I leave a message for?"

Marco shook his head. "I don't know."

Her eyes filled with tears. "Oh, God, you're going to fire me, aren't you?"

"Carly…"

"Oh, you are. Oh, you should. I'm terrible at this job." The tears fell, running her mascara.

Marco started to say something, but Devan appeared on the other side of the glass door. He pulled it open and stepped into the precinct.

"D'Angelo."

"D.A."

He gave Carly a concerned look. "Is something wrong?"

"I'm an hour and a half late and I called voicemail, but we don't have voicemail."

"No, the precinct has voicemail, but it's *your* job to get the messages each day. I don't check it."

"Oh!" She threw up her hands. "I can't even call in late the right way. You should so fire me."

Marco gave Devan a helpless look. Devan didn't offer any solutions.

"Did you need me?"

"Uh, yeah. You gotta minute?"

"I'll just pack up my desk." She went over to it and began reaching for her things.

"You're not fired," Marco said. "Just don't be late again."

She clasped her hands to her mouth and gave him a watery smile. "Oh, thank you. Thank you. I'll do better. I promise."

"Sure." Marco motioned Devan into his office, then beat a hasty retreat himself, closing the door at his back. He leaned against it, watching Devan take a seat.

"You have to fire her."

"I know."

"So why aren't you?"

"Because every time I try, she cries."

"She's manipulating you."

"I know."

"Then stop letting her do it."

"It's not that easy."

"Do you want me to fire her?"

"No, I'll do it."

Devan gave him a disbelieving look. "She's gonna wind up retiring from here, isn't she?"

"Probably." He pushed away from the door and crossed around the desk, sinking into his chair. "Why do I feel like you're not going to make my day any better?"

"Because I'm not. The NRA posted bail for Will Cook."

"He's out?"

"As of this morning."

Marco shrugged. "We knew that would probably happen. He's still going to stand trial for murder."

Devan reached into the inner pocket of his jacket and pulled out his phone, turning it so Marco could see the display. Taking the device from him, Marco pressed the video play button. A crowd had gathered outside the courthouse. Some held signs demanding gun control and others held signs supporting the Second Amendment. The camera panned over to a pretty female reporter standing on the courthouse steps. She explained to her audience about Cook's release, his bail, and who had put up the bond.

Then she turned to a man in a business suit. Marco recognized him from the courtroom. He'd been standing in the group on the other side of the door. The reporter asked him what he thought of the case.

"Our thoughts go out to the family of Gavin Morris. We feel the same sense of loss they must feel, the same pain and sorrow at the death of such a promising young man, but this isn't an issue for the courts. Mr. Cook was protecting his home and his daughter. He was exercising his Second Amendment rights provided by the U.S. Constitution. We understand any loss of life is a tragedy, but you can't blame the gun for the fact that Gavin Morris entered a home without the homeowner's permission, and you can't blame Mr. Cook for protecting what was his."

Marco sighed.

"Oh, there's more," said Devan.

The reporter shifted suddenly and hurried down the steps of the courthouse, picking out a man watching from the sidewalk. Marco leaned forward. It was Ryan Morris. "Mr. Morris," she called. "Mr. Morris, wait!"

Morris had started to turn away, but he stopped and allowed her to come alongside him.

"What do you think about William Cook making bail, sir?" asked the reporter, shoving the microphone in his face.

"What do I think?" snarled Morris. "I think he's a filthy murderer and he deserves the same thing my son got!"

"What do you mean, sir?" she asked, shoving the microphone in his face.

He shoved it back violently, making the reporter gasp, then he slipped into the crowd and disappeared.

Marco lowered the phone.

"You're going to have to put someone on Cook."

"Morris is just upset, Adams. He didn't mean it."

"You sure about that? Seemed to me that's a man who doesn't give a damn about anything anymore, except justice for his son."

"Look, I'll call him. I'll talk to him. If necessary, I'll go out to the house and sit down with him, explain how things work."

"All right, D'Angelo, but I still think we need to put a body on Cook."

"I'm working two cases right now. I can't spare the manpower. Besides, I don't really believe Morris meant what he said."

Devan took back his phone, giving Marco a skeptical look. "I sure as shit hope you're right."

So did Marco because looking at Ryan Morris on that screen, he didn't see much but hatred simmering in his eyes.

*　　*　　*

Marco braced his hand on the desk by Carly and pointed to the buttons on the phone. "No, this one connects you to voicemail. Then you have to enter our code."

"What's our code?" She blinked up at him, giving him doe eyes.

"Didn't Maria train you on any of this?"

"She tried, but she was so anxious to get out of here."

"Our code is our phone number."

She gave him a worried look.

"The precinct's general number?"

Still blank.

He grabbed a business card off the front of her desk and laid it down before her, pointing at it. "This number."

"Oh!" She gave a laugh and placed her hands over her mouth. "It was right in front of me."

"Yeah."

"As my mama used to say, it would have bit me if it was a dog."

"Yeah. Look, press the button, listen for the beep and then punch in the number. After that…"

He looked up as Tag and Holmes entered the precinct. They took in the scene, then they both gave him a frown. He straightened. "Well?"

Tag pushed open the half-door and leaned against the back of the counter, facing Carly's desk. "Sherry Morris, Gavin Morris' mother, says she hasn't seen her ex-husband all day. She's trying to get him on cell, but he won't answer."

Marco rubbed the back of his neck. "What about Cook?"

"He's home. With his guns."

"What?"

Holmes leaned on the counter next to her. "They left him with his guns. He made bail."

"If Morris goes over there, he'll shoot him."

"I know. We explained that to Sherry Morris," said Tag. "Can we put a BOLO out on Morris?"

"For what? He didn't commit a crime." Marco shook his head. "This just gets worse and worse. Two desperate fathers who feel they've somehow failed their children…" Marco's voice trailed away as something clicked in his mind.

"Captain?"

Desperate fathers who failed their children? *Desperate fathers?*

"Put Bartlet and Smith on Cook's house. They can split the shift. You keep looking for Morris. Bring him in so I can talk to him if necessary."

"How?"

Marco started toward the back of the precinct. "I don't know. Resisting arrest. Anything."

"Okay."

Marco turned the corner, limping toward Cho and Simon's desks. "Ryder!" he shouted.

Jake popped out of his cubicle. "You bellowed?"

"Get over here." Marco pointed at Simons. "Remember that other list we had."

"We had three lists."

"Yeah, one of current customers, one of customers who moved out of the area, and one of people who died."

"Right."

"We decided that the last list was a waste of time, remember?"

"I remember."

"But you'd called the father of a kid on the list. The kid's name was Calvin Delacruz."

"He had AIDS," offered Jake.

"Right, but he was killed in a robbery." Marco turned back to Simons. "You were supposed to call the father and tell him not to come in, remember?"

"I did call him."

"But he lost his cell phone and didn't get the message. He came in and I interviewed him."

"Where you going with this, Captain?" asked Cho.

"He was big, at least six feet, two hundred pounds, give or take and…" Marco pointed at Jake. "He was an air conditioner repairman."

Cho let out a whistle.

"Look up his driver's license record, Ryder. His first name was Al."

Jake clicked on his tablet.

"What motive would he have for killing Greer?" asked Simons.

"He blamed pot for his son's death. I called it medicine and he corrected me."

"So he might have blamed Greer?"

Marco held out a hand.

"Alfonso Delacruz," said Jake, looking up. "Six feet one and two hundred and fifty pounds."

"All of this is circumstantial, Captain. We can't even get a warrant to search his place, let alone bring him in."

Marco rubbed a hand along his jaw. "We need that video from Stan."

"We can't get a warrant and we can't bring him in, but we can go out and talk to him again, see how he reacts," offered Simons.

"You do that, and Ryder, go light a fire under Stan's ass."

They moved off to do as he said.

Marco watched them go, feeling a rush of adrenalin that was almost as good as going after the perp himself.

*   *   *

Pacing his office wasn't helping. It was almost 8:00PM. Cho and Simons were searching for Delacruz, Tag and Holmes were looking for Morris, and no one was where they should be. Sherry Morris had called twice worried about the father of her son, but Marco couldn't tell her anything.

Then there was Stan. Stan Neumann, who'd always come through for Marco before, couldn't seem to come through for him now. He couldn't clean up the video. He couldn't get a clear shot of the person in the hood, and without that, without Delacruz, they had nothing.

He turned and stared at his phone. Then there was Peyton. He'd agonized over the thought of Peyton with someone else almost obsessively. He couldn't stand the thought of anyone else touching her, sharing the intimacy they shared. It made his skin itch, it made his stomach sour. She was his, she was supposed to be his wife, his partner, forever.

He grabbed the phone and dialed her number before he could count off all the reasons why this was a bad idea. She picked up on the second ring.

"Hey?"

"Hey," he said, then just held the phone to his ear. The sound of her voice gave him a gut-check.

"Marco?"

"Hey," he gasped out. "How are you?"

"Okay. Is everything all right?"

"Yeah." He wanted to tell her about Dr. Chamberlain, about the TENS and the surgery, but something stopped him. "I just wanted to see how you were."

She fell silent. He waited, gripping the phone so tight it dug into his fingers. "I'm fine. Busy."

"Yeah?"

"I had dinner with Cho and Maria the other night."

"Oh."

"They're getting married."

He sank into his chair, absently rubbing his leg. "Really? Cho didn't say anything."

"Really? He wants you to stand up with him. I mean, Simons is his best man, but he wants you to be there too."

"Wow. Uh, no, he didn't say anything."

"Maria asked me to be a bridesmaid. Abe's helping her plan the wedding. You don't think they're going to dress me in bows, do you? Pink bows?"

Marco laughed. God, he missed her so damn much. "I don't know. It's Abe. He was wearing hot air balloon pants the other day."

"Now that I would've liked to see. This wedding's in two months."

"Really? They sure aren't waiting."

"No."

They both fell silent. Marco realized this was a bad idea. It made the wanting of her come back in full force. This wasn't a woman he would ever get over, ever stop loving. She was his. "Who's Mike?"

The moment it left his lips, he wanted to bite it back, but it was too late.

"What?"

"Who's Mike, Peyton?"

He felt the tension in the line. "What the hell did Abe tell you?"

"Not much. Who is he?"

"He's none of your business."

"Are you seeing him?"

"What?"

"This Mike. Are you dating?"

He wanted to stop himself, but the jealousy, the fear was pushing him relentlessly.

"That's none of your business."

"How isn't it?"

"You left me, Marco. You walked out on me."

"I didn't have a choice. I left to get well."

"You left." That and nothing more. "You left."

He drew a deep breath and held it. This wasn't how he'd wanted this conversation to go. "Peyton, I just thought…"

"You thought what? That I'd wait forever. That I'd just sit on a shelf hoping you'd realize you love me."

"I do love you."

"Funny way you have of showing it, bucko. What was the real reason, Marco?"

"What?"

"The reason you left. Was it too real? Did you feel suffocated because we had something special?"

"It wasn't any of that, Peyton and you know it."

"Then what was it? What was so terrible that you couldn't let me work through it with you?"

"I wanted you to quit your job!" There, he said it. He wished he hadn't, but there it was. "I wanted you to quit and I wanted you to stay home where I knew you were safe."

She didn't respond. He wasn't sure if she was still on the line.

"Peyton?"

Still no answer.

"Peyton, please."

"I thought we were equals."

"We are."

"Are we? How so? You know firsthand what sort of cop I am, and yet you don't trust me enough to be who I am."

"It's not that. I saw you hurt and I couldn't stand it."

"You always stood it before."

"It's different now. Then I was there with you. I put myself on the line with you. I thought that if something happened…"

"What?"

He couldn't say it.

"Marco?"

He forced himself to continue. "I thought it would happen to both of us. Like the explosion in Berkeley that time. I figured if it was our time to go, we'd go together. But now, now I'm not there. I can't be there. In fact, I'd be a liability if I was there." He braced his forehead in his hand. "I'm not the same man I was, Peyton, and sometimes, lately, I saw that in you."

"What?"

"Sometimes, sweetheart, the way you looked at me wasn't with love or lust or anything else. Sometimes you looked at me with pity."

She let out a sigh. "Marco, I never pitied you. What you saw was frustration, worry, pain that I couldn't do more to help you. What you saw was a woman who felt afraid for her man."

He didn't know how to respond.

"Where does this leave us?"

"I don't know." He raked his hand back through his hair. "I sure as hell know I don't want you seeing other people."

"Marco."

"No, Peyton, listen to me. Whoever this guy is, it's just wrong. It's too soon. I know you hate being alone, but come on, sweetheart, it's only been a few weeks and…"

"You think I'd jump into bed with someone new just so I wouldn't be alone."

Marco closed his eyes. They'd been so close to a real connection, a real understanding, and he'd ruined it. "Peyton…"

"No, now you listen to me, buster. I'm not some two-bit whore sniffing around for my next score…"

"I didn't say…"

"But if I did decide I was going to move on, that would be my business and my business alone."

"Peyton…"

"Because what I can't forget, what I'll never forget, is that you walked out on me, Marco. Not the other way around. I never left you. I never gave up on you, but you gave up on me!"

Marco tried to answer, but she gave a furious, "Good bye!" and the phone went dead. He sat and stared at the display. He could call her back, but he knew she'd never pick up now. Shit. He'd screwed up and there was no way to go back and fix it. She wasn't going to let it go. She wasn't going to forgive him for leaving her.

Because what I can't forget, what I'll never forget, is that you walked out on me, Marco. What I'll never forget, what I'll never forgive. She would never forgive him.

Jake poked his head inside the door. "You gotta see this," he said, stepping over the threshold with Stan in tow. He set the tablet down on Marco's desk and pointed at the screen. "Is this the guy who came into the precinct the other day?"

Marco stared at the blurry image on the tablet. Stan had done a good job, but the image was still pixelated, still grainy. He leaned closer and tried to remember the features of the man he'd interviewed two days before. Then his gaze focused in on the scar smack in the middle of the man's chin.

He looked up at Jake and Stan. "Yep, that's Alfonso Delacruz all right. I'll never forget him."

CHAPTER 20

Wednesday

Radar gripped the Suburban's steering wheel in both hands, staring at the wooden gate blocking the road. Two young boys stood on the other side of it, holding rifles. *No Trespassing* signs were plastered on trees, the gate, and the wooden box built beside the dirt track leading back into redwood trees.

Peyton glanced at him. "You okay?"

He didn't respond, just stared. She couldn't see his eyes behind his sunglasses, but his posture was tense, alert.

She glanced over her shoulder at Tank and Bambi. They both looked worried, but Bambi gave her a nod of reassurance.

"Radar?" She touched his arm. "You okay?"

"I should go alone."

"No, we already discussed this. We go as a team. We're wired. If things get hinky, this place will be swarming with agents."

"And shots start flying."

"It's gonna be okay, Radar." She looked back at the gate, uncertain. The boys didn't look more than fifteen or sixteen, still in that invincible stage of youth, certain they could survive anything, and without the ability to count costs.

Radar touched the headset in his ear. "We're going in," he said.

Rosa's voice echoed in Peyton's own headset. "Tell Brooks not to surrender her gun."

Radar glanced over at her. "We're going to have to discuss this at some point. Why does she keep saying that?"

"No idea," said Peyton, shifting away from him.

"Right," came his guarded response. "Let's go."

316

They pushed open the Suburban's doors and exited. The boys came together. Peyton could see they wore the same brown baggy clothes the two women at the farmer's market had worn. One of them still had acne across his nose and forehead. The other had a badly cut head of curling brown hair.

As they got closer, Tank leaned in to whisper in Radar and Peyton's ear. "The kid on the left has a cleft lip."

Peyton marked the defect.

Radar reached for his badge. "Special Agent Carlos Moreno of the FBI. We'd like to speak with Thatcher."

"Why?" said the boy with the curly brown hair.

"We'll take that up with Thatcher."

The boy went to the box and opened it, pulling out an old fashioned walky talky. Peyton hadn't seen one of those in years. He pressed the button. "FBI here to see Thatcher," he said into it, then released the button. Static fed back to him, but a moment later, another voice answered.

"How many?"

"Four."

"What do they want?"

"Don't know. They want to see Thatcher."

They waited, listening to the static crackling through the walky talky. Radar shifted weight, casting a look into the trees. Peyton couldn't deny her skin was crawling. She had the sensation that someone was watching them.

"Send them up," came the response.

The boy replaced the walky talky, then he and the other boy dragged the wooden gate back to let them pass. The brown haired boy pointed up the dirt road.

"About a quarter mile in."

Radar shot a look back at the Suburban, but clearly they weren't going to be allowed to take the SUV. The boys had only pulled the gate back far enough for foot traffic. Radar's jaw clenched, then he started walking. His team followed.

The dirt path cut through a densely growing grove of redwood trees. Peyton could see tire marks where rain had turned the road into mud and hardened again. It must be difficult getting in and out during the winter.

Just as the boy had said, they came upon the farm about a quarter mile up the road. The trees had been cleared to create a circular space. One-room shacks circled the periphery of the clearing with a larger house dead center before them. In the middle of the circle was a large steel barbecue and two clotheslines with more of the brown fabric items flapping in the breeze. A fire-pit sat on the other side of the circle, surrounded by redwood stumps, and a horseshoe tossing pit lay beyond it.

Behind the circle of shacks was a large area cleared for a garden and a number of very young children worked the garden under the supervision of an older boy. A quick count revealed seven adult women and five teenage girls, setting two picnic tables under a brown canvas awning to the left of the barbecue. Two other women were hanging sheets on the clotheslines.

All motion stopped at their appearance, but no one approached them. Radar exchanged a look with his team. Instinctively they spread out, searching the perimeter for any other young men that weren't readily visible.

A screen door on the main house opened and a tall man with brown hair stepped out, followed by a teen with a rifle. They jogged down the steps and approached Radar, the man holding out his hand.

"FBI?" he said, coming to a halt before them.

Radar extended his own hand and shook it. "Special Agent Carlos Moreno. Are you Thatcher?"

He wore the same brown, rough-spun clothes of everyone else on the property. He was in his mid to late forties, spare of frame, long, narrow face, wide chin and a scar where his cleft lip had been surgically repaired.

"I am."

"Franklin Thatcher?"

He smiled, drawing his scar tight. "Franklin Thatcher's dead to me. I'm just Thatcher now, a humble servant of the Lord."

Radar tilted up his chin. "Convenient."

"How may I help you, Agent Moreno?" He glanced at the rest of Radar's team.

"We're looking for a young man named Finn Getter."

At the mention of that name, one of the women stepped away from the picnic tables, her hands clasped in her apron.

"Finn Getter has gone into the world to find his fortune. He left here about three weeks ago."

"Where did he go?"

"I believe he planned to go to San Francisco. I do hope he isn't in some trouble."

Radar shrugged. "You didn't seem much concerned about throwing him out on his own before this."

Thatcher clasped his hands in front of him and gave Radar a beatific smile. "It is our philosophy, Agent Moreno, that young men need to learn to survive. They are well equipped for it, since, unfortunately, in your civilization, it is still primarily a man's world." He cast that smile on Peyton and Bambi. "Finn was well prepared."

"How?"

"We sent him forth with around $400. He was well read, had an inquisitive nature, and boasted many very unique skills."

"Like making clothing from hemp?"

Thatcher's smile never wavered. "I don't believe our young men engage in that pastime, but if you're asking about our clothing, I will admit we find hemp to be the most durable of natural fibers."

"I'm sure you do. Do you have a grower's license, Mr. Thatcher? I couldn't find one."

"We don't grow our own hemp, Agent Moreno, we barter for it."

"With what?"

319

"Our produce is in demand and we weave our own cloth. We are self-sustaining, environmentally sound, and independent."

"Independent? Meaning above the law?"

"Certainly not."

Radar's expression hardened. "Then I want to see permits for every gun on this property, Mr. Thatcher."

Thatcher's look never faltered. "Certainly. Won't you come with me?" He motioned to the house. "I'd be happy to offer you refreshments."

Radar gave Peyton a firm look, nodding at the women. Peyton gave him a nod in return. "Tank, you're with me," he ordered and followed Thatcher and the armed boy toward the stairs. If Thatcher was concerned that Peyton and Bambi didn't follow, he didn't show it. He pulled open the screen, motioning Radar inside, then followed him without a backward glance.

As soon as the screen closed, Peyton turned toward the young woman in the apron. She had curly red hair, nearly as wild as Peyton's own. "Janice?"

The woman shot a frightened look at the house, then turned wide eyes back to Peyton. She gave a jerky nod. Peyton and Bambi approached her slowly. As they did so, a little girl darted out from under the picnic table and threw her arms around the woman's legs. By her curly red hair and the scar on her upper lip, Peyton knew she had to be Little Gina.

Peyton held out her hand. "I'm Agent Brooks…"

Janice shook her head, motioning her closer. They stepped under the awning and Janice indicated they should sit at the picnic table. As Peyton and Bambi climbed onto the bench, the other women hurried off toward the shacks. Janice and Gina sat down across from them, Gina climbing into Janice's lap. Peyton noticed that Gina had Thatcher's longer chin and wide-spaced eyes. She held a rag doll in her hands with a green dress and bright red yarn hair.

"I'm Peyton," she said, then pointed at Bambi. "And this is my partner Emma."

Janice nodded. "You're looking for Finn?"

"Right."

"Is he in trouble?"

"That's why we're trying to find him. Did he tell you he was going to San Francisco?"

Janice nodded, tightening her hold on Gina. "He said he'd write, but he hasn't. I went to town the other day to ask the librarian if she'd heard from him. He was close with her."

"Mrs. Elder?"

"Yes."

"She hasn't heard from him either."

"How do you know about Finn?"

Peyton smiled at Gina. The little girl smiled back, brushing her red curls out of her face. "A man named Jeff King brought me some letters Finn wrote to his mother Aster."

Janice smiled for the first time. "Finn was so fascinated by the world outside Horizon. He liked computers and movies and the internet. He wanted to go to college."

"To study medicine."

Janice glanced up at her. "Yes."

"He wanted you to go with him," said Bambi. "Why didn't you?"

Janice's expression shut off. "All the things that intrigue Finn scare me. It's a violent world out there. Murders and assaults. Women get raped all the time."

Peyton and Bambi exchanged a look. Bambi made a face and glanced away. If what Peyton feared was happening on this farm proved true, women didn't just get raped out in the greater world. She looked back at Little Gina, studying the girl's scar.

"I like your doll. What's her name?"

Gina lifted the doll for Peyton to see. "Fiona. Finn says she's a princess."

Peyton nodded. "She's lovely." She reached over and fingered the green dress. "This is really well done."

Janice smiled. "I made it."

"Really? What's the material? It's so soft."

"It's a special blend. Hemp's a bit rough, so I combine it with mohair."

"Mohair? Angora goats?"

"Yes."

"I came to the Farmer's market on Saturday and I saw a woman who made ragdolls out of mohair. She showed me a picture of her goats. Is that where you get yours?"

"Yes."

Peyton braced her chin on one hand and rubbed the fabric between the fingers of her other hand. "What else do you make with this?"

"Sweaters, vests, blankets…"

"Blankets. Really? It's so incredibly soft. Do you ever sell the blankets at the market?"

"Sometimes."

"My fiancé has a bad leg. Sometimes he has to sleep in a chair, it aches so badly. I was just thinking a blanket made from such soft material might be really comforting." She beamed a smile at Bambi. "Don't you think?"

Bambi gave her a puzzled look, then understanding dawned. "Yeah. Oh, he'd really like this."

"I might have one I can give you."

"Really? That would mean the world to me."

"Just wait here." Janice started to climb out of the bench. "Come on, Gina."

"We'll watch her," said Peyton. "You won't be long."

Janice hesitated, but Gina looked up at her. "I'm okay, Mama."

Touching her daughter's bright head, she hesitantly walked toward one of the shacks. Peyton fingered a red strand of the doll's hair. "So Fiona, huh?"

Gina nodded, hugging the doll to her. "Finn says Fiona has red hair."

"She does."

"Like mine, but it's not curly like mine. It's like hers." She pointed at Bambi. "I wish I had hair like her."

"Why? I like curly hair. I have curly hair like you."
Peyton pulled the clip out of her hair and let it spill to her shoulders. "See."

Gina smiled and climbed on the bench, so she could reach over and touch one of Peyton's curls.

"Curls are beautiful," said Bambi, brushing the curls off Peyton's shoulders. "Especially red ones."

Gina slumped back on the bench and pressed her lips to Fiona's head. "She married an ogre. Fiona did. That's what Finn says."

"That's right. Do you know what an ogre is?" asked Peyton.

Gina nodded. "A monster."

"Right, but he was a good monster."

"Not this one." Gina rubbed her cheek on Fiona's red hair. "He's mean to her."

"How? Does he yell?"

"Sometimes. Sometimes he yells a lot."

"I see. Does he hit Fiona?"

"Hit her?"

"Yeah. Does he ever use his hands on her?"

"I don't know, but sometimes she cries."

"Why does she cry, Gina?"

"Because she's sad."

"What makes her sad?"

"People leave. Her grandma left and other people."

"Like Finn?"

"Yeah, like Finn."

Bambi shifted on the bench, looking around. Peyton stayed focused on Gina. "Does the ogre do anything else?"

"I don't know."

Bambi turned back to the little girl. "Did Finn tell you what the ogre's name was?"

"Huh?"

Peyton picked up Bambi's thread. "The ogre, Gina? What's his name?"

"Name?"

"Yeah, what did Finn say his name was?"

"Finn didn't say."

Peyton looked away. Everything appeared all right on this farm. The area was clean, no signs of neglect. Gina wasn't thin, didn't show outward bruises. And yet, everything felt off. "Okay."

"I know what it is though," offered Gina.

"You know what the ogre's name is?"

"Yep."

"What is it?"

"I can't tell you."

"Why can't you tell me, Gina?"

The little girl looked over her shoulder. Her mother was hurrying across the circle with a blanket in her hands. Turning back around, Gina pressed her lips to the doll's head again and said nothing more. Peyton gathered her hair and wound it back into a bun, shoving the clip in to hold it up.

"How's this?" asked Janice, extending the blanket to Peyton.

"It's beautiful." The blanket's intricate weave was a mixture of brown and cream fibers, and velvet-soft to the touch. "How much do I owe you?"

Janice shrugged. "Twenty?"

"Twenty? That's not enough, Janice."

Bambi reached into her pocket and pulled out a wallet, removing a hundred dollar bill and passing it over. "Here. This is more like it."

Janice's eyes widened, but she didn't take the bill. "That's too much."

Bambi shook it. "Take it, please. It'll buy you more yarn. Clothes for Gina."

Janice glanced around, then took the bill and shoved it into the bodice of her dress. "Why are you looking for Finn?" Her jaw firmed, but she wound her hands in her apron. "The FBI wouldn't come out for nothing."

Peyton pushed herself to her feet and faced her. "We found a child at Natural Bridges, floating in the surf." She glanced at Gina. "She was different, Janice."

"Different? How?"

"She had a birth defect that made her look like a mermaid."

"Ariel," said Gina. "She had red hair too. Finn told me about her."

Peyton smiled at Gina. "See, a lot of princesses have red hair."

Janice moved closer to her daughter. "What does that have to do with Finn?"

"We aren't sure. When we went to Natural Bridges to view the body, I saw a Horizon van there in the parking lot."

"And?"

"It seemed coincidental, especially after I got Finn's letters. He mentions…" Peyton glanced at the little girl with the scarred lip. "He mentions a number of birth defects. He said you lost a child after Gina, he talked about a boy named Ezekiel who also had a cleft palate, and the boy at the gate today…"

"Things like that happen. No one knows why."

"Actually, we do know why. It's most often genetic. Thatcher clearly had surgery to repair the defect himself."

"So?"

Peyton couldn't be sure how much Gina knew about her parents, but she couldn't think of any other way to pursue this. "Thatcher's Gina's father, isn't he?"

"That has nothing to do with the baby you found."

"Is Thatcher Ezekiel's father, and the boy at the gate?"

"I've seen other children with varying degrees of cleft lip since we've been here, Janice," offered Bambi.

Janice pulled Gina to her, fidgeting with the collar of her dress. "This is why we choose to live apart from society. All of your television and movies and internet cloud your minds, make you think evil things."

"If he's raping girls on this property, Janice, we can stop him."

"We live a simple life. It suits us. Do you see any sign of abuse? Any sign of neglect? We're happy here."

"Why does he send the young men away at 21, Janice? So he doesn't have competition? So he can keep his own harem?"

"That's a vile thing to say. He sends them away to make their fortune in the world."

"Like Finn? Was Finn capable of making his fortune in the world, Janice? You thought about going with him. Finn thought you would. What changed your mind? What made you decide to stay? Did Thatcher threaten you?"

Janice stroked Gina's hair. "I chose to stay. I didn't want to go." She glared at Peyton and Bambi. "I knew I'd never survive out there. I'm happy here. Isn't that enough?"

"Happy! You watched your mother die in agony! You did nothing to get her help! You let him throw your brother out into a world he didn't understand!" shouted Bambi.

Janice took a step back, pulling Gina with her.

"Emma!"

Bambi fought to gain composure. Glancing around, Peyton saw that the women had come out of the shacks and were looking at them. The young children had stopped working the garden and two more teenage boys materialized from the trees, carrying their guns.

"I'm sorry."

Peyton placed a hand on her arm, while she reached for a business card. She held it out to Janice. "We want to help you, Janice. There are things we can do, help we can get for you if you want it. Just call me. I will do everything I can for you and anyone else who needs us."

Janice took the card. Her fingers trembled, but she stuffed it in her bodice with the money. Peyton gave Gina a reassuring smile and gathered the blanket off the picnic table. At that moment, the screen door opened and Thatcher led Radar and Tank into the yard.

Peyton motioned Bambi before her as they circled around Janice and met the men in the center of the clearing. Thatcher's smile was still in place, but his eyes lighted briefly on the blanket in Peyton's hands.

"I'm glad everything's in order, Agent Moreno," he said. "As you can see, we do very well for ourselves."

Radar inclined his head, but didn't respond.

"I hope we provided you with the information you sought and I wish you all the best in trying to discover the identity of that poor unfortunate babe. Terrible shame." He graced Peyton and Bambi with his smile. "I'll just have Edmund here escort you to the gate."

The boy with the rifle moved around them and started toward the dirt track. Tank and Bambi followed him, but Radar hung back. Peyton stayed with him. Thatcher raised his brows in question, but Radar had nothing to say. Turning abruptly, he stalked toward the trail, following the others.

"Did he have permits for the guns?" asked Peyton in an undertone.

"Yep."

"How? He's a convicted felon."

"The permits weren't in his name."

"The boys?"

"Yep."

"Did you ask him if he fathered half the children on that farm?"

"Yeah, right after I asked him if he was a rapist."

"Really?"

"In so many words."

"What'd he say?"

"He just smiled and said those thoughts were the purview of our tainted, sick society and the very reason he chooses to live apart from it."

"I hate that smile. What did you say after that?"

"I reminded him that Franklin Thatcher had no problem sleeping with underaged women."

"And he said?"

"Franklin Thatcher is dead." They said it together.

"What did you get?"

Peyton held up the blanket. "A little something for Igor."

"Nice." He reached out and fingered it. "Was that Janice?"

"Yep."

"How'd you get her to part with it?"

"Told a sad story, then Bambi gave her a hundred dollars. Thatcher didn't seem pleased to see me with it."

"I noted that." Radar fell silent. The wooden gate had just come into view with their Suburban waiting behind it. "Something's not right. I don't believe they barter for hemp. I think they grow it right on site."

"What makes you think that?"

"Why the guns? This is like a military compound. I get having a gun for protection, but why guards?"

"You have a point. Bambi went after Janice a bit, got heated."

"Yeah?"

"Suddenly two boys appear out of the trees, carrying rifles."

Radar stopped walking and looked up the road. "We aren't going to get a warrant with this circumstantial shit. We need something more."

"Maybe the blanket?"

"That just links them to the baby, but I'm telling you there's something bigger going on here."

Peyton glanced toward the Suburban. The others had stopped and the three teenagers seemed to be discussing something. "What if we find pot fields?"

"We'll get our fool selves shot wandering around in these trees." Radar shook his head. "We can't sneak in. That gets us nothing but a bullet."

"What about a drone?"

Radar's gaze snapped to her face. "A drone? Fly one over?"

"Yep, with a camera. Come on. The FBI has got to have some neat gadgets like that, right?"

Radar gave her a slow smile. "Now you're thinking, Sparky," he said and started walking rapidly toward the Suburban.

Peyton followed him, pleased despite herself with that glimmer of praise. As she climbed into the passenger's seat, she folded the blanket on her lap and clicked on her seatbelt. Her eyes caught motion at the side of the road just as Radar threw the Suburban in reverse and started backing up.

Peyton leaned forward, squinting into the shadows beneath the trees. Just for a moment, she thought she saw a young girl's face looking back at them, watching them from behind the massive trunks, then she was gone.

*　*　*

Peyton hated coming home to an empty house. Pickles met her at the door and danced around her feet, but even he acted like he was feeling lonely. She emptied her pockets onto the sofa table and settled the blanket beside them. She'd take it to Igor at the lab tomorrow. By the time they got back to the City, he'd already left for the night. She wondered if he had a wife and little Igors to go home to.

She picked up Pickles and cuddled him as she moved to her bedroom and changed into Marco's jersey and a pair of shorts. She knew she should probably stop wearing the jersey, but every time she told herself that was it, she found herself reaching for it again.

She fed Pickles, walked him his one block, then carried him for another block because she didn't want to go home, but failing light forced her to return, shutting and locking the door behind her. Then she cooked a TV dinner, ate only half of it, grabbed a beer and plunked herself down before the television. Pickles curled up beside her with a doggy sigh of discontent.

She absently stroked him while she tried to get lost in some reality drama that held no interest for her. Janice had a point. Was she really missing out on so much by not having television and the internet? Peyton had never felt so alone, while Janice had a daughter and other people to fill her days.

The phone rang and she grabbed it without looking at the display. Whoever was calling was better than sitting here moping. "Hey?"

"Hey."

Her grip on the phone tightened. *Marco.* The silence lay like lead between them. "Marco?"

"Hey, how are you?"

"Okay, is everything all right?"

"Yeah. I just wanted to see how you were."

Peyton couldn't speak. She wanted to tell him how lonely she was, how badly she missed him, how his jersey no longer smelled like him, but she couldn't. She couldn't give him that much satisfaction. "I'm fine. Busy."

"Yeah?"

What did she say? How did she prolong this call without looking desperate? Weak? "I had dinner with Cho and Maria the other night."

"Oh."

"They're getting married." She was reaching and she knew it. She didn't really want to talk about Cho and Maria, not with him, but it was the only thing that came to mind. Probably the worst thing she could have said, reminding him that at one time they'd planned to marry.

"Really? Cho didn't say anything."

"Really? He wants you to stand up with him. I mean, Simons is his best man, but he wants you to be there too."

"Wow. Uh, no, he didn't say anything."

More awkward silence. She gripped the phone with both hands and closed her eyes, wishing the ease they once shared was still there. Now they were reduced to talking about other people, avoiding anything meaningful. "Maria asked me to be a bridesmaid. Abe's helping her plan the wedding. You don't think they're going to dress me in bows, do you? Pink bows?"

Marco laughed. God, she missed that sound. Even when he'd been angriest at her, she could make him laugh. "I don't know. It's Abe. He was wearing hot air balloon pants the other day."

Peyton smiled. Abe was something they both shared, someone they both care about, someone who connected them. "Now that I would've liked to see. This wedding's in two months."

"Really? They sure aren't waiting."

"No."

They both fell silent. When had this happened to them? They used to spend whole days together. Sometimes in silence, but it hadn't felt like this, weighty, full of portent.

"Who's Mike?"

Peyton went still, uncertain she'd heard him right. "What?"

"Who's Mike, Peyton?"

Peyton stared at the television screen. A sick feeling caught her low in the gut. "What the hell did Abe tell you?"

"Not much. Who is he?"

"He's none of your business."

"Are you seeing him?"

He might as well have slapped her. What the hell did he think about her? That she was some whore looking for the next guy to warm her bed? "What?"

"This Mike. Are you dating?"

Rage and panic moved through her. Was he dating? Was that why he was asking? Had he already turned to someone else? "That's none of your business."

"How isn't it?"

She rose to her feet, startling Pickles. "You left me, Marco. You walked out on me."

"I didn't have a choice. I left to get well."

"You left." She started pacing between the couch and the coffee table, unable to believe he was saying this. Hurt bubbled up, made thinking difficult. "You left." She wanted to say something more, something clever, but this is all that would come to her.

"Peyton, I just thought…"

"You thought what? That I'd wait forever. That I'd just sit on a shelf hoping you realized you loved me." The words tore out of her. She didn't have control over them anymore. They were speaking without her knowing what she was going to say.

"I do love you."

"Funny way you have of showing it, bucko. What was the real reason, Marco?"

"What?"

"The reason you left. Was it too real? Did you feel suffocated because we had something special?" She knew she was breathing hard, almost sobbing and she so didn't want to cry, she didn't want him to get the satisfaction of hearing her fall apart.

"It wasn't any of that, Peyton and you know it."

"Then what was it? What was so terrible that you couldn't let me work through it with you?"

"I wanted you to quit your job!"

Peyton stopped pacing, shocked.

"I wanted you to quit and I wanted you to stay home where I knew you were safe."

She didn't respond, she couldn't. This was all about the job. This hurt, this loneliness, this devastation was about her stupid damn job.

"Peyton?"

Still she couldn't answer.

"Peyton, please."

"I thought we were equals." The words slipped out beyond the tightness in her chest. It hurt her to say them. She'd always thought that. She'd always thought he was one of the few men who believed they were equal, who believed she was as capable as he was.

"We are."

"Are we? How so? You know firsthand what sort of cop I am, and yet you don't trust me enough to be who I am."

"It's not that. I saw you hurt and I couldn't stand it."

"You always stood it before." Her mind wasn't processing this. Never in the eight years that they'd been partners had he treated her as if he didn't think she was capable of protecting herself…and him if it came to it.

"It's different now. Then I was there with you. I put myself on the line with you. I thought that if something happened…"

"What?"

He fell silent.

"Marco?"

"I thought it would happen to both of us. Like the explosion in Berkeley that time. I figured if it was our time to go, we'd go together. But now, now I'm not there. I can't be there. In fact, I'd be a liability if I was there." His voice trailed away. "I'm not the same man I was, Peyton, and sometimes, lately, I saw that in you."

"What?"

"Sometimes, sweetheart, the way you looked at me wasn't with love or lust or anything else. Sometimes you looked at me with pity."

She sighed. Damn it, how had they gotten so confused with one another? Missed so many cues, so many things that should have been obvious to the both of them?

"Marco, I never pitied you. What you saw was frustration, worry, pain that I couldn't do more to help you. What you saw was a woman who felt afraid for her man."

He didn't respond.

"Where does this leave us?" she asked. She feared asking, but she knew she couldn't go on like this, longing, wanting him back, needing him the way she did. Either they had to try, or she had to let him go. She couldn't stay in this limbo.

"I don't know." Her heart caught. She wanted him to say they'd try, they'd make it work somehow, but that's not what he was saying. Then he made it worse.

"I sure as hell know I don't want you seeing other people."

"Marco."

"No, Peyton, listen to me. Whoever this guy is, it's just wrong. It's too soon. I know you hate being alone, but come on, sweetheart, it's only been a few weeks and…"

Anger sparked again. She clenched her jaw until it ached. "You think I'd jump into bed with someone new just so I wouldn't be alone."

"Peyton…"

"No, now you listen to me, buster. I'm not some two-bit whore sniffing around for my next score…"

"I didn't say…"

"But if I did decide I was going to move on, that would be my business and my business alone."

"Peyton…"

"Because what I can't forget, what I'll never forget, is that you walked out on me, Marco. Not the other way around. I never left you. I never gave up on you, but you gave up on me!" She sucked in a wild breath to stop the sobs, then held the phone away from her face and shouted into it, "Good bye!"

Tossing it on the couch, she glared at it. She wasn't sure what she wanted to happen. She didn't know if she wanted him to call back, or go straight to hell where he belonged. Then the sobs came, wrenching up inside of her. She fought them, but it was impossible to stop it.

She sank to the floor, putting her back to the couch, tenting her knees and covering her face with her hands. Pickles jumped down and crawled into her lap and she cradled him, burying her face in his fur and giving way to an ugly sobbing session.

She wasn't sure how long she sat there, eventually the torrent passed, but she continued to sit, her face pressed to Pickles' fur. The drone of the television filled her aching head with meaningless sound.

When her phone rang, she reached over the arm of the couch and located it, thumbing it on. She pressed it to her ear, expecting Marco, uncertain what she would say to him now.

"Peyton?"

Mike. Shit. Just what she didn't need now.

"Yeah." Her voice came out rough, husky from tears.

"Peyton, are you all right?"

"Yeah, I'm fine. What do you want, Mike?"

He hesitated. "Uh, I just wanted to apologize for the other day. I'm sorry I overstepped my boundaries."

"It's fine. Don't worry about it."

"Peyton, you sure you're all right? You sound funny."

She sighed and stroked Pickles' damp fur. "I'm fine." She clenched her teeth and pushed back her hair. "Look, Mike, how 'bout we meet for pizza Friday night? I hear Serrano's on 21st has the best dough."

"Yeah. Yeah, that sounds great. Should I pick you up at your house?"

"I don't know when I'll be done with work, so let's say I meet you there. I'll call you that afternoon and we'll pick a time."

"That's great. Hey, Peyton, thanks. Thanks for giving me another chance."

She started to tell him they were just meeting as friends, but she decided not to. She could tell him when she called him on Friday. Right now she was just too damn tired to go around and around with him about it.

"Great. I'll see you then."

"See you then, and Peyton…"

"Yeah."

"I'm here if you need to talk. Know that, okay?"

"Sure. Bye, Mike."

"Bye, Peyton." The line disconnected.

Peyton sat and stared at the phone in her hand. Suddenly she didn't think this was such a good idea. She sure as shit didn't need any more complications right now and Mike was a complication with a capital C, except she knew it would piss off Marco if it got back to him and pissing off Marco felt pretty good right now.

She looked at Pickles and gave an aggravated growl. He pricked his ears. "What the hell am I doing?" she asked the little dog.

He cocked his head.

She settled him on the ground and climbed to her feet. "What the hell am I doing?" she said loudly, holding out her arms. Of course, no one responded. "Just what I thought," she said, then walked to her bedroom door, leaving the television blathering to an empty space.

CHAPTER 21

Thursday

Marco leaned against the table in the viewing room, watching Cho and Simons escort the huge Alfonso Delacruz into the interrogation room. After Cho and Simons started poking around, looking for him, he'd called first thing this morning and agreed to turn himself in.

Marco was trying to force himself to concentrate on the man, but he kept thinking about his fight with Peyton and wishing he could call her and smooth it over. What the hell had happened to them that they couldn't even carry on a simple conversation without it becoming a shouting match?

Stan stepped into the room, his eyes fixed on the two way glass, watching as Cho read Delacruz his rights. He was wearing a t-shirt with a weather report in the middle of it and the word Alderran across the top, a pair of jeans, and red converse sneakers. The red converse were new.

"What's up?" Marco asked him, crossing his arms over his chest. Stan never came into interrogation.

"Hey, Captain. I just wanted to see if I really did get our man."

"You did. Good work. But I knew you'd do it."

Stan beamed a smile at him. "Thanks, Captain. Hey, there's a Star Wars convention at the Cow Palace this afternoon. I was wondering if I could check out a little early and attend it."

Marco smiled. "Sure. You earned it. Star Wars?" He nodded at Stan's shirt. "Dressed to impress, huh?"

"Oh, no, for that I have a Boba Fett costume. The women love it."

Marco laughed. "I'm sure they do."

"Well, I'll just go finish my report for the ADA."

"Thanks."

As he turned to go, Devan loomed in the doorway. Stan ducked his head and scurried past him.

Devan looked over his shoulder, watching him go. "Strange little guy."

"Brilliant little guy. He got us the damning evidence on this case."

Devan nodded and moved into the room, leaning against the table beside Marco.

"He's also crazy in love with Peyton."

Devan's brows lifted and he looked back at the door. "Man's got taste."

Marco chuckled and reached out, turning up the sound in the interrogation room. Cho and Simons left Delacruz where he was and came into the viewing room.

"How do you want us to play this?" asked Cho.

Marco considered a moment. "Let Simons question him. He's got kids. Try to connect with him, find out what happened."

Jake appeared in the doorway with a folder in his hands. "I found the murder weapon in his tool chest on his truck." He held the folder out to Cho. "It's a hose removal tool."

Cho opened the folder and glanced at it, then showed it to Marco. The tool was a long round column with a wickedly pointed end.

"Usually it has a hook on the end for grabbing the hose, but he straightened this one."

"Straightened it?"

"Yeah." Jake nodded at the next page. "I printed a copy of what it should look like."

"Why'd he straighten it?" asked Marco.

Jake shrugged.

"Could be the difference between premeditation or not," said Devan.

Marco looked at Simons. "Get him to explain it."

"On it, Captain." He took the file from Cho, then he turned and left the room. A moment later he appeared next to Delacruz. "I'm Inspector Bill Simons, Mr. Delacruz. I want to ask you a few questions, but first, I wanna make sure you understand your rights." He set the folder down on the table and opened it, showing him the picture of the weapon.

Delacruz's eyes focused on it. "I want a lawyer."

"That's fine. We'll get you one, but once he or she gets here, I won't be able to talk to you anymore."

Delacruz closed his eyes briefly, then glanced at Simons. "Look, it doesn't matter. None of it matters."

"What do you mean?"

"My son's gone. What difference does any of this make?"

Simons folded his hands and rested them on his stomach. "I have kids. They mean everything to me. I can't even imagine losing one."

Delacruz fixated on the murder weapon. "I didn't mean to do it."

"Do what, Mr. Delacruz?"

"Kill the pot guy. I didn't mean it."

"What happened?"

Delacruz gave a humorless laugh. "My son recommended me to him, told him I was good at fixing heating and air. Pot grows in hot, humid climates, you know?"

"I know."

"My son had been dead for a month or so when he calls me, asks me to fix his heater." Delacruz rubbed a hand over the stubble on his chin. "I don't know why I took the job. I shouldn't have, but he told me Calvin recommended me." He blinked to fight his tears. "Calvin and me, we didn't always see eye to eye."

"Because he was gay?"

"Right." Delacruz fell silent, staring at the file. "I threw him out when he told me. I threw my own kid out for being gay."

"A lot of fathers have made that mistake."

Delacruz's eyes snapped to Simons' broad face. "Would you, Inspector? Would you throw your son out if he told you that?"

Simons drew a breath and held it, then he slowly let it go. "I don't know. I want to believe I wouldn't. I want to believe I'd be understanding, but we don't really know how we'd react in that situation."

Marco shifted. He knew. Nothing his child could say would ever make him turn away from him. *Nothing.* If you were going to have children, you loved them unconditionally, no matter what, no matter who they were. You just loved them. He drew a shaken breath. He wanted children. He'd always told himself he didn't, but he wanted them and he wanted them with Peyton.

"What happened with Greer, Mr. Delacruz?"

"I'd been working in his shop for a couple of days." He spat the word *shop* as if it were dirty. "I had the tool box open and I was taking apart the heater. I forgot something in my car, so I went back out for it."

"What did you forget?"

Delacruz nodded at the photo Jake had taken. "That. I use it to grab the old duct tubing, so I don't have to squeeze behind the unit."

"That tool? It's usually curved, isn't it?"

"Usually."

"Did you straighten it?"

"Yeah."

"Why?"

"Sometimes I need it straight. I have another curved hose tool, but this one I had a buddy straighten for me in his metal shop. I was going to just jab it in the duct and pull it out."

"But?"

Delacruz tilted back his head and curled his hands into fists. "I shouldn't have gone there. I was too raw from Calvin's death still. Hurting too much."

"What happened, Mr. Delacruz?"

"The day before, he told me what a nice kid Calvin was. What a shame it was that he was killed like that." Delacruz shook his head slowly. "That he was killed like that? He was killed because of the pot he carried. He was killed because he went to that man's store and he sold him that shit."

"Then what?"

"Nothing. The argument ended. I left that night, but I was so angry. I went back to the store after it was closed and I saw the security cameras. He had security cameras there to protect his business, but where were they when Calvin was killed?"

"You broke the camera."

"Yeah, then I felt bad about it. The next day I was going to tell him, offer to pay for it, but we got into another argument over the pot. He said he was doing a social good. He was helping people. Helping them get killed on the street? Helping them become addicted?" Tears filled Delacruz's eyes. "I don't even remember doing it."

"What? What don't you remember doing?"

Delacruz lifted his eyes to Simons. "I stabbed him." A tear raced down his cheek. "I just hauled back my hand and I stabbed him. That was it. That was all."

Simons shifted in the chair and looked back at the two-way glass.

Marco rubbed a hand along his chin. "Get him a lawyer, Cho," he said.

*　*　*

"It was a crime of passion," said Derek Smythe, the court-appointed defense attorney Cho had called. "Come on, Adams, you know it was. He was under duress from his son's death and he snapped."

Devan glanced at Marco. They were sitting in Marco's office, the two attorneys occupying the chairs across from

Marco's desk. "He destroyed the security camera the day before he killed him, then set the guy on fire while he was still alive, burned the entire place down. He might have killed other people."

"He panicked. He didn't know how else to clean up what he'd done. Besides, he was burning up the drugs he thought got his son killed."

Devan gave a bark of disbelieving laughter. "Are you shitting me? If he had stabbed him, then called for help, I might be lenient, but as it is I've got him for Murder One."

Smythe gaped at him. He was young, handsome, idealistic, a blond, blue eyed, all-American boy who thought he could change the world by defending people accused of the most heinous crimes.

"This is Second Degree and you know it, Adams. You're just busting my chops."

Devan continued to stare at Marco. "What do you think?"

Marco drummed his fingers on the desk. Group meeting was in an hour and Dr. Ferguson had been very adamant that he attend. "I think you'll get a conviction on Second Degree," he said.

Devan glared at him, but Smythe smiled in triumph. "That's playing softball," growled Devan. "I thought you were all about going balls to wall with these cases."

"When it makes sense. This doesn't make sense. You go for First and the jury listens to his story, hears how much he regrets throwing out his kid, how devastated he was at his death, well, you're not going to be able to prove he premeditated Greer's murder and he'll walk. You go for Second, they may be sympathetic to him, but they won't be able to deny that he killed a man, then set him on fire to hide the evidence."

Devan considered for a moment. "Fine, we go Second, but he pleads guilty. Let's avoid a trial and a media circus." He cast a sidelong look at Marco. "I've got enough of that with the other case."

"I'll talk to my client," said Smythe, rising to his feet. He shook hands with Devan, then held his hand out to Marco. "Thank you for being the voice of reason."

Marco shook his hand in return.

"I'll call you as soon as I get an answer," he said to Devan, then let himself out.

"What's with you?" said Devan, turning on Marco. "You're all fired up to take on the NRA, but this guy, you're gonna let go with a slap on the wrist."

"How is it a slap on the wrist? He's going to prison." He pointed to the door. "He didn't premeditate that, Adams. He lost it."

"He fashioned the weapon himself."

"You don't believe that."

Devan sank back in the chair. "What about the other case? I hear you got men watching Cook and you're looking for Gavin Morris' father."

"He's in the wind. We can't locate him, but so far he hasn't approached Cook."

"Cook has his guns?"

"That's what I've been told."

Devan shook his head, scrubbing a hand across his face. "Doesn't make a damn bit of sense, that."

"That's what I've been saying."

"Let me know when you locate Morris. I don't want anything happening to Cook before we get him to trial. I gotta have at least one win this month."

Marco smiled. "I'll let you know." He pushed himself to his feet. "Now, if you don't mind, I've got a group meeting to attend."

"Group meeting? I thought you didn't go in for that new age psychobabble crap."

"I don't, but Dr. Ferguson does. If I don't go, he'll pull my badge and I won't be here to make your life a living hell."

"Well, that would be all bad, now wouldn't it?"

Marco reached for his cane. "When's that baby of yours going to be born?"

"No idea. Rani doesn't seem to want to let her go. They're gonna induce her next week if something doesn't happen."

Marco chuckled. "Good luck with that."

"Yeah, thanks. Can you imagine me a father?"

"Not even a little."

"Neither can I. Besides, I always thought…"

Marco hesitated at the door to his office. "You thought what?"

Devan met his gaze, then gave a violent shake to his head. "Definitely not going there with you, D'Angelo. Definitely not." He walked in front of him into the precinct.

Marco frowned. Had he really thought he'd have children with Peyton? They'd only dated for a short time. What the hell! Stepping out after him, he marked that Carly happened to be at her desk.

"I'll be on cell," he told her.

She looked at the clock. "All righty then."

He didn't bother to suggest that she might make up the hours she'd missed the previous day. He figured she'd be bolting out the door about five minutes after he got in the Charger. He and Devan walked to the precinct door.

"Later, D'Angelo," Devan said, giving him a wave as he hurried to his sporty Mercedes in the distance.

Marco lifted a hand to him and unlocked the car, then climbed behind the steering wheel. As he drove to the meeting, he fought with himself the whole way. He didn't want to go. He didn't want to sit in that room with other people who were so depressed they thought the answer was talking with an entire group.

When he arrived, he climbed out, feeling irritable and out of sorts. What he really wanted was to go home to Peyton, pretend none of this had happened, and go back to the life he had. Still, he entered the building and limped his way down the hall.

The same group of people were gathered around the refreshment table, talking when he stepped inside. They paused and looked at him. Tricia, the group leader, detached herself and came over to him.

"Captain D'Angelo, I'm so glad you came back."

He gave a tight nod.

"Well, let's get started," she said, sensing he might bolt again. "Please, everyone, take your seats."

He moved to the same chair he'd had before between the kid who'd been in the military and the middle aged teacher. He was trying to remember her name, when she turned toward him.

"Barb Harris," she told him. Then she picked up a chocolate chip cookie off her plate and held it out to him. "Cookie?"

He took it because he couldn't think of a reason not to. "Thank you."

She smiled and passed him a napkin. He held the cookie and looked around the group. Everyone stared back at him, including the lady with the dead cat. Tricia looked at her. "Linda, how are you feeling this week?"

She gave Marco a severe glower, then studied her clasped hands. She wore a long, plaid skirt with a light pink sweater. "I don't think I should mention it, since it upsets some people."

Marco drew a breath and released it. "Look, I'm sorry about last week. I wasn't being very sensitive to other people."

He felt everyone's eyes on him, judging him.

"I really am sorry about your cat."

Her look softened. "Thank you." Her eyes went liquid. "Some people don't understand, but Bob meant the world to me."

"I'm sure he did."

"Especially after Buster died."

"Buster? Another cat?"

She reared back.

Tricia winced and Barb made a sympathetic groan. Marco looked over at her. Slowly Barb shook her head.

"Buster was my husband!" said Linda angrily. "He was killed in a car accident a year ago."

"I'm sorry…"

"I'll bet."

"Ease up, Linda," said the African American man in his mid-fifties, a man whose name Marco couldn't remember.

"Ease up? This is supposed to be a safe group. We come here to feel secure in sharing our problems." She turned to Tricia. "We don't need someone judging us."

"I don't think Captain D'Angelo is judging anyone."

"Really?" She glared over at him. "What's your story anyway? You come in here acting superior and looking down at us. I heard what you said last week. You're here because you have to be here. Not because you want to be. So, tell us why."

"That's not how this works, Linda," said Tricia. "We don't force people to talk if they don't want to."

"Well, then I'm not talking anymore either." She crossed her arms and her legs, giving him a death stare.

Marco glanced around the group. No one else would meet his gaze. His eyes lowered to the stupid cookie he still held in his hand. What the hell was he supposed to do now? Not only did he not want to be here, but he'd ruined it for everyone else. He didn't need this shit. He didn't need more guilt. "My fiancée loves sweets," he said because he didn't know what else to say. "She'd eat them for every meal." He smiled over at Barb. She smiled back, encouraging him. He drew a breath and held it. God, he didn't want to do this. He'd been taught that men didn't go around sharing their feelings with anyone, but especially not with strangers. Slowly, he exhaled. "Funny thing is I still think of her as my fiancée. I can't stop."

He looked up at Linda. She had her arms crossed, but her expression had softened a bit.

"I walked out on her. I left in a fit of anger and confusion and...and I can't go back. It was the biggest mistake of my life, but I can't fix it." He looked at the cookie again. "I just can't fix it."

"Why not?" asked the light haired man. Marco remembered he'd left an abusive relationship with his boyfriend. "Can't you talk about it with her?"

"I've tried. It doesn't work."

"Try again. Anything worth having is worth fighting for," he said, looking to Tricia for encouragement.

She nodded at him.

"It's not that simple. It's not that easy."

"Why not?" asked Linda. "What's stopping you?"

Marco considered that. What was stopping him? What was making everything so damn hard?

"I got shot seven months ago. Shattered my leg. I always thought I was this...I don't know. Tough guy, I don't know, that sounds so stupid, but I got by with my size, my strength." He glanced at the kid next to him. *Kurt.* That was his name. "You know?"

The kid nodded.

"And there I was, suddenly. Broken." He scratched at his jaw, then held out his hand in a gesture of futility. "I'm not good with this stuff."

"You're doing fine," said Tricia.

He gave a frustrated laugh. "We don't talk about feelings in my family. I mean, the men don't. Actually that's not true. My dad and I don't. I've never been comfortable with this stuff." He shook his head, unable to continue.

"Have you told your fiancée this?" asked Barb.

He glanced at her. "All we do is shout at each other. Every time I try to talk to her, I say the wrong thing. It was always so easy between us. We were partners for years and it was always so easy. She's my best friend. She's everything to me, but I can't explain this. It's easier for me to talk to strangers than her."

"Why?" asked Tricia. "Why is that, Marco?"

He scraped his teeth across his bottom lip. Why? It always came back to why. "She knew what I was before. That's the man she loved, but now…" He gave a pained laugh. "If you knew her, you'd know what I mean. She takes in strays – people, animals. I'm afraid I'm just another stray and I can't be that with her. I can't."

His voice trailed away, the weight of his admission laying heavy in the room. Now that he'd said it, he didn't know what to do with it. And now that he'd said it, he realized how silly it sounded. How self-absorbed it was. Peyton had told him over and over again that she didn't feel that way, but he didn't hear her. He heard only himself, heard only his own self-doubt. All this time, he'd been thinking of *his* pain, *his* loss, *his* depression.

He lifted his head, meeting Linda's gaze. "I'm sorry, Linda," he said, touching the center of his chest. "You're right about me. I came here for the wrong reasons and I'm sorry. You deserved better than that."

Her eyes went liquid and she covered her mouth with her hand. Tricia placed an arm around her.

"Thank you," she whispered, burying her head on Tricia's shoulder.

Barb reached over and laid her hand on his arm. It was a simple gesture, from a stranger, but it grounded Marco like nothing had in a long time.

* * *

Marco walked to the Charger feeling a mixture of things – humiliation warred with a strange sense of relief. He still wasn't sure he believed in this group shit, but something about it had taken a weight off him. He sure as hell didn't want anyone else knowing he'd opened up like that, told them things he'd told no one else, but still, he felt lighter, more at peace. It didn't hurt that Dr. Chamberlain's TENS device let him have a few hours where the pain in his leg wasn't front and center in his mind.

Staring at the traffic on the street, he realized he hadn't thought about taking a drink all day. Now that was something.

His phone buzzed in his pocket. He pulled it out, not recognizing the number. The time flashed at him. 7:00PM. He thumbed it on and held it to his ear.

"I heard you're looking for me."

Morris.

"Yes, Mr. Morris, your ex-wife's been trying to find you since yesterday."

"Cook's out on bail."

"I know."

"The NRA got him out."

"Just temporarily. Look, Mr. Morris, I'm concerned about you. I think we should talk. I can meet you at your ex-wife's house."

"No. I'll meet you at the precinct."

"Okay, that's good. I'll be there in about fifteen minutes."

Without saying another word, Morris disconnected the call. Marco stared at the display. What the hell was he going to say to this father to make him understand how the law worked? As he walked to the Charger, he put in a call to Tag.

"Hey, Captain," came her voice.

"Morris called."

"Bartlet thought he saw him outside Cook's place. We came over here to check it out. Cook's holed up in that house, sitting on his couch with the damn rifle in his lap."

"Wonderful. Look, Morris is coming to the precinct. I'll talk him down." He pulled open the Charger door and slid behind the steering wheel, dragging his bad leg into the car. He tossed the cane on the passenger's seat.

"You want us to meet you back there."

"Sure."

"I'm gonna talk to Cook again. Remind him that he doesn't need another felony on his record, then we'll be on our way."

"See you soon."

Night had fallen by the time Marco pulled the Charger into the precinct parking lot. He was tired, but today had been a relatively productive day. They'd caught Quentin Greer's murderer, got Devan on board for a guilty plea of Second Degree murder, and now Morris was coming in of his own volition. If things kept working out this way, Marco might start believing he'd turned a corner of some kind.

He climbed out of the Charger, grabbing his cane, and locked the car. Then he moved toward the precinct. Cho and Simons' cars were gone, so was Carly's little sporty Scion, but Jake's Daisy still occupied its space in the closest spot to the precinct stairs. A dark blue Toyota pickup sat next to it.

He frowned at the sight of Jake's car. Jake only stayed late when absolutely necessary. Usually, as soon as five o'clock hit Jake fought Carly to be the first one out the door. What the hell could be keeping him tonight? Marco was afraid it had something to do with *him*, some damn request that Abe had made, some social something that he and Jake wanted him to do. Abe had warned him that morning not to go to a bar after the group meeting. This was probably some damn scheme the two of them had concocted to keep him sober.

Marco grimaced as he climbed the stairs. It had been a long day and the longer the day, the greater the ache. He tapped a finger against the TENS device, glancing down at it as he pulled open the door of the precinct.

Then he looked up.

Ryan Morris stood beside Carly's desk with a gun pointed at Jake's head.

Jake closed his eyes and swallowed hard. "I'm so sorry, Adonis," he murmured.

CHAPTER 22

Thursday

Radar sped down Highway One toward Santa Cruz. No one had spoken since they left the FBI building at 7:00AM that morning. Peyton hated the quiet. They were all tense, all worried about what the day would bring, and whether they were going to have to go back on that spooky-ass farm again.

"How about a round of 100 Bottles of Beer on the wall?" she suggested, looking over the seat at Bambi and Tank.

They looked puzzled, but Radar's expression never changed. Not that Peyton could see his eyes beyond the sunglasses. She realized she wasn't really sure what color his eyes were.

"Okay then, what about *I Spy*? I'll start. I spy with my little eye something that begins with the letter u?"

Radar clenched his jaw. "Unemployment, which is where you're going next."

She looked out the window. "Fine. No *I Spy*," she said, drumming her fingers on the armrest.

"My brother and I used to play 20 Questions," offered Bambi tentatively.

Peyton shifted and looked back at her. "Yeah? Remind me."

"I think of something, then you try to guess it. Usually the first question is animal, vegetable, or mineral."

"The professor and I play this on road trips. We usually mix in elements from the periodic table," added Tank.

"So heavy on the mineral?" offered Peyton.

"Well, we also limit it to animals discovered in the last twenty years, you know like the Atewa dinospider, the gola malimbe bird, the Indonesian flasher wrasse…"

"The flasher wrasse. That's my favorite," she said. From the corner of her eye, she caught the upward tilt of Radar's lips. "Okay, Emma, think of something."

Bambi tilted back her blond head and thought. "Does it have to be real or can it be imaginary?"

"Probably real."

"Shoot. I just always find myself thinking of the chimera. It's a fire breathing monster with the head and body of a lion, a goat's head growing out of its back, and a snake's tail." She punctuated the last with her index finger. "And it's a girl."

Peyton realized her mouth was hanging open, but before she could respond, her phone rang. She fished it out of her pocket and thumbed it on. "Brooks?"

"Hello, Agent Brooks, this is Igor."

Peyton smiled. How many people could say they had a man named Igor calling them early in the morning? "How's my blanket?"

"Still in one piece as you requested, but I did get a sample off the back of it and ran some tests."

"Tell me it's a match to the fibers you found in our mermaid's fingernails, Igor."

"I can do you one better, Agent Brooks. When I went over the body a second time, I found fibers caught around the wee lass's umbilical cord."

Peyton's fingers tightened on the phone. "And?" Before he could answer, her phone buzzed, indicating she had another call coming through. "Hold that thought a minute, Igor."

"All righty."

She clicked over to the other line. "Brooks?"

"Agent Brooks?"

"Yes."

"This is Cheryl Watts from the Santa Cruz Public Library. You gave me your card when you were here the other day."

"Yes, Cheryl, how can I help you?"

"I was wondering if you'd be able to come in today."

"Why? Mrs. Elder made it clear she had nothing to tell us."

"Well, Lois has changed her mind. I think there's someone here you really want to meet, Agent Brooks. Will you come?"

They'd found Finn. That had to be it. Peyton felt a wave of relief wash over her.

"We're on our way. See you in a bit." Radar made a grumbling sound, but Peyton ignored him and clicked back over to Igor. "Igor? What do you have for me?"

"The fibers I found under our mermaid's fingernails match the hemp on the blanket you brought me, but there's more."

"Dazzle me, Igor. I need a win right now."

"The fibers caught around the umbilical cord?"

"Yes?"

"Mohair."

"Sweet, sweet man, I owe you a drink."

He laughed. "I'm partial to Prosecco, Agent Brooks, very partial."

"Done." She disconnected and turned to Radar. "We've got to go to the library right now."

"No, Officer Brannon and Reynolds have cordoned off an area near Horizon in the forest for us to use. Our guys are already there setting up the drone as we speak."

"Cheryl Watts has someone at the library she says we want to meet. I'm sure it's Finn."

"They can wait, then."

"Radar, the fibers on the blanket match the fibers on the baby. All of the evidence is adding up. The drone is just final confirmation. Let's go to the library and talk to Finn first."

He blew out air in frustration and his hands tightened on the steering wheel.

Peyton gave him an arch look. "You just want to play with the remote controlled plane."

He shot a glance at her. "It's a drone, not a plane."

"You want to play with remote controlled drone."

He gave her a glare. She knew only because his brows drew down below the sunglasses. "Who doesn't," he grumbled, then he slammed a hand on the steering wheel. "Fine, we'll go to the damn library first."

*   *   *

Cheryl met them at the door to the library, unlocking it and waving them inside. She cast a look toward the street, then locked the door again. Peyton frowned at her.

"The media have been here every day since you came the last time," Cheryl explained. She motioned to the stairs. "Come on."

"What's going on, Cheryl?" Peyton asked, jogging to catch up to her longer stride. Radar and the rest of the team followed behind them.

"You'll see."

They found Lois Elder standing outside the door to her office. Her windows had been covered by curtains. Peyton realized she didn't really like this woman very much as Mrs. Elder gave her a critical look from behind her spectacles.

"Before you go in, I just want to reiterate that I believe in freedom of religion, Agent Brooks."

Peyton gave her an aggravated look. "This isn't about freedom of religion, Mrs. Elder. It's about human rights."

"You need to know that I do care about Finn. I care about him a great deal. I will do anything to help him."

"I'm glad to hear it. Now, we don't have a lot of time, Mrs. Elder. The door, please."

She reached for the knob and pushed the door open. Peyton stepped into the darkened office, straining to see the slight figure sitting in one of the armchairs before Mrs. Elder's desk. The rest of the team crowded in behind her, but Peyton held up a hand to stop them.

She recognized the face looking back at her with the wide, frightened eyes. It was the same face that had watched them from the trees when they left Horizon yesterday. Peyton took a step closer, holding out her hand.

"Molly? I'm Special Agent Peyton Brooks."

The girl shot a terrified look at Mrs. Elder. The older woman came over and wrapped an arm around her shoulders. "It's all right, Molly. Agent Brooks wants to help you."

Molly ducked her head, but she peered up at Peyton through her lank brown locks. "I want to find Finn, Agent Brooks. Can you help me?"

Peyton moved to a chair directly across from the girl and took a seat. "I'll do everything I can. How did you get off Horizon, Molly?"

"I hitchhiked. Finn brought me here, to the library, a couple of times, so I knew where it was."

"When was the last time you saw Finn?"

Molly closed her eyes briefly, reaching up to curl her hands in Mrs. Elder's sweater. "The day we threw the baby into the ocean."

*　*　*

Peyton faced off against Radar in the Young Reader's Lounge. "You can't arrest her, Radar. She didn't understand what she was doing."

"That's not for you or me to decide, Sparky. That's what juries do."

"She did nothing wrong. She gave her baby the only burial she knew how." She pointed back to the office. "That girl has been raped and abused and tortured by that monster, Radar. He's the one we should be arresting."

"And we will, but it doesn't change what she did."

"What was she supposed to do?" asked Bambi, moving to Peyton's side. "She saw what happened with Finn's mother when they couldn't pay for burial. She didn't want that for her baby."

"She's just a kid, barely twenty-one," continued Peyton.

"Old enough to know what she did was wrong."

"If she's suffering from Stockholm Syndrome, Radar," said Tank, "she may not be capable of seeing her actions as wrong. Most psychologists agree that victims of Stockholm Syndrome are not responsible for themselves."

Radar looked back at the office door. "She'll be safer in custody. Where else is she going to go?"

"Mrs. Elder agreed to help her. She'll take her in for now," said Peyton. "Please, Radar, don't traumatize her any more than necessary. If Sarge decides to turn this over to the prosecutors, so be it, but right now, leave her here. Let's go after Thatcher."

Radar hesitated.

"We can go fly your toy plane."

"Drone."

"We can go fly your drone."

"Fine," he said, whipping around on a heel. "Let's go fly my drone."

The ride out to the drone site took thirty minutes over rough roads, dirt tracks and across one dry creek bed, but the Suburban had little difficulty navigating the terrain. Peyton marveled at the beauty of the Santa Cruz mountains – dense, old growth redwood forests, ferns, and a dappling of sunlight sneaking through the branches to touch the loam of the forest floor.

When they reached the clearing where the FBI had set up camp, Peyton marveled at the number of people moving about, talking on phones, working off remote computer terminals. It was a command center in the middle of a forest.

As the Suburban bounced to a stop, Lieutenant Brannon came over to them. "They've got it all set up."

She pointed to a strange looking plane resting in the open part of the clearing. It looked like a weird space alien with four vertical propellers on top, four thin legs, with a surveillance camera hanging off its belly. Radar and Tank made a beeline for it, stopping beside Sergeant Reynolds, both of them exclaiming in wonder. Sergeant Reynolds gave them each a high five.

Brannon shook her head. "Boys and their gadgets."

Peyton smiled at her.

"Come on. We can watch the display over here." She led them to one of the laptops set on a camp table. A man in an FBI jacket nodded at them. Peyton nodded back.

"We're just about ready to go," he said, pointing to another man with a remote control. "If we pick up anything, it'll show here. It's being beamed directly into Judge Lewis' chambers in San Francisco. Sarge is standing by to get the warrant."

"Great."

They crowded around him and watched as the man with the remote started the drone and brought it to a low hover over the ground. An exclamation of delight rose from the men. Peyton and Bambi exchanged a smile.

Then the drone rose higher and higher until it cleared the tree cover. A moment later, the agent in charge banked it to the left and it took off, disappearing from sight. Peyton focused her attention on the monitor. A moment later the men were crowded around behind them, looking over her shoulder.

"I've got a visual feed," said the agent with the remote.

The agent at the laptop clicked on a program and a window opened, showing the tops of trees. Peyton held her breath as the drone passed over them, showing more trees, a break where a stream cut through the hills, a few dilapidated outbuildings, an old truck rusting on bare rims, then suddenly they were gliding over Horizon.

Peyton held her breath. The center circle became clear, the covered picnic tables, the clotheslines, and Thatcher's house. They passed over the gardens. The children looked up at the drone. Peyton couldn't see their features, but she could catch the motion, the shift of colors.

"What's over there?" asked Radar, pointing beyond the house.

The agent holding the remote banked the drone and flew to the right of the screen. A wood pile, a shed, and the Horizon van were stored behind Thatcher's house, then the forest took over. The agent banked the drone back over the compound, taking in the circle, the clotheslines, the shacks, the garden...nothing.

"Shit!" swore Radar, slamming his fist on the camp table. "I thought for sure we'd find something." He pushed through the crowd around the laptop and paced out into the clearing. Peyton watched after him, but she didn't know what to say. They might have enough for a warrant if they brought Molly in to testify.

"What's that?" asked Tank, pointing to a spot on the screen that led into the trees just behind the garden.

The agent leaned closer, squinting at it. "I'm not sure. Slim, can you bring the drone lower? Skim it just over the garden again."

Slim, the agent with the remote, angled himself so he could see the screen, then he brought the drone in low. Peyton could see the children scattering as the little plane banked over the top of them. An older boy was shouting, waving his arms back toward the house. The drone picked up the spot that Tank had noticed and sped along it.

"It looks like a path of some kind."

"Can we follow it beneath the tree cover?" asked Tank.

"I'm worried we'll lose contact," said the agent at the laptop.

Slim shook his head. "She can do it. She's the most sophisticated model money can buy."

Radar pushed back into the crowd, his gaze fixated on the screen, following the wobbly flight path of the drone beneath the trees. Peyton glanced at Slim, worried they might lose control of it before they found anything, but his concentration was fixed.

The drone skimmed along, over the top of the trail, going deeper and deeper into the forest. Radar's hand tightened into a fist on the table, his breath coming faster. Then, just when Peyton was sure this had to be a simple deer track, the drone skimmed over the top of close growing green, bushy plants with distinctive serrated leaves.

"Yes!" said Radar.

A cheer went up among the group. Peyton closed her eyes, exhaling in relief. Opening them again, Peyton watched the drone bank over the entire field, beaming the evidence directly to the judge's chambers in San Francisco.

* * *

Radar pulled his team around him. The FBI squad, Lieutenant Brannon, and Sergeant Reynolds were pulling on their riot gear. Peyton adjusted the brim of her FBI cap and fixed the strap on her flak jacket, her hand trembling. Now that the moment was upon them, she felt like she was going to be sick.

"Look," said Radar, drawing their attention. "I don't think we get out of this without shots being fired. I've seen how these things go down. It happens fast and it gets out of control faster. Don't lose your heads. Don't start shooting until absolutely necessary, but when it starts, shoot to kill."

Peyton swallowed hard. She wanted to take down Thatcher, but she didn't want to be in the crossfire. Shit. There were women and children on that farm, and the men were all boys, babies, unable to understand what the hell they were doing.

"Radar?"

"It's okay, Sparky. It'll be okay."

She tried to stop her rapid breathing, but she couldn't. She felt the beginnings of panic seep into her. Radar placed his hands on her shoulders.

"Look at me, Sparky."

She did, focusing on his dark eyes. A deep, deep brown. A brown almost moving to black.

"It'll be okay. We go in, we control the situation, we get the guns. Okay?"

She nodded, unable to speak.

"Okay," he said again, releasing her. Then he motioned to the group. "Move out," he shouted.

They walked up the road from where they'd left their SUVs. Peyton's heart was hammering so hard in her chest, she could feel it pounding in her ears. Sun dappled over their faces, birds called in the trees, but everything else was silent.

The gate had been vacated.

Radar motioned and the agents spread out, moving off the road and into the trees. Radar walked to the barricade and unhooked it, dragging it back. Then he pressed the radio on his shoulder. "We're going in."

"Careful," came Rosa's voice in Peyton's earpiece.

Bambi touched her arm as she moved past her. Peyton could hear the engines on the vehicles start behind them, creeping up the road to block off any exit. She followed her team down the long drive, feeling like it was warping and lengthening as they walked. The trees seemed to be crowding in on them, pressing down on them with their silence and density.

Just as they reached the opening to Horizon, Radar held out his hand stopping them. Peyton edged up to his side, her fingers flexing on the handle of her gun. Thatcher stood in the middle of the circle, his boys behind him all carrying rifles. Peyton quickly counted eight boys, eight rifles, but Thatcher himself seemed to be unarmed. The women and children huddled behind the boys, crouching on the stairs, but still in the line of fire.

"Franklin Thatcher!" shouted Radar, holding up the warrant in his left hand. "I have a warrant to search these premises and the surrounding forest for contraband or other illegal activity."

Thatcher's hands were loose by his sides, his expression bland, but Peyton noted the annoying smirk was gone. "You are trespassing on private property, Agent Moreno. We have done nothing wrong to necessitate such an intrusion."

"Tell your followers to drop their guns. We don't want trouble, Thatcher! Tell them to lay down their weapons!"

"They are exercising their Second Amendment rights, Agent Moreno. Are you denying them their right to bear arms?"

"We don't want anyone hurt, Thatcher. Tell them to lay down their weapons."

"Unfortunately, I can't do that. I have no way of knowing what that paper is that you're waving around. You'll have to come forward and show it to me."

Radar exchanged a look with his team.

"Radar, don't do it," Peyton pleaded.

"I don't have a choice. Stay here. Remember what I said."

"Radar…"

"Just do what I said."

"I'm going with you," said Peyton, not sure where she got the courage. "You're not going alone."

Radar started to protest, but Peyton turned back to Thatcher. "I'm coming in. Hold your fire!" she shouted.

Radar hurried to her side. "We need to work on your obedience."

Peyton cast a quick glance at him as they continued walking. They came to a stop before the Horizon leader and he gave Peyton that self-serving smirk of his. Radar snapped the warrant out at him.

"There. Take it."

Thatcher took the paper and read it over, then he held it out again. "I'm afraid I don't recognize the United States government as my sovereign. Your warrant is denied."

Radar gapped at him in astonishment. "What?"

Thatcher's gaze fixed on Peyton's eyes. "You'll have to take us by force."

Radar made a strangled sound, but Peyton knew he wasn't kidding. Thatcher wanted a blood bath, he wanted to go out in a hail of bullets. He wanted another Waco, Jonestown, Ruby Ridge. She could see it in his eyes, she could hear it in his voice. He wanted to die a martyr. Radar had been right all along.

She moved before anyone knew what she was going to do and whipped out her gun, then she stepped into Thatcher and shoved the gun under his chin.

CHAPTER 23

Thursday

Marco went still. Jake sat in Carly's chair, the muzzle of the gun pointed directly at his temple. Between Marco and him was the counter. Ryan Morris's expression was grim, the hand on the gun steady.

Marco leaned the cane against the counter, holding up both hands. He could feel the weight of his gun hanging below his left arm, but he knew he wasn't steady enough on his bad leg to grab it before Morris pulled the trigger.

"Mr. Morris, I thought we agreed to meet and talk."

"I'm done talking. Cook is out, home, enjoying his freedom, and my son's dead, rotting in a coffin."

Marco glanced at Jake. Jake's shoulders were hunched, his head turned at an odd angle to avoid the gun, his eyes narrowed. Marco could see the tremors that coursed through him. He wanted to reassure him, but what the hell good would that do now?

Suddenly Tag and Holmes appeared from the back. They caught sight of Morris and whipped out their guns, pointing them directly at him.

Marco signaled frantically with his hands. "It's okay. It's okay."

Tag and Holmes gave him panicked looks, but their guns never lowered. Morris shifted just a little to see them, but his gaze snapped back to Marco. The gun against Jake's head remained.

"This isn't the way, Mr. Morris."

"Isn't it? The NRA wants guns, well, let's give them their guns and the violence that goes with it. If I can walk into a police station and shoot it up, maybe they'll realize what they've caused with their gun proliferation. What happens when even the authorities are outgunned? What then?"

Marco forced himself to draw a deep breath. "It won't change anything, Mr. Morris. It won't stop them or make them reconsider. You'll be chalked up as a deranged father and your fight ends here."

"I don't care. My son's dead. What does any of it matter now? Everything I dreamed for him, everything I hoped for, gone like that. In an instant. While Cook sits at home, becoming a folk hero."

"No, he isn't. He may be home now, but he's going to stand trial. He's going to prison, Mr. Morris."

"You can't possibly know that. The NRA got him out, they'll get him off too."

"I don't believe that. I don't believe they'll get him off. I believe Gavin will have justice, Mr. Morris. I believe a jury will make sure your son didn't die in vain."

"How can you say that? He was seventeen. Seventeen. Just starting his life. How can it not all be in vain? The time we put into keeping him safe. The worry, the care, watching over him, making sure he never got hurt. It meant nothing."

"That's not true and you know it." Marco swallowed hard. "I can't begin to imagine what you're feeling, Mr. Morris. I can't. I'm not a father. I don't know the pain you're experiencing. I wouldn't presume to understand, but what I do know is this – every day on this job, I see parents like you, grieving, devastated, unable to accept what has happened to them."

"Then you know why I have to make this stand." He looked down at Jake, tightening his grip on the gun.

Jake closed his eyes, shuddering.

Marco gave Tag and Holmes a barely perceptible shake of his head. He couldn't have them taking a shot now. Morris would kill Jake through reflex.

"Look at me, Mr. Morris, please, sir. Look at me."

Morris turned tortured eyes to him.

"Every day I meet people like you and Gavin's mother. I tell them their children are gone, and I watch them fall apart. I can't completely feel what they do because it's not me, it's not my life, but I know this." He pointed at Jake. "If you pull that trigger, you take away the hope of every parent who's lost a child in this City. You ruin the chance they have to get answers, to get justice. You take away the closure they need, the ability to lay their children to rest knowing that another child won't share their same fate."

Jake opened his eyes and looked up at Marco.

Marco took a step closer to the counter, holding Morris' gaze with every ounce of his will. "The man you're holding with that gun is the first line of defense we have in this precinct, Mr. Morris. That man has solved more cases, found more evidence to convict more killers than any of the rest of us. If you take his life, you take away the hope of other parents like yourself, you take away their closure, their peace of mind, their ability to get some measure of relief from their unrelenting pain. You deny them the justice they deserve. You kill that man, Mr. Morris, and the NRA wins, Will Cook wins, and the rest of us…well, God help us all, sir."

Morris clenched his jaw and for the first time, his hand wavered. Then he lifted the gun into the air. Holmes was on him in the next instant, slamming him into the counter and wrenching the gun out of his hand.

Marco closed his eyes and dropped his arms, feeling a wash of vertigo sweep over him.

*   *   *

"Just what will this accomplish, little one?" said Thatcher, staring down the barrel of the gun at Peyton.

"A whole lot I'm thinking."

"Do tell."

Peyton could feel the tension vibrating around them. Radar stood with his hands out flung, signaling for everyone to stay still. The boys behind Thatcher were exchanging looks, uncertain what they should do.

Peyton pressed the muzzle of the gun tighter against Thatcher's jaw. "Seems to me all I have to do is cut the head off the snake."

"Do you really believe I'm afraid to die?"

"Not a moment ago, but now, yeah. Now you've had time to wonder just how painful it will be when my bullet carves a path through your skull, into your brain, and blows the top of your Goddamn head off!"

He gave her that smirk of his. "I don't believe you have it in you."

Peyton narrowed her eyes on him. "That's what the last bastard said before I emptied my gun into him."

The smile dried.

"Tell them to put down the guns, Thatcher!" ordered Radar.

Thatcher's scarred lip twitched.

"Tell them!"

"Put down your guns," he said, looking away from Peyton. "Put them down!"

Peyton didn't move until the last boy lowered his gun and laid it on the ground.

"Tear this place apart," said Radar, replacing his gun in his holster and grabbing Thatcher by the shoulder. Peyton stepped back as he yanked his arms behind his back, slapping cuffs on him, then he shoved him toward the picnic tables. "You okay, Sparky?" he said over his shoulder.

"Fine." She holstered her own gun, her hands shaking.

Bambi stepped in front of her. "Damn girl, that was crazy!"

Peyton nodded, still unable to believe she'd done it. Tank gave her a stunned smile, cuffing her lightly on the shoulder, then he walked off to help with the search.

Bambi continued to stare at Peyton with a mixture of bewilderment and respect. "That was freakin' ass crazy!"

"I know."

Grabbing her face in her hands, Bambi planted a kiss on Peyton's forehead, then she followed Tank toward the house. Peyton made eye contact with Janice as she followed Radar to where he was forcing Thatcher into a chair.

"Get a forensic team in here to bag up the weapons. I want them dusted for fingerprints and I want to know the last time they were fired."

Then he braced a hand on the back of Thatcher's chair and stared him in the eyes. "Do you wanna tell us just what we'll find when we take this place apart? If my people stumble on a shotgun trap or anything else, I'm gonna make sure you get the death penalty, Franklin, so anything you can tell me will go a long way toward saving your sorry ass."

"I don't know what you mean, Agent Moreno. As I told you, Franklin Thatcher is dead to me. We are a peaceful community that simply wants to be left alone. We ask for nothing from the government and we expect the same in return." He leaned closer to Radar, as if he wasn't aware of the handcuffs on his wrists. "You'd think the FBI would be more careful about approaching private citizens living peacefully on private land. Your track record with such things is shameful."

Radar's jaw clenched and his hand curled into a fist. "I promise you, Thatcher, that I will be there when they stick the needle in your arm. I will be there and I will watch you draw your last breath and then I will tell all these women exactly how you died."

"Radar," said Peyton, moving to his side and touching his arm. "He's not worth it."

Thatcher smiled.

Radar straightened and took a few steps back as the radio crackled on his shoulder.

"Radar," came Tank's voice.

Radar pressed the button. "Yeah?"

"We found a shallow grave near the woodpile."

"What?" Radar turned toward the house.

Peyton felt her heart catch.

"We're uncovering it now."

Peyton's gaze met Janice's as she moved away from the stairs toward the picnic table.

"Are you sure it's a grave?" asked Radar.

"Yes. The smell of decomposition's strong and we have insect activity. It appears to be calliphoridae flies, which are present during active decay."

Radar shifted toward Thatcher. "You've got about thirty seconds to tell me what the hell's going on."

Thatcher met his look, but he didn't say anything. A clammy, nauseous feeling rose inside of Peyton. She started toward Janice, but before she could move, Radar's radio crackled again.

"Radar?"

"Yes, Tank."

"It appears to be a Caucasian male. Late teens, early twenties by the dentition." He paused. "Red hair."

A keening wail rose from Janice and she ran at Thatcher, her hands raised. She slammed into him, knocking him and the chair over, then she fell on him, her fists pummeling him while he tried to scramble away.

Radar grabbed her around the waist and threw her off. She landed on her backside, but was up in the next moment. Before anyone could move, she darted at the agents cataloging the weapons and lunged for one of the rifles. Without hesitation, she brought it around, cocking the hammer and leveling it on Thatcher.

"Hold your fire!" shouted Radar as cops and agents drew their weapons. "Hold your fire!"

"You said he went to San Francisco!" she screamed at Thatcher, moving toward him.

"Janice!" cried Peyton. "Don't do this!"

"You said he went to San Francisco!"

"He did!" shouted Thatcher, kicking backward with his feet, trying to get away from her.

"Liar!" she screamed. Then she pulled the trigger.

Peyton ducked, closing her eyes, but nothing happened.

Nothing happened. The gun didn't fire.

Radar lunged for her and tore the rifle from her hands, then he broke it and looked inside. For a moment, he didn't move, didn't seem to breathe, then he whirled on the agents. "Check the others!"

They scrambled to do his bidding, breaking the rifles and looking into the barrels. "Empty," came the response.

Radar shoved Janice out of the way and reached for Thatcher, hauling him halfway to his feet, then he backhanded him, sending him sprawling again. "You set them up! You sonuvabitch, you set them up!"

Thatcher tried to roll over and escape, but Radar advanced on him. Peyton threw herself in front of him, bracing her hands on his chest. "Radar! It's over!"

"He set them up!"

Peyton shoved against him. "It's over, Radar! It's finished!"

Radar tore his eyes from Thatcher and stared into Peyton's face. He tried to say something, but nothing came out.

"It's over!" said Peyton, fighting the rush of tears. "It's over."

*　　*　　*

Marco leaned against the counter, arms crossed over his chest, watching Abe take Jake's blood pressure. Abe was dressed in tangerine orange from his dreadlock beads to his pointed-toed shoes. He tugged the blood pressure cuff off and adjusted the blanket around Jake's shoulders.

"Blood pressure's back to normal, Jakey," he said, rising to his feet. He wound the cuff up, stuck it and the stethoscope into his medical bag, then snapped it shut. "I'll just go to the break-room and brew you some of my famous chamomile tea…" He smiled into Jake's face. "…with a touch of bourbon in it."

"Thanks, Abe," Jake said, hugging the blanket tighter about himself.

After Abe walked away, Jake shot a sidelong look at Marco. "I'm sorry, Adonis. Carly left early and asked me to watch the phones. I was just finishing up my report on Greer's murder weapon when Morris showed up. I didn't even know what was happening before he pulled the gun on me."

"Did it look like I was blaming you?"

"I just feel bad that I didn't warn you and you walked in on that."

"What were you supposed to do, Ryder? You did everything right."

Jake fiddled with the fringe on the blanket. "I thought he was going to kill me. I really thought he was going to pull that trigger."

"Yeah." Marco scrapped his bottom lip with his teeth. "So did I."

Jake glanced up at him. "Did you mean it?"

"What?"

"What you said?"

Marco shook his head. "Ryder, I don't know half of what I said just then. I was spit balling, trying to keep from seeing your brains on my office wall."

"It sounded like you meant it. The stuff about me being your first line of defense."

Marco gave a growl. "I keep telling you you've got to stop hanging out with gay guys."

Abe came back with the tea and held it out to Jake. "Careful, it's hot. That microwave works wonders back there."

Jake sipped at the tea, watching Marco from the corner of his eyes.

Marco shifted weight. Shit. He hated this stuff. Why was he always being put in these situations where he had to share his feelings and shit? Maybe he needed to stop hanging out with gay guys himself.

"How's it taste?" asked Abe, fussing over Jake.

"Good. Thanks, Abe. I appreciate it. I don't know why it shook me up so bad, but it's nice to have someone care."

"You had a gun pointed at your head, Jakey. That would make anyone lose it. Dear God, I'd probably piss my pants. How you stayed so calm amazes me. I'd be a puddle of piss. That's what I'd be. Just a big old puddle of piss."

"Okay!" snapped Marco.

They both looked over at him.

"I meant it, okay."

They continued to stare at him with alarmed expressions.

He jabbed a hand at them. "Fine. You want me to say it. You want me to spill everything."

Jake and Abe shared a bewildered look.

"Without you, half these cases wouldn't get solved. There, I said it. We need you. We need your smarts and your quickness and...we need you. There."

And then it happened, just as Marco knew it would. Jake's lips turned up into a grin and Abe rushed over to him, throwing his arms around his shoulders and kissing him on the side of the face.

"That was beautiful, Angel. Just beautiful!"

"Okay!" said Marco, trying to extricate himself. "Okay, Abe."

"Wasn't it beautiful, Jake?"

"Yeah, really poetic and all, Adonis."

"Shut up, Ryder!" he hissed, glancing around the precinct to see if anyone else heard.

"I knew it. I knew it all along," said Jake to Abe.

"Please don't say it," begged Marco

"What did you know, Jakey?"

"Adonis and me…"

"Don't," he pleaded.

"We're friends."

Abe pealed off into laughter and clapped his hands.

Marco fought a smile, but in the end, damn them, they won.

*   *   *

Peyton took a seat beside Radar on the stairs of Thatcher's house. Agents swarmed the farm, bagging and removing evidence. Thatcher and the boys had been taken into custody and transported into Santa Cruz for questioning, while the women and children were being interviewed by representatives of a women's shelter. Dusk had crept onto the farm, casting long shadows over everything, including the Coroner's van, which held the remains of Finn Getter.

Radar hadn't moved in more than an hour, sitting in his flak jacket, combat boots, and black FBI ball cap. He hardly acknowledged Peyton as she sat down next to him, staring at his sunglasses which he twirled back and forth in his hands.

"What's going on, Radar?" she asked.

"Just trying to decide if it's time for me to retire."

Peyton made a scoffing sound. "Retire? You're way too young. What are you, twenty-five?"

He glanced over at her with a frown. "I'm younger than you, Sparky? Really?"

"I was going to say thirty-five, but I thought you might not see that as a compliment."

He laughed and Peyton felt something ease in her chest.

"I'm sorry about Finn," he said, twirling the sunglasses.

"So am I. I really hoped he'd made it out of here." She couldn't quite process the futility, the horrible sadness of that.

Radar sighed. "He set them up. That sonuvabitch Thatcher, he set them up. His own people. He wanted us to slaughter them. He wanted us to come in here guns ablazing and massacre his people. There's no part of it that makes sense."

"It does if you realize he wanted to be martyred. He wanted people to talk about him for generations like Jim Jones or David Koresh. He wanted to be a folk hero."

"And it almost happened."

Peyton bumped him with her shoulder. "But it didn't because you were here, because you were our leader."

He gave her a faint smile. "What you did, shoving your gun under his chin, damn it, woman, but that was the gutsiest, craziest thing I've ever seen anyone do."

Peyton returned his smile. "Sarge said not to surrender my weapon."

"We still need to talk about that."

"We don't really. It was nothing."

"Apparently it was something."

Peyton pushed herself to her feet. "It's an incredibly boring story. It'll put you to sleep."

"I'm beginning to think nothing surrounding you is boring, Sparky."

She held out her hand. "Come on, old man. Let's get the hell out of here. This place is getting creepy."

He chuckled and took her hand, letting her yank him to his feet, but when she started to pull away, he kept hold. "You're going to make a good leader someday, Sparky, you know that."

"Well, not today. Today we have a leader, who happens to be decades away from retirement."

"Decades?"

"At least one decade."

"I don't think Mrs. Radar is going to want to hear that."

"Well then, I'll just have to talk to her, won't I? I mean I'm certain Mrs. Radar and I will get along famously."

"I'm sure you will."

"And Mitten and Bootsy, they're going to love me too."

"That's not their names."

"Tiger and Pixie?"

"Not even close."

"Lula and Jezebel?"

"Those are stripper names, Sparky," he said, rolling his eyes.

EPILOGUE

Peyton climbed out of the Suburban, carrying a wooden box. The sun shone brightly and the brilliant green grass of the cemetery waved in the ocean breeze. She looked up the incline to where the small group gathered at the gravesite, then waited while the rest of her team exited the SUV.

Radar straightened his suit jacket, his sunglasses in place. Bambi came up beside him and slipped her arm through his, letting him help her over the rough terrain as they climbed toward the service. Tank offered Peyton his arm.

She smiled at him and took it, wishing she'd chosen her pantsuit and combat boots instead of a black skirt and heels for today. Shifting his hold to her elbow, he steadied her as they followed Radar and Bambi to the top.

"The professor finally figured out the coin," said Tank conversationally.

Peyton gave him a quizzical look. "Coin?"

"Lance Corporal Daws' mystery coin?"

Peyton stopped walking. "Really? What did she find?"

"It dates back to the Sassanid era from 225 BC to 640 AD."

"What? From where?"

Tank gave her a pleased nod. "That's the interesting part."

"What, Tank? What's the interesting part?"

"They're Iraqi."

Peyton opened her mouth to speak, but Radar called to them. "Are you coming or not?"

She held up a hand and they climbed the rest of the way. Janice separated herself from Lois Elder and Cheryl Watts, coming to her and hugging her. Peyton hugged her in return, then bent down and hugged Gina. As she straightened, her gaze met Molly's. The girl held out her hand and Peyton took it, squeezing her fingers. Standing a little separated from them was Jeff King with a woman who Peyton guessed was his wife. She waved at him, then the pastor called them all together for the service.

It was a simple, lovely ceremony. Once the pastor finished the final prayer, Finn's coffin was lowered into the grave. Janice came forward with a plain porcelain urn, which she opened and sprinkled into the grave, laying her mother to rest with her son. Bambi handed Peyton a tissue, slipping her arm around Peyton's waist as Molly came forward and dropped a flower onto the casket.

The four women walked over to Peyton and her team, exchanging hugs. Janice held Peyton tightly and whispered in her ear, "Please thank everyone for helping me bury my brother."

Peyton held her off and smiled at her, then reached down and stroked Little Gina's bright red hair. "I'm so sorry for your loss, Janice. I wish things had turned out differently, but I promise you, Thatcher's going where he can't hurt anyone again."

Janice's eyes filled and tears spilled down her cheeks. "I'm glad."

"What are you going to do now?"

She held out her hand and Mrs. Elder took it, coming to her side. "Mrs. Elder has offered to help us, Gina and me. We're going to stay with her for a while."

Peyton gave the older woman a grateful nod, then her eyes landed on Molly, standing with Cheryl Watts. Cheryl had her arm around the girl and was comforting her while she cried. "What about Molly?"

Janice glanced at her. "Cheryl's letting her stay with her family. She's helping them with the kids and she's going to school. Community college for now." She shot a look at Radar. "Thank him for us, for not charging her with anything."

"I will."

"Goodbye, Agent Brooks."

"Goodbye, Janice." She smiled at Gina and tucked a red lock behind her ear, then she watched the four women and the young girl wander back to their car.

As soon as they climbed inside, Peyton approached Jeff King, accepting his offered hand.

"This is my wife, Ruth, Agent Brooks."

"Nice to meet you," said Peyton, taking her hand.

"Same here."

Peyton turned back to Jeff. "Finn's sister Janice was very grateful to get the letters Finn wrote to your mother."

He smiled. "It was the least I could do."

Peyton extended the wooden box. "This is for you. When Janice went through her brother's things, she found the letters your mother wrote to him. She thought they might help you remember her better."

Ruth covered her mouth with her hand, her eyes going liquid. Jeff blinked rapidly a few times as he accepted the box. "Thank you, Agent Brooks. You don't know what this means to me."

Peyton smiled. "I can imagine, Mr. King. I hope it brings you some peace."

He nodded at her and held the box close. "I'm certain it will. Best of luck to you, Agent Brooks."

"You too," she said, watching as he and his wife moved off toward their car.

Turning back around, Peyton hesitated. A tall man in a suit with a cane stood beneath the trees a little distance away from the grave. She would recognize him anywhere. Despite herself, her heart kicked up speed and she caught her breath, only half aware that the rest of her team had moved up behind her.

"Peyton, is that…" began Bambi.

Peyton nodded.

"What's he doing here?" growled Radar.

"I don't know."

"Do you want me to tell him to leave?"

Peyton glanced at him, then gave him a faint smile. "No, I'll take care of it." She squeezed Bambi's hand. "It's okay. Really. I'm fine."

"We'll just wait for you here," said Radar.

Peyton nodded distractedly as she picked her way around the grave and climbed up to his spot under the trees. He gave her a sheepish look.

"What are you doing here?"

"Abe told me what you were doing today and I know how hard these things can be." He nodded at the grave. "I wanted to be here for you."

Her eyes swept over him. He looked so much better than the last time she'd seen him. His hair was cut short, his jaw clean-shaven. His eyes seemed brighter, less bloodshot. She was still angry with him, still hurt and confused, but he was here and right now that's all that mattered. He was here. "I appreciate it."

He glanced beyond her to her team. "So that's Radar, huh?"

"Yeah."

"He doesn't look happy to see me."

"That's how Radar always looks."

He smiled and Peyton felt her heart pick up speed. God, he still could make her giddy with just a look. "I was hoping you'd let me take you to dinner, drive you home."

She hesitated a moment. She wanted nothing more than to accept, but every time she let him back in even a little, he hurt her again. She hated being a fool for any man, but with him it went so much deeper, hurt so much more.

"It's just dinner, Peyton. Please."

For so long, he was as integral to her as her next breath and the truth was, she still loved him, would probably always love him no matter what he did. That didn't mean she trusted him, or that she'd ever be able to trust him again, but he was right. It was just dinner. It was a start.

She glanced at the others. "I guess that'd be all right." She waved to them, indicating they could go.

They hesitated, but finally turned and started toward the Suburban.

"Where do you want to eat?"

"I don't care."

"Chinese, Thai?"

Peyton shook her head. "No, I want a hamburger," she said, starting toward the Charger parked on the road above them.

"A hamburger?"

"Real beef, not soy."

"Okay."

"And a milkshake."

"A milkshake?"

"Yeah. With whip cream and a cherry and...chocolate. I want chocolate."

"Of course you do. Anything else would be ridiculous."

"And after dinner I want pie."

"Pie? Boston cream?"

"No, apple."

"Apple?"

"Gotta have my daily allowance of fruit."

"Right. That's important."

"It is." She stopped and looked up at him.

He stopped beside her.

"Thank you, Marco."

"For what?"

She tucked her arm through his and started him walking again. "For knowing me so well that you're here today."

He pulled her closer and pressed a kiss to the top of her head. "I wouldn't be anywhere else, sweetheart," he said.

The End

Now that you've finished, visit ML Hamilton at her website: authormlhamilton.net and sign up for her newsletter. Receive free offers and discounts once you sign up!

The Complete *Peyton Brooks' Mysteries* Collection:
Murder on Potrero Hill Volume 1
Murder in the Tenderloin Volume 2
Murder on Russian Hill Volume 3
Murder on Alcatraz Volume 4
Murder in Chinatown Volume 5
Murder in the Presidio Volume 6
Murder on Treasure Island Volume 7

Peyton Brooks FBI Collection:
Zombies in the Delta Volume 1
Mermaids in the Pacific Volume 2
Werewolves in London Volume 3
Vampires in Hollywood Volume 4
Mayan Gods in the Yucatan Volume 5

Zion Sawyer Cozy Mystery Collection:
Cappuccino Volume 1

The Avery Nolan Adventure Collection:
Swift as a Shadow Volume 1
Short as Any Dream Volume 2
Brief as Lightning Volume 3
Momentary as a Sound Volume 4

The Complete *World of Samar* Collection:
The Talisman of Eldon Emerald Volume 1
The Heirs of Eldon Volume 2
The Star of Eldon Volume 3
The Spirit of Eldon Volume 4
The Sanctuary of Eldon Volume 5
The Scions of Eldon Volume 6
The Watchers of Eldon Volume 7
The Followers of Eldon Volume 8
The Apostles of Eldon Volume 9

Stand Alone Novels:
Ravensong